The Getaway That Got Away

To Oscar,
Enjoy!
with love,
Vicki

The Getaway
That Got Away

A Novel

VICKI SOLÁ

Full Court Press
Englewood Cliffs, New Jersey

First Edition

Copyright © 2011 by Vicki Solá

Published in the United States of America
by Full Court Press, 601 Palisade Avenue
Englewood Cliffs, NJ 07632

This is a work of fiction. Any similarities to persons
living or dead are purely coincidental.

ISBN 978-0-9833711-4-4

Library of Congress Control No. 2011927085

Editing and Book Design by Barry Sheinkopf for Bookshapers
(www.bookshapers.com)

Cover Design by Jay Hudson (www.yojayhudson.com)

Cover Illustration Copyright © 2011 by Jay Hudson

Author photo: Vicki Solá with friend Brian Pagan and the real
Gneeecey. Photo Credit José Pagan, 1989

Colophon by Liz Sedlack

DEDICATION

For Salvador F. Solá, M.D., Samuel Blanc,
Mara Walden, Tony Rodriguez, and Stanley Bernstein,
and my pets, Gneeecey, Sooperflea, Flubbubb, and Altitude

FOREWORD

I am honored to have been asked to write this by someone who is a mentor, protector, hero, and also my beloved sister, not to mention many other things (all of them wonderful) to me.

As we Earthlings attempt to maneuver through the corn mazes that seem to make up our paths in these uncertain times, when we can easily be made to feel as if we're targets in some scary video game, with really dumb rules, being played by an expert sharpshooter (of course), one could say that this story is just what the good diroctor ordered. And I couldn't think of a better person to make us laugh as we stumble along—picking bits of corn out of our teeth, to help us forget, at least temporarily, about the worries and struggles that could easily turn our umbrella smiles upside down, getting us really wet in the process, too—than Vicki, because I've watched her throughout her adult life, my jaw agape with awe as she deftly navigates the aforementioned corn maze while, at the same time, juggling axes, flaming washing machines, bowling balls with whipped cream and a cherry on top, and expensive porcelain sculptures—never dropping any of them or even making the cherry on the bowling ball go lopsided, and somehow managing to keep the mother of all juggling objects—the trapezoid of sanity—in the air as well. Wow!

It has been a great privilege for me to have borne witness to this book from its inception—to have been present at the birth of this unique world, the convoluted county that is Perswayssick, and its wacky, and somehow familiar, inhabitants. Through the years in which this project has been taking shape, Perswayssick County and its denizens have become so real to me, if not more real, and a helluva lot funnier, than the so-called "real" world and all that it entails* that, many times, I'd prefer to hang out there, with them, most of them, anyway, heh-heh.

---

*I like "entails" because it has "tails." There are many "tails" in this tale.

There are those who would compare this book to works such as *Alice in Wonderland* or *The Wizard of Oz*. And yes, I too can see that, especially if you can imagine Alice and her whole Wonderland colliding with Oz and all of its characters at a very high rate of speed, with no helmets, of course. . . .

—Alexandra Solá
Park Ridge, New Jersey
February 2011

Acknowledgements

My friend the late Latin music promoter Tony Rodriguez, always said, "We never do it alone." How true.

You wouldn't be holding this book in your hands if not for my brother, Salvador F. Solá, III, who has supported me in every project I've ever undertaken, in every way possible.

Working with Barry Sheinkopf's BookShapers and Full Court Press has been marvelous. Thank you, Barry, for sharing my zany vision. And I express deep gratitude to the disproportionately cool Jay Hudson, whose awesome art graces this book's cover.

Special thanks to my mother, Hedda B. Solá-Westhead, for believing in me long before it was fashionable; my late father, Salvador F. Solá, M.D., for instilling in me his love of the written word; and Alexandra C. Solá, my twin-sister—born-in-a-different-year, and heck of a writer in her own right (as opposed to being a heck of a righter in her own write)—for her touching foreword, unwavering belief in this endeavor, and discovery of Gneeecey's neurological affliction, Redecoritis. And I must thank my son, Frank S. Grillo, for his patience, and for naming two of my characters, B.M. Bonbeeederhead and Yammicles. I remain grateful to David Rosenthal for taking the time to critique my work, and to Miriam Fajardo, Craig Mandeville, Max Salazar, Louis Laffitte, Patricia Duarte, Louis Delgado, Gloria Feliciano, Norman Alberts (who loved this story from its inception), Susan Kaplan, Ivan Velez, Jaime Rodriguez, Joe Hutlak, Esther Diaz, and Evan Toth. And I'll never forget my dear friend, the late Mara Walden, who encouraged me at every turn. I express utmost appreciation to Carl J. Kraus and "Captain of the Airwaves" Barry Sheffield, for their technical advice and supportiveness throughout the years, and I offer thanks to Kathy Stein-Smith and Maryann Sena, for their time and kindness.

Latin Beat Magazine's Rudy and Yvette Mangual, and *Descarga*'s Bruce Polin, first gave me an opportunity to write; I thank them, as well as my teachers Jon Brancato, Beulah Warshaw, Vincentine

Cundari, and Marian Shelby, who nurtured my literary passions.

I owe debts of gratitude to E. J. Rand, Jeremy Salter, and also the Pascack Valley Writers Workshop, especially Angela Artemis, Janet Dengel, Betty Vallone, Valerie Gross, Christa Holder Ocker, and Alexandra C. Solá, for their invaluable suggestions. I must also credit Michael Potter's For the Love of Words Workshop—in particular, our generous leader Michael, and Elly Ochiise, whose encouragement has been phenomenal, and Marva Woods Stith, Joe Del Priore, Ana Doina, Steven Swank, Lynne Cheson, Kyle Chu, Anne Langer, and Alexandra Solá (I've heard that name before. . .).

Connie Grossman Leviatin, her husband Daniel Leviatin (inventor of Gneeecey's "hollow graphics"), and Connie's mom Audrey Grossman have enthusiastically egged me on, from the very beginning. I offer a heartfelt "Gracias!" to Richie Bertrán for overseeing second-generation Puerto Rican Nicki Rodriguez's usage of the Spanish language, and I appreciate Michele Bertrán's enthusiasm. I thank fellow writer Ayme Butavia for her love of bratty ol' Gneeecey, and acknowledge Dr. Michael Vargas for ensuring Sooperflea's proper execution of chiropractic techniques, Robert Moll and Candice Ellington for advising Gneeecey about which motorcycles taste best, Robert Reitman for disapproving of Gneeecey's questionable financial dealings, and Kevin Walsh for declaring the Mierkolatory a fire hazard.

My fuzzy-faced pets taught me unconditional love: the feisty Chihuahua-terrier Gneeecey (who walked upright whenever I held out a five-dollar bill), beagle-terrier Sooperflea (this superhero could spell—and taught me how), dopey-but-beautiful beagle-terrier Flubbubb, high-jumping mouse Altitude, and Cookie, my Flubbubb-look-alike shepherd–hound. I'm happiest when she sleeps by my chair as I write (and eat 72% dark chocolate).

To all of my radio listeners, thank you from the bottom of my heart—you have energized and inspired me with your love and support. *A todos mis radio audientes, les doy las gracias desde la profundidad de mi corazón—con su amor e apoyo, me han dado energía e inspiración.*

Finally, I thank the fine citizens of Perswayssick County, whose cooperation helped make this book a reality.

—Vicki Solá
Teaneck, New Jersey
April 7, 2011

About The Author

Vicki Solá and her long-running radio program *Que Viva La Música*, heard on 89.1 WFDU-FM, provide the New York metro community with Salsa and Latin jazz produced by a singular mix of famous performers, plus artists rarely heard on commercial stations.

Featured on *American Latino TV*, a program hosted, at the time, by Daisy Fuentes, Solá has served as an advisor to the Smithsonian Institution, and her articles have appeared in internationally circulated trade periodicals, like *Latin Beat Magazine*, for which she writes the column "A Bite from the Apple."

As she established her show, Solá worked full-time at a New York Spanish commercial station and part-time at a faraway one that offered oldies along with local fishing reports, and she took evening classes in which professors apologized for keeping her up. She also performed freelance audio production, usually at three a.m.

In short, she spent years guzzling black coffee, gulping down cold pizza, and walking into walls.

After she banged her head against a particularly hard cinder block, it dawned on her that the stories she was cranking out during her spare time were autobiographical. And she felt compelled to share them.

Solá lives in Teaneck, New Jersey, with her son Frank and rescued canine Cookie (a shepherd-hound mix certified by the county shelter as having been born on Earth).

"Vicki Solá knows how to tell a story."

—*late playwright and Obie Award
winner Louis Delgado*

PART 1

CHAPTER 1

SOOPERFLEA AND ME

T HE WHOLE MESS BEGAN one early September Saturday. Fiery horns and blistering percussion—from my almost-boyfriend Carlos Santiago's new Salsa CD—worked overtime, keeping me awake as I sped toward a little white house down by the Jersey Shore, one I hadn't seen in five years, thanks to my workaholic ways.

I'd managed to cram in a whole three hours of shut-eye before hitting the highway. Checking the rearview mirror, I caught sight of my red-rimmed eyes, framed by windblown blond hair—and a couple inches of dark roots.

My so-called career in radio—working at two different New York stations—wasn't nearly as glamorous as most people imagined. What with seventy-hour weeks, plus the freelance production I did on the side, I had no life. I have to admit though, it had been my choice. Long ago, I decided I didn't want to live an ordinary life—a decision I grew to hate.

Sighing, I hit the gas harder. As miles of hot, black pavement flew under my tires, and parkway exit numbers grew smaller, I swore I could smell the sea.

Traffic was light. Glancing at my watch, I declared, "Three forty-two, skies are blue!"

That split second, something—it sounded like a bomb—detonated overhead, slamming my '64-and-a-half Mustang—my late dad's last gift to me—into a wild spin.

Deafened by the blast, blinded by a fluorescent flash, I dug my fingernails into the cushioned steering wheel cover and struggled to regain control of my bucking red bronco.

A nightmarish squeal sliced through the sulphur-laced air when I finally managed, bearing down with all the force of my one-hundred-ten-pound frame, to floor the brakes with both feet. Eyelids squeezed shut,

I braced myself and waited.

It was over. The maniacal maelstrom had run its course, leaving be-hind a vacuum of silence, save for the stray buzzing between my ears.

My body crumpled down into the bucket seat. Dazed and drenched, tears criss-crossing my face, I sat motionless as my heart hammered my ribs like a machine gun and forced gallons of blood through my veins. I thought I was going to blow up.

Only when my head stopped spinning did I dare open my eyes.

Things looked pretty routine. No signs of mass destruction, no ev-idence of calamity—no raging fires, blackened terrain, or scorched craters. Not even a fallen tree. Traffic, although sparse, flowed in an or-derly fashion. When my legs stopped shaking, I got out and checked the car. Odd. Not a scratch.

Feeling like a little kid, alone and scared, I drove off the dirt shoulder and headed for South Seaside Park.

A couple boring miles later, an enormous green sign appeared. Hung from a nondescript overpass, it proclaimed in bold white letters that I was enjoying my trip on the recently resurfaced Perswayssick Thruway.

"Perswayssick Thruway!" I shouted, squinting.

As I freaked, the six-lane highway dissolved unceremoniously into an unpaved ramp leading onto the Perswayssick River Bridge, a structure that didn't simply cross the zigzagging river—dull and narrow, it spanned its entire length.

My new wristwatch twinkled on the seat beside me, its sterling band snapped. The cracked face read three forty-two. Hadn't even paid for the damned thing yet—I'd charged it. Scowling, I jammed the timepiece in my pocket and peered down at the murky river, surprised by scores of luminous, cobalt-blue ovals splashing about.

As I gazed, amazed, a muddy mist rose, obliterating the blobs—and everything else. In seconds, the dank vapors—accompanied by an un-familiar, gut-wrenching stench—painted my windshield green.

Ticker thumping up in my ears, I steered toward what I hoped was the road's edge and eased to a stop. Before I could close my windows, Carlos's CD ejected itself, disintegrating as it whizzed past my nose, and words shot out from all four speakers like snipers' bullets.

"We'll be comin' right back at'cha wit' 'The Line to Your Heart's Al-ways Busy,'" shrilled a dentist's drill of a voice. "It's been number one for six months! Okay, peeps, it's five p.m.! Your dial's mutated to 1780 AM, WGAS, part of the Gas Broadcast Network!"

I gasped.

"Our live mierk cams show we're havin' a inversion! Yee haw! I love inversions! Out there on the bridge, your visibility's a big fat zilch—an' so's your mother's!"

My jaw dropped.

"Let's hope," continued the screechy piece of chalk, "this inversion sticks 'round for our Annual Mierk Fest nex' weekend!"

Annual *what?*

"Y'know, I love this planet—even though I miss mine."

Acid rose into my throat, burning my tonsils.

"The river's overflowin' an' the goonafish are jumpin'! Whatta soooper Snatturday!"

At least it was still Saturday. Maybe.

"Now, here's the toppa the charts for yuz!" A tone-deaf cowboy, accompanied by twangy, out-of-tune guitars, began caterwauling, "The line to your heart's always busy, I call it all da-a-a-a-y long. . . ."

My fingers never reached the dial. A thundering wallop from behind slammed me back against my seat and blasted the Mustang through the guardrail.

Airborne, I tumbled through pea soup, praying that my dad was watching over me. Then, a sharp tilt forward smashed my skull into something hard, and I found myself floating. From above, I stared as my vehicle hurtled through the lifting fog.

Below, on the mucky riverbank, a red-caped black dog stumbled upright on paddle-shaped feet. Forelimbs extended, he took a giant, clumsy leap into the sky. His pendulous ears whipped in the wind.

My doomed automobile continued its slow-motion descent, listing to the right, bags and books streaming out of the passenger windows in a hideous arc. Old magazines and my flat spare spilled from the open trunk. As each item splashed into the foul waters, the blue things sprang up, annoyed.

The caped canine zoomed underneath my car moments before impact with solid ground, and hoisted it back into the air.

Gravity began to tug at me. I felt leaden, and the pain returned. From the corners of my consciousness, gleaming clusters of disembodied eyeballs glared my way, then vanished into the returning haze.

Shivering, my agony replaced by dull throbbing, I drifted through damp dreariness.

THE MUSTANG ROCKED GENTLY. As I came to, I noticed the protruding peepers of a panting black hound plastered to me. Atop his whipped cream-splattered snout sat a shiny wet nose. A shiny, wet running nose.

Microscopic dots obscured my vision as I pushed the door open and stepped out. Swaying, I collapsed upon the creature.

He spoke English. "Here, sit down," he suggested, guiding me toward a flat rock that sat in the middle of a muddy gully.

"Th—thanks. . ." I stuttered.

"A pleasure, Nicki."

"I—I don't recall telling you my name—"

"Oh, din'cha?"

My eyes remained fixed on him. "No."

"I'm Sooperflea, at your service." He pointed to the triangle-enclosed backward "S" embroidered on his navy shirt.

The canine-humanoid's voice boinged like a rusty spring. He was just about my height—when I sat.

"Real name's Fleaglossity," he continued, wiping his schnozz on his sleeve. "Fleaglossity Floppinsplodge. But'cha can call me Flea. All my friends do."

"I'm Nicki—as you already seem to know," I replied, gazing into his concerned cocoa eyes. "Nicki Rodriguez."

He extended a furry, four-fingered hand. "Pleased t'meet'cha."

"Likewise," I replied, catching a glimpse of my own lavender-tinged hand.

"Don't worry, that'll go away," Flea assured me. "Your face, too."

"Whaa—"

"The purple, I mean—y'know, your *dimension burn*."

"Huh?"

"You're only twenty-four," he continued. "You'll heal fast."

"How'd you know—"

"You're lucky. I was jus' passin' through on my way into the city, to meet a buddy."

"City? What city?"

"Perswayssick City," he answered, matter-of-factly.

Silly me, I should've guessed.

THE GETAWAY THAT GOT AWAY —5—

He shook his oversized head. "Nah. No way y'coulda guessed." My mouth opened wide.

"Come wit' me—y'need a good meal."

I forced a smile.

"'Zig'll take care of ya. He's my bes' friend—we grew up together. C'mon."

My eyes wandered down to Flea's gargantuan high-tops. Circled X's decorated each ankle.

The superhero studied his red sneakers self-consciously.

I pondered my fate—silently. *Where the hell was I, and how could I get back home?*

"Don't worry," said Flea, "we'll answer all your questions before y'leave." Leave. Just what I wanted to hear.

A hurt expression crossed his face. He stumbled face first into the dirt, mumbling.

His shoes are too big, I thought.

"Nah—they fit jus' fine," he insisted. Astonished, I watched him stagger to his feet. As we trudged toward my car, a lump rose in my throat. My vintage Mustang sat dented and gashed.

"Don't worry, Nicki, they can be banged out an' painted over."

Just get me back to the parkway, I thought, blinking back tears.

"I *said* I'd get'cha back to your parkway—later." He smacked my trunk shut.

I stopped in my tracks. Flea kept walking, and tripped right into the driver's seat. He could just about see over the dashboard.

Consoled by the presence of my handbag, its strap tangled around an inner door handle, I took a shallow breath and flopped into the passenger seat. Breathing hurt.

"Now lessee, howd'ya start this thing? Oh, yeah." Next, he grasped the gear shifter. "Hmmm. . .kinda like prndl, but on the floor. Wow, I can jus' 'bout reach these pedals. The long one on the right makes it stop. . .this shorter, sideways one makes it go—"

"No!"

Flea tapped the gas, then hit the brakes full force. Smash went my head on the dash. Curiously, he had no problem finding the clutch.

He chuckled. "It's jus' the opposite on my planet."

"*Your planet?*"

"An' where *I* come from, Prndl is a girl's name, too."

"I'll drive!" I yelled, coming to my senses.

"Nah—you're in no shape."

"IT'S MY CAR!" I began blacking out as I reached for the wheel.

He shot me a "told-you-so" look and clicked the radio on. "Better put on that seatbelt. We gotta backtrack a few miles to get on the bridge." We lurched forward.

That same flat voice droned, "—the line to your heart's always busy." Flea hummed along as he hit every pothole and curb in sight. He had to be the worst driver on any planet.

"I'm not the worst driver," he protested. "Jus' a little—whaddaya-callit—rusted."

"Who said you were a poor driver?"

"Y'thought it—an' y'thought *worst*, not poor!"

"I—I—"

"An' stop wonderin' where the parkway is!"

I tried not to think aloud.

When that corny, twangy song ended, a familiar, grating voice began to pitch an ad: "An' now, an importan' message from us here at Gas Radio! My kingdom for a horse! My corporation for a brief! Ah, the age-old lament of the busy, squirmin' executive! Whaaat could be worse than ill-fittin' underwear?

"I'm Doctor B. Z. Z. Guhneeeecey, an' I wanna talk t'ya 'bout somethin' personal! It's sad but true—eighty per cent of corporate blunders are produced by 'executive squeeze'—the torment of ill-fittin' underwear! There's no tellin' how many financial tragedies can be attributated to chafin' an' itchin'! Well, I've done somethin' 'bout it!

"I've invented an amazin' new revolutionary formula! Jus' *one* application of clinically proven Bend-A-Britch, an' I unconditionally quarantine that your very personal undergarments'll conform to you!

"Even works on tail holes! Call I-T-C-H-Y-B-U-T-T-S today to find out more! Remember, y'heard it here, on 1780 AM, Gas Radio!"

Flea smiled.

I hoped it was just a bad dream. "I'm changing the station."

"It's your car," he snapped. "But y'know, that underwear stuff's pretty good. An' no—you're not dreamin'."

I slapped the button to FM. The same high, nerdish voice babbled on. "Bad afternoon, everyone! It's a soooper Snatturday here on 109.3 FM, WGAS, Gas Radio! Yee haw—"

I punched one of the knobs so hard it popped off into my hand. Grunting, I chucked it over my shoulder.

"Flyin' objects are dangerous," Flea admonished as he sped onto the bridge.

My eyes rolled upward.

Suddenly, he jammed on the brakes and his bulbous nose struck the wheel, honking like a Model T's horn. We skidded hundreds of yards, trailing stinky clouds of burning rubber. Splattered on the passenger-side windshield was one of those luminous blobs from the river.

"Aw, I tried not to hit him," cried Flea. "Poor goonafish. Little guys are really jumpin' this time of year."

My neck had locked, forcing me to stare at the road kill. The globby thing was actually a fish, strange and two-tailed, with no apparent head. "Ugh—can't move," I moaned.

The superhero reached over and grabbed me by my shoulders. After a rapid succession of twists, pulls and yanks, I was able to turn from the grisly mess.

"Th—thanks, Flea!"

"Been studyin' to be a chiropractor—can't keep this superhero stuff up forever." He stepped out, scraped the smooshed goonafish off the glass and tossed it back into the Perswayssick, giving it a proper burial at sea.

THE BRIDGE RAN OVER dry land for the last mile or so.

"Why does this bridge span the length of the river?" I asked. "Why doesn't it cross over like a normal bridge? And why does this part go over land?"

"Jus' the way it is," answered Flea, stony-faced. He gunned the gas and the Mustang flew down the ramp, smoke billowing from behind.

"Don't say it," he warned, cheek muscles twitching.

"I didn't," I snarled, through clenched teeth.

He glanced up at the rearview mirror. "Hmmm. . .blue exhaust. . . engine trouble—"

Did the creature ruin my engine?

"I didn't ruin it. I merely observed that the smoke comin' from your tailpipe is blue. Y'might be burnin' oil. Remember, Nicole, if it wasn't for *me*, y'wouldn't be here to *give* a deck of vlecks!"

"Sorry, Flea—I mean, I just—"

"I know what'cha meant. An' I'm not a creature!" He made a sloppy turn onto Street Road, an industrial thoroughfare neither scenic nor smooth. Never-green traffic lights adorned each corner. Each stop smacked my soggy gray matter up against the inside of my head. The flop, flop, flop became a steady rhythm, a distraction of sorts. Almost made me forget his driving.

Flea's head whipped around. "Did'ja say somethin'?"

"No—not a word," I replied, in the most convincing tone I could muster.

"Oh. Okay."

I decided I'd better think as quietly as possible. But wasn't I entitled to the privacy of my own mind? Wasn't that a most basic right?

I faked a cough to cover those last couple thoughts.

"Y'oughtta get that checked," advised Flea. "Sounds bad."

Uncomfortable with my deception, I turned my attention to the world outside. Street Road, more country-like now, had been graced by an early autumn. A chaotic carpet of riotous hues crackled under our sporty tires.

"Perswayssick County's so pretty this time of year," proclaimed Flea, misty-eyed.

"Uh-huh." Vision blurred by my own tears, I cradled my pounding head and cursed my luck.

Since graduation two years before—still grappling with my dad's death the summer after freshman year—I'd been toiling away for pennies. Didn't have time or strength to look for another "dream" job.

My part-time gig at the left end of the FM dial, hosting and producing a noncommercial Salsa show, wasn't bad, although the pay was. Management gave me free reign pretty much, as long as I didn't blow the place up, and local bands were grateful for the exposure I gave them. And I'd met Carlos. But I worked thankless twelve-hour shifts at the other end of the dial, at slick Spanish commercial station WUGG, where I yearned to lock myself inside a soundproof studio, stuff a rag in my mouth, and scream at the top of my lungs during my twenty-minute lunch. Only thing stopping me was that my boss would probably be hiding with me, videotaping my meltdown.

Freelance production augmented my slim earnings. Doing odd jobs for showbiz wannabes helped chip away at my student loans, and my sanity.

I'd just pulled an all-nighter, recording a client. Now, here I sat, nursing a migraine, talking to a driving dog.

I coughed so loudly, Flea almost drove off the road.

THE SINKING SUN SHOT glistening copper highlights across the acres of tall fields that surrounded us, making them shimmer and click in the cool breeze.

Enraptured, Flea pulled over and parked. "Ah, rindom, the source of life! It's harvest time!" Clusters of raspy arrows protruded from each weapon-like plant.

Bucolic calm shattered abruptly when a tornado of black feathers exploded up from the stalks, followed by an outraged raven, thrashing to free itself from the hostile crops' clutches.

After a prolonged, ear-splitting battle, the bird sputtered into the sky, shrieking "Nevermore!" and set down atop a nearby billboard.

Mierk Fest on the Perswayssick! advertised the sign, picturing a motley assortment of humans and canine-humanoids mingling happily. *Mierking, Goonafishing, & Picnicking! Fun for the Whole Family! Snatturday & Someday, September 16th & 17th!*

Fluttering about, still delivering its soliloquy, the Poe crow fell off its perch. Flea giggled, then started the car, hit the wrong pedal and climbed the curb.

My jaw tightened.

He glanced my way. "My telepathy stopped workin 'bout three miles ago."

"Oh?"

"It's been kinda spotty," he added, leaning closer, "like summa my other powers. Some days, my ESP doesn't work at all. But I do know, your dad *is* lookin' out for ya."

MINIATURE CLAPBOARD HOUSES, THEIR arched doorways boarded up by knotted planks, dotted Boulevard Avenue's hillsides. Paint peeled off the single-storied, windowless dwellings, and their half-shingled roofs resembled checkerboards.

Between shacks, weeds towered over broken bottles and crushed cans, and crumpled bits of newsprint skimmed the ground, turning like pinwheels.

Up ahead, a lone, matted schnauzer—a tiny, regular dog—eyed us furtively, then ventured from its spot smack in our car's path, dragging a brown paper bag. Flea leaned on the horn, and the animal became a dirty blur. A couple miles later, we rolled past a tall cyclone fence that guarded an expansive yard heaped with overturned shopping carts, many missing wheels.

"Shoppin' Cart Orphanage," volunteered Flea, bearing right onto Murgatroyd Avenue—a main drag.

It took forever-and-a-half to pass a broken-windowed, smoke-vomiting plant known as the Mierkolatory, an architectural disaster of pachydermian proportion, coated by centuries of soot. I wound my window up and Flea stepped on the gas.

By the time I'd stopped retching, I found myself gaping at a semicircle of sleek, mirrored buildings, surrounded by twisted shrubbery clipped like kangaroos, giraffes, and anorexic hippos.

"Freak O'Nature Foods' Corporate Headquarters," Flea informed me. Gothic, three-headed hawks, their stone beaks gushing thin arcs of water, stood at each end of the central, dozen-doored entrance.

"A sign for the turnpike!" I exclaimed, bolting upright. "I could drop you off, then—"

"It's not *your* turnpike!" shouted Flea.

A SPARKLING CITY FILLED the windshield. Everywhere, skyscrapers rushed up into the night skies, their myriad lights indistinguishable from the stars.

I craned my neck to stare up at one particularly surreal edifice. "Why do they call it Seemingwhale *Towers* when there's only *one?*"

"Uh. . .well, y'see," stammered Flea, "they started buildin' two, but, uh, had a recommendation to put one on top of the other—y'know, turn it into a single buildin'. They kept the original sign, though—it was easier than orderin' a whole 'nother one."

"Easier?"

"Jus' the way it is," growled Flea, screeching to a stop when a cluster of jaywalkers began a leisurely stroll. Perswayssick City's pedestrians— and drivers—reflected the diverse mix represented on Street Road's Mierk Fest billboard.

Nearby, an elderly, tweed-jacketed Flea look-alike tripped, recovering his balance seconds before his ankle-high, leashed brown-and-white puppy could escape. A group of human youngsters howled. The superhero flashed them a dirty look.

As the last stragglers sauntered past, the light turned red. Flea took the opportunity to point out a ritzy restaurant across the street. A scarlet carpet ran from door to curb, and its marquee's thousands of micro-sized bulbs spelled out "Les Pantalons de Napoleon," in elegant script.

"That's a real high-class bistro," explained Flea, "named after Napoleon's pants. There's a real pair of his trousers on display—in a locked case nexta the men's room."

"Really."

"His *Waterloo* pants," he whispered, awe-stricken.

Moments later, a white, fully-articulated stretch-limousine slithered, snakelike, around the corner, each segment sliding smoothly from view. It appeared to have more than thirty doors on each side. "Grate 1" was the moniker engraved on its Jersey tags.

"We're almost—HIC—there—oh, no—this—HIC—always happens—HIC!" spluttered Flea.

"Hold your breath," I suggested. I didn't know him well enough to scare him.

"Never—HIC—works!" A look of helplessness washed over his face. Equally pathetic were his attempts to park between two ambulances. He jerked back and forth for ten minutes, hitting a trash can. Its contents spilled across the sidewalk.

I groaned.

"I think—HIC—I'm finally gettin' used'ta your car," he announced, ramming both emergency vehicles, incredibly, in a single stroke.

Averting my gaze, I noticed that same ethereal limo parked across the street. It took up an entire block. Hand-scrawled "out of order" signs covered each adjacent meter.

Meanwhile, my measly Mustang cowered curbside, illuminated by orange-and-puke-pink neon, flashing the name "Gneeezle's." Purple calligraphy below read *Fine Family Dining Since 2005*. Filthy, half-drawn venetian blinds languished behind the gaudy lighting.

Flea leapt out of the car, unaware that he'd caught his cape in the door.

"Flea!" I called out, too late. Fabric ripped as his nose hit the pavement, blaring like a trumpet on steroids.

He squirmed his way upright and, whistling a carefree tune, hopped onto the sidewalk, only to stumble over the trunk of an uprooted tree.

My legs had gone numb, and my back felt stiffer than a petrified two-by-four. I staggered over to Flea and helped him to his oar-shaped feet.

Clutching onto each other, we hobbled toward the eatery.

"This is—HIC—a real high-class joint," Flea boasted from under my armpit.

Looks more like a high-class dump, I thought. My empty stomach rumbled.

CHAPTER 2

ME AND GNEEE

GNEEEZLE'S," I WONDERED ALOUD. "Three E's in a row—"

"Spare a vowel, spoil the food!" shrieked a familiar voice from under a deflated chef's hat.

"Huh?"

Jet ink spattered both sides of this canine-humanoid's cranium and triangular ears, dipping down over his right eye. Dingy white fuzz carpeted his scowling snout. A soiled apron covered his T-shirt.

"You're purple," he observed, staring me up and down. "Y'should see an epidermicist."

"I—"

Flea pinched me. His hiccups had disappeared.

"C'mon in, I *guess*," snarled the surly critter. He flung the plate glass door open and shoved past us. "Last one in's a rotten egg!"

Flea flew in after him.

Seconds later, a grungy index finger pointed my way. "Yooou!" whooped the voice attached, "yooou're the rotten egg!"

I bit my lip.

"Heya, 'Zig, whazzup?" inquired Flea, ignoring his buddy's antics.

"Price of vowels."

The two slapped high-fours, sprang up and down rubbing elbows, pranced in clockwise, then counterclockwise circles—hopping on alternating feet—a half-dozen times.

Afterward, Flea turned to me, winded. "What's your name again?"

"Nicki, who needs to get back to the parkway."

"Icky!" shouted Flea's friend. "Icky Parkway—whatta stooopid name!"

"Nicki," began Flea, nodding in the loudmouth's direction, "this is Dr. B.Z.Z. Gneeecey—we jus' call him Bizzig—or 'Zig."

I gasped. "You mean—*that's*—"

"That's Guh-neeecey," stated Gneeecey, "wit' three E's—but'cha only pronounciate two, 'cause one's a spare. Spares are good—in case y'get a flat."

My stomach growled.

"An'," he informed me, before I might commit any phonetic blunders, "y'pronounciate the *G*, but it ain't spare—ain't got another."

"Y'know," bragged Flea, "'Zig's known as 'the Grate One'—"

"That's G-R-A-T-E," interrupted Gneeecey. "Wouldn't wan'cha to picture it wrong."

Didn't think I would.

"I s'pose," he said, scratching his noggin through his hat, "I could use that G as a spare, but it might not fit—it's too used to bein' near different letters."

I extended my hand. "Pleased to meet you, uh, Doctor Gneeecey." Hmmmph. Doctor. Doctor of what? Vowels and consonants? My dad was a doctor. A *real* one, who had run a clinic in East Harlem.

Gneeecey's snoot wrinkled.

"C'mon 'Zig," coaxed Flea. "I can vouch for her."

After an awkward moment, Gneeecey's hand grasped mine. His bristly fur made me itch.

"'Zig owns this place," said Flea, peering into the dining room, "plus the WGAS Broadcast Network."

I perked up. "*I* work in radio."

Gneeecey, still shaking my hand, scrutinized me through narrowed lids. "Guess they're lowerin' standards everywhere."

"*What?*"

"Keep tellin' 'er how g-r-a-t-e I am, Fleaglossitty."

"'Zig's an inventor, too."

Gneeecey's left sneaker tapped impatiently. "Aaaaan'?"

Flea adjusted his tattered cape. "He's also Perswayssick County's Quality of Life Commissioner."

"An'," interrupted Gneeecey, still pumping my arm, "I was jus' elected Grate Gizzy–"

"Perswayssick County's highest office," explained Flea.

Gneeecey pounded his sunken chest. "Now—even before my official inordination nex' week—the freeloaders gotta answer to meee."

"Y'mean, *freeholders*."

"Stinkin' whatever, Fleaglossitty. Y'know, *I* shortened Gizzy-galumpaggis to Gizzy 'cause it wasted consonants. No word needs three spare G's. It was that conversationalist platform that got me elected."

"Y'mean *conservationist*," said Flea. "That, plus y'swore you'd be held accountable for returnin' us to—"

"Enough, Fleaglossity." Leaning closer, the white-and-black wonder confided, "Mos' folks say I can do no wrong."

Flea grinned.

"An' as Grate Gizzy," squealed Gneeecey, "I oversee myself as chair-person of the Quality of Life Commission—so even *I* gotta answer to me. An' I get to ride horseys!"

Reeling, I leaned against the wall.

"It's tough bein' me all day," added Gneeecey.

"Start a support group for yourself," suggested Flea, as he lowered himself into the chair I'd been eyeing.

"Hey," inquired Gneeecey, only just noticing the superhero's scruffy condition. "Wha' happened to *you*? Your cape an' nose—"

"Ain't nuthin', 'Zig."

"Did sheeee do that?"

I gazed down at my muddied maroon mules.

"Nah, 'Zig—I kinda fell outta the car—"

"Well, y'better go put quarters in that meter 'fore they ticket'cha. If they do, don't expect help from *me*."

"Wait, Flea." With my free hand, I began digging for change.

"Y'let *her* call ya Flea?!"

Sooperflea shuffled past his slack-jawed pal. "S'okay, Nicki—I got it."

"GETTIN' BACK TO MEEE," continued Gneeecey, still shaking my hand, "I do mosta the cookin', too."

"Really?" I answered, my legs crumbling beneath me.

"I gotta," he added, in a martyred tone, "till Altitude's trained. He's a mouse."

"Oh my." The room began spinning. "Uh, could I sit some-where—"

"That's in addition to everythin' else in my hectic life. Us important people got it rough." Suddenly, he cast my hand aside with enough force to dislocate a shoulder, and covered a small, round object with his foot. As he lurched down, he bashed his honking schnozzle on a tabletop.

"Y'hunka garbage!" he screeched, kicking it till splinters and hardware flew. "DIE!"

The little table stood on one leg, defying him.

Gneeecey snatched up a steel rod and smashed the remaining post until it exploded into a fine powder.

On its belly, in a cloud of dust, the piece of furniture seemed to plead for mercy.

Bulgy peepers glazed with hate, Gneeecey displayed a dime. "Finders keepers, losers weepers! Why're y'lookin' at me like I'm nuts?"

As I collapsed into a nearby chair, I tried to quell the small but nagging notion I had died.

"Need that lousy chair inside," said Gneeecey, as he pulled it out from under me.

Mouth gaping, I stumbled backward.

"Y'look like y'smell somethin' rotten—whaddaya think this is, Denmark?"

The place did smell strange. "Now that you mention it—"

"Let's sit," suggested Flea, just walking in and steering me toward the very same seat that had been yanked out from under me, and a table much like the one just murdered.

Meanwhile, Gneeecey grinned at a jumbo, wall-mounted TV, and his own blabbering likeness, amateurishly superimposed, flying over the Perswayssick River.

"Vote no to Question 345 this Octvember 68th—stop the riverfront divlopment!" shrilled his onscreen image, flapping unwashed off-white arms. "An' save the engendered goonafish!"

"That was meeee!" exclaimed the good doctor. "Wasn't that 'nouncement 'bout votin' 'gainst the divlopment cool?"

"Uh, yeah, 'Zig," replied Flea. "Y'sounded very, uh, natural, speakin' up against the *development*."

"Mark an' them'll love it!"

"Who?"

Wearing a cat-that-swallowed-the-canary grin, Gneeecey swaggered into the kitchen.

INSIDE GNEEEZLE'S, PEPTO-PINK, neon-orange, and fluorescent-purple tie-dyed, Haight-Ashbury flower-power ruled, juxtaposed shamelessly with quasi-classical Greek furnishings.

Scores of poorly-reproduced vases, repainted in brilliant black light colors, sat scattered throughout the lava lamp-infested dive. Some housed raspy rindom stalks, others contained drooping ferns. Our table, lit by a particularly lurid violet fixture, tottered precariously whenever we moved so much as an elbow.

A framed caricature of Socrates gripping a goblet engraved "Hemlock" graced a nearby wall. Captioning underneath read, "Sock it to me!"

Its companion piece, an illuminated, life-sized Bacchus, clenched a froth-filled mug. Each time the jovial immortal's mechanical fist hoisted the vessel over his head, he winked, and his motorized mouth opened, exposing a neon ad for Perswayssick Breweries' full-bodied, rindom-based Slog.

The schizophrenic scheme extended back to the kitchen's chipped steel doors, where two Greek pillars, obviously plastic, stood guard.

FRAMED BY HIS FAKE columns, Gneeecey stared into space, wielding an oversized ladle.

I held up a cruddy, bent utensil. "Fork's a tad dirty."

"Ain't nuthin' wrong wit' that utensicle—it's jus' a little oxidated. Ya oxidate when ya breathe."

"I just meant—"

"An' a few germs won't kill ya, neitherwise—they immunizate'cha."

"She jus' meant," began Flea, "y'know—"

"I stinkin' *know* what the Iggleheimer meant! Everythin' here's quaquaversically quarantined to be clean, unless it ain't."

My bleary eyes rolled up to the ceiling, one high enough to accommodate the six-foot-plus, waxy-skinned humanoid staring our way.

Flea tugged on Gneeecey's apron. "Why's that creepy dude wit' amber skin keep lookin' at us?"

"That's my friend Mark."

"You've never mentioned him before."

"He's a *new* friend."

"Why's he keep lookin'?"

"Maybe," suggested Gneeecey, waving to the humorless gray-suited man, "he wants to order take-out for his brothers."

"Don't think so," replied Flea, as Mark disappeared into the gloomy shadows.

LEAFING THROUGH GNEEEZLE'S MENU, I wondered if I *was* on my own planet.

"Y'know, 'Zig," began Flea, patting his round belly, "the malted cauliflower sounds delicious."

"We're outta that."

"Okay—make that Surprise Stew. An' bring me a mug of Slog. Wit' extra pulp. Put it in the freezer first, for 'bout ten minutes."

"Gotta charge y'for the extra pulp," growled Gneeecey, scribbling away. His ladle protruded from under his arm like an extra appendage.

Flea licked his shiny black lips. "An' bring me some Swillsville crackers."

"Don't eat wit'cher eyes, Fleaglositty."

"An' gimme a coupla squirts of Zurt."

"I'll hafta charge ya the extra buck for each squirt."

"An' tell me, are your slothflogs fresh today?"

Gneeecey crossed his arms. "Y'think I'm gonna say *no?*"

"I'll find out for myself."

Gneeecey jammed his face in mine. He had dog breath. "Well, whaddaya waaant awready?"

"Y'know," I replied, backing away, breathing through my mouth, "I'm really not very—"

"Course ya are," interrupted Flea. "Your stomach's rumblin'!"

Turned off by alien aromas wafting through the air, and a sign that warned, "Don't Wake the Food!" I closed my menu.

"Nicki, it's on *me*," declared Flea. "Don't even *look* at prices."

"Whaddayathink this is?" screamed Gneeecey, pounding a fist on our table, causing it to rock. "A soup kitchen? Your account's delinquent— an' now I'm s'posed to eat *her* dinner?"

All things considered, that last suggestion wasn't bad.

"An'," he bellowed, "when Planet X uploads my books, your account gathers *thirteen months'* interes'!"

Flea shrugged.

"Thirteen months, daily *compounderated* interes'!"

The superhero rose to his size-thirteen paddles. "Do I hafta remind y'bout the time I saved your—"

Gneeecey reached back and grabbed his backside. "How dare y'mention that?! Why yoooou—I'm gonna—hmmm—grfff—" The good doctor's arms and legs sliced through the air as his threats deteriorated into unintelligible shrieks. Gneeezle's patrons didn't raise their heads. Maybe the food had deadened their senses.

After several minutes, Gneeecey slumped over our table, spent. He'd bent his ladle into a Z.

"Election took a lot outta him," whispered Flea. "Everyone wants a piece of him."

"Whaddaya waaant awready?" demanded Gneeecey, firing spit into my face with each syllable.

"Uh. . .I think I'll have some of that Chinese take-out from next door," I replied, squirming. "Listed here, under Entrées."

"Wong's is CLOSED!"

A STEADY STREAM OF high-decibel expletives—punctuated by crashes and smashes—poured out of the kitchen.

I glanced over at Flea.

"Be charitable," he advised, crunching on appetizers that resembled the rock collection I had when I was seven. "He's had lots to overcome in his life."

Just then, Gneeecey, an avant-garde vision in soot, burst through the doors. "A boiled pot never watches," he grumbled, plopping down next to me.

Before he caught his breath, a brass band struck up a dirge-like rendition of "Four-and-Twenty Blackbirds."

He and Flea shot up so fast, they nearly toppled the table. Facing the television hung over the Slog bar, the two placed their hands over their hearts.

As their tragic anthem blared, a lone tear streamed down Gneeecey's cheek. "My plaaanet," he bleated, blowing his nose in his hat.

Onscreen, cameras panned across an orange-and-green octagonal field. Its vivid patterns created an illusion of movement, making my woozy head swirl.

Commentators marveled at the legions of fans that packed the arena, waving purple-and-orange "X" banners in support of their visiting planet's underdog team.

"Those X's," Flea informed me, "are short for E-C-C-C-H-S."

"Saves lotsa C's," added Gneeecey. "Reminds me, tomorrow, after the Alphabet Exchange, I gotta go down to piss."

I blinked.

"That's short," explained Flea, "for Perswayssick Interplanetary Stocks an' Securities."

I blinked again.

"Game's startin'!" shouted Gneeecey.

Emblazoned on a huge scoreboard was "Planet Eccchs Gnorks vs. Home Planet Zoid III."

Gneeecey shot me a haughty, sidelong glance. "*I'm* from a consonant-rich planet. Where are yooou from?"

"Earth." Couldn't believe I'd just said that.

"Earth—sounds so puny—"

"C'mon, 'Zig—"

"Say it over an' over again! Earth! Earth! Sounds meanin'less after a while, don't it?"

Sighing, I glanced up at the screen.

Attired in baggy purple-and-orange suits, matching football helmets, and monstrous kelly-green masks, the Gnorks rushed the field. Zoid III's smug players, already in formation, sported streamlined silver uniforms.

Flea stuffed an onion-like, three-legged slothflog in his kisser. "Our Gnorks are finally contenders."

"Congratulations." I knew what it was like to root for the New York Mets.

"We're playin' the toughest team in the quadrant. But we got Gronkle."

"Highes'-paid player this side of the universe," added Gneeecey, tearing past with a toilet plunger.

"But," cautioned Flea, "we're not used to Zoid III's zloggy atmosphere. Our fans are wearin' masks. See all those purple nurkzoog particles floatin' 'round?"

"Yes," I replied, hoping a football game might steady my nerves before I hit the parkway.

"No—zorgle's more like football, baseball, an' bowlin' combined," stated Flea.

"Hey—you said your telepathy wasn't—"

"Sorry—I jus' guessed wha'cha were thinkin'."

"PLAY ZORGLE!" bellowed an argyle-tuxedoed referee as whistles screeched.

Roars erupted from the stadium, and Gneeezle's Slog-chugging crowd.

Gneeecey tossed plates and bowls at our table as he dashed from the dining room to the kitchen.

"Watch it!" warned Flea, dodging a plum-colored flying saucer.

Egg-shaped eyeballs glued to the screen, Gneeecey pitched a jumble of unmatched utensils our way, coaching his team all the while. "ZORG! DON'T LET 'EM PLOOK! DEFENSE! DEFENSE!" He ran backward through the kitchen doors and landed on his butt. It honked loudly.

Seconds later, he emerged, hauling a steaming, mustard-colored bucket across the orange tiles. Teeth clenched, he lifted it up to our table. "Here's your lousy stew."

Flea salivated as cloudy amber broth rained into Gneeecey's over-sized dish, along with a canvas upper, some bottle caps, a seaweed-covered tire gauge, and several blue blobs from the river.

"I'm givin' me an' you the bes', right offa the top," proclaimed Gneeecey, pouring out a smaller portion for Flea.

A gallon or two later, the chef turned to me and, swearing under his breath, dumped remnants into my cup—an athletic sock, some screws, and a clump of something green.

The two canine-humanoids took little notice of what they gobbled so ravenously—and noisily. Folks here obviously had different nutritional requirements. And strong tooth enamel.

Gneeecey accidentally stuck his elbow in my soup and shot me a dirty look.

I didn't give a deck of vlecks. I'd pick up a snack soon, at a parkway rest stop. Or hopefully just wake up and raid my own refrigerator.

Suddenly, my dinner companions bounced up, slapping high-fours.

"Second time *ever*," exclaimed the sportscaster, "the Gnorks have plooked a triple-boinger!"

"Is that like a grand slam?" I asked.

Gneeecey sneered. "Better."

"And there's Gronkle," added a second TV commentator, "circling the field as his fans cheer, many wearing big, floppy ears like his. He's a huge guy, about eight-vlurd-five."

Flea grinned. "Gronkle's triple puts us ahead, three-zip!"

"Y'know, Fleaglositty," began Gneeecey, slurping his slop, "this reminds me of the time I threw up in Seemingwhale's—remember?"

"Yeah. Last year, in Electronics."

"The Gnorks had just plooked their first triple-boinger. They showed it over an' over, on every TV in the department."

Flea stuffed a fistful of wiggly slothflogs in his face and washed 'em down with a hardy gulp of Slog. "I hadda find a janitor."

Queasy, I turned my attention to the game. It appeared that when a zorgler managed to run through a line of tacklers and toss a wooden bat over his adversaries' goal post, he'd attempt running eight bases placed helter-skelter across the field, and then try to roll a heavy black ball into his own team's net.

All the while, his opponents chased him. His own teammates did little more than hurl insults at the enemy. Each hard-won, completed task was considered a "boinger" and earned one "zoing."

When a player completed all three boingers, he'd have zorgged, or plooked, a triple-boinger. The referees would yell, "Go fish! Boing three!" Most players never got past the first boinger.

"Let's celebrate," suggested Gneeecey. "Let's have pizza for dessert— it rhymes wit' our dinner."

I looked at him. "Pizza doesn't rhyme with stew."

"It's the *taste*," he explained, eyeing me with a mixture of pity and contempt. "Pizza rhymes wit' our dinner's *taste*."

"I want ice cream on mine," said Flea.

"One scoop or two?" asked Gneeecey.

"Two. Any chicken flavor left?"

"Yupperooney—that's my favorite, too."

"Don't forget the whipped cream!"

Gneeecey sprinted into the back and returned schlepping a corroded aluminum tray that dripped with red sauce. In the center, atop two triangular slices of cheese-covered dough, sat four mounds of a frozen, whipped cream-topped gray concoction that smelled like a supermarket's meat aisle.

Flea's eyes widened with delight. The two plunged in, muzzle-first, surfacing only for air.

Grossed out, I turned my attention to the TV, where a blinking, eight-hosed, high-suction vacuum slithered around, devouring everything and anything in its way—including a lamp. "Commercial's kinda long, isn't it?" I asked.

Gneeecey wiped his mouth on his sleeve. "It's a infomercial, ya Ig."

"My name's *Nicki*—"

Flea raised his glop-covered snout. "Whaddabout the game?"

"Halftime," replied Gneeecey. "I'm runnin' this OctoVac spot while the bands play."

"OctoVac musta paid ya top dollar."

"Yeah—I'm rerunnin' it later, insteada the news."

Flea licked his fingers. "'Zig, thinkin' of tomorrow, an' our recital at the rally—"

"Yeah?"

"Well," the superhero ventured cautiously, "Flubbubb still wants to play. He'd only hit his triangle a coupla times—y'know, ding, ding. Wouldn't really hurt nuthin'—"

Gneeecey slammed his fist down. "Y'mean, when me an' you perform Shriekensobb's 'Plight of the Goonafish'?"

"I jus' thought—"

"When I dramatize the plight of dyin' goonafish, on my 'lectric voaline?"

"*Violin.*"

"Stinkin' whatever. He'll even putrificate your piano part—if y'don't ruin it yourself, always playin' aheada me 'causa your lousy ESP."

"No need to get personal."

"Although your ESP ain't workin' like it used'ta—"

"No need to rub it in. I jus' thought y'could give Flubbubb a chance—I mean, he's worshipped the ground y'walk on since we were kids."

"Got no use for freelance percussionists. Subjec' closed."

Flea stared down at his lap. "Need a favor."

Gneeecey burped. "WHAAAAT?!"

"Uh, my roommate's havin' a buncha people over. Nicki an' me need somewhere to stay tonight."

I shot up. "What?! I'm not staying anywhere! You *said*—"

Flea shook his head. "Sorry, Nicki—"

"I'm leaving—tonight!"

"I been observin' ya. It's too *soon*."

Tears stung my eyes. "You promised you'd get me back on the parkway—*tonight*!"

Flea cracked his knuckles. "No way—it could kill ya."

Overtaken by a sudden wave of nausea, I fell back into my chair. "I—I don't understand—"

"Get'cha Ig elbows offa my table," ordered Gneeecey, picking his teeth with a bottle opener. "Ain'cha got no manners?"

"'Zig—"

"Let 'er *go*—maybe she'll end up like Julio."

"'Zig!"

"Who's Julio?" I demanded. My head was killing me.

"Tell 'er, Fleaglossitty."

Flea's eyes misted over. "Y'mean, who *was* Julio?"

Gneeecey let forth with another belch, followed by a wicked laugh. "Julio croaked trynna go home. Like yooou will—"

"'Zig!"

"Holy crap!" I exclaimed, clutching my sides. I felt faint. "Tell me all this'll go away if I close my eyes."

"It won't," replied Flea.

Our gracious host leapt to his feet. "Yuz two better get goin'. I'll get your check. Hotels, motels—even all the dumps—are fillin' fast causa the Mierk Fest."

Flea jumped up. "Hotel? Motel? I'm your bes' friend!"

"Don't matter—I treat everyone alike."

"Y'remember the time I saved your—"

"Don't keep bringin' that up!"

Flea's jaw tightened.

"Okay, daaammit—y'can stay wit' *me*."

"Thanks, 'Zig."

"Well, actually, y'can stay at my dog's condo."

I looked at him. "Your *dog's* condo?"

Gneeecey turned to Flea. "Her too? *She* gotta stay?"

"Do I hafta remind ya—"

"Awright, y'can both stinkin' stay." Gneeecey glared my way. "But jus' tonight. An' make sure she's stupervised at all times."

"'Zig, I don't think y'hafta worry."

Gneeecey stuffed a cold slothflog in his mouth. "I don't usually allow people from other planets."

"His dog's condo," I muttered, regarding my fate in a curiously detached manner.

"Spot's got his own condo," snapped Gneeecey. "His own phone, his own big boy life. Whole derangement works out priddy good—I get all the fun of pet ownership, but none of the responsibilities."

Sick to my stomach, I staggered to my feet. "Uh, where's the restroom?"

Gneeecey pointed in Bacchus's direction. "Hope y'fall in."

Shooting him a disapproving glance, Flea rose to steady me.

GNEEECEY SNATCHED A NEWSPAPER from under an astonished customer's nose and waddled to the back.

"Pardon the indelicacy," I whispered in Flea's ear, "but, what was that plastic thing attached to the back of the seat in the, y'know, privy? It fell off and wouldn't go back on."

"Oh, y'mean the sploggle," he replied, blushing through his fur. "Sploggles, uh, keep our tails high and dry."

"Uh, Flea, we've gotta talk—I've gotta get back home—"

A blood-curdling yelp let forth from the bathroom. Seconds later, Gneeecey appeared, nostrils flared. Before he could unlatch his poisonous muzzle, patrons began cheering wildly.

"It's an upset!" exclaimed the TV announcer as Flea leapt up. "With Gronkle completing a second triple before the clock ran out, Planet Eccchs has beaten Zoid III, six boing to one zoing! First time an expansion team's taken a berth in the Zyphon finals and gone on to win the Intergallactic Championship!"

Flea and Gneeecey skipped in circles, chanting, "Six boing to one zoing, six boing to one zoing!"

When the two flopped into their seats, drunk with ecstasy, Gneeecey turned to me. "Y'made me miss the enda the game, plus y'didn't eat'cha dinner."

"I—"

"There's hungry people on other planets."

"'Zig—"

"Waste not, want not—early bird eats the worm."

Groaning, I pulled out my watch. It still read three forty-two.

The timepiece flew out of my hands when Gneeecey shrilled, "Bad evenin', Altitude!"

"Bad evenin', Boss," replied an oversized mouse. Black-and-white, he was a negative of his similarly-marked employer, to whom he stood elbow-high.

"You're two hours late, Gingivitis-head!"

"Weren't my fault."

"I hadda cancel all the deliveries!"

Altitude studied his filthy sneakers. His dilapidated Gnorks jersey bore the name of everyone's hero, Gronkle.

Gneeecey smashed his tankard at the teenager's feet, spraying my bare ankles with wet shards. "This is posilutely, absitively disgustin'! Remember which side of the carpet your bread's buttered on! Y'wanna end up back in that sploggle factory, workin' for Broken Nose Tommy?"

Altitude raised his head. A chewed-up yellow pencil dangled from his lips. "It was the ol' Splodge. Muffler fell down on Vompt Boulevard. Boy, am I lucky it didn't come down by St. Vlad's, wit' all dem tombstones!"

Gneeecey bared his unbrushed teeth.

Altitude set down his "BZZG"-monogrammed violin case. "Hadda walk all the way back to Summer Vacation Street for my bike. Its tire was only flat on top. But every time I pedaled, it went flat on the bottom. So I hadda half-ride it back home an' jump off every time the bottom went flat."

Gneeecey twisted his ladle.

"Was good I went home," Altitude pointed out, "'cause I forgotted to lock my door. Since it was open, I went in an' sat down. Then Gronkle plooked a triple boinger."

Gneeecey's spoon snapped in half.

"Then," continued the mouse, "I said, geeez, the boss probably wonders where in Hemlock Heights I am. So I went outside, but went back in when I saw I was wearin' my watch wit' the dead battery I couldn't find another one like."

Gneeecey listened, bug-eyed.

"Searchin' under my bed for my other watch, I found one of dem flushable cameras—it still had a coupla shots lef' on it."

Gneeecey began frothing at the mouth.

"Then," added Altitude, "Zeke's Pizza an' Transmissions called, an' after I reminded 'em it was *your* car, they said it's the whole exhaust system an' transmission too."

The good doctor fell to his knees.

"Too bad," concluded the mouse, "it wasn't jus' half the exhaust system an' transmission, y'know, like jus' half my tire goin' flat. Two of those halves wouldn'a cost as much as two wholes of one thing each."

Altitude swaggered over to Flea. "Great game, huh? Did'ja see Gronkle zorg—after Obble couldn't block 'im?"

Gneeecey lunged in Altitude's direction. Howling bloody murder, the mouse tore toward the kitchen, his boss hot on his heels. The two crashed through the doors like a train wreck.

GNEEECEY FLICKED THE LIGHT switch. "Eat up!"

Cutlery clanked as customers bolted down their meals.

"Line up by the register when you're done," he ordered, snatching a dish from under an elderly human's poised fork. "I think you've had enough for now, sir, don'chooo?"

The gray-haired gentleman gawked.

"Take it wit'cha, why don'cha?" Gneeecey dumped the entrée into a paper bag and tossed it into the man's lap. "It'll keep—it's kept for months awready."

Hoping to kick some life back into my limbs—and convince Flea that I was strong enough to leave—I limped over to Gneeecey's Greek columns.

As Bacchus winked my way, I reached out to touch one. It crashed to the floor and cracked in half.

"*Iggleheimer!*" shrieked Gneeecey as he ran toward me and climbed me like a ladder. He dug his sharp, skinny feet into my shoulders and plastered his face against mine.

"Get offa me," I pleaded.

"Y'broke my restaurant—y'busted my column! Y'know how much this is gonna cost me?"

"OW—all I did was touch it lightly—with one *finger*—"

"Even if they stinkin' fix it," he yowled, yanking a fistful of hair out of my scalp, "it'll never be the same!"

"FLEEEEA!" I hollered.

"Whole place is ruint! Permutantly disfigurated!"

Flea zoomed across the room and peeled his crazed pal off me. "'Zig, it was an accident."

"Accident, shmaccident—she did it on purpose!"

Seeing stars, I sank back into my chair. Altitude, pleased to see someone else in the doghouse, smirked.

"Y'jus' need some glue, 'Zig," insisted Flea. "It'll be good as new."

"But the crack'll still show," sobbed Gneeecey, long, blond strands of hair hanging from his clenched fists. "My column'll look ancient!"

GNEEECEY KICKED HIS REGISTER open and began scooping greenbacks and coins into a King Oggle Supermarket's sack. After a couple seconds, he jerked the entire tray out and turned it upside down.

"Tips in the bag too," he instructed diners. "An' once your mon-ney's in, I can't give out change—it's 'gainst my policy. An' I'm watchin' yuz—I count it *all* at home."

The way Gneeecey pronounced the word "money," exaggerating the word's two syllables, sounded really silly to me.

As each departing patron paid, he shouted angrily, "Bad night!"

Flea, last in line, opened his purple rubber billfold. "Gee, 'Zig, prices really rose since las' week."

"Inflation hits everyone, even business maggots like me."

I opened my purse. "Here, Flea—"

"No," he replied, handing Gneeecey a pile of rumpled bills. "I tol' you, it was my treat. Besides, you didn't eat nuthin'."

The good doctor tapped his foot. "That's thirty-five *twenny-six*."

Flea scrounged through his pockets. "Here—two quarters."

"Can't give out change." Gneeecey quadruple-knotted his bulging satchel's drawstring, then marched over to a metal box and threw three giant switches.

Gneeezle's ghastly interior disappeared into darkness—a euthanasia of sorts, albeit temporary.

CHAPTER 3

LET'S HAVE ANOTHER
PIECE OF COFFEE,
LET'S HAVE ANOTHER CUP OF PIE

"WATCH OUT FOR THAT TREEE!" warned Gneeecey, to no avail. Flea was already down. "Y'got astinkmatism in your lef' eye, don'cha?"

"GAROOOGA!" replied the superhero's nose.

"Y'wore glasses when we were kids," continued Gneeecey, money bag wedged between his knees as he secured Gneeezle's dozen locks and alarms. "Big, thick, funny-lookin' ones. Y'better thank your lucky gizzards that science came up wit' contractin' lenses."

"An' you, 'Zig—you're still allergic to fracas trees."

"Yeah—sneezed down four tonight."

As the two conversed, Altitude tiptoed over to his famous red bike, roped to a nearby lamppost. Both tires appeared to be fully inflated.

Stealing furtive glances, he unfastened the two-wheeler, hopped on and flew down Murgatroyd Avenue, out of sight.

"Let's go," barked Gneeecey, slinging his sack over his shoulder. He tossed a handful of crumpled papers onto the sidewalk, at Flea's feet.

Snout crinkled, the superhero pointed to the heap of trash.

"Someone else'll pick it up," stated Gneeecey, with his usual air of self-importance.

"Yeah." Flea whisked up the litter and dropped it into a nearby receptacle.

"Tol' ya someone else'd pick it up. I'll meet yuz at the condo." Gneeecey shot me an icy glare, then crossed the street and began ripping "out of order" signs off meters.

MIRACULOUSLY, WE ARRIVED AT Seemingwhale Towers intact. Flea's driving skills had deteriorated after only a couple hours away from the wheel.

"Prndl was the prettiest girl in third grade," he recalled, scraping the Mustang's tires against the curb.

By the time we stepped out, Gneeecey was already dragging his loot up the walk, toward the skyscraper's entrance.

"Bad evening," simpered a patent leather-haired doorman, leaping out of the way when Gneeecey smashed the door open. The fellow's accent and long, pointy incisors reminded me of a certain Transylvanian nobleman's.

Gneeecey pushed past him. "Bad evenin', Bogelthorpe. I ain't greasin' your palm—y'didn't hold the door."

"Very good, sir."

We followed Gneeecey through the marble-floored lobby, into an elevator. Its neutral shades were most welcome, after Gneeezle's.

I studied the blinking, gold-toned control panel and gulped. "Four-hundred-fifty floors?!" This *was* one heck of a dream.

"Only the highes' for my dog—I can afford it. He lives on the four-hundred-*fourteenth* floor."

"Really."

"When we built this place, we were real astoopt—we skipped from four-twelve to four-fourteen, so there wouldn't be no four-thirteen." He smiled condescendingly. "Woulda been bad luck, y'know?"

I bit my tongue.

"It was my idea to make this one buildin' insteada two."

My stomach plummeted through the soles of my feet as the elevator continued its high-speed ascent. And Gneeecey suddenly appeared thoughtful. "Don'cha wonder," he asked, studying the ceiling, "what'd happen if y'jumped real high when y'were goin' down real fast? Would the ceilin' hit'cha?"

He jumped, until our rocketing capsule, which he'd forgotten had been soaring upward, slid to a smooth halt. We exited into the plush corridor.

"We put Suite 414-A all the way down the hall, to fool burglars," Gneeecey explained, as we waded through ankle-deep crimson carpeting. "The front woulda been too oblivious." He dropped his sack and began fumbling with keys.

When he finally opened the door, there, on four paws, stood a tiny white-and-black pooch, absolutely identical to him. The little yapper, who couldn't have weighed more than two pounds, bounced into the air like a spring. His wildly wagging tail created a small windstorm.

Gneeecey caught his look-alike in midair. "This is Oxymoron. I call him Spot for short."

"I DID THE DECORATIN'," bragged the good doctor. "Did it up the same way I did the restaurant—wit' lotsa classy downtown sophistication an' junk."

Gneeezle's had indeed metastasized its way uptown. Purple walls, orange beanbag chairs and hot pink shag reigned supreme, accented by color-coordinated lava lamps and Grecian end tables. It wasn't wise to look in any one direction too long.

"Spot loves it here, don'cha Boy?"

"Grrrrr!"

"Did the doorman feed y'that new food I sent?"

"Grrrruff! Ruff ralph!"

"You'll get used to it—it's a inquired taste. Freak O'Nature gave me fifty free cases."

"Urf!"

"Did Bogelthorpe walk ya?"

"Riff raff!"

"I wish you'd learn to use your own bat'room. I better call down an' remind him I'm jus' visitin'—he might think I'm gonna take care of ya."

"Grrrrrrrrrr!"

The air was thick with doggie smells, and mountains of shoes cluttered the living room. Crouching down, I read labels. The chewed-up pumps and oxfords were actually pricey French and Italian imports.

"Spot takes after me," declared Gneeecey. "He's too cultural an' discrimulatin' for toys."

Dizzy, I braced myself against the wall.

He peered down his nose at me. "I only bring back the *bes'* luxurities when I visit your mudball planet."

My eyes widened. "*You* visit *my* pl-pl—"

"Why don'cha siddown?" He pointed to two squat orange blobs. "They're occasional chairs—sometimes they let'cha sit in 'em."

Before Flea even finished lowering himself, his seat threw him, like a defiant stallion.

But luck smiled upon me for the first time that day—I sat and wasn't thrown. Sighing, I watched Oxymoron nose around in a box labeled "Puppy's First Chemistry Set." Excited, he galloped over and deposited a slimy red microscope in my lap. Although riddled with bite marks, the polyurethane instrument appeared fully functional. We engaged in an exuberant tug-of-war.

"Don't play wit' him—he'll get used'ta it!" scolded Gneeecey. "Spot, go watch TV."

The pup dropped his toy and trotted purposefully to a switch partially hidden in the shag. With a click of his paw, he activated a screen that transformed the wall into a vividly-hued test pattern.

"Put on *my* station, Spot—s'more ignorcational."

Oxymoron clicked to Channel 3½ and flopped down, fascinated by the sight of a singing scarecrow.

"This film's 'bout a wizard of ounces," Gneeeecey informed me. "Y'know, a sorcerer of measurements. Cute little documentary."

"One of my all-time favorite movies," I replied. "But it's not a—"

"Who aaasked ya?" Scowling, Gneeecey glanced at his watch. "Can't stay—got lotsa important junk to do. That's how it is wit' us busy, important people—we're real busy an' important. Y'want some coffee 'fore I go? Well? Tell me quick—yup or nope? Nope or yup? Will somebody answer awready?"

"I'll have some," replied Flea.

I nodded in agreement. "Me too—some caffeine would really hit the spot."

Gneeecey aimed his clenched, revolving fists at my kneecaps. "You're gonna hit my dog wit' coffee? Why, I'll have ya arresticated—"

"That's *not* what I meant—"

"Y'GONNA HIT SPOT WIT' COFFEE?"

My muscles tensed. "'Hit the spot' is a figure of speech, an expression we use back on Earth, to indicate that something—like a cup of coffee—would really be great." Shuddering, I realized I'd just referred to my planet as being somewhere else.

"You're not gonna throw hot coffee on Spot?"

"I'd never harm Oxymoron—"

"Y'wouldn't *harm* him, but would'ja *hurt* him?"

"'Zig, 'harm' means—"

"Shaaaddup, Fleaglossitty—"

"I meant," I shouted, "I'd never *hurt* Oxymoron—"

"Nebberd-kinnezzard?" demanded Gneeecey.

"Nebberka-*what?*"

"Nebberd-kinnezzard. Means 'extra-never.' It's a, uh, igspression—like yuz use on Earth."

"Nebberd-kinnezzard," I assured him, "would I ever hurt your dog, or any other dog! I love dogs!"

He unballed his fists. Hoping our relationship might be on the verge of becoming friendlier—or at least less hostile—I ventured, "Flea calls you 'Zig.' Is that short for—"

"Only my friends call me 'Zig," he shrieked, shattering any illusions of impending camaraderie. "So that means yooooou can't."

Staring at him through narrowed eyelids, I massaged my sore scalp. "I wasn't asking if I could—"

"Y'CAN'T!" He stomped into the kitchen.

Flea shrugged. "Y'can still call me Flea."

"Sorry it took so stinkin' long," snarled Gneeecey, toting a tray containing three tottering mugs and a heap of cutlery. "Sorry for *meeee*, that is—it's *my* valuable time bein' wasted—hadda make this from scratch." A molasses-like stream trickled down his left elbow. Flea and I exchanged glances.

Gneeecey shoved a gooey mug filled with a solid, gelatinous material into my hands.

Balancing the burning beaker on my knee, I shifted uneasily, turned off by the brown goop's sickly-sweet smell.

"Whattsamatter?" he demanded, irritated by my scientific approach. "Ain'cha never ate coffee?"

"I was just, uh, looking at how different—"

"It's Merk Perk, the coffee y'eat wit' a fork," he explained, a hint of defensiveness creeping into his shrill tone. "Another fine Freak O'Nature food! Like it says on the package, 'Look for the three-headed hawk!'" Slobbering, he and Flea attacked their wobbly mud with glee.

Aware that caffeine deprivation wouldn't help my migraine, I took a stab, literally, at the jiggly java, and put fork to mouth. My eyes popped out and my cheeks sucked in. The two canine-humanoids gawked.

"What's that?" jeered Gneeecey. "Some kinda fish imitation?"

The bittersweet flavor and gruesome aftertaste sickened me. A single word came to mind. I was unable to prevent its escape from my pursing lips. "Yiccch!" Without apology, I rested the vessel on an end table.

Like a heat-seeking missile, Oxymoron's pint-sized body fired across the room, straight into my cup, knocking it to the floor. Only the tip of his ceramic-battering tail was visible.

"SPOT—WHAT BAAAD MANNERS!" howled Gneeecey, as he wiped his honking schnozzle on his left wrist. "OW—stinkin' watch always hurts my nose."

Having gulped down every last glob of gelled joe, Oxymoron backed out of the rolling mug and zoomed down the hallway.

Without warning, Gneeecey hurled himself to the floor, convulsed with sobs.

Flea struggled to pull his pal's rigid body up off the carpet. "C'mon, Bizzigsickles."

Clutching clumps of frizzled shag, Gneeecey resisted, with all his might.

After a good ten minutes of bawling, he crawled into my lap. His pear-shaped body was light.

"In school," he blubbered, swollen eyes gazing into mine, "everyone always made funna me 'cause I loved mon-ney. They called me 'Cash Register-head.'"

I listened, rapt.

"They'd put a dollar on the floor—wit' invisible string tied 'round it—then they'd pull it an' make me fall. Once, in chemistry class, they set my propeller beanie on fire."

Flea chuckled. "Y'wouldn't take that hat off, even though your head was burnin' up."

"Couldn't. Lousy thing cost ten zork—that's 'bout twenny Jersey bucks today."

"Lotsa moolah, back then."

"For a whole year—thirteen months—I delivered the *Daily Prognosticator* an' sold Rindom Doodles door-to-door, plus schlocked grongoids on weekends, to earn enough to send away for that hat."

"What," I asked, "are grongoids?"

"They're these hairy gourds that grow on fracas trees," explained Gneeecey. "Ya eat 'em."

Flea swallowed another mouthful of coffee. "Your allergies really kicked up, schlockin' those grongoids."

Tears trailed down Gneeecey's dirty cheeks. "It was worth every lousy sneeze—whadda beautiful stinkin' hat!" He punched my kneecap. Hard.

"Had red, multidirectional propellers," recalled Flea. "Turbo-driven—not bad for somethin' advertised on the back of a cereal box."

Gneeecey bunched up his shirt and blew his nose. "I ran down the hall, fas' as I could. The fire was outta control—set off all the alarms!"

Flea nodded. "My geometry test got canceled—"

"Stop interruptin', Fleaglossitty! So I stuck my head in the janitor's bucket. Even underwater, I heard everyone laughin'."

"We got dismissed early—"

"Fleaglossitty!"

"Sorry 'Zig—"

"When I finally came up for air, my hat was ruint. All that was lef' was melted propellers."

Flea patted his buddy's shuddering shoulder.

"Look." Gneeecey pointed to a microscopic, paisley-shaped scar on his lowered dome. "I still got a mark, right here. It's permutant—hair don't grow there."

"I'm sorry, Doctor—"

He slapped my thigh. "An' yooooou. Y'come an' bust my beaudiful column—accident, schmaccident—"

"I really didn't mean to—"

"Then y'threaten Spot an' tell me my lousy coffee stinks!"

"*I* never—"

"I've worked like a *dog* to get where I am today!" He leapt off my lap. "An' I shown 'em all! I'm a zillionaire! Y'hear me?"

I reached into my purse for a roll of antacids.

"I'm MEEE!" He smacked my leg for emphasis.

Wincing, I popped a chalky, cherry-flavored Tumm-Eaze.

"Look, Fleaglossitty—she was lyin' 'bout havin' no food."

"This isn't food," I protested. "It's—"

"Who asked ya?"

Flea rose. "'Zig—"

"Lemme keep tellin' her how much better'n everyone else I am."

Flea fell backward into the violet sofa.

"Everyone loves me—*I* love me! Y'HEAR me?"

"Yes," I replied, chewing on a second tablet.

THE GETAWAY THAT GOT AWAY

"An' I got lotsa education an' junk. On your dopey planet, I'd win a Nobular Prize."

"Uh-huh."

"Uh-stinkin'-*huh*? That's all y'can say? Y'know what I do when I'm bored? Brain surgery!"

Eyelids clamped shut, I visualized myself helpless on an operating table, Gneeecey's chainsaw poised over my skull.

"Whatsamatter, Ig?"

"Stop calling me—"

"I'm GRATE!" he screamed, hurling an end table at me. "G-R-A-T-E! Y'hear me?"

"Uh-huh," I replied, ducking.

He pounded his fists on his chest. "I'm stinkin' filthy rich! STINKIN' AN' FILTHY AN' RICH!" He collapsed into a bean-bag chair.

After several moments of sweet silence, my empty stomach roared, and Oxymoron jumped sideways. Under most other circumstances, I would have been embarrassed.

Flea ripped open a bag of Freak O'Nature Rindom Doodles and held out a handful. "Try one."

Noticing the razor-sharp quills that covered each rust-colored arrow, I declined.

Even so, the superhero dumped a mound in my lap. "Y'know what they say—'One day, that three-headed hawk's gonna bite'cha.'"

A flake punctured my thumb.

Gneeecey gaped at my wound. "In all my years sawin' skulls open, I ain't never seen real Ig blood. It's red—like ours!"

I scowled.

Flea threw a doodle up in the air, caught it on his tongue, and scarfed it down. "Rindom's a valuable grain, right 'Zig?"

"Extremely valoolable."

The superhero's jaw dropped. "'Zig—y'jus'—"

"Whaaat?"

"You're exhibitin' symptoms of infected speech! Plus, y'claim y'seen chairs an' trees walkin'—"

"Awready tol' ya, I ain't goin' to no nervologist."

"But Dr. Idnas is s'posed to be really—"

"Y'know," continued Gneeecey, "y'can actually see our planet's golden rindom fields from space."

"Speaking of space," I began, "would someone please tell me what's going on? I mean, I can't actually be on another planet—"

"I tol' ya, all your questions'll be answered," said Flea. "Later."

"I need to know *now*—"

"LATER!" He cracked his fur-covered knuckles. "It's not as simple as y'think."

Gneeecey's piercing peepers drilled through me. "Ain'cha gonna make nice an' try a Rindom Doodle?"

I thought it best to change the subject. "My luggage!" I exclaimed, actually only just remembering it. "All my stuff's at the bottom of the river." Grimacing, I pictured slimy goonafish swimming through my panties.

"Couldn't save you, your car, *an'* your stuff!" shouted Flea. "I hadda prioritize—that's one of the first things they teach at the academy."

"I—I didn't mean you should've—"

"He's a superhero, not a porter, ya Ig!" exclaimed Gneeecey, delighted to have an opportunity to take a shot at me without incurring Flea's disapproval.

I plucked a doodle from my sleeve, ripping it. "Flea, you saved my life—I can never, uh, *nebberd-kinnezzard* repay you. And I'm certainly not criticizing you."

Gneeecey screwed up his snout like he smelled rotten eggs. "She certaincerely did criticalize ya!"

"S'okay, Nicki—I know what'cha meant. I understand—"

"I know y'know I meant y'knew what I understand we both knew y'were sayin'," cackled Gneeecey, shoving a finger down his throat.

"Thanks, Flea," I replied, ignoring Gneeecey. "Y'know, I do think I've lost some important stuff. Confidential stuff. I can't remember exactly what—my head hurts and I'm so dizzy—"

The superhero's eyes widened with concern.

"Do you think there's any way I can retrieve my bags?"

"Not likely," answered Flea. "Aren't too many divers worth their salt who'd swim in those waters—for any price. Way too dangerous, what wit' all the sudden inversions."

"Isn't there gonna be that festival by the river?"

"Yeah—but no one goes *in* the water."

Gneeecey's eyeballs had taken on the appearance of cash register windows, displaying actual dollar-and-cent signs. And suddenly, he seemed much friendlier. "What was in your luggage? How valoolable was your stuff?"

"'Zig—y'did it again—"

Gneeecey's noggin spun around. "Fleaglossitty—for Bogelthorpe's sake!" Lowering his voice, he turned back to me. "Maybe *I* can help."

"You mean—"

He spoke fast. "Y'lose any mon-ney? Any jooooolery? Any secret formulas? All your luggage fell in? How many pieces? What'd they look like?"

My fuzzy mind drew blanks. "I think I had a coupla small suitcases, and my green duffel bag. And—I think—my maroon leather portfolio." I groaned. "I sure hope *that* didn't end up in the river—"

"What parta the river?" inquired Gneeecey, doodles crackling in his mouth like fireworks. "Wasn't it by the middle of the bridge? Y'went off halfway, right? Well, stinkin' answer me awready!"

Flea stood. "It's late. Let's call it a night."

Gneeecey's dark eyes bored into mine, with a spooky intensity. "Didn't your car go off halfway? Yup or nope? Nope or yup?"

A feeling of dread gripped me. I'd already given him too much information. "Yeah," I answered casually. "I guess."

"*Y'guess?* Were y'goin' north or south?"

"I dunno."

"Enough, 'Zig."

A nefarious grin illuminated Gneeecey's begrimed face. He stared into the distance through narrowed lids, rubbing his palms together.

PERWAYSSICK COUNTY'S GRATE GIZZY-elect plunged a last wiggly forkful of coffee into his pie-hole. "Gotta go count my mon-ney, plus I gotta call Mark—"

Flea's head tilted.

Gneeecey didn't notice. "An' I gotta put the final touches on Petey's papers."

"Things workin' out wit' the foster family?"

"They're adoptin' him, thanks to me, philanthropoopist that I am—"

"'Zig—y'jus'—"

"As I was sayin', I completely rehabituated Petey—replaced his busted handle an' straighted out his bars. Groceries'll never fall through him again."

Flea smiled. "How carin' an' selfless."

"Bes' of all, the family's payin' me top dollar."

"Oh."

"Gotta go—also gotta work on my altercatin' plans 'gainst the divloppers, in case the election don't go the way we're tryin' to rig it—I mean—"

"Y'mean *developers*, 'Zig. You're tryin' to keep the *developers* from—"

"I was wonderin' when ya'd finally get it," barked Gneeecey. "Even Flubbubb understands that redivlopment would ruin the county's ekookology—"

"There y'go again—"

"I mean, whaddabout the goonafish? Where could they swim in pieces an' have happy, produckative lives? Poor dopes ain't got heads."

I had to speak up. "I couldn't help noticing goonafish entrées listed all over your menu. You say you care about 'em, then you *eat* 'em?"

Gneeecey waved his finger in my flinching face. "We wouldn't eat 'em if we didn't like 'em. An' we're helpin' Ol' Mother Hubbard thin out their population—makes more room for the res' of 'em. An' havin' more room makes 'em happier—it's a vicious cycle."

"Isn't your logic muddled?"

"If our side does stuff to 'em, it's different. We got the right reasons. It's the reasons that count—not what we do."

"I don't under—"

Gneeecey peered down his snoot at me. "I'm a crusader. One day they'll name a turnpike restroom after me."

"'Zig," began Flea, "y'jus' said Flubbubb understands. So how 'bout lettin' him—"

"Certaintifically not. He suffers from xylophobia."

"Xyla-wha'?"

"He's afraida xylophones."

"But—"

"I refuse to disgust it any further."

"Put yourself in his place, 'Zig—imagine how he feels."

Gneeecey looked up at the high, sparkle-painted ceiling. "Like a spigot-brain, I guess. Hmmm. . .I wonder how much divin' lessons cost?"

Flea sank back into the couch, and Gneeecey shuffled over to his money sack. "C'mere, Spot."

Oxymoron trotted over, obediently.

"Don't spend this right away," warned Gneeecey, depositing a wad of bills in the pup's mouth. "An' don't use too much 'lecricity—remember to turn off that air conditioner. Don't forget, *I* make your lifestyle possible—I'm your bent factor."

"Woof—scrrrimp!" Oxymoron replied, through his cash-clogged muzzle.

"Call the office if y'need anythin'."

His face suddenly contorted with fury, Gneeecey addressed me. "Y'may be leavin', but'cha ain't seen the last of me. An' that story 'bout my hat an' the fire—happened to someone *else*. Bad night, Fleaglossitty."

"Bad night, 'Zig."

The good doctor stormed out, nearly slamming the door off its hinges.

CHAPTER 4

CRASHIN' AT OXYMORON'S

MORNING'S LIGHT MOUNTED A ravaging assault on my raw eyeballs. I'd fallen asleep on the floor, shoes still on. Awareness of my predicament trickled back in increments, like a bitter wine poured slowly. I sighed and was startled to hear the sound of my own voice.

The air conditioner still chugged away full blast—I felt like I'd camped out in a freezer. The fact that Gneeecey would end up paying for my goose-bumps made them just tolerable.

Several feet away, Flea snored vigorously, Oxymoron nestled under his chin. The superhero's occasional nose honks jolted the paw-twitching pup but didn't wake him. The orange-and-purple tie-dyed curtains seemed more disturbed, drawing in and out with each guttural gust.

As I forced myself into a sitting position, memories of Friday night rushed back.

Lounge lizard Maurice L'Orange—real name Bobby Escovedo, about as French as *arroz con pollo*—rice with chicken, that is—needed two months of his radio programs prerecorded. All so he could grab his bad toupee and inflict his sour notes and matching personality on another unsuspecting group of ocean-faring hostages cruising to Alaska, Antarctica or Arkansas. Somewhere starting with an "A."

All the while, he'd be broadcasting drivel-in-absentia—thanks to me. . . .

He still owed me a bundle.

My eyes opened wide. Hadn't L'Orange finally coughed up some cash?

The blood drained from my face. God help me, I couldn't remember—I really, really didn't know. . . .

I *did* know that I was desperate. Desperate to escape. To rethink my life. By the ocean, where, despite the heartbreaking memories, I knew I would feel closest to my dad. I'd just about had enough of everything.

Where I'd gotten the wacko notion I'd also have time to read a suitcase worth of books in a single weekend, I have no idea. Now, schools of headless goonafish were reading 'em, down at the bottom of a foul, extraterrestrial river.

Terrified I'd lost my mind, I staggered over to the window. As I clutched at the drapes, they fell to the floor, rods and all, creating a clatter loud enough to rouse the dead. The commotion elicited only a soft, high-pitched woof from Oxymoron.

Four-hundred-plus stories below, Murgatroyd Avenue bustled with pedestrians and a steady stream of cars, trucks and rumbling motorcycles, all microbe-sized.

Teary-eyed, I hoisted the psychedelic rags back into their brackets and checked my watch. Still read three forty-two.

I'd take that shower I'd been dying for, then wake Flea. We'd have that conversation. The one about leaving.

Rindom Doodles crunched under my shoes as I hobbled down the hall, sticking my tongue out at each of a dozen or so framed portraits of Gneeecey. When I reached the last doorway, I just stared.

I was looking at a bathroom alright—one whose Lilliputian purple porcelain fixtures, including a doll-sized shower, had been custom-built for Oxymoron.

Stung by defeat, I knelt on the tiles and, using my thumb and forefinger to turn a microscopic golden faucet, let lukewarm water dribble into my cupped palm. When I'd collected enough, I slapped it on my face.

Hardly made a difference.

Twisting into a pretzel, I viewed segments of myself in a miniature mirror. I gasped—shag imprints welted my lavender skin, and my hair resembled Einstein's. I would've appreciated his take on this whole situation. He'd most likely chalk it up to relativity. Relativity gone horribly wrong.

My bloodshot eyes followed the maroon runner that swept from the washroom's threshold right up to a tiny toilet equipped with a platinum sploggle. A ten-carat, marquise-cut diamond sparkled from a crown-shaped setting in the lid's center. A white rubber yacht sailed the bowl's calm seas.

Flaxen fringe bordered the edges of spool-sized toilet paper hanging from a moronically-grinning ceramic jester's fingers. A brush disguised as a scepter stood guard. The royal chamber lacked only a monarch.

Overcome by a rush of anxiety, I lumbered out of the room, trying, for the life of me, to remember what it was I'd been trying to remember.

I DIDN'T KNOW WHETHER it was the stink or the swinging doors that whacked me when I entered the kitchen.

Overflowing trash cans, crusty utensils, and moldy lumps sprouting technicolor shoots surrounded a disconnected, displaced stove. A sled—ridden by a murky bowl housing two motionless goonafish and a plastic deep-sea diver—jutted out of the oven.

A toaster claimed squatter's rights on the cooker's top level, most likely enchanted by the property's oceanfront view. Grisly vegetative matter cascaded from its four slots, onto the three-headed-hawk percolator perched below. Dark globs dripped from each chrome beak, indicating recent usage.

Against the wall, alone and aloof, stood a pristine ivory refrigerator. The tall, good-looking appliance must've been slumming.

Hope sprang, but not eternal. I flung the fridge doors open, only to be met by a wall of pungent odor packing a punch so powerful that it solidified my sinuses and hurled me several feet backward, landing me atop a mountain of rubbish.

From my lofty new perspective, I studied the icebox's vividly colored contents, concluding that they might possibly be dangerous if taken internally. My empty stomach whined.

"Bad mornin'," chirped Flea, skipping into the room.

"Mornin'."

Noting my glum mood, his demeanor changed. He pointed to a green spaghetti dinner pasted to the wall. "I've already cleaned this place twice."

"Uh-huh."

Up on the ceiling, a leggy insect labored fruitlessly to free itself from a web. When a spindly spider moved in for the juicy kill, I had to look away.

"'Zig," continued Flea, "could afford to hire someone."

While he prattled on about the kitchen's disgraceful condition, thoughts of home flooded my mind. Everyone—my mother, sister, brother, even my landlord—knew I'd headed for the shore. Nobody'd miss me till I wouldn't show up for work Monday morning. And no-body'd ever find me. Not in a gazillion years.

I barely felt Flea tapping my foot. "Din'cha hear me?"

"Yeah," I answered, invisible steel pliers squeezing my brain. "This place is gross—"

"No—"

"It's *not?* You just *said*—"

"I jus' said, lessee if you're ready to travel home."

I raised an eyebrow.

"If y'learn to do it safely, y'can come back an' visit."

I'd rather have malaria, I thought.

Frowning, he extended a hand. "Lemme help ya down."

"OKAY, NICKI, WALK A straight line. Again."

"What're you, the walking police?"

"I hafta judge whether you're strong 'nough to leave."

I trudged across the living room for the twenty-ninth time.

"Can't let'cha go if y'not steady."

"C'mon, Flea—you promised—"

"You're swayin'."

"I'm exhausted! And there's nothing in this whole county I can eat—"

"Your legs are still weak."

"Please, I gotta leave—*today!*"

"I dunno."

I fell to my knees. "I'm begging."

"Stand on one foot again."

"I feel so stupid—I hope no one can see me."

"Jus' do it." He pounded his fist on the table. "I'm responsible for ya. Y'don't wanna end up like—like—"

I crossed my arms. "Julio?"

"Jus' do what I say," growled Flea. "Stand on your right foot. Ready? Go!" He clicked his stopwatch.

"There," I shouted, struggling to maintain my balance for five seconds, "is *that* good enough for you?"

He clipped his timepiece back onto his utility belt. "Sit."

First time a dog had ordered *me* to sit. I lowered myself and tumbled backward, landing in a heap. I glared at the occasional chair. I didn't like its attitude.

Before I could pick myself up, Oxymoron was all over me, licking my face. It was disconcerting to receive comfort from someone who bore such close resemblance to Gneeecey.

CHAPTER 5

THREE LOUSY NUMBERS
AN' A COLOR

"I, UH, DIDN'T MEAN—um, I'm sorry for, y'know, when I said—I mean, thought—I'd rather have malaria than come back," I stammered. "I really didn't mean—"

"S'okay," replied Flea, patting my arm.

"Thanks for understanding."

"*De nada.*"

My jaw dropped.

"Been waitin' to use that—we studied alien languages at the academy. Trouble speaks in many tongues."

"I—I imagine it does."

"Let's go, Nicki. Time to get'cha home." He crouched down to rub

Oxymoron's snowy tummy. "Don't worry, Spotsickles—Bogelthorpe'll be up soon."

Hands shaking, I stroked the pup's lightbulb-sized head.

OXYMORON'S YELPS RICOCHETED OFF the walls as we lumbered down the corridor. My numb legs kept giving way—I had to stop every few yards.

"Bad morning," gushed Bogelthorpe, as he bounced out of the chiming elevator. A choke chain dangled from his pasty fingers.

"Bad mornin'," replied Flea, his eyes fixed on my gimpy limbs.

The doorman inserted an arm back into the car after we entered, and pressed the button for the lobby, to save us the trouble. His open hand, ignored by Flea, narrowly escaped being severed at the wrist by the closing doors.

I clutched the icy railing and braced myself for the ear-popping descent.

DAYLIGHT GLORIFIED THE MUSTANG'S new streaks and dents. My dad had spent years restoring that car. Tears welled up as I flopped into the driver's seat and pulled the door shut.

Flea leaned into my open window. "You're trapped," he whispered, glancing over his shoulder, "between *worlds*."

"Whaaa—"

"Perswayssick County was created when our two dimensions collided."

"This isn't funny—"

He fiddled with his long ear. "It was an accidental interface."

"C'mon—"

"Our scientists call it an 'EDE'—an Exponential Dimensional Event. It's complicated—hasta do wit' time warps an' the time-space continuum, an' tripled dimensional displacement."

"*Tripled dimensional displacement*," I repeated, praying that Flea wasn't some kind of nut.

"I'm *not* some kinda nut!"

"Hey—"

"Y'wanna go home?"

"Aren't you supposed to be telling me *how*?"

"Displacement formulas are so complex that 'Zig thinks 'bout 'em when he has trouble sleepin'—works better'n countin' herds of vlork vaultin' over vlonkets."

I winced. I couldn't picture Gneeecey counting anything but cash.

"'Zig'll 'splain the technical part better, some other time—"

"Some other TIME? There isn't gonna BE—"

"SSSSSH! I know this is hard to wrap your head 'round."

"You got that right."

"When y'think of it though, we're lucky."

I licked my dry lips. "We are?"

"Well," replied Flea, laughing so hard he began crying, "if one of those collidin' dimensions, say yours, was antimatter, we wouldn't be havin' this conversation."

I shot him a sidelong glance.

"Anyway," he continued, regaining his composure, "when the outer reaches of our atmospheres touched, it created a new dimension incorporatin' elements of Earth *an'* Planet Eccchs."

"Strange universe. You'd better not be pulling my leg."

"I'm not. An' actually, our scientists say it's a multiverse—at least a tripliverse, possibly a quadrupliverse."

My eyes widened.

"You'll be shocked to hear this," he informed me. "Perswayssick County's parta New Joisey."

"Oh?"

"Planet Eccchs—actually, our richly-historic Commonwealth of Bozovia—brushed by your Garden State, quite accidentally."

"How come the rest of Jersey doesn't know?"

"Perswayssick County's not detectable by *your* dimension."

"So then you don't pay state taxes."

Flea's face lit up. "Or federal. But we do maintain our own taxation commission, to ensure county safety an' services. Taxation's one of the things our Grate Gizzy oversees."

My jaw tightened. Gneeecey would tax a dead horse and enjoy it.

The superhero noticed my pained expression. "'Zig's not all that bad."

I remained silent.

"D'ya understan' so far?"

"Honestly, Flea, I'm trying."

He rubbed his chin, searching for the right words. "Y'can't see these other dimensions from here or there—it's kinda like not bein' able to see somethin' that's 'round the corner.'"

"Uh-huh."

He raised an index finger. "Like radio waves—y'can't see 'em, but'cha know they're there."

I nodded. "Okay. Got'cha. But how do I return to, y'know, *regular* New Jersey?"

"Well, that all depends on what'cha consider regular—"

"Please—"

"Awright, awright." He scribbled something on the back of a business card.

"What's that?"

He slapped his hand over my mouth, squashing half my nose. "These words are your passport home. Don't say 'em aloud till you're in a deserted area! Nebberd-kinnezzard say 'em when you're sick, or wit' anyone—it could be disastrous."

Trying to breathe through one clogged nostril, I grunted.

"I'd suggest those woods, on Street Avenue," he advised, finally removing his hot, prickly mitt.

"*Four words'll* get me home?"

"Yup—like 'Zig says, three lousy numbers an' a color."

"You mean, *he* knows how to—"

"Now put that card away!"

"How do I know that this, uh, incantation, won't transport me to your planet?"

He gazed heavenward. "It can't. Nuthin' can."

"You can't return to your planet?"

"Nope." The superhero wiped his wet peepers on his sleeve. "Us Eccchsers—canine-humanoids, humans, an' other folk, like Altitude—have no such way of goin' home."

"Why not?"

"Has somethin' to do wit' our planet bein' the PDT—the Primary Dimensional Transgressor. Our scientists say we caused the EDE. Quantum Electrohypernuculational Globulization or somethin'—I'm not sure. Ask 'Zig—"

"You mean, *he*—"

"He's the expert," declared Flea.

"Can't your, y'know, ESP help?"

"Even when it works, it never gives me the answer to this."

"Does your planet know you're stranded?"

"Yeah. Our technology's more advanced than yours," he answered, apologetically.

"Anybody from Jersey stuck on your planet?"

"Not that we know of—although some of our citizens have reported sightin' rogue tomatoes. Giant ones."

"How many of you are stuck here?"

He lowered his head. "At last census, fifteen million."

"That's more people than in all of—"

"New York City," he proclaimed, finishing my sentence. "More folks than y'got in some countries."

"So, you do communicate with your planet."

"We maintain an electronic link-up—our computers have a twenny-seven-zillion-point-two terafluroflop capability," he replied, sniffling. "We can even transfer certain light materials back an' forth, like rindom seeds."

My own eyes had misted over.

He blew his honking nose on his cape. "Our scientists—here *an*' on our mother planet—are workin' day an' night, thirteen months a year, to find the right formula to bring us home."

I took his hand in mine.

The hint of a smile suddenly illuminated his tear-stained face, much like sunshine peeking through clouds after a soaking storm. "Y'know, as Grate Gizzy, 'Zig'll not only be accountable for our safety an' welfare—he'll be spearheadin' efforts to return home."

"You mean, *he*—"

"FLEEEA!" screamed a sign-carrying figure, zigzagging across the street, as horns blasted and tires shrieked.

Flea's eyeballs popped out. "FLUBBUBB—WATCH OUT!"

A split-second later, a speeding brown Freak O'Nature truck plowed into a swerving kelly-green taxi.

Oblivious to the fact that Murgatroyd Avenue had, in his honor, just tied itself into knots, gift-wrapping him a smash-up complete with sparkling confetti, the jaywalker stepped up onto the curb.

As the drivers emerged from their crumpled vehicles, cussing each other out, Flea grabbed his pal by the shoulders. "For Bogelthorpe's sake—y'almost got hit!"

"Lousy drivers," muttered Flubbubb. His golden, iridescent fur reflected subtleties of the rainbow with each movement. A cinnamon widow's peak capped his lustrous dome, and he possessed a magnificently silky buff tail.

He set his handmade "Stop the Divlopment" sign down on the sidewalk. The "S" had been scrawled backward.

"I see," Flea shouted over the whining sirens and clanking tow-trucks, "you're demonstratin' 'gainst the *development*."

"Yeah—I been protestin' all mornin', all by myself, to impress 'Zig."

"Nice threads," commented Flea, noticing Flubbubb's electric-blue "Save the Goonafish" T-shirt.

"Been wearin' it everyday—I mean, how'll the poor goonafish learn if their underwater schools get bulldozed? An' we can't let those mean divloppers steal 'Zig's money—"

"Flubbubb," interrupted Flea, looking my way, "Nicki Rodriguez. Nicki, Flubbubb Finial."

"Hi." I extended a hand.

"Oh, hi." Flubbubb glanced absentmindedly in my direction for all of two seconds, then addressed Flea, in his Gneeecey-like voice. "Can't wait till our big rally tonight, in Circle Square!"

My teeth hurt, picturing the good doctor playing his electrically-amplified violin.

"Uh, Flubbubb—"

"Did 'Zig say I could play wit' yuz? Did he? Did he?" Flubbubb's tail revolved so rapidly, he resembled a helicopter, ready for take-off.

"Uh—"

"Got my triangle professionally tuned, 'specially for tonight. An' I'm takin' these anti-xylophobic tablets—the pharmacist says they're herbicidal."

"Flubbubb, we gotta talk—"

"I love talkin' 'bout 'Zig! He's so cool!"

Steering Flubbubb up the walk, Flea pointed to a chrome-plated railroad car across the street. "Nicki, we're headin' over to the diner. Can I buy ya brunch?"

"Uh, no—please don't! Um, I mean, no thanks!"

"Okay, nex' time."

"Uh—there won't *be* a—"

"Oh, an' here." Flea handed me a wad of bills.

"What's that for?"

He grinned sheepishly. "Your bumpers."

"Thanks, but I can't take that—you saved my life."

He stepped back. "I insist."

I tucked the money into his red utility belt. "I'm gonna miss you— you're a class act."

"Aw, that's the nicest thing anyone's ever tol' me."

"I mean it."

"You be careful, Nicki."

Nodding, I fastened my seatbelt.

The superhero tossed a Rindom Doodles SnacPac through my window. "Y'gotta be hungry!"

"Thanks, Flea. Nice meeting you, Flubbubb. If I run into Julio, I'll tell him you guys said hi."

Flubbubb's chin clunked to his chest, his spinning chocolate eyes stilled by terror.

I WAS READY TO roll.

I'd lost track of how many times I'd peered down at Flea's card, to make sure it was still there.

Hyperventilating, I turned my key, comforted by the Mustang's distinctive idle, that is, until voices exploded from my speakers—sassy and harmonized, like my grandmother's favorite group, the Andrews Sisters—belting out, "Nuthin' could be stoopider than a week away on Jupiter, with you, joop-joop-a-joop, stoop-stoop-a-stoop!"

I slammed the radio's remaining knob with my fist—popping it off—and screeched out of my parking space.

Murgatroyd Avenue remained littered with broken glass and bumper-to-bumper traffic. Overhead, tangles of unchanging red lights, multi-colored blinkers, and odd signs decorated intersections, like carelessly hung holiday ornaments.

What did "Look before you stop to start before you go," and "Left turners may not, unless not specified not to, especially in this lane. Otherwise move into the next left-turn-only lane before trying not to do it again," mean?

My damp clothes glued me to my seat as the midday sun transformed the car into a greenhouse.

Exhaust mingled with street vendors' steaming, rindom-laced munchies, manufacturing a hanging stink. Nausea stole up into my throat.

LEAVES BLEW DOWN THE road sideways, their sharp points scraping the pavement. The sweet smoke that swirled through the crisp air conjured up phantoms of autumns past.

Before I knew it, Street Road's flame-colored woods filled the windshield. Jelly jiggled through my veins as I drove over layers of crunchy foliage and parked.

I scrutinized Flea's chicken scratch, until the words meant nothing. His card's flip side pictured him high in the clouds, cape billowing as he clutched a model of a spine. Embossed letters below read:

Fleaglossitty Floppinsplodge, Superhero
In a jam? Call 3-3-3—S-O-O-P-E-R-F-L-E-A
Chiropractic office opening soon
on Shnoggleshnook Road & Achilles Avenue!
Ask Flea or visit xxx.ifyoucryfleawillfly.zoom or xxx.ouchmyback.click

Cold perspiration gathered on my upper lip as I recalled other times I'd sat frozen—across the street from the midtown Salsa club where I was emceeing.

Each time the light went red, I'd promise myself, next light. Next light, I'll get out and go in. I'd play that game until it was nearly time for the band—and me—to be onstage.

Once inside, I'd always wonder why I'd stayed in the car so long. It wasn't because I was afraid to meet anyone named Julio.

Heart racing, I lowered my head onto the steering wheel, then bolted upright and opened my mouth. Out tripped Flea's four little words, "Three, forty, two, blue!"

After the blinding flash, I saw nothing.

CHAPTER 6

DRAGONS AND DOODLES

THERE WAS NOTHING but blackness. Blackness, accompanied by a suffocating woodsy scent. Whatever pinned me felt soft, yet crackled whenever I stirred the slightest bit.

Freaked, I began thrashing, until it dawned on me that I might be inside my car. Leaning to my left, I groped for a handle, and one resonant click later, tumbled sideways into harsh daylight.

My watery eyes focused slowly. The Mustang was packed solid with leaves—bushels of vivid autumn leaves.

Stumbling upright, I brushed myself off and looked around. Somehow, I'd materialized on the Garden State Parkway's northbound shoulder, headed for home.

I CLEANED OUT MY vehicle as well as I could with two hands, and, flummoxed, pulled out onto the highway. My wristwatch smiled up at me from the passenger seat. Its cracked face, circled by a jerky second hand, read four twenty-three.

I tuned in my all-news station—an ordeal, manipulating razor-sharp screws that should've been covered by knobs.

"It's seventy-five degrees, and we've got sunshine this gorgeous late-summer afternoon," proclaimed WXNY's Autumn Raines. "But we'll cool down tonight—temps'll plummet through the upper forties. For back-to-work Monday, we can expect highs to recover only into the mid-fifties—if we're lucky."

Great.

"And get your umbrella out," advised the meteorologist. "Drizzle will be steady tomorrow. With this system stalled over us, we can expect a pretty chilly, dreary week."

I hit the gas.

To this day, I have no memories of paying tolls. Or exiting. I do recall pulling onto the driveway, thrilled to see every crack and pothole, even the unsightly oil slick created by my Mustang's leaky engine.

And I recollect plucking leaves off my sleeves as I hobbled past my lanky, silver-haired landlord. Rico mentioned something about my terrible sunburn, then asked if I'd gone upstate instead of to the shore. I think I mumbled something about borrowing a rake.

Floating down the creaky staircase into the welcome darkness of my basement apartment—on my way to total shutdown—I must've brewed some coffee. Probably slapped something between a couple slices of bread, and gobbled every last crumb.

I do remember, in the shower, gazing lovingly at the holes where the old faucets used to be.

THE CONSTANT PATTER OF rain outside sounded more vigorous than Raines' drizzle.

Hulking silhouettes, cloaked in the charcoal of dawn, played tricks on my eyes. Huddled under my covers, savoring the smoothness of my sheets, I watched meek lamps and benign coat racks morph into savage, book-devouring dragons, their barbaric intentions reflected in my damp dungeon's mirror.

Unclenching my right fist, I became aware of a burning sensation. Gripped by a sudden nostalgia for something vague, something dream-like, I pulled my monster-lamp's chain and examined my hand underneath the warm, yellow light.

A rust-colored, quill-covered Rindom Doodle stared up at me, from the center of my bloodied palm.

PART 2

One month later. . . .

CHAPTER 7

THE PURLOINED PORTFOLIO

T HE TRAIN WHISTLE'S MOURNFUL strains pierced predawn's quiet, its minor chords wailing tales of woe from places far away, with a weary but determined urgency.

After a minute, the blaring trailed off, leaving in its wake a sense of unease. I stared, transfixed, at the clock's obscene red digits, suspended in darkness.

I drew in a deep breath of dank basement air and pulled the cool sheets up past my sniffling nose. My miserable, month-long cold-that-wasn't-really-a-cold wouldn't go away.

Despite my malaise, I was getting up and going to work, six, sometimes seven days a week, holding down two jobs.

I threw off my covers and forced my weary bones into a sitting position. Since that lost weekend, I'd all but abandoned my own business, NickelRod Productions, managing to dodge clients—something my incredibly screwed-up budget wouldn't allow much longer. Not that I was in imminent danger of starvation. Truth was, I had little desire to eat, and all my clothes had become baggy—a new, not entirely unpleasant phenomenon.

Shivering, I dangled my tingly legs over the floor. Any day, Maurice L'Orange would steam back into port, ego towed by a small fleet of overtaxed tugboats.

I sat up straight as an arrow. A dim, half-memory floated through the cloudy space separating my ears—that of L'Orange forking over cash to cover his last batch of programs plus his outstanding balance. At sunrise, after a hellish all-nighter in my makeshift home studio, I didn't think I was imagining it. . .but couldn't be sure I wasn't. . . .

One thing I did know for sure: Like my clothes, my life didn't fit right anymore.

But it was the *missing* thing that drove me craziest, that vital something that eluded me, even as I chased it through my waking dreams.

I whacked the whining alarm clock and sprang out of bed. I was already late.

Displaying my usual allergic reaction to mornings, I walked into a wall. The shower refreshed me—until the last sliver of soap slipped down the clog-prone drain when the "no sting" baby shampoo blinded me, and I dropped my five-ton, economy-size bottle of no-name conditioner on my foot.

Frigid air slapped my wet body as I leapt through the plastic curtains. A lopsided hop became an ungainly trot when my feet hit the cold cement. Fumbling with an uncooperative bath towel, I made a beeline for the pre-set coffee maker and scalded my tongue taking a greedy, on-the-run sip. At least this morning, I hadn't poured the joe into the instant oatmeal.

Back in the bathroom, WXNY's sports report informed me I was losing my race against time—by a quarter-past-seven, I should've been curling my newly-dyed, what-was-I-thinking ash blond hair. Instead, I'd assaulted my cornea with a mascara wand. Several black rivers trickled down my cheek. Damn—the stuff was only waterproof when you tried to get it off.

I scrubbed my face raw and slathered on more foundation, careful to conceal a strange, purple-tinged complexion. I had yet to call Dr. Acevedo.

Eye still tearing, I balanced the coffee cup, comb, and jar of gel on the basin's edge, and switched on the dying blow-dryer. If you happened to shut the thing off by mistake, you had to wait twenty minutes before it would restart.

The phone rang, and everything—including the overfilled mug—tumbled into the sink. Who'd call this time of morning? Whoever the hell it was would be sorry—I'd make sure. I yanked the cordless phone out of my pocket, ripping my robe. "Whaaat?!"

"It's me—Carlos! You okay?"

"Carlito!" Instantly, my anger dissolved. "Where are you? I mean, it's so early." I held the dryer as far from the phone as the length of my arm allowed.

"Wow—I totally forgot the time difference! We're in Amsterdam—I haven't slept in two weeks."

"Don't worry—it's good to hear your voice. When are you coming home?"

"Friday. Day after tomorrow—the thirteenth."

"Can't believe you guys have been gone two weeks."

"The trip's been amazin', Nicki. London's 'Salsa City!' The promoter wants us back next spring. They want us back in Paris, too. Maybe you can come an' emcee—think about it!"

"I will—"

"Paris was off the hook! Papo Martínez sat in with us—on congas."

"*The* Papo Martínez?"

"The one an' only. Now, maybe after all this freakin' European stardom, we'll be able to get a decent gig in New York. Y'know, home, sweet home?"

"Carlito, it's sure about time—you've paid your dues—and a few other people's, too."

"Oh—I wanted to ask you, can I come up to the radio station Saturday? Y'know, to play some of our live stuff with Papo?"

"That'll work out great—I don't have anyone else scheduled."

"Cool! An' I picked up somethin' special for you in Paris— I'll bring it Saturday. Be good. Ciao!"

I could feel his broad grin.

The prehistoric hair dryer still roared. I was late, but suddenly in less of a hurry. Visions of the Eiffel Tower peeking through spring blossoms drifted between me and the fogged-up mirror. Hmmm. . .still couldn't find my passport. . . .

The phone rang again, interrupting a new stream of thoughts.

Like before, I held the dryer at arm's length, answering more gently this time. No one seemed to be on the other end. One of *those* calls. My eyes narrowed.

Suddenly, high, squeaky words fired out of the earpiece.

"Bad mornin', it's MEEEEEEEEE!"

The dryer coughed out a puff of pungent gray smoke and died.

"Ig," inquired the shrieky voice, "are y'there?"

I felt the top of my head being pulled upward by some invisible force.

"Y'didn't think you'd stinkin' get away wit' this, did'ja?"

"Hah," I managed to croak, "whaaa—"

"Ya owe me big time, Ig! Big an' Ig rhyme! Plus they both have I's an' G's that could be spares—horizontally or vertically! Even verticazontically! But forget that—you're gonna *pay*!"

The nightmarish image of a cracked, puke-pink plastic Greek column reentered my consciousness. "Your *column?*"

"Yeah, Iggarooney, plus I got this here invoice—hadda dredge the river to recupetrate your junk!"

"Who asked you to?" I shouted, emboldened by wrath.

"Hadda make sure your toxic trash wasn't gonna deregenerate our river an' poison the goonafish!"

"Whaaa—"

"Want'cha stuff, y'gotta *buy* it back! Where else could'ja get a deal like that?"

"I've got news for *you*—"

"Nope, Iggleheimer, I got news for yooou—if y'don't buy it back, I'm sellin' it!"

I stumbled backward, slamming my spine into the sink's unforgiving porcelain.

"I know how y'got to our dimension, too," continued the screechy voice, "an' I know all your other secrets."

"What secrets?"

"Your little game's over."

"WHAT GAME?!" The telephone, propped between my chin and shoulder, slipped and became airborne, plunging into the waters of the open toilet. As the beige buoy bobbed, its antenna stuck straight up, like a periscope.

"Y'know," screamed the voice, oblivious to its nautical fate, "you'll pay back summa what'cha owe by preforatin' commonoonity service—that's a fryable option. Look at all the abandoned shoppin' carts lyin' HOMELESS in the STREETS! Jus' cast aside! RUSTED! Missin' WHEEEELS! YOU'RE gonna get 'em ready for ADOPTION!"

Vision obscured by white spots, I dropped to my knees.

"An' ya owe me for INCORNVENIENCE! INCORNVENIENCE is very INCORNVENIENT!"

I flushed the toilet, knowing full well that the phone wouldn't go down.

I TRUDGED UP THE driveway on leaden legs, squinting to shut out arrows of late afternoon sun as they shot between leaves and clouds.

Still breaking my head trying to remember exactly what had knocked me for a loop earlier that morning, I clicked my key in the lock, shoved the door open, and scooped up the mound of mail piled on the ledge. Scrambling down the steps, I made a dive for my oversized swivel chair and slumped over my paper-covered desk.

Slowly, I summoned the courage to raise my head and sift through the day's heap of bills and ads. Tore open my mechanic's statement. Had to keep getting the car fixed or I couldn't get to work to keep getting the car fixed—to keep getting to work. Maybe the Mustang could be trained to wait tables. Another income would come in handy—help pay off those pesky student loans.

And there was the car insurance. Anytime I thought I had a couple extra bucks, there it was, without fail.

Muttering, I rifled though the usual assortment of insipid ads, repeats of one-time-only offers to send away for genuine replicas of things you wouldn't want in the first place, even if they weren't fake, and catalogs so dumb they flunked their entrance exams to get into bathrooms.

One last piece remained: a plain, white envelope bearing only my first name, sloppily typed and misspelled—without the "N." No return address, no stamp, no visible postmark.

After examining the mysterious missive under the lamp—additional illumination revealing only a brown smudge streaked across the back— I ripped the thing open.

It appeared to be a ransom-style note. Glossy letters of various fonts, sizes and colors, cut crookedly from magazines and glued with lumpy paste, read [sic]: "Wancha stuff bak? Start puttin green piktshures of Grover an Ben together for me. Yull be gettin further instrukshuns whutta dooo necks."

The letter was signed neatly, in purple ink, "Verrry turly yers, Dr. B.Z.Z. Gneeecey."

With a dull thud, my head dropped to the desk.

I WOKE WITH A start and lurched forward, upsetting a Styrofoam cup and spilling icy, week-old coffee in my lap. In front of my bloodshot eyes sat the *missing* thing—my maroon leather portfolio. It was swollen and weatherbeaten.

Holy crap—it all came rushing back! I'd stashed L'Orange's dough, plus payments from other clients—around 10G in cash—into a secret compartment inside the case. Zippered inside the main section were a shorthand outline of my unwritten novel, and my passport.

Gulping, I extended a trembly hand.

"Now y'see it, now Y'DON'T!" shrilled an all-too-familiar, furry white-and-black apparition, whisking the case away in less than a wink.

My mouth opened.

The creature lifted a red high-top in my direction. "Trick or treat, smell my feet, gimme somethin' good to eat!" Anger crept into his voice. "Well, ain't that how yuz Earthlin's greet each other this time of year?"

I jumped up.

"Y'surprised to see me? Did I scare ya? Haaah? I certaincerely hope so!" He hugged the portfolio to his chest. "Geez, don't look so oogdimonious."

"Dr. Gneeecey," I whispered, memories of that lost weekend flooding back, "how the hell did you get here?"

"WHAAAAAAAT?"

"How the *hell*," I repeated louder, articulating each word clearly, "did you *get* here?"

"Hell had nuthin' to do wit' it—y'left a window open."

Smiling defiantly, Gneeecey hoisted my treasure high above his head. "Y'know, I've always prided myself on sneezin' correctly—phonetically. Watch—AAAAH, HAAAH, HAAAAH, HAAATCHOOOO!" An ear-splitting nose honk followed, as papers and other light objects flew off the desktop.

"Bless me!" He tossed the portfolio into the air and laughed fiendishly as it grazed the low, rough-textured ceiling. Scurrying across the room, he made a grandiose catch, then looked my way as if seeking approval.

My stomach churned audibly.

"Entertaineratin', huh, Ig? Y'like vaudeville? I visited once—gave my regards to Broadway."

"Okay," I growled, "give me back the case."

"Nope—y'gotta earn it back, the ol' fascist way, jus' like I earned everythin' *I* got!"

"I said, give it back."

"I said nope—I'm takin' it back home wit' me!"

"You'll do no such thing."

"I'll do YES such thing!" he countered, leaping out of range and flying smack into the side of a tall bookcase, toppling it.

A deafening deluge of hardcover books pounded the floor.

I clenched my fists.

Oblivious, Gneeecey skipped up the mountain of fallen tomes and kicked one down. After executing several hideous somersaults, Aristotle's *Metaphysics*—leather-bound, a gift from Dad—landed open, face up, its gilt-edged pages mangled.

"Spilt books are worth two in the bush. Don't cry over 'em," he philosophized gleefully. "Cry for Argentina instead."

He must've realized I wasn't amused. Maybe he sensed homicide hanging in the air. Still clutching the case, he took several steps back.

I lunged at him.

"TOOOODLES!" he cried, bolting.

As I flew up the stairs and out the door, my head spun in fifty directions, searching the darkness for any sign of the little creep.

Swift on his sneakered feet, Gneeecey was already halfway down the block, emitting high-pitched squeaks.

My ankle nearly turned as I tottered down the uneven sidewalk in delicate red pumps. The October air had frozen my coffee-saturated jeans to my thighs, and my cramping calves threatened mutiny.

Just as my right knee buckled into a backward collapse, Gneeecey screeched to a halt. "Real EARTH pumpkins!" he squealed, eyeing a neighbor's stoop. "Jus' like in the BOOKS!"

Pivoting, he headed west, toward the railroad tracks.

Crumbled steps on each side led down into an unsavory tunnel, one that had a reputation for radiating putrid odors on *nice* days.

My heart plummeted through the pit of my stomach when I saw the parked freight train. Losing no time, Gneeecey scampered underground, whooping, "A TUNNEL! WHAT FUNNEL!"

I froze.

"Wan'cha stuff?" he taunted. "Come GIT me!"

Tearing in after him, slop walloping my shoes, I ran hard, desperate to escape the stink, and the hellacious passageway's fabled legions of vile, subterranean reptiles and multiple-legged insects—and two-legged thugs.

Still breathing through my mouth, I threw myself up the steps and rolled onto the sharp, debris-littered stones outside.

Gneeecey stood over me, victory flashing in his bulgy eyes.

Before I could get up, the cackling cur howled something undecipherable and vanished with the portfolio into thin air. Five magic syllables, propelled by blind fury, exploded up from my depths.

CHAPTER 8

TOO BAD, THREE EGGS

MY SLIT OF A right eye opened. At least I think it did—all I saw was sludge. Then I heard squishy footsteps, as two luminous orbs—a pair of sickly-yellow eyeballs, not inside anyone's skull—came into view. Lumpy raised vessels circling their shiny whites, they floated toward me.

The ovals glowed and glimmered and dipped down low, intrigued, as a brown, rubbery blob took on a life of its own, rising up from the ground and moving in midair, stretching itself into a taut membrane.

Gradually, the force made itself visible as a pair of amber-tinged hands, slathering and caressing more muck, building the eyes a head to live in. And a waxy face wearing an expression made malicious by its slanted, sardonic smile.

The hands grew arms. Muscular, chiseled arms. And legs. And a naked body that, pleased with having created itself, stole off into darkness.

"GEDDUP, IG!" SCREAMED A familiar voice.

"I'm stuck in this—ugh—skunky brown stuff," I replied, choking. "I can't move."

Gneeecey was as sympathetic as a washing machine. "Course y'can, Ig. But may ya? An' don't say 'skunky'—mierk's our county's most precious resource."

"Leave 'er alone, 'Zig," implored Flea, peering down at me like I was some half-baked school science project. "She's jus' dimension-jumped. Way too soon, wit'out the protection of a vehicle."

"Veeehicle, shmeeehicle—*I* didn't have none neitherwise, an' nuthin's wrong wit' *me*."

"You *know* her species is, well, uh, biologically *different*."

"Fleaglositty Floppinsplodge, maybe all them consonants ain't wasted on ya after all. Us Eccchsers are superior—in all ways. Now GEDDUP, y'dopey subspecies!" He kicked me.

I moaned.

Flea sighed. "'Zig, don'cha have a single shred of compassion runnin' through you?"

"Nope, Fleaglossitty, I'm proud to say I don't." He yanked a strand of mierk from his sneaker and let it snap back like a rubber band. "Not a stinkin' shred."

As my right arm flailed uselessly, vestiges of a disturbing dream—one with devilish undertones—haunted me. Couldn't recall much. But the evil lingered.

"I'll dig ya out," volunteered Flea, kneeling on a ragged piece of cardboard. Gently, he began to peel away the latex-like mask that covered half my face.

"Thanks," I whispered.

"Y'know, Nickels," he said, calling me by a nickname only my younger brother Dave used, "my ESP musta kicked in—I had a feelin' someone was in trouble. Hadda walk all the way. My flyin' feature's hardly workin'."

I raised my newly freed head. *How come*, I thought, *all the crummy stuff happens to good people?*

The superhero looked at me. "Doesn't always."

Gneeecey reached into his bulging T-shirt pocket, whipped out a translucent orange flip-top phone, and punched in numbers with a vengeance. "Answer awready! This is a state-of-the-art Binky the Clown phone—victims are s'posed to answer immediately. Culvert—what TOOK y'so stinkin' long? Come get me—NOW! An' I got a coupla Iggleheimers wit' me."

Flea shot Gneeecey a glance that could've withered an oak tree.

Gneeecey kept barking into his cell. "Don't make me wait—that's why I fired Ogglebert. . .I don't care if he's maaaad—two bad, three eggs. Listen up—we're on the riverbank, near the new Grubble Grange service road. By Belcher's Mill Run. . .no, not Hoosegow Road—we're on the other end, by Dweebner Boulevard—a mile south of Frogless Flatts. . .y'can't miss us—one of the Iggleheimers has a purple face."

I groaned.

"Later," continued Gneeecey, "I got a meetin' wit' Mark. . .yeah, the older, fraternically identical twin. Then I got my brain surgery club down at Ferguson Memorial. It's my turn to bring sandwiches—we'll swing by the restaurant an' see what Altitude's saved from customers' plates."

Flea's nose wrinkled.

"Whaaat, Culvert?" demanded Gneeecey, squeezing a soft marble of mierk between his thumb and forefinger. "How many times does a duck need to *go*? Drink less. Yeah. . .okay, since now you're my only driver, I'll pay ya extra, but your checks won't refluctuate it. In fac', they'll seem smaller—wit'holdin' taxes are a killer. G'bye!"

"ARKKETTYSMASH!" yelled Flea, still bent over me. "My back!"

"Stop cussin', will ya!" ordered Gneeecey. "I'm the only one authorizated to swear in this here county—I'm the only one who does it wit' any stinkin' class or dignity."

"Flea," I begged, "take a rest."

"I'm okay," he replied through clenched teeth, as he released my lifeless left leg from the gunk's grip. "Sorry 'bout the swearin'—"

"I'm more worried about your back."

"It's embarrassin'," he declared, steadying me as I rose. "Y'ever heard of a chiropractor who needs one? That's bad marketin'."

"Certaintaneously is," agreed Gneeecey. "It's her fault—y'proboobably hurt'cha back liftin' her Mustank."

"C'mon, 'Zig—"

"C'mon y'self." Gneeecey plucked a glob of mierk off his shirt, stuffed it into his kisser, and chewed noisily. "Look at this from *my* angle. What's the use of havin' a superhero friend wit' failin' powers? What's in it for *meeee*?"

Flea's moist eyes met mine.

Gneeecey blew a basketball-sized bubble and sucked it back in before it burst. "Plus, you're afraida heloolicopters."

Flea remained silent.

Gneeecey spit out his coffee-colored wad at my feet. "Pure mierk—ain't bad. I think it's okay to keep puttin' it in our food. I don't feel guilty even more now—I certaincerely don't believe we're poisonatin' our community."

"'Zig, scientists need to study this whole thing more before we—"

"I *am* a scientist, Fleaglossitty—an' who asked ya? An' speakin' of askin' ya stuff, is that whoop cream on your nose?"

Flea whisked the offending substance off his snoot with his long tongue. "What was that all over your face the other night at rehearsal?"

"Shavin' cream. . .I was, uh, tryin' out this new, uh, Freak O'Nature shavin' cream, y'know, 'specially formulizated for, uh, shavin'."

"Y'don't shave, 'Zig."

"Might start." Squirming, he changed the subject. "Uh, hey Ig, y'woulda loved our Mierk Fest!"

"What's to love 'bout mierk?" grumbled Flea. "Walkin' in this mess can't be healthy—maybe that's why I can't fly!"

"WHAAAAAAAT?" shrieked Gneeecey.

"Nuthin'."

"Mierk's our future—it's our civoovic duty to eat it an' play in it—"

"Over there!" I shouted, gripped by déjà vu—and a palpable sense of doom. "Under the bridge, over the water—floating eyeballs!"

"Wit' my astigmatism, all's I see's a blur," replied Flea.

"Look!" I insisted. "Hundreds!"

"It's jus' her Iggleheimer imagination," said Gneeecey.

"It's not! They're moving—aw, they're gone!"

"What'cha got, Ig, Redecoritis?"

"Redeca-*what?*"

"Redecoritis—it's a neurolongitudinal disorder—"

"*Neurological*," interrupted Flea.

"Whatever," growled Gneeecey, regarding him with disgust. "I was addressicatin' the Ig. Redecoritis is a nervological disorder—y'gotta take these special tablooblets—"

"Y'mean, *tablets*—"

"That's what I stinkin' SAID—an' stop tellin' me what I MEAN! Now, like I was sayin', y'gotta take these special tablooblets 'cause stuff starts movin' 'round, trynna get'cha. First, your furniture starts movin'. Then bad Mr. Tree in the backyard starts movin' 'round."

"Strange," I replied. "I've never heard of—"

"C'mon! I got a full schedoodle. Tonight, me an' Dr. Yupnope are perpoopetratin' a partial inclopitation—kinda like a Earth lobotomy." He pointed to my head. "Gotta get to the hospoopital early to stupervise—it ain't his specialty. He's a heemahoologist—y'know, one of them blood doctors. So, c'mon awready!"

"Awright," snarled Flea, surveying the yards of mierk we still had to traverse in order to reach the service road.

"Me an' the Ig landed here 'bout the same time, but *I* awready got so much done! I lef' her here, flat on her dopey face—"

Flea's mouth opened wide. "*Y'what?*"

"I thought'cha proboobably might save her—if y'were havin' a good day. Will y'stop lookin' at me like that! Anyways, I went home to do my mornin' aberrations. Then I hid her stuff, an' when Ogglebert dropped me back here—before I fired him—here she was, the lazy Ig, still hardly movin'. But yooou were here, so that made everythin' okay."

Flea shook his head.

And I remembered why I'd uttered those four words. "Where's my portfolio? The one you dangled in my face to trick me into coming back here—the one you just admitted you hid? Where is it, Doctor Gneeecey?"

"That's stinkin' *Director* Gneeecey! I jus' been officially inordinated Grate Gizzy—director of this county. Bein' a doctor *an'* a director makes me a diroctor."

"Okay, uh, stinking—uh—*Diroctor* Gneeecey. Where's my portfolio?"

"What poopfolio?"

"You know what I'm referring to."

"Y'jus' ended your sentence wit' a propooposition."

"You know which portfolio—"

"The one I dredged outta the river, put in your face, an' hid? Never heard of it."

CHAPTER 9

LIKE A DUCK ON FIRE

GNEEECEY WAS THE ONLY one smiling. His goose steps easily ruptured the molasses-like sheets that connected his sneaker bottoms to the mierk-covered ground.

Flea handed me a penknife. "We'll take turns cuttin' this gump from our shoes."

Leaning on the superhero, I snipped and inched forward, then passed the blade back to him.

"How," he mumbled, "can anyone call this fun?"

Gneeecey's head spun around. "WHAAAT?"

Flea was saved by the bell, or to be more exact, the "Pop Goes the Weasel" tune tinkling out of Gneeecey's phone.

"What'chooo starin' at, Ig? Mind your own stinkin'—smello. . . heya Mark. . .yup, sure was an interesticatin' conservation we had. . . yeah, things are fallin' into place—got somethin' here that'll knock your socks off! Yuz got a big payday comin' your way—an' so do I!" Blinking rapidly, Gneeecey glanced my way. "Even better'n that—I got the *source*."

My purple skin grew clammy, despite the chill in the air.

"I know—I promised yuz," Gneeecey continued, his voice rising several octaves. "Uh-huh. . .I'm sure the whole Merchants' Association, even Councilwoman whassername *an'* her freeloadin' sister'll vote our way. It's in the bag! See ya tonight. . .yeah, it *is* funny how yuz always seem to know 'zactly where I am."

Flea stopped in his sticky tracks and gawked at Gneeecey, who looked right through him, as his white limousine slid up alongside us, pristine in contrast to the slop that surrounded it.

"C'mon," Gneeecey challenged us, hopping onto the blacktop. "Las' one in's a rotten sclogg!"

I eyed him quizzically. "What's a sclogg?"

"A three-legged, sneaker-wearin' mollusk."

"Of course."

"Culvert," he hollered, galloping toward the elongated Lincoln, "y'gonna sit inside all day, QUACKIN'?"

A startling albino mallard—a giant of a bird—emerged from the driver's compartment. Wingless but two-armed, the gawky six-footer waddled, with an air of efficiency, down to the limo's last segment. Around his neck, above his tan tweed jacket's velvety black collar, sparkled the hint of an opalescent, cream-colored ring.

With a dramatic flourish, the dapper drake flung open the vehicle's thirty-first door. As he did, his cap sailed off his feathered dome. He hooked the hat in midair with his webbed foot and inadvertently mashed it down into a mierky puddle.

"Clumsy duck," muttered Gneeecey, hurling himself into the car with the grace of a dump truck.

"I'M F-F-FREEZING," I STAMMERED through chattering teeth.

"You're f-f-freeeeezin'?" Gneeecey stuttered back, seated across from Flea and me.

"S-stop imitating m-me."

"Y'know what'choo Earth people say—'imitations are the mothers of invitations.'"

"Can't Culvert put up the heat?" inquired Flea.

Gneeecey punched his fists in the air. "Heat's too 'SPENSIVE! I never put it up at home _or_ work—_I_ feel warmer when I pay less."

The superhero unsnapped his cape and draped it over my shaking shoulders.

"Thanks." My shivers stopped instantly. I looked at him wide-eyed. "Y'know, I'm amazed—how can we have a _duck_ for a driver?"

"Easy," snapped Gneeecey, before Flea could reply. "They're so easy to take advantage of, it's embarrassin'."

I looked him in the eye. "Director, just for once, I want you to give me a straight answer—"

"Why—are there crooked answers jus' for twice?"

"Just answer my question—tell me once and for all where my portfolio is."

"That's not a question, Ig—it's a regoogoolar sentence. I only answer askin' sentences."

"I'll make it an 'asking' sentence. Where's my portfolio?"

"Oh, that—dunno. But that was a askin' sentence."

We hit a long stretch of bumpy road.

"Whaaat, Fleaglossitty? Ain't my fault your back's messed up. Anyways, I got worser troubles'n you—the Ig here owes me big time. BRAAAP!"

"Uh, 'scuze you?" Flea prompted him.

"Whooo? Yooou? Okay, Fleaglossitty, you're 'scuzipated. As I was sayin' before bein' so rudely interrupticated, the Ig owes me, an' she'll stay as long as it takes her to—"

"As long as it takes me to find my portfolio."

"How dare ya? I'm talkin' at Flea! The Ig here'll stay at my place—"

"Stop talking about me like I'm not here. I'm not staying anywhere—you're giving back my case, then I'm history."

"Nope. You're stayin' wit' *me*."

"Oh, not at your dog's condo?"

He fixed his eyes on me. "You're gonna stay where I can watch ya. An' you're gonna work till y'pay off every cent."

"Oh, really?"

"You're comin' to the office every day, plus you'll help out at the restaurant. An' y'ain't stealin' no more menus. Thought I wouldn't notice, huh, Ig?"

"Uh—I'm sorry. I did take one." My purple face burned with shame. "I thought it would be, y'know, a cool souvenir."

Flea bit his lip to keep from giggling.

"Y'want souvoovenirs?" shrilled Gneeecey. "You'll have plenny when *I* get through wit'cha!"

"When I get home—after you've returned my portfolio—I promise I'll mail back your menu—"

"Y'ain't goin' nowheres. Not till I say ya is."

"Nicki," began Flea, "you're gonna be here a while—you've got severe dimension burn. Bet'cha can hardly feel your legs."

I smacked my dead thighs and the soles of my feet began to tingle. "But my family—and my jobs—"

"Remindicate the Ig 'bout Julio—he was Hispanical too."

"And what exactly happened to Julio?" I demanded.

Flea stared straight at me. "He jumped too *soon*."

Gneeecey tilted his head thoughtfully. "When y'really stop to think 'bout it though, Julio did have some luck in his short little life—ownin' a name startin' wit' a unauthorized J impersonatin' a H."

We'd been riding for an hour, in what seemed to be circles. Bored studying my coffee-stained, mierk-splattered jeans, I turned my attention to a newspaper Flea had absentmindedly tossed onto the floor—the *Perswayssick Pooper-Scooper*. The slogan beneath its Gothic masthead proclaimed, "All the Poop That's Fit to Scoop."

Two headlines vied for attention. One stated that a local whale, beached on the Perswayssick's banks, had given birth to a litter of purebred kittens who solved algebra problems underwater, scribbling on waterproof chalkboards. "Whales are, after all, mammals," began the article.

The other banner blared, "Embattled Grate Gizzy Defends Environmental Stance." Gneeecey's face scowled up from the page.

Shooting me daggers, the good diroctor crumpled the entire section and shoved it out the window.

Just then, our duck driver stopped short. Flea, who'd been dozing, cried out in pain.

"Some chiproctologist you'll be."

"Well 'Zig, at least I'll understand my patients' pain."

"Stooopidest thing I ever heard! BRAAAAAAP! Aaah, that one's been trapped all mornin'," said Gneeecey as he extracted a striped, oblong potato-like object from his shirt pocket.

Clenching it tenderly between unclean choppers, he flipped open his phone and pressed Binky's red nose. A yellow flame shot out of the tongue-shaped nozzle below. Sighing, he ignited his two-toned tuber. The lit end crackled and exploded, filling the limo with black smoke and a stink suggestive of an overpopulated zoo.

"'Zig! Y'trynna kill us?"

"It's a health cigar—s'posed to help my, y'know, *problem*. This one mus' be deflective."

FLEA AND I COULDN'T stop coughing.

But Gneeecey was fine. Happily humming Planet Eccchs's tragic anthem, he plunged his fist into a box. "Rindom Doodle anyone?"

No one answered.

"Good—more for meee." He crunched his doodles rhythmically. I swore he'd had microphones implanted in his molars since my last visit.

My sister Alex would've despised Gneeecey's slovenly smacking—a passionate hatred of eating noises was one of many things we shared. She'd be crushed when she heard I'd gone missing. Twenty years old, Alex was my "younger twin," as we joked. My partner in crime. And our poor mom, Anna—I couldn't bear to think of what this would do to her, so soon after my dad's death. This would be one time my sixteen-year-old brother Dave wouldn't just shrug and offer his stock reply, "Stuff happens."

I prayed that my father was watching over me, as I was driven around by a duck wearing tweed.

"SHAAADDUP, IG!" bellowed Gneeecey. "I CAN STINKIN' HEAR YA THINKIN'!"

I wanted to jump out of the window.

"Don't even try it," Flea advised sternly. I forced a face-hurting smile.

As Gneeecey ingested the last bits of his snack—cardboard container and all—we reached the northernmost end of Murgatroyd Avenue, and the Mierkolatory. The dingy dinosaur's colossal pistons slammed up and down, shaking the ground beneath us as it puked poison into the atmosphere.

Gneeecey rolled down his window. "Stuff that goes in our food comes from there."

"CLOSE THAT, WILL YA 'ZIG?!"

Gneeecey leaned out of the vehicle. "Mark, ol' buddy, I'll buzz ya after my meetin' wit' Mark! An' hi, Mark! An' Mark—call y'later! An' thanks, guys—driveway's beaudiful!"

Flea and I exchanged puzzled looks. "'Zig, din'cha jus' talk to him on the phone? How many Marks d'ya know?"

"Lots." He lowered his mierk-spattered behind back onto the swanky white seat. "The Mark I talked to before has brothers—a couple are rare almost identical fraternically internal triplets, born in different years."

"Huh?"

"He has sevooveral identical twins that look jus' like him too, 'cept they're taller an' have smaller noses, plus one has redder hair than the other one, who has a bigger chin but browner hair that's shorter."

"Huh?"

"They even share their hair. After a few times, y'can tell 'em apart."

"They're all named Mark?"

"Yeah. Accordin' to Mark—or was that Mark?—since there's so many of 'em, leasin' such a consonant-rich name's cheaper."

STREET ROAD'S WOODED AREA, a palette of wild color only weeks before, had decayed into a lifeless collage of bare sticks and brown leaves. I couldn't imagine how I'd escape this time. My life was over, totally over. I slumped down in my seat.

"Look!" exclaimed Flea.

Reluctantly, I raised my head, as we rumbled down the dusty road, past a black-spotted white building.

"Dalmation Brewery's finally open," he said. "Jus' hired a buncha people. You'll love their beer—it's a white malt, filled wit' these yummy, three-dimensional licorice spots that dissolve in your mouth."

Feigning interest, I nodded. I just wanted to wake up in my old, battered swivel chair, hunched over the mound of unpaid bills piled up on my desk.

"Their brewin' technique's a marvel of physics," added Flea. "It's a secret formula—no matter how you pour or store the stuff, the spots remain evenly distributed."

"Yeah, but it has a flat taste," complained Gneeecey, ripping open another carton of doodles.

"It's made wit' skips, not hops."

"I s'pose it is a revoovoolution in brewin'," Gneeecey conceded grudgingly, "but the way they operate is cost-defective. They should make fewer workers do more—that's how I *got* to be a business maggot."

Yawning, I looked down at my purple hands, then back up at Gneeecey's smirking face. Our eyes locked.

"We borin' ya, Ig?" Suddenly, he screamed into the intercom. "RUN THAT LIGHT!"

"Boss," protested Culvert, his quacky-but-concerned voice barely penetrating the radio static, "it's *red*!"

"SPEAK UP, DUCK, SPEAK UP!"

"I SAID, LIGHT'S RED!"

"Don't take that tone wit' MEEEE! I SAID, RUN THAT LIGHT!"

"We'll get a ticket!"

"Tickets, shmickets. I fix 'em—make 'em into tax decapitations.

That's one of the perks of bein' Grate Gizzy. AN' STOP SHOUTIN'!"
Turning to Flea, he shouted, "WHADDA *DUCKS* KNOW?"

"He's right, 'Zig. Runnin' lights is 'gainst the law—an' jus' plain
dangerous—"

"Law, shmaw—I AM the law 'round here. RUN THAT LOUSY
LIGHT LIKE YOU'RE A DUCK ON FIRE—OR I'LL FIRE YOU
TOOOO!"

"Okay Boss!"

I squeezed my eyelids shut, as all around us tires screeched and glass
shattered.

"Tol' yuz it was safe," said Gneeecey. "Nobody hit *us*. Furthermore,
hitherto, in any event, be that as it may—may that as it be—the law can
kiss my left foot." He ripped off a sneaker, revealing a foul-smelling,
green-and-purple polyester sock embroidered with runs and snags.

I came to, in time to be informed by a snooty sign that I'd just been
afforded the revocable privilege of entering St. Bogelthorpe Parke, an
exclusive and historic suburb of Perswayssick City.

Barren trees shivered along the roadside, their brittle branches clat-
tering in the chill winds. Everywhere, rindom stalks had been chopped
down close to the ground. Frost-covered mounds of the harvested arrows dotted stubby fields for miles. The skies above were overcast, and
you could almost smell snow. I hated winter.

Culvert barely negotiated the sharp turn onto Paper Plane Avenue,
then nearly missed Horsey Street, stopping so short that the limo's thirty-
two segments clunked against each other in a violent, repeating chain
reaction. I felt Flea's pain.

"WATCH IT, DUCK!" howled Gneeecey, spraying half-chewed doodles all over the intercom. "SHE'LL DISLOCATE!"

Culvert answered with a lone, forlorn "quaaack," as the traumatized
vehicle began a harrowing hula dance, ascending Bimbus Crack Drive, a
perilously narrow road that wound round and round a double-peaked
mountain. The higher we climbed, the more fallen trees I saw.

Halfway up, a rotting wooden duck mailbox, a "three" painted on its
wing, listed toward the weeds on a rotting wooden pole, perhaps seeking
a rotting wooden lake.

Several hundred yards later, a parked Good Intentions Paving truck
blocked our way.

"EVERYONE OUT!" barked Gneeecey, pointing to a stone mansion just visible atop the miniature Everest's dimpled summit, its four chimneys partially obscured by heavy, dark clouds. "We WALK the resta the way."

Flea and I groaned.

"Too bad, three eggs," sympathized the good diroctor. "An' walk on the grass—driveway's jus' been done."

Flea's eyes traveled up the half-mile of glistening black ribbon. "Musta cost a deck of vlecks!"

"Mark an' his brothers all chipped in to gimme this, as a token of their depreciation. I jus' hadda pick out the pavin' company. Close your mouth, Fleaglossitty." Gneeecey slapped the side of limo. "Duck, be back by five-stinkin'-thirty."

"Okay, Boss."

"An' don't drive like a duck on fire!"

SLOPING ACRES OF LUSH tartan plaid surrounded Gneeecey's four-story castle. I collapsed into the dreamlike lime, emerald and olive grass.

"Welcome to Three Bimbus Crack Drive, situated on toppa scenic, double-mounded Bimbus Hill," sputtered Flea, gulping for air.

"Don't *welcome* her. She hasta stay, but I don't want her to feel *welcome* in my gigantical, unsinkable mansion."

"Y'must be confusin' your mansion wit' your yacht."

"I'm sicka ya constantly corrugatin' me!"

"Sorry, 'Zig."

"Has this stinkin' house ever *sunk?*"

The superhero bowed his head.

"THEN DON'T KEEP TELLIN' ME WHAT I MEAN!"

CHAPTER 10

BAD FANG CHEWY

I GASPED. GNEEECEY'S HEDGES matched the half-dozen blue jays bloomping around his lawn. "Blue bushes are a luxury only us rich can afford," Gneeecey informed me, as he threw a rock at the birds and missed. "Ain't fair for them to enjoy stuff I pay for. GIT!"

They paid him no mind.

Suddenly, my legs gave way beneath me and I fell into a fluorescent flower bed. "*Electric-orange* hydrangea—"

"Y'see them hydrants plugged in anywhere, ya Ig?"

"Stop calling me 'Ig'."

"Okay, Ig, what's your name again?"

"It's—"

"Time's up—y'don't know. I'll call ya Icky!"

"That's not my—"

"Then I'll jus' call ya Ig, so we'll both know who ya are."

I stumbled upright. "Uh, Diroctor, can't we go inside?"

"See them hardy, all-tempooperature plants?"

"*Please*—"

"Lemme igsplain the colors," he continued, in a condescending, "aren't you a simp?" tone. "The seeds for the bushes an' hydrants come directly from Planet Eccchs. On my planet, these same bushes would come out green—well actually a green-an'-three-quarters— an' the hydrants would be red—a *whole* red."

I began breathing warm air into my blouse.

"But here, Ig, your single sun confuses our plants' chloroflop. Your planet only has one sun. Mine can afford *two*." He shot me one of those patronizing "my planet's superior" looks.

I groaned.

"My blue bushes are really green—on a normal planet, that is—an' the orange hydrants are, like I said, red—that's proboobably why they're called hydrants—an' as everyone knows, when y'subtract one inferior sun's yellow from green, y'get blue bushes."

"Huh?"

"When ya add that subtracted yellow to the red hydrants, y'get orange. Not that I'm complainin'. Orange is neutral—goes wit' everythin'."

The winds had picked up and my teeth began chattering. I was not dressed for winter. "S-subtract yellow? D-doesn't the sun sh-shine on b-both?"

He rolled his eyes. "Flopposynthesis works different here. Our bushes' cloroflop don't absorb your dopey sunlight. So that rejected light reflects back onto the hydrants. Why d'ya think I plant 'em nexta each other? The bushes have a synoonergistic effect on the hydrants."

I sat. Everything was spinning.

"My planet's two suns are strong 'nough to counteract the green plant that's not really blue from reflectin' away the yellow to the red plant that's not really orange."

"What?"

"On my planet, the blue plant hasta stay green. An' the orange plant that's really red can't get orange 'cause our second sun cancels out the yellow from the first sun, but only from the red plant—y'know, the one that the green plant that wasn't blue didn't reflect yellow onto." He smiled.

I began rocking back and forth.

"So, we got lotsa blue food. Y'poor Earthlin's hardly got none."

I decided not to ask about the plaid grass.

"C'mon, Ig—you're makin' me late."

Staggering to my feet, I gazed up at the gleaming, arched windows that graced all four stories of Gneeecey's silvery-stoned McMansion. Inside, an opulent crystal chandelier illuminated a golden-railed, circular staircase. Sliding glass doors above led out to a generous balcony, one my entire dinky basement apartment could fit in.

For all of the elegance, something was amiss. I scrutinized the stately front entrance—polished, red-stained mahogany doors, accented with sparkling brass handles, and not one, but four, doorbells. Gilt italics above spelled out, "Residence of The Grate One."

After about a minute, I realized what was wrong. The slate staircase that belonged in front of the entranceway was positioned fifteen feet to the left of it, underneath a low, open first-story window. A chintzy green-and-white rubber doormat, monogrammed "GIT," languished in the mud, where the steps should have been.

"C'mon—ain't got all day!" Gneeecey yanked a rusty pogo stick, along with a handful of cobalt branches, out of the shrubbery.

"Shouldn't those steps be underneath the doors?"

"Arkookitect built it like that to fool burglars," he answered, peering down at me with disdain, lamenting my pathetic stupidity.

The pogo stick sounded as corroded as it looked, but Gneeecey boinged his way up expertly, yowling, "YEE HAW!" On his third bounce, he managed to grab onto a handle. Balancing the stick's tip on a skinny stone ledge, he turned a dozen keys in a dozen locks, then tumbled through the doors. His nose honked loudly. "Here, Ig. A stick in time saves nine!"

The thing whizzed past my face and crashed in the bushes, smashing 'em flat.

"No thanks, Diroctor. I'll use the side door—it's open."

"That's the out door—but suit yourself."

I FROZE, PLASTERED AGAINST the wall, as two snarling, prehistoric-yet-futuristic chrome beasts snapped at my ankles, ready to rip their razor-sharp, metallic fangs into my flesh. "GNEEECEY!"

"THAT'S DIROCTOR GNEEECEY!" he bellowed from the other end of the hallway.

"DIROCTOR, CALL 'EM OFF!"

"You wanted to use the side door."

"HELP!"

"Stop perspiratin'. It's only Ozzy an' Vizzy. Haven'cha never seen goths?"

"No—can't say I have! They're foaming at the mouth—"

"Ain't they cute?"

Moth-eaten patches of coarse brown fur speckled their shiny, dachshund-like bodies, and a series of hairy handles ran from their necks to their spiked tails. Eight or nine ocher eyes circled their rhino horns, and their slimy snouts housed walls of wolflike teeth. They had too many legs and smelled like little garbage dumps.

"Lovable, ain't they, Ig?"

"Uh, how's Oxymoron these days?"

Gneeecey's face went blank.

I shook my head in disbelief. My sudden movement caused the techno-beasts to rear up on the eleven hind limbs they owned between them. "Your puppy, Spot—"

"Oh, he ain't called lately. Anyways, these guys were a present from Mark. An' Mark. They got chrome-covered steel chassis, but their choppers are iron—gotta be inspecticated regoogoolarly, for rust. Their dentist over in Plackettsburg gave me these barbed-wire toothbrushes to use on 'em, twice a day."

"Vizzy's gonna bite me—"

"That's Ozzy—don't worry, you'll learn to tell 'em apart. He has a bigger horn an' smells like spoilt meat. An'—OW—he's FRIENDLIER! Can'cha tell?"

"NO!"

"Ozzy's a male—they're called gazooongas. An' Vizzy's a female— a gaaah-gaaah. She's smilin'—see? When they have babies, it'll be like gettin' more of 'em, for *free*. Goths are easy to take care of—they'll even eat car batteries."

"Really."

"An' they love cans an' scrap metal. I don't even bother wit' recyclin'—not that I ever did. What's the environment ever done for *meee*?"

"YAAAAAA—HE JUST SLASHED MY SHIN!"

"Anyone ever tell ya, Ig, y'look priddy stooopid hoppin' on one leg?"

"Would you put 'em back—"

"They're jus' showin' off 'cause you're here," Gneeecey insisted, grabbing them by their handles. "OW! C'mon, y'little tykes—Ig's afraida yuz."

He dragged the clanking, slime-oozing critters down the hall and tossed them, along with a shovel, into their room. "Try not to eat your other chair!" He slammed the door shut. You could hear their heads butting against it.

I gave him a stern look. "We've gotta talk."

"First I wanna show y'round so y'don't get lost an' scare nuthin' in the middle of the night."

"But—"

"Now, here's my Hall of Clox—spelled 'C-L-O-X.' It's more economical for one X to do a job that takes a C, K, *an'* S to do."

"Diroctor—"

"Look!" He waddled over to a framed Mona Lisa, one sporting an added-on, clock-infested abdomen. Her mysterious eyes moved back and forth. And so did her tail.

"She jus' gotta look down to see what time it is. See her waggin' tail?" He sighed. "Proves she's happy!"

To the right of da Vinci's altered masterpiece mooed a full-sized Hereford cow, a standard analog clock implanted in her tummy. I jumped when her red eyeballs flashed.

"Installed them infrared security sensors myself." He patted himself on the back. "No intruder'll make it past her."

"Uh, Diroctor—"

"Y'smack her rump—resets the whole system." He smacked her rump.

Nearby, a bespectacled iron hog rocked in his rocker, cradling a book in his hooves. A digital clock grazed in his belly. According to Gneeecey, the scholarly beast oinked on the half-hour.

"Art that ain't functional's a waste. Waste not, want not—there's hungry people on other planets."

A stark, gunmetal clock—"BLIRG" printed across its face—towered over us. "I've never seen a clock like that before."

"Y'mean y'seen all these other clocks before?" asked Gneeecey.

"No—I was just wondering, what's—"

"Y'won't understand, but I'll igsplain anyway." He took a deep breath. "Blirg's a almos'-month-long holiday season where time reverses, on accounta us havin' two suns an' a thirteen-month year. That's when this here clock runs, counterclockwise. An' all these other ones jus' stop."

"Huh?"

"Bein' entangulated in your one-sun, twelve-month stooopidness rotates our whole dimension backwards on its axis."

"Backwards?"

"Yup. Every year, startin' on Octvember 40th, it's legal to eat dessert before dinner. When Blirg ends, we celebrate Grimace an' give each other purple rubber wallets. Season's interestin'—time actually marches forward backwards."

I held my pounding head. *"Marches forward backwards?"*

The corridor, which had been silent save for audible springs, gears, and ticks, exploded with moos, oinks, whinnies, dings, dongs, gongs, chimes, horns, sirens, engines, train whistles and crowing roosters. I covered my ears.

Suddenly, a wild-eyed cuckoo bird lunged out of a brown house, a clock embedded in his stomach. "Now, Ig, how many people—or whatever carbonated life forms y'got on your planet—own a cuckoo that's also a clock that lives in his own house that's *not* a clock? He don't hafta come out to see what time it is—he *knows!*"

"I feel faint—"

"He comes out to tell us that he knows that he knows when to come out, 'cause he aweady knows!" Rapture lit Gneeecey's grungy face.

"Please show me where I can—"

"An' look!" he cried, admiring a three-dimensional rendering of Goya's ravenous Cronus, hoisting a partially devoured timepiece up to his mouth. "One of his kids he's devoooveratin' is named Timex!"

"With all these clocks, how do y'know what time it really is? If I had more watches, I'd always wonder which one was right." I tapped my wristwatch. Strangely, it was working.

"Y'better start wonderin'—here, your watch automatically becomes parta *my* more."

I looked down. "My leg's really bleeding—"

"Hangin' here's some paintin's by a coupla famous identically fraternical twins—Dippenshmeer an' Rippenshmeer Knottvermeer. They're 'zactly like the ones hangin' in the museum, 'cept they're different. Notice how they paint in complooplementary colors. Dippenshmeer paints in orange, an' Rippenshmeer paints in purple."

"Diroctor—"

"As his name suggesticates, Rippenshmeer tore up his canvasses an' pasted 'em into colleges."

"I don't feel well—"

"I got a Renoyer in my foyer 'cause it rhymes. An' your Van Gogh—after he cut his ear off, he had trouble hearin' what he was lookin' at."

"Please—"

"An' this is my that, that's my this, an' I'm the only one who has one of them! C'mon, Ig—y'makin' me late. Lemme show ya the stinkin' bat'room. Like yuz Earthlin's say, 'Cleanliness is nexta Goldilocks.'"

I slid in goth slime.

"How entertaineratin'!"

"Instead of laughing, you should be trying to help. You're a doctor, and my leg's bleeding because your, uh, pets—"

"That's only a stooperficial wound—y'can clean it in the bat'room. Jus' don't bleed on nuthin'. C'mon."

I shuffled behind him, on numb feet.

"Okay, Ig, this first-floor bat'room's the only one we can use—all the others are busted. So be stinkin' careful in here."

I stinkin' would, I assured him.

"This is a seat-warmer." A lit, life-sized replica of Rodin's Thinker sat thinking on the toilet. "For the W.C."

"Water closet—how quaint."

"THIS IS NOT A WATER CLOSET!" he boomed, stepping over mounds of debris. "IT'S A ELECTRONIC WATER CYCLONE 3000! HIGH-TECH, STATE OF THE ART—THREE-THOUSAND CY-CLONES PER FLUSH!"

I pointed to the stainless steel commode's panel of hypnotically winking, multicolored buttons. "When it breaks down, who do you call—a plumber or an electrician?"

"A computer geek. An' it won't break down. Y'know, it was a choice between this an' the Mechanical Bull 2000. I tried the display Bull in Squiggleman's front window, but it threw me. Embarrassin'—made Squiggleman's look bad."

"Diroctor—"

"This here Cyclone 3000 electronically detects *me* as its only regis-tered user." He frowned. "Guess I'll hafta give yooou the guest code. There's a fine for visitor over-usage—it beeps three times, then y'gotta use *that*." He smacked the side of the tank. "Coin slot only takes dol-lars—Susan B. Anthonies."

"How much usage is over-usage?"

"You'll find out. An' don't forget to replace the lousy sploggle." Glaring at me, he hurled his plastic philosopher into the shower stall.

"He's still plugged in—isn't it dangerous to put him in there?"

"Only if ya use water. Now, speakin' of art, I ordered Rodin's beaud-iful *Balzac*, wit' a clock where his appendix belongs. He'll never get 'pendicitis, an' it ain't life-threatenin' to have your clock removed."

"Diroctor—"

"I also ordered a chrome Harley wit' a clock in *his* stomach—I can pick at it when I'm hungry. It's not by Rodin—don't think he ever rode a chopper."

"Can you show me how the shower works?" The system of faucets, levers and multiple shower heads was more complex than any I'd ever seen.

"Dunno—never use it."

Something behind the Cyclone whined.

"That's Klunkzill—wit' two K's an' three L's. Got a great deal on him!" An aura of misery surrounded the bag of bones that clunked out from behind the throne. A rainbow of grays, the feline's sunken eyeballs matched his sunken sides.

Sideways, I thought, *Klunkzill resembled a xylophone.*

"Sideways, don't Klunkzill resembooble a xylophone?"

"Uh, yes, actually, he does," I agreed, hoping fervently that *grate* minds didn't think alike.

"Flubbubb's afraida xylophones. Whenever he visits, I gotta lock Klunkzill in the basement."

"Thought you didn't want the responsibility of owning pets."

"Klunkzill's real low-maintenance. He's half motorcycle."

"Uh, Diroctor, could I have a coupla minutes in here?"

"How can anyone have minutes?"

"I meant, a coupla minutes alone—"

"Privooovacy—why din'cha say so? Yeah, but hurry. An' y'better do somethin' wit' that leg—looks bad."

A REAL FREAK O'NATURE STARED back at me, from under blond, blender-styled straw. My skin glowed violet, and smudged mascara blackened my lower lids, giving me that sought-after zombie look.

I splashed icy water on my face and rubbed. It didn't help. And the stiff, once-white towels scratched more than they dried.

Under the mirror, several squashed toothpaste tubes had glued themselves to the basin. A fossilized, amber-bristled toothbrush stood upright in a crater of glop, like a flag claiming territorial rights.

Grossed out, I turned away and leaned against the sink's cold edge. I had to find some bandages.

Stuff was strewn all over the grimy gray tiles—Tolstoy's *War and Peace*, a mangled Perswayssick County phone book, and a handwritten, coffee-stained manuscript entitled *My Unauthorized Autobiography*, by Dr. B. Z. Z. Gneeecey.

Spray cans of Atomic Blast Deodorant, labeled "Gift Set" and still sealed in shrink-wrap, mingled merrily with a wide array of laxatives— pills, tablets, Laxa-Patches, and brown bunnies made of that-special- kinda-chocolate.

As I plucked a box of Ouch-O Strips off the floor, my eyes wandered over to the windowsill, piled with prescription bottles.

I read labels. Millvill, "for *your* ailment. Take 2.5 milligrams three times daily with food, but *not* other meds. If dose is missed, contact Dr. Yupnope immediately." Repulsid, "formulated for the way *you* live. Take 50 milligrams twice daily on an empty stomach, *with* other meds. Pre- scribing physician, Dr. Matt Hazz." Bumpex, "1,000 milligrams—take three times daily with meals, but *not* other drugs. Prescribed by Dr. Alexandra C. Idnas. If inanimate objects begin speaking, report to near- est emergency room."

Oh boy.

I turned my attention to my goth-gashed leg. Each time I attempted to apply an Ouch-O, the gauze center tore down the middle before even making contact with the wound. After several tries, I gave up.

"Your minutes are UP!" shouted Gneeecey, pounding his fists on the door. "An' I hope y'ain't usin' too many stinkin' Oucho-O's!"

"I'm not using *any*—and they *do* stink," I replied, limping out into the hallway. I longed to dive into a soft bed and pull the covers up over my throbbing head.

Gneeecey flung open a narrow door situated between the bathroom and Hall of Clox. "C'mon!"

I stepped into the windowless closet of a room. A thin, spring-pop- ping mattress—two-thirds the size of a standard adult bed—covered half the stained parquet floor. I didn't see a pillow or blanket. Just a swamp-green bath towel.

Nearby, a cardboard carton bore a printed warning: *Do Not Store On Floor!* A beige ceramic lamp, crowned by a crooked shade, made its home-sweet-home atop the box, lighting walls painted no particular color.

The room reeked of chemicals.

"Y'like it, Ig?"

Before I could answer, something buzzed past my ear. Glancing up- ward, I spied two tiny Lear jets flying circles around a broken light fix- ture. Airplanes didn't usually fly indoors. Definitely time to turn in.

Gneeecey chuckled. "They're insects that mutated—y'know, as a natural defense—to look like high-flyin' planes, so nobody'd bother 'em. They're a real problem out here in the suburbs."

I stared, amazed.

"An' they bite!" He threw a flyswatter at me. "There's a can of plane repellent in the bat'room. Yup, when these guys get ready to bite'cha, their pincers shoot straight outta their little cockpits."

Gneeecey's phone tinkled. He ripped it out of his pocket. "Mark? Oh. . .Flubbubb—it's *yooou*. Y'made me bust my shirt. Nope, ain't got time for ya. What? Y'got me a present? I gotta go meet Mark, but'cha can come by—throw it through the window—y'know, the one over the front steps? Gotta leave! G'bye!"

As Gneeecey checked his watch, a loud thump startled us. He tore up the hall and returned a spilt-second later, ripping open a silver-papered package. "Ooooooooooh! Look!" He lifted a purple knit snake from the box. "A monogrammed tail-warmer from *Seemingwhale's*!" He pulled it up over his tail. "Hand-knit in Booolabeeezia—musta cost a decka vlecks! Flubbubb can't afford stuff like this."

"Isn't he a percussionist?" I asked.

"He plays triangles an' does experimental junk like throwin' shoes in washers an' dryers—calls it prepooperated percussion. By day, he works in a bread factory, tyin' twist-ties on loaves—y'know, them little wires that'cha can't never get off, so y'rip the lousy package open?"

"Uh, before you go," I began, pointing to the mattress, "could I move this further into the room so my feet won't stick out through the doorway?"

"NO! You'll discomboooobulate the flow of energy in this entire house—that would be bad fang chewy!"

"And what about this box on the floor that says 'Do Not Store On Floor'?" I asked, whisking the mattress away from the door.

"Don't believe everythin' y'read, Ig," he replied, not noticing. "Jus' make sure y'don't *touch* it."

"But, what if in the middle of the night, I—"

"DON'T! An' here!" He tossed a ball at me—a beanbag clock, upholstered in grimy white-and-black fake fur. Its yellowed face frowned, through cracked plastic, at its bent hands.

Attached in back, beneath sharp levers, was a fuzzy, striped tail, stuffed with bells.

"Set it to thump at six a.m.! Y'better sleep fast!"

"We've gotta talk—"

"GOTTA GO! BAD NIGHT!"

CHAPTER 11

BAD MORNING TO YOU, TOO

S UNLIGHT STREAMED IN THROUGH the picture window, illuminating the junkyard of a kitchen. I suddenly felt grateful that black holes might, one day, swallow everything up.

"Bad mornin', Ig," droned Gneeecey, peering over the top of his *Perswayssick Tims*. Its front page headline cried, "BAKERY BANDIT STRIKES AGAIN—DETECTIVES FOLLOW WHIPPED CREAM TRAIL!"

"Bad morning to you, too," I replied, butterflies fluttering in my stomach. It was my first day of work.

Gneeecey grunted and reached across the table for his Crack O'-Dawn Cereal. The slogan on the box read, "If we don't wake you, you're dead!" A grinning vampire urged eaters to search for the toy surprise inside.

"Breakfast's all 'round ya, Ig—scrape some offa the counter."

You could barely see the gray granite for all the fast food bags, junk mail, and swatters decorated with squished planes.

The scent of newsprint mingled with the bittersweet stench of Merk Perk. Every few seconds, projectile chunks of the chewable java sizzled as they hit the merkolator's heating element. The triple-beaked appliance hiccupped atop a mound of magazines that covered two gas burners.

I was hungry, but I wasn't.

"Why," I asked, hating myself the instant my mouth opened, "is that last S in *Tims* printed backward? And shouldn't it read '*Perswayssick Times*'?"

Gneeecey's newspaper lowered slowly, exposing dark, narrowed eyes. "A vowel saved is a vowel earned—the S keeps the invisible E it saved the resta the word from payin' for. Keeps it for free if it's stinkin' backwards!"

"I—"

"An' it's pronounciated '*Tims*'—why'd the E bother bein' invisible if the vowel was gonna be long?!" He hoisted his vowel-harboring publication back over his snout. "SHEEESH!"

A bereft meow, accompanied by a pungent litter box odor, announced Klunkzill's arrival. The motorized feline clanked over to his bowl, slurped up a quart of high-viscosity engine oil, then sniffed at some chrome pebbles in his saucer. Wrinkling his silver nose, he clunked out into the hallway.

My legs gave way and I collapsed into a chair. Gneeecey's rindom-based toothpaste's bitter aftertaste made my cheeks suck in.

"Lickin' your chops, Ig?" he inquired, between thunderous chomps of Crack O'Dawn. "Noises annoy me when I'm readin'."

"*I'm* not the one making noise—"

"Geez—where's the toy surprise?" He poured more rocks into his dish. "Y'know," he mumbled through his gravel-filled muzzle, "his tail will be in our neck of the woods any day now. Any day."

I tilted my foggy head. "Whose tail?"

"Our spiritual leader's," he answered, standing on his chair.

"Your spiritual leader's *tail?*"

"Our spiritual leader's *comet*, ya Ig," he snapped, elbow-deep in his cereal box. "Every year, when Blirg ends—on Octvember 69th, Grimace Day—our Grand Oogitty-Boogitty arrives on a comet's tail, from deep in outer space. We have a big concert an' parade, an' I get to ride a horsey!" He belched. "Tol' y'not to make noise, Ig!"

"*You* just—"

"Y'stinkin' made me topple the salt!" Eyeing me with disgust, he jumped down, spun in circles chanting, "Where it goes, nobody knows," and hurled the crystal shaker over his left shoulder. It sailed across the room, shattering against the mountain of pots and pans piled in his triple sink.

"Spilt salt, your fault," he growled. "*Your* baaad luck!"

Gritting my teeth, I stared out at a majestic oak that towered over Gneeecey's white gazebo.

He turned on the radio, and crunching contentedly behind his wall of newsprint, sang along with what sounded like a bunch of deranged ducks.

When the song ended, an unmistakable, grating voice blasted from the speakers. "Deranged Ducks' 'We Ain't Got No Money and Can't Get No Gigs' is number two this week here on Gas Radio!"

I glanced over at Gneeecey. All I could see was the top of his grimy head. And his matching, tabloid-clutching mitts.

"If you're jus' tunin' in," continued the high, nerdish voice, "bad mornin', it's meeee, The Grate One! An' now, some headlines an' weather! In today's news, yesterday. . . ."

"Dirroctor! That's you on the radio!"

"Yupperooney."

"You prerecord news and weather?"

He threw down his paper. "Sometimes sevooveral weeks in advance." My jaw dropped.

"Shut'cha mouth, Ig—planes'll fly in."

"But—"

"I rerun news an' weather too."

"How can you *possibly*—"

"All has to do wit' mathemetratical proboobability!" he shouted. "In my News Guessin' seminars, I learnt everythin's fifty-fifty—either somethin'll happen or it won't. I'm a Senior News Guesser!"

An unidentified morsel of something unsavory dangled from his shiny, black lower lip, waving up and down with each syllable.

"Uh," I ventured, "you've got something on your mouth."

He whisked his wrist past his yapper, and caught the offending blob on his watch. "Always bein' half-right's priddy good—an' bein' only half-wrong ain't bad neitherwise."

"What about reruns?"

He pounded his fist on the tabletop. "How many times do I gotta igsplain?! Stuff happenin' again's fifty-fifty, too! Either stuff'll happen again or it won't!"

"But—"

"If somethin' fifty-fifty happens again, I'll be twice as right, an' if it don't, only a quarter as wrong."

"Surely," I argued, "there's less than a fifty-fifty chance that, say, a five-hundred-pound purple pelican'll fly out of the skies with a policy in its beak and try to sell me life insurance today, isn't there?" I crossed my arms and waited for an answer.

"Y'never know, Ig. It's all fifty-fifty. I got proof! Ain't somethin' always either happenin' or not happenin'?" The disgusting glob had migrated to the crook of his right arm.

"Turnin' to the weather," screeched the-Gneeecey-on-the-radio, "this mornin's torrentializin' rains'll continue all day! So far, this month of Octvember, we've had ten inches of rain—that woulda been fifteen *feet* of Merk Perk!"

I scowled.

"An' when barometers fall, it's easier for yooou to fall—there's less air pressure to help y'stand! Now be carefoofal in that rain—we got reports of a crash on Sciatica Street, an' a multi-vehikookular pile-up on the Laconic Highway."

I leapt to my numb feet. "The sun's shining!"

"Coulda rained today—if it did, I'da been covered. Am I wastin' my bad breath on ya? EVERYTHIN'S FIFTY-FIFTY!"

My barometric pressure had sunk to an all-time low. I flopped back into my seat. A half-stuffed brown teddy, slumped over in what I'd thought was an empty chair, caught my attention.

"Forgot to introducerate'cha. Yammicles, meet the Ig. Unfortoonately, she'll be stayin' awhile. An' Ig, meet Yammicles. He's better'n a imagooginary friend—y'can *see* him."

The bear's permanently-crossed peepers gazed crookedly into space.

"Oh—Flea said to give y'this here crummy junk." Gneeecey tossed a gold Seemingwhale's bag into my lap.

It was bursting with goodies. Turtlenecks—my favorite colors, maroon, midnight-blue and black—plus jeans and a down-filled, navy jacket trimmed with silver zippers and too many inner and outer pockets to count. And, thank the heavens above—or wherever they were—a new, *unused* toothbrush.

"Wow! 'Face-in-a-Bag'! Make-up—to cover my purple face!"

"What'cha want wit' make-up? Made-up junk ain't real."

"You should talk."

"An' you stinkin' shouldn't."

Out of spite, I read Flea's note aloud. "Nickels, here's some stuff to get you started. Before you leave P.C., you can take me out to lunch—wherever YOU choose. Your friend, Flea."

I smiled. "How sweet—how thoughtful."

Gneeecey scowled. "UGH! Hope nobody nebberd-kinnezzard says that 'bout *meeeee*."

Moos, oinks, and the clock-bellied cuckoo's looney cries drowned out my reply.

"Eat, Ig—you'll be workin' *hard*." Gneeecey threw a cellophane package at me. "Try some flummery."

"Flummery?"

"Rehydrated flumm gizzards."

"Think I'll skip breakfast."

"*Your* decision." Gneeecey pitched his mug at the sink. "C'mon—y'makin' me late again."

Suddenly, his body went rigid.

"What's wrong?" I asked, not really wanting to know.

He gaped out the window. "Mr. Tree jus' snuck closer to the gaze bow!"

"How can a tree—"

He tossed three brown bottles at me. "One of your jobs is to re-mindicate me to take my meds. They keep Mr. Tree away—better'n a restraineratin' order. An' make sure I take 'em on time."

"If I cooperate, I suppose you'll return my portfolio, and help me contact my mom and my bosses—"

"*I'm* your boss now."

CHAPTER 12

TIME WILL SMELL

OH, GOD!" I EXCLAIMED, wincing as the limo wound its way down Bimbus Crack Drive. "It's *Friday*!" Gneeecey crumpled his newspaper. "Yeah, it's FriedEgg, Octvember 13th. Now stop inter-rupticatin' my readin'." An unlit health cigar hung from his mouth. "Market's volatile—if I don't stay ontoppa this, I'm gonna take a real bath in stinkin' alphabet soup."

A bath in any kind of soup would be an improvement, I thought.

"What'chooo lookin' at?" He pulled the *Tims*' business section back up over his schnozz.

I sighed. It was indeed Friday, the 13th. I'd be a no-show at WUGG, never even calling in. Never putting final touches on weekend public affairs programs or adding sound effects and music beds to the fifty-million commercials stacked in my bin.

That would delight our soon-to-be former sponsors, and my boss, Bill Fernández, who was already mad at the world because his sensible stockbroker daughter had just run off with a green-haired tattoo artist.

And the next day, I'd never make it into the city to host my Salsa program.

"Diroctor," I began, digging my fingernails into my palms, "sorry to interrupt you—"

"WHAAAAAT?!" He flung the FriedEgg entertainment section in my face.

"Can you help me phone home? You called *me* from here just the other day. If I could just make *one* call, to my mother—"

"Y'can't! Blirg disrupticates all communications! Can't even get *Brady Bunch* reruns!"

"You—you watch—"

"Not no more. Not since yesterday, when our gravoovitational anti-whaddayacallit poles began neutralizatin', in prepooparation for their annual electronical shiftin'. Sorry."

"But—"

"Look, nobody, not even meee, the stinkin' Grate One, can call outta Perswayssick County till Blirg ends, an' our poles snap back."

"But, there has to be *some* way—"

"Ain't. Anyways, our county's revoovolutional reversal's your fault. Blame Earth for gettin' our dimensions all entangulated."

"I've gotta reach my mom—"

"If *I* can't call my mommy, you can't call yours!" Eyes glistening, Gneeecey hoisted the classifieds up over his face.

My stomach knotted up. Alex would phone tonight. When she didn't reach me, she'd assume I was out. Out on a Friday night.

Saturday at noon, when Carlos arrived at WAOK, I wouldn't be there. It would be the second time I'd stood him up.

And nobody else at that radio station knew how to cover my show. The program I worked so hard to establish, for five years of my life, would vanish from the airwaves, and from the face of the earth. Like me.

My mom, Alex, and Dave would take turns calling me. Monday morning—hearing I hadn't made it to work since Wednesday—they'd go to my place and find my car, but not me. They'd file a missing persons report and be thinking the worst. Planning a funeral without a body.

"Stop mumblin', Ig!" snarled Gneeecey.

"What? I'm not—"

"You are, an' it's gettin' on my nerves!"

I closed my eyes and continued freaking.

Fernández would fire me. Can me, posthumously. My full-time job was a killer, with its staggering production load and monotonous rotation of overly-commercial Salsa, Merengue and Bachata "hits." And working with my well-meaning-but-carping boss was no walk in the park either. He was constantly breathing down my neck.

But the gig kept a roof over my head.

I'd lose that, too. True, it was only a basement apartment, crowded, chilly and damp—I was forever battling mildew—but it was *mine*.

My landlord was exceptional, as landlords went. Rico was always checking to make sure I was okay. Said I reminded him of his grand-daughter. Every time he saw me, he'd mention he wanted to give me an album by his brother's friend, who'd led a Latin jazz band back in the sixties. He was still looking for the old vinyl recording.

The six hundred bucks a month Rico charged was pretty reasonable, considering that the house was located up the street from the bus stop, minutes from Manhattan.

What if I didn't make it back in time to pay my November rent?

I couldn't picture Rico chucking my possessions out onto the curb. But I could envision him, bewildered and apologetic, asking Alex and Dave to come empty out my place.

And my creditors. Would my family be responsible for my debts? I bit my finger so hard, it bled.

"Y'wouldn't try my flummery, but you're eatin' your fingers?"

Lost for words, I gazed out the window. What if the little hairball had already slid his slimy fingers into my case's secret sleeve and swiped my ten grand?

"Why're y'cryin', Ig? Ain't no spilt milk here."

"Diroctor, let's just cut to the chase."

"How can y'cut a chase? Didn't nobody never tell ya y'shouldn't run wit' scissors?"

"Stop calling me 'Ig.' I insist you return my portfolio."

"Return it? Where'd I buy it?"

"Let's cut all the nonsense—"

"Nonsense is easier to cut than a chase—"

"If I cooperate with you today, will you give me back my portfolio?"

"Time will smell, Ig. Time will smell."

The limo's stuffy passenger compartment could've turned the strongest stomach. I rolled my window down and gulped in the cool air.

Sunlight ricocheted off other vehicles and anything else remotely reflective, imprinting my retinas with brilliant spots and curved lines that didn't disappear even when I squeezed my eyelids shut.

When the long light at Pheasantbelly Road turned green, street crossers scrambled as we sped onto Murgatroyd Avenue.

By the time Culvert double parked alongside several dozen cars, I felt like I'd already slogged through an entire workday. I stumbled out onto the sidewalk.

"C'mon, Ig—gotta see GUS!" Gneeecey shoved me into a sea of bustling, briefcase-toting pedestrians. Most held huge black umbrellas over their heads.

As I stepped forward, a minuscule football bounced off the side of my nose and hurtled into my left eye, point first.

My hand shot up to shield my injury. High-pitched whistles screeched.

"YA IG!" Gneeecey dug his fingers into my arm.

Through stinging tears, I saw only a blurry flurry of flapping wings. A sharp beak stabbed my cheek.

A growing crowd circled around me, chanting "DEE-fense! DEE-fense!"

"What the—" I stammered.

"It's championship mini-sparrow football," shrilled Gneeecey. "Y'gotta stand still until they complete play!"

"But—"

"If y'move, y'can get fined for interference—"

"Huh?"

"County ordinance BS396.3 clearly states that birds may use people as goal posts an' playin' surfaces, wit'in city confines as they determine fit, durin' all post-season play—play-offs an' championships."

"I don't—"

"They mighta been attracted to your purplish skin. Jus' stand still— let 'em finish. I don't wanna hafta make a snitizen's arrest."

I stood cross-eyed as the diminutive descendants of dinosaurs—sparrows the size of overgrown bumblebees—executed a flea-flicker pass across my face. Their itty-bitty, needle-sharp cleats scratched and pinched.

A few more jabs, penalties, tackles, huddles, and feathers poking me, and it was over—my part, anyway.

The team wearing little fire-engine-red helmets made a first down, then, along with their white-uniformed rivals, took off into the sky to play somewhere else, on someone else's nose.

"You're lucky, Ig," said Gneeecey, surveying my scraped-up, tear-stained countenance. "Sometimes they poop on ya!"

SOCK REPAIRS BLAZED NEON letters hanging above the drab storefront. Five or six pairs of artlessly displayed socks adorned its dusty window.

Bald industrial carpeting, colored several shades of gray, covered the floor. The acrid odor of dry cleaning fluid permeated the place.

A notice taped to the wall read: "On Premises Sock Repair, Cleaning & Storage." Another sign warned: "NO SOCKS RETURNED WITHOUT CLAIM TICKET! *NO* EXCEPTIONS!"

Left eye still running, I traipsed behind Gneeecey, who, with great authority, marched up to the establishment's crazed Formica counter and pounded the service bell with both fists. "GUS! I NEEEEED YOU!"

A gaunt, nearly bald old human emerged from behind a shabby olive curtain and took his place behind the cash register. Cobalt eyes peered out from underneath his unruly salt-and-pepper brows, contrasting with a sallow complexion that resembled baked clay. His face matched his counter top.

"Bad mornin', Gus." Gneeecey pulled two limp, green-and-navy socks from his T-shirt pocket. An uncharacteristic tremble had hijacked his vocal chords.

"Bad mornin' to you too, Diroctor," drawled Gus, looking me up and down like I was a bad auto wreck. His voice was as dry as his skin.

Gneeecey's hands quivered as he laid down his shiny knee-highs and stroked them flat. Riddled with runs and snags, they stank. "Can y'fix 'em?"

"Dunno." Gus held them up to a bare hundred-watt bulb that dangled from the ceiling. The harsh light rendered his features more severe.

"Well, *can* ya?"

"Yep." Gus was a man of few words.

Gneeecey exhaled audibly.

"But they'll just tear again. Y'ever considered replacin' 'em?"

Gneeecey recoiled in horror. "They're my lucky socks!"

"Doesn't UniGeek's carry 'em?"

"Nope."

"I see they still stock those, uh, shirts y'wear. Y'ever tried Martian's, on Wet Cactus Street?"

"They don't got 'em neitherwise. Nobody does."

Gus flicked the foul foot coverings with his bony thumb and forefinger, wrinkling his gourd-like nose when a cloud of dust exploded from the fabric. "Want 'em cleaned, too?"

"Nah, jus' fix 'em. Can I have 'em back today?"

"Yep." The old man removed a handkerchief from his pocket and dabbed at his watering eyes.

"Well, Gus, y'know that ol' sayin'—'y'weep when y'sew.'" Gneeecey snatched his yellow ticket and waddled toward the door.

"Welcome," muttered Gus, draping the horizontally striped skunks over a doll-sized wire hanger.

Gneeecey stopped short and spun around, smashing into me. "One more thing," he shouted, cramming his claim ticket into one of my new jacket's five-thousand pockets. "I'll proboobably send in my new assistant here, the Ig, to pick up my stinkin' socks."

"Yep."

"Uh, hi. Name's *Nicki*." I forced a smile.

"Okay, Ig. Later." Holding Gneeecey's stockings at arm's length, Gus disappeared behind his curtain.

"C'MON—I'LL SHOW YA a little trick." Gneeecey pushed me back into the limo. "It's faster gettin' places from inside this baby. Follow me!"

I ducked my head down, and on buckling legs chased Gneeecey through one segment after another.

"Door number eight!" he shouted. "Puts us right outside Shisskey's!"

Greeted by a heavenly-sweet aroma, we floated out of the limousine, between the bumpers of two parked police cruisers, and into a bakery.

"Bad mornin', Burt." Gneeecey threw down a couple coins. "The usual."

"Comin' right up, Bizzig. How ya doing?" Six foot six, with thinning blond hair that went gray at his temples, the white-clad, human Burt's rugged good looks and muscular build conjured up visions of a high school football star gracefully weathering middle-age.

"Busy as usual, Burt. Y'know how it goes wit' us business maggots—we got it rough. Even wit' all our mon-ney, we still got probooblems. Whazzup wit'choo?"

"Well," replied Burt, "Mary and I are kinda jittery—did you see the paper? That 'bakery bandit' broke into another place, on Stromboli Street. Two blocks away—too close for comfort." His deep-set emerald eyes settled on Gneeecey.

He squirmed. "Yeah, I read all 'bout it."

"Sometimes this guy even leaves money on the counter. A guilty bandit."

"Chump. *I* wouldn't leave nuthin'." Drooling, Gneeecey inspected the goodies inside Burt's glass case.

"We're installing a new, high tech alarm," said Burt, stooping low to hand Gneeecey an ornate cathedral constructed of whipped cream-covered angel food cake, topped with a plump red cherry.

"*I* got a cow-wit'-a-clock-in-her-stomach," proclaimed Gneeecey, sucking the cherry up like a vacuum cleaner. "She's a high tech alarm—installed her infrared sensors myself."

"You installed 'em yourself—"

"Y'know, Burt, I'm gonna force Altitude to dress in white uniforms like you an' Mary. I'm sicka that crummy ol' Gnorks shirt."

"How's Altitude doing—"

"I'm teachin' him to run Gneeezle's. I'm formin' him into my own moldiness—he's my protogheeghee."

"He must be glad not to be making so many deliveries, driving that tired ol' Splodge and constantly breaking down—"

"Hey, Burt," began Gneeecey, plunging his muzzle deep into his cream-covered piece of heaven, "you an' Mary comin' to our nex' Quality of Life meetin'?"

"We'll be there. We're very concerned about—"

"We're gonna put a lid on riverbank divlopment—once an' for *all*! Divlopment's very detrootimental for us entrepreneuters. I'm hopin' the whole Merchants' Association'll back me up."

"There are actually a couple sides to this."

"That's right," agreed Mary, tying back her honey, shoulder-length hair as she joined her husband behind the counter. The slim, delicate-featured woman's smile lit up her face, softening its many worry lines. "Approving Question 345 would protect our environment *and* save the goonafish from extinction." Her intense gray eyes locked with Gneeecey's bulgy peepers.

Looking away, he pulled a battered pamphlet from his shirt pocket and tossed it onto the counter. "Mark gave me a buncha these, to knock some sense outta people's heads. Read it." He crammed the rest of his snack into his yapper.

"Isn't he one of those guys who stands by the door all night, watching our meetings?" asked Burt. "He's your friend?"

Gneeecey licked his goopy fingers. "One of my bes' friends."

"Those guys are weird—they always wear the same gray business suits," observed Mary. "And their eye whites are yellowed, like they all suffer from jaundice."

Burt nodded. "Complexions are kinda weird, too."

"Yeah, sort of translucent and waxy—almost amber," added Mary, as she filled in a shelf with freshly-baked apple strudel. "They're not real friendly, either."

"Mark, Mark, an' Mark are okay," Gneeecey assured them.

"They're all named Mark?" asked Mary.

"They're rare-but-almost-identical fraternical sets of triplets," explained Gneeecey. "They stand in for each other at meetin's. Most of 'em are cops."

"Well," said Burt, inscribing "Happy Birthday Frank" on a cake, "getting back to riverbank development—actually redevelopment—miercoles production and mierk are really at the heart of this. I, for one, think it would pay to clean up all the mierk and look into zodd."

"PAY WHO?"

Burt laughed. "Not those guys who run MierkoZurk Mining— that's for sure."

I gaped as actual steam poured from Gneeecey's ears.

"Give zodd a chance, Bizzig. We've got a plentiful supply—it's in our soil. It's everywhere!"

"It'll *kill* yuz!"

Burt handed Gneeecey back his leaflet. "C'mon—it's a benign, natural compound!"

"But—"

"And it's cheaper," chimed in Mary.

"Y'can't tell MEEE nuthin' 'bout CHEAPNESS!" shrieked Gneeecey, springing up and down. "I'm the EXPERT!"

"Out of curiosity," asked Burt, "where does Gus stand on this?"

"Dunno," replied the good diroctor, panting. "If I bother him 'bout it, he might not wanna fix my socks."

"Well, in the end, it's up to us voters."

"Fixin' my socks?"

Burt and Mary exchanged amused glances, then looked my way. "Burt, what bad manners we have!"

"Yeah, Bizzig—you never introduced your friend."

"She ain't my friend—she's only my new stinkin' assistant, the Ig. She's, uh, not from 'round here. She'll be workin' for me for a while—indefiantly."

"Name's *Nicki*. Pleased to meet you."

"Nicki, it's a pleasure," replied Mary.

"Yes," piped in Burt. "Can we get you anything this morning?"

"Nah, Burt, the Ig don't want nuthin'—she's too nervoovous to eat. It's her first day of work—her stomach's jumpin' 'round tyin' itself in knots."

"Everything looks so delicious," I answered, devouring the oversized muffins, pastries, and croissants with my eyes. "But, I haven't, uh, been paid yet." I looked at Gneeecey. "Diroctor, maybe you could advance me a coupla bucks?"

Gneeecey stared up at the ceiling, whistling an off-key rendition of Earth TV's *Jeopardy* theme.

Burt handed me a hot, buttered blueberry muffin, the size of a small cake. "On us. Good luck on your first day!"

"This is on us, too," added Mary, presenting me with a giant Styrofoam cup filled to the brim with freshly brewed coffee. Normal-smelling coffee.

"Thanks!"

"Yuz'd do better sellin' Merk Perk insteada that igspensive, organical mud." Gneeecey pulled a glossy, full-color Freak O'Nature brochure out of his endless pit of a pocket.

Burt folded his arms. "Anyone wants a cup of Merk Perk, there's a Freak O'Nature kiosk on practically every corner."

"Try it—your profits'll fall offa the charts! I can work it out on a calcoocoolator for ya. Y'got a calcoocoolator?"

"Listen, we've got orders to fill. Take care, Bizzig. And it was nice meeting your friend. Bye, Nicki."

Mary smiled. "Good luck!"

Gneeecey swallowed the wax paper that had covered his treat. "SHE'S NOT MY FRIEND! SHE'S A TEMPOOPORARY EMPLOY-EEEE!"

I followed Gneeecey as he stomped out of Shisskey's. "Y'embar-rassed me—y'behaved TERRIBOOBLY!"

"*What?*"

"Try not to act like such a ALIEN nex' time I bring y'somewhere," he yelled, elbowing my ribs. "Get in the CAR awready!"

I cleared my throat and took a sip of coffee. "We haven't discussed my salary or hours."

"We'll disgust financial derangements later."

CHAPTER 13

THAT'S FIFTEEN CENTS THIS WEEK

D UCK!" SHRIEKED GNEEECEY, "STOP!" The limo screeched to a dead halt, slamming us to the floor. Possibly mistaking me for Rapunzel, Gneeecey clutched fistfuls of my hair, to pull him-self upright, and dashed out into the street. As profanities spewed from drivers' mouths, he squatted down and snatched up a shiny ob-ject.

"A *dime*!" he squealed, doing cartwheels all the way back to the car. "That's fifteen cents this week!"

Shooting him daggers, I massaged my sore scalp.

"One day," he squawked, lowering his scruffy behind, "this spectack-ookular period of history'll be known as 'The Bizzigian Era'. I'll be in-stitootionalized!" He stuffed his rescued coin, along with clumps of my hair, into his T-shirt pocket.

Our ride continued uneventfully until we entered an intersection where six two-way streets converged, and twice as many signs and signals contradicted each other. Culvert quacked in confusion.

"JUS' STINKIN' TURN!" Gneeecey shouted into the intercom. "They'll automatically HAFTA stop for US!" He turned to me. "I'm gonna fix this intersection! Red lights slow y'down an' create confusionism—I'll paint 'em all green!"

I just looked at him.

"Then everyone can jus' go at their OWN risk—y'know, survival of the fittest—an' the BIGGEST an' FASTEST!"

Desperate not to join the ranks of the unemployed, the beleaguered mallard turned left—from the lane furthest to the right—onto Edgar Vompt Boulevard.

I dug my nails into the leather seat as the limousine slithered, like a caffeine-crazed snake, through a high-speed obstacle course, leaving behind a trail of yelping brakes, shattered glass, and crumpled fenders.

We'd just cut off eleven lanes of traffic.

Gneeecey raised a grubby index finger into the air. "Edgar Vompt," he informed me, "was Planet Eccchs's greatest business hero."

The financial icon's thoroughfare, a monotonous industrial roadway, dragged on forever, making even that sunny morning seem gloomy.

Just as I began to drift off, my eyes opened wide.

The barren strips of land bordering the boulevard were suddenly populated with elephantine stone ironing boards and irons, the latter exquisitely detailed with switches and electrical cords.

Some appliances sat perched atop building-sized boards, while others stood on the parched earth, pointy noses facing skyward. Still others rested face down, scorching, for all eternity, whatever they'd been pressing.

"Who made these?" I asked. "How on Earth—or *whatever*—did they get here?"

Gneeecey threw down his shredded *Tims*. "We're jus' drivin' through The Iron section—we call it 'The Irons.'" He whisked the sports section back up over his snoot.

"But, I—I've never seen anything like this!"

"They're jus' lousy rock formations," he snapped from behind his paper. "Nobody knows how they got there. An' nobody really cares."

Evidently, no one did give a deck of vlecks. Traffic just whizzed by the Stonehenges-with-steam-settings.

CULVERT FLASHED HIS LAMINATED ID.

After a white-haired, sleep-walking security guard motioned us to proceed, we rolled up to a sprawling office complex.

Its centerpiece, a fantastic structure, wide as it was tall, appeared to be constructed mainly of glass, with lustrous strips of ebony tile separating oversized, dark-tinted windows. Silver art deco characters floated above the dozen-doored entrance, heralding our arrival at the Edgar Vompt Pavillion.

Scores of satellite dishes and antennas sprouted from the glossy wonder's flat roof. A patched-up purple-and-orange helicopter cowered on a grassy triangle below, sporting droopy rotors, one blade bent so as to render flight extremely perilous, if not impossible. Peeling white letters identified the flying machine as GAS-TV's Chopper 3½.

"What'chooo lookin' at, Ig? GEDDOUT!"

Gneeecey's high-tops squeaked across the expansive, marble-floored lobby. My gimpy legs barely kept up.

Mutilated newspaper wedged under his wet armpit, cigar clenched between his unbrushed teeth, he grunted and nodded, spitting out the side of his mouth every several feet and muttering an occasional "Bad mornin'."

During the course of our ear-popping, stomach-dropping ten-minute ride to the skyscraper's top, we changed elevators five times, as each packed car traveled fifty floors.

"Two-hundred-fiftieth floor," announced a robotic female voice, as bells chimed and golden doors slid open, depositing us outside WGAS Broadcast Network's executive suites.

"Top four floors are *mine*," boasted Gneeecey. "You'll be workin' at AM, FM, plus TV—till y'drop!"

"But, I've never worked in television—I've only—"

"You're LATE," he bellowed, stomping through the scarlet-carpeted lobby, into his office. "Don't look too good on ya first day, does it?"

He slammed his door in my face. Its mangled venetian blinds swung from side to side, obstructing my view of what sounded like file cabinets being dragged about and smashed against walls.

Taking a deep breath, I leaned against the unmanned reception desk and waited.

"Okay, Ig—get IN here!"

My blood ran cold.

"NOW!"

I turned the knob slowly and stumbled over the loose wooden threshold. Planes could've flown into my mouth. Gneeecey's majestic mahogany desk sat in the middle of a garbage dump.

"Copy a squat, or whatever yuz Earthlin's say."

"Huh?"

"Over there, Ig, in that itsy-bitsy purple chair in fronta my desk. It'll make y'feel even insignificanter than ya are."

Scowling, I sat.

"Be right back, Ig—forgot somethin'."

After fidgeting for fifteen minutes, I hauled my bones out of the puny chair and tripped over an overturned GAS-TV mug bearing Gneeecey's grinning image—one of dozens glued to the once-beige carpet.

Framed documents and licenses hung haphazardly along the orange walls, including a degree from St. Bogelthorpe's University of Medicine and Dentistry—located on Planet Eccchs—and a diploma from the Perswayssick University of New Ideas, conferring upon B.Z.Z. Gneeecey a doctorate in advanced gasometry.

Across the room, ethereal scarlet digits morphed fluidly on yellowed green drapes—on the fabric's very surface—displaying the time. Window treatments with clocks in their stomachs. The stiff fiberglass panels weren't synchronized. The curtain hanging to the left read nine-forty a.m., while its companion lagged behind by twenty-two minutes.

Five dented file cabinets stood nearby, topped by an evenly distributed mound of future landfill. Cables, braided with miles of runaway audiotape, and videocassettes vomiting yards of tangled film, spilled into open drawers below.

I tripped over a soldering iron that had melted into the rug's synthetic fibers. One knee landed in a Styrofoam container filled with stiff fries, and the other in a wilted salad garnished with leaky batteries.

As I staggered upright, I found myself gawking at a memorandum that detailed the network's sick-day policy. It stated that an employee must give two weeks' notice prior to calling in sick, and in the event of one's sudden demise, a relative must contact the office beforehand.

Sidestepping an upside-down box labeled "SPESHUL FUZES—STORE UPRIGHT," I bumped Gneeecey's desk. An avalanche of paper and other assorted items tumbled down, including the solid brass dollar sign paperweight that fell on my left foot.

As stars and birdies orbited my skull, I read the memo that floated before my purple face. Entitled, "Regarding Malicious Gossip," Gneeecey warned:

If you must say anything about co-workers, you must say it close enough to my office that I can hear it too. Of course, gossip about ME is grounds for immediate dismissal, whether I overhear it or hear it through the grapevine.

After I unknotted the insulated spaghetti twisted around my ankles, and heaped all the debris back onto Gneeecey's desk, things looked pretty much the same as before.

As my eyes settled on a coffee-stained engineering log, I reached into my pocket for Gneeecey's sock repair claim ticket. It wasn't there.

Heart pounding like a jackhammer, I rummaged through the dozens of inner and outer pouches and secret compartments—some disguised as seams—hidden throughout the body and sleeves of my reversible jacket.

The little piece of cardboard was nowhere to be found.

I tore the coat off and slid my fingers into every visible opening. Still nothing. Nothing but a little slip of paper informing me that my new article of lifetime-guaranteed apparel had been rigorously tested and approved by Inspector #3.

For ten more gut-wrenching minutes, I searched. And came up empty. Empty, that is, until I did find *something*—a hole in the bottom of a front pocket.

I'd have to spend my lunch hour looking for the ticket.

Head throbbing, I studied Gneeecey's dinosaur of a desktop computer. The monitor was so big, he could probably read his e-mails from Mars—or Planet Eccchs. Its printer beeped continuously, flashing an "out of paper" warning.

A laptop rode an adjacent tsunami of rubble. The gash on its screen created the illusion of a sad, down-turned mouth.

Two phones sat on the desk's northwest end. One, a chunky gray model—labeled "NEWS," with a backward S—appeared to have been run over. Its healthier, more streamlined red neighbor was tagged "HOTLINE."

The latter began wailing like a siren. Fifty lights flashed under its keypad.

Acid flooded my stomach.

"DON'T TOUCH IT!" ordered Gneeecey, as he barreled through the door, waving a copy of the *Perswayssick Pooper-Scooper.* "JUS' LET IT RING!"

A well-built, dark-skinned black human sprinted into the room behind Gneeecey, obviously distressed, clutching his abdomen and a quart-sized bottle of antacid.

Only when he slowed down did I detect his slight limp. He looked to be in his mid-twenties.

"WHO MOVED MY STUFF?" demanded Gneeecey.

Face flushing, I slunk back into my seat.

Gneeecey stomped over to his desk, grabbed a battered sheet of paper, and tossed it at me. "Y'gotta fill out this here job aplooplication."

"You mean, I don't have the job yet?" Maybe my father had been right—where there's life, there's hope.

He lobbed a pen at me. "FILL IT OUT!"

I began writing. Gneeecey shook his newspaper in the distressed man's face, distressing him further, no doubt. "Look, Cleve," he yowled, "no wonder this paper's named after poop! That jerk Imbroglio's trynna pass a idiotronical editorial off as a objectionable report!"

Cleve took a long swig from his blue-green bottle.

"Look what he writes!" shrilled Gneeecey. "'Mierk's a highly-hazoozardous byproduct of miercoles, a unstable element mined in our northwestern hills, used in the manufacture of pavin' materials, automotive an' aircraf' parts, fuel additives, an' plaastics, an' even pumped into foods!' Y'listenin', Cleveland?"

"Uh-huh," he replied, gulping down a couple more ounces.

"Iggleheiemer says, 'The county's monstrous Mierkolatory churns out tons, poisonin' our air an' waterways!'"

Cleve sighed.

"An' listen—'Environmentalists, an' a growin' base of alarmed citizens, are supportin' 345 an' riverbank reedee—reedee—reedeeevooolavlop—howd'ya say that word again?"

"Uh, *redevelopment.*" Cleve's deep voice was made for radio.

"Oh, yeah. Reeedeeevooolavlopment."

Cleve stared at a looseleaf that tottered on a shelf's edge, contemplating suicide.

"Y'listenin', Cleveland?"

"Huh? Uh-huh." Cleve's eyes remained fixed on the despondent notebook.

"Refooferendum's comin' up soon—I'll hafta knock it offa the ballot!"

Cleve raised an eyebrow.

"If it stinkin' passes, it'll ruinate EVERYTHIN'!"

"Uh-huh."

"THEY'LL REPLACE MIERK WIT' ZODD IN SIX MONTHS!" Gneeecey kicked a file cabinet with all his might.

Cleve gazed at a terminally ill blue fern, living out its last days in an undersized clay pot stuck to a sawed-in-half, vintage manual Smith Corona typewriter.

"Creep writes, '345 would create a level playin' field for certain corpooperations' COMPETITORS, much to the vexation of some nearsighted, profit-driven entrails!'" added Gneeecey, hopping in pain.

Cleve blew a thick layer of dust off a framed portrait of a white-and-black canine-humanoid couple. Embossed script underneath read, "Froop & Fritzl Gneeecey, Celebrating Thirty AngRangs of Wedded Bliss." It was inscribed, "To our darling little Bizzig, with love from Mommy and Daddy."

Gneeecey punched a hole through the wall. "OW, DAAAMMIT! Y'KNOW HOW MAAAAAD THIS MAKES ME?"

"Uh-huh." Cleve's bleary eyes focused on the supermarket tabloids piled up outside Gneeecey's executive privy.

The good diroctor threw his newspaper down at Cleve's black wingtip oxfords.

The young man guzzled some more liquid chalk and blotted his thin mustache with a crisply folded handkerchief.

"These environmentalists ARE mental! I'll GET Imbroglio! Don't yooou EVER air a story on this till I put MY spin on it!"

"I—"

"Stories like THIS ain't never gonna smell the stinkin' daylight of fresh AIR!"

Cleve's finely-chiseled cheek began twitching.

"Wait til that Frank Salvador gets ahold of this on his jackassical station—whazzit called again?"

"Uh, 98.6, *Normal Radio*," replied Cleve, running a hand over his closely-cropped head of hair.

"If I ever catch y'listenin', y'can go ask THEM for a job—y'won't have one HERE!"

A smile illuminated Cleve's face as he glanced down at his maroon silk tie. Monogrammed with the initials "C W," it hung limp and askew, contrasting with his immaculate white shirt, tucked into creased gray slacks.

A gleaming watchband circled his right wrist. The timepiece's rectangular, ultramarine face was distinctive—I'd never seen one like it.

Gneeecey kicked my chair. "YOU better not listen to that station neitherwise—or ELSE!"

Resisting the urge to ask, "What?", I looked up at Cleve.

"Keep fillin' out that aplooplication—you'll meet Cleveland later."

"I've just met him now," I replied, rising. "Hi, I'm Nicki. Nicki Rodriguez. We'll be working together."

Gneeecey stepped between us. "Y'AINT GOT THE JOB YET!"

"There's still a chance I won't? Cool!"

Cleve's facial muscles relaxed, and he let go of his belly. Stifling a guffaw, he reached behind Gneeecey to shake my hand. "Name's Cleve Wheeler—and I'm real glad to meet *you*."

Gneeecey sucked in his teeth.

"I see you've just arrived," continued Cleve, no doubt noting my discolored skin and mierked-up shoes.

"Yesterday, as a matter of fact. What do you do here at WGAS?"

"A little bit of everything. Engineering, production, and administrative stuff, like toilet-unclogging. You name it, I do it."

"Don't act so martyrannical," admonished Gneeecey. "*I* do all the work here! Now git downstairs. Stuff the VCR carousels wit' commercials an' garbage."

"Diroctor," began Cleve, "it would really pay off in the end if—"

"Pay off in WHOSE stinkin' end?"

"Uh, what I meant is, it'd make life 'round here a lot easier if we'd invest in more modern equipment—stuff like computer storage. Everyone else has it. Nobody else really uses these outmoded—"

"WHO'S 'EVOOVERYONE ELSE'? FRANK SALVADOR? IF EVOOVERYONE ELSE JUMPED OFFA SEEMIN' WHALE TOWERS, WOULD YOOOU?"

"I might," muttered Cleve, heading for the door.

"Besides, TV's goin' three-dimensional—wit' high-definition holography. I'll wait till THEN to modernizate."

Cleve's head turned. "Holographic TV?"

"Hollow graphics are cheaper."

"One more thing, Diroctor. I see reception's empty. Have you heard from Fraxinella?"

"She called in SICK again—second time in SEVENTEEN YEARS! An' she only left a MESSAGE! Somethin' 'bout bein' rushed into surgery for some rupturated appendage."

Cleve's brow wrinkled. "Last night, she was doubled over with this sharp pain on her right side. But she wouldn't leave till she finished some correspondence for you."

"She looked fine to *me*—worked through lunch as usual. Hope she didn't take her work home again—it'll be real incornvenient if we're missin' any paperwork."

"Shouldn't we really be thinking about—"

"Oh—an' I'm havin' lunch wit' Mark again."

"Whatever," Cleve replied, loud enough for only me and his boss's dying plant to hear.

"An' call Ferguson Memorial. If Fraxinella's really been admitted, ask her or her daughter Margoogaret if they got any of our files over there."

"But—"

"An' if she's really in the hospoopital, send her a packa Rindom Doodles, from all of us—a small bag."

"But Fraxinella *hates*—"

"Oh, call Seemin' wale Towers—see if Oxymoron needs more food. He don't like his new chow—hopefully there's plenny left."

"Uh-huh."

"An' at lunchtime, put the Ig here at Fraxinella's desk. Show her how to make out outvoices—we mus' have FIVE ZILLION sittin' there! She can get lunch from the vendin' machine downstairs an' eat while she works!"

I was doomed. "*Work* through *lunch?*"

"Y'think I'm payin' ya to EAT?"

"And what," I asked, "are outvoices?"

"Opooposite of invoices. We got all these bills we delay payin'—we contesterate 'em. Oh, Cleveland, almost forgot—the Ig here's from 'round *your* parts—she's from Turtleneck. Ain't that near Piscataway?"

"That's *Teaneck*, and no, it's not," I answered. "Where are you from, Cleve?"

"He's from Sackenhacky—ain't that kinda near ya, Ig? Would sure 'splain a lot."

Cleve grinned. "That's *Hackensack*—we're neighbors!"

Another human—from regular New Jersey! I couldn't wait to ask him how he got here. How did he cope? Could he communicate with family and friends back home? Most important of all, would he be returning home soon?

But that limp—did it have anything to do with dimension burn?

"Stop DREAMIN', Ig—that's not allowed here. Take these papers to personnel. Cleve, I wan'cha to go up in Chopper 3½—"

"*I'm* not riding in that deathtrap. Flea's right—one day it's gonna drop to the ground like a rock. Why don'cha ask Mr. Pitt. He's itching to go."

"Stu? No, it's too dangerous."

"But it's okay for me? Well, thanks. Right back at'cha."

"Hah?"

"I'd better get downstairs to check—"

"Cleve, why're y'jus' standin' there? GIT TO WORK!"

"WHATSAMATTER, IG? Y'LOOK like y'jus' been chased by a three-headed gazoonga."

"I—I—"

"Stop holdin' on to the wall, perspiratin' like that—you'll scrungle our new paint job. Green-an'-three-quarters is extra igspensive—gotta be specially mixed wit' rare sclogg pigmentations."

"I—I went to p-personnel like—like you asked me to—n-nobody was there, so I w-was j-just g-gonna leave—and suddenly, this—this—"

"SPIT IT OUT, IG!"

"This huge purple pelican—it—it must've been five-hundred pounds—tried to sell me this life insurance policy it was carrying in its—its beak!"

"That's jus' Cleopatrick, our human resources director," explained Gneeecey, shooting me a smug "told you so" look. "Sells insurance on the side. We take a cut."

I followed him back into his office.

"Wit' the job *you'll* be doin', might not be a bad idea to buy a su-plooploomental policy." Gneeecey took a flying leap into his oversized chair. "Now, don't forget to pick up my socks tonight. Don't lose that ticket! Gus won't ever release socks—not even mine—wit'out a ticket."

Suddenly nauseated, I flopped into my seat.

"Y'didn't hapoopen to bring a resoosumay wit'cha, did'ja?"

"Do I look like I brought a resoosumay—ugh, I mean, resumé—with me?"

"Don't get intelligent wit' ME, Ig. I'll jus' hafta judge ya by your aplooplication here, plus what I foun' out from schnooglin' ya."

"Huh?"

"Schnooglin's like your googlin'. Now, despite your obvious deficiencies, I can still utilizate ya."

I bit my tongue.

"Like I said, you'll do radio an' TV!"

"I told you, I've never worked in television—"

"TV's jus' radio wit' pictures." He slapped at a Lear jet as it zoomed past his honker.

"Y'know, Director, I'm not interested in working for you—I just want my—"

He smirked. "You ain't goin' nowheres for a while. Jus' ask Cleve. Or Julio."

I bolted upright, almost toppling my wimpy chair.

"Plus, y'ain't got no mon-ney."

I groaned. I didn't.

"I'm givin' ya a title," he said. "I'm makin' ya 'VLAM'."

"*Vlam*," I repeated, scratching a plane bite on my left wrist. "What's *vlam*?"

"Very Low Assistant Management. You'll be workin' lotsa extra hours, but'cha won't get no overtime."

"What?"

"Then y'can look yourself in the mirror wit' a empty conscience—y'won't hafta lay awake nights worryin' 'bout deprooprivatin' the network of revenue."

A blood-spattered twin prop cruised past my nose.

"Now," continued Gneeecey, "so there's no confusionism 'bout

chained-up command, LISTEN GOOD: Y'REPORT DIRECTLY TO
MEEE AT ALL TIMES!"

"*Right.*"

Next thing I knew, a legal pad sliced through the air, nearly decapi-
tating me. "I'll read off your duties. Write 'em down." He threw a dull,
inch-long remnant of a pencil at me.

"Every mornin', you'll run into the newsroom. We use the same
one for AM, FM an' TV, even though they're on difooferent floors, at difooferent ends of the buildin'."

I made a face.

"Y'might wanna get yourself a pair of them motorized sneakers."

"What?"

"PAY DETENTION! You'll run down all the news—from the *Tims*,
the wire, blogs, an' podcasts. But NOT the *Pooper-Scooper!*"

"Uh-huh."

He spat on the floor. "You'll check my computer for satellite feeds
from Planet Eccchs." He smacked his ancient behemoth of a monitor.
"Print out everythin' from our bigger moon, FishVendor 4. We don't
get nuthin' useful from the smaller one. Cronon's more for vaca-
tionin'—my folks sent me away there to Camp Bingaboonga every summer."

"By the way, Diroctor," I ventured, trying hard to imagine him as a
child, "your printer's out of paper—"

"AM I PAYIN' YA TO TELL ME OBVOOVIOUS JUNK I
AWREADY KNOW? SO PUT IN S'MORE! Now, this is REAL IM-
PORTOOTANT—put any stuff 'bout 345, an' of course, anythin' 'bout
MEEEE, on my desk. *I* decide what airs."

My fingers cramped as I scribbled away.

"Nex', y'call the Perswayssick City Police Department—you'll usually get Mark. Or Mark. Or even Mark or Mark."

"How many—"

"Have 'em check their blotters, then write down whatever they say."

"Whatever they *say*? Shouldn't I ask a few questions?"

"DOOO WHAT I SAY! NEVER ASK WHY!"

"Which phone should I use?"

"DON'T EVER TOUCH THE HOTLINE! Only use these gray
phones. They're all over the crummy place. Now, nex' y'gotta do back-
ground production research to execute potential stories—an' ya gotta

talk to our editor—that's *me*."

My eyelid began twitching.

"Then," Gneeecey continued, hurling a prehistoric black walkie-talkie into my solar plexus, "use this here two-way devicicle to dispatch your engineerin' crews to cover junk. If I make up news, y' can skip that step."

"Uh-huh."

He leaned back, put his feet up, and stuffed a cigar in his mouth. A squashed white commuter jet decorated his left sneaker sole. "You'll run audio boards an' master control switchin'. Every hour, you'll check base current readin's for AM, an' log FM's total wattage outpoop."

"Yes," I replied, staring at a gooped-up bottle of Bend-A-Britch.

"Then you're off to TV, to clean heads an' lenses, vacuum out equipment bays, an' empty trash cans. Make sure Merk Perk's always mercolatin' on all four floors, an' there's always fresh Freak O'Nature snacks out front—"

I stopped writing. "What am I—a janitor and waitress?"

"Both! An' y' gotta provide studio audiences for game shows, an' derange for their transpooportation an' refreshments."

I exhaled slowly.

"Plus," he boomed, chewing his cigar as he pointed to his laptop with the damaged screen, "you'll check this here computer every hour, for personal messages. If they ain't personal, don't bother wit' 'em. But if they are, don't *read* 'em, jus' print 'em out. An' leave 'em here on the floor."

"If I have to decide what's personal and what's not, how can I not read them?"

His eyes bulged with fury. Shuddering, I glanced down, barely able to decipher my notes. My stub of a pencil scratched more than it wrote.

"An' you'll get us outta make-goods to all them sponsors whose commercials we forget to run," he added, swallowing his cigar.

"Right."

Suddenly, he sat up straight, kicking a pile of papers to the floor. "An' another thing, Ig—"

"Name's *Nicki*—"

"When it snows, Ig, an' it's gonna, any day now—you'll climb up on the roof an' shovel out them satellite dishes."

I hated snow.

"An' check the programmin' an' engineerin' logs daily—leave 'em on my desk."

"Uh, could I have another pencil?"

Flinging a chewed-up, eraserless yellow stick my way, he continued inventing my position. "Hmmm. . .lessee what else. . .an idle mind is Santa's workshop. . .okay, once a week on, lessee, FriedEggs—why, that's today—y'clean out the big goonafish aquarium in the lobby."

"You mean—"

"Before y'scrub out the tank, y'gotta fish 'em all out an' put 'em in their wadin' pool. It's filled wit' distillerated, alkookaline water. It's right nearby in the electrical closet— y'can't miss it. Sign says 'DANGER! HIGH VOLTAGE! LIVE WIRES!'"

I flinched.

"Feed the goonafish three times a day. There's a coupla barrels of live gloortworms in the electrical closet. Y'can't miss 'em—they're green an' slimy an' smell like Limburger cheese. Plus they light up, an' sometimes they crawl outta the barrels."

"How do goonafish eat, without heads?" I asked, grimacing.

"Good question for a Ig."

"Don't patronize me."

"But it *is* a good question for a Ig. Their bodies are covered wit' these itsy-bitsy ingesticules—that's how they take in nutrition. Them little openin's are what make 'em look phosphoosphorescent. Put in five gloortworms for each fish."

My eyes had glazed over.

"An' make sure y'change the hourly survooliance tapes—they're in the electrical closet too. Don't touch no wires when you're standin' in puddles. We got a cardiac defribroobrillator, but'cha can't always depend on it bein' here—sometimes people from other offices borrow it. Close your mouth, Ig. Now, you'll assistipate me wit' prerecordin' news an' weather—"

"How can I possibly—"

"Now for the stuff you'll do on your time—"

"*My* time?!" I longed to dump my new boss into his goonafish tank, shove a fistful of gloortworms down his gullet, and toss him a plugged-in hair dryer.

"If y'wanna get what'chooo want, y'gotta play a little basefootball wit' me. Y'don't got much choice, dooo ya?"

I didn't. Not until I found my portfolio. Then I'd quit, on the spot, and go rent a room somewhere—bide my time in peace, until I was healthy enough to leave.

"Oh—every WetNooodlesday's 'Upside-Down Radio Day.' We stand on our heads an' walk on our hands—then whatever we say comes out upside-down. Cuts up the dull drums of midweek."

"Count me out."

"But if I'm on-air speakin' upside-down an' yooou engineer me right-side-up," he whined, "everything'll come out sideways!"

My hands curled into fists. "I've heard enough. Now I—"

"You'll come to work wit' me every mornin', Mondistinks through FriedEggs. AN' Y'BETTER NOT MAKE ME LATE NO MORE!"

Visualizing my fingers tightened around his neck, I grinned.

"Y'GOT NUTHIN' TO SMILE 'BOUT! You'll work Snatturdays an' Somedays too. Don't worry—you'll only work four or five weekends a month, an' the good thing is, Mondistinks won't even feel like Mondistinks. You'll feel like you're further along in the week."

"You've gotta be—"

"I don't do weekends—all work an' no play splits soup chefs' britches."

I pictured planting one of my mierk-splattered shoes in his moth-eaten keister.

"Weekdays, y'won't be leavin' wit' me unless it's your night to help at the restaurant—"

Not Gneeezle's.

"Don't look so oogdimonious—I'm really not obloobligated to help ya."

I dug my fingernails into my palms.

"Thirsty nights, you'll put in a coupla hours as a volunteer at the Shoppin' Cart Orphanage, feedin', oilin', an' shinin' the little guys. I've awready registered ya—"

"What?!"

"An' you'll be takin' official minutes at Quality of Life meetin's. Reminds me—you'll stuff envelopes today so I can mail out them ten-thousand pampoophlets Mark printed."

"But—"

"You'll be doin' it on compoopany time, but'cha can't go home anyways till y'finish your work, so it'll wind up bein' on your time."

"I—"

"I hope your spit ain't defective, like Cleve's. Stu usually hasta re-lick his envelopes."

"Ugh—"

"Y'get a twenny minute lunch hour an' two ten-minute breaks. Durin' Blirg, I dock ya douboobble time—I'll igsplain later. Study this in your free time—CATCH!" He pitched a humongous hardcovered volume, *Broadcast Engineering & Production for Iggleheimers*, into my lap.

"An' Ig, I'll need your signature here, sayin' you'll waive your company physical, so y'can get right to work."

"I'm not signing *anything*—"

"Then I'll hafta take the time to igzaminate'cha myself, an' I'll hafta dock y'for—"

"Give me that," I snarled, snatching the form from his dirty mitts.

"That's a good Ig—put'cha John Shuttlecock right on that line there."

"Is there a health plan?"

"Yeah. Plan not to get sick."

A tiny 747 zoomed past my spinning head.

"No personal calls in or out, an' no fraternalizatin'. An' water my plant here—twice an hour." He shook his dying fern.

"Uh-huh."

"Oh, what's this here? Want a snack?" He threw a small, silica gel-filled bag at me.

"Uh, this says 'Do not ingest.'"

"Aaaah—don't believe everythin' y'read, Ig."

"Uh, I'll need some sort of cash advance to tide me—"

"Gimme a second," he mumbled. "I'll work it out on my cal-coocoolator. Lemme figure out how much your first check'll be. First, I gotta figure out your base salary." He began crunching numbers.

Stomach acids began eating me alive.

"Five buckerooneys should get'cha to payday nex' WetNooodles-day—"

I leapt to my feet. "*Five dollars?!*"

"Y'get paid every other WetNooodlesday—"

I moaned. "Every *two* weeks?"

"That way, y'don't get paid less more—y'get more less. Oh, y'gotta fill out a second income tax form—you'll hafta pay tax on any refund y'might be receiveratin'. . .fill out this 1040-FU an' bring it over to Cleopatrick."

I broke into a cold sweat.

"Now, there's what'cha owe for the river dredgin'—"

"I never asked you to—"

He looked up. "Y'don't got much choice in all this, *do* ya?"

"I'm gonna make the choice to find my portfolio and leave!"

"Suit y'self. But don't forget, you're makin' igsclooosive concessions here that won't be offered to ya anywhere else."

The fur ball had that right.

"There's my finder's fee, your fines for pollutin' our river an' damagin' our bridge. . .an' there's my busted column. . .an' there's your rent, paid weekly—every WetNooodlesday—"

"*Weekly?*"

"Some months got more payin'-up days—more WetNooodlesdays. Y'wouldn't wanna cheat me, would'ja?"

"And how much is my—"

"I'll give ya a printout later."

I collapsed back into my chair.

"My washer an' dryer are coin-opooperated. But there's your projecticated use of water, gas, 'lectricity, an' oxygen. An' your kitchen-usage fee. Plus, transpooportation—one extra person's weight impactuates fuel inefficiency. Vehicles are very 'spensive to run."

"No—I had *no idea.*"

"Now, there's my bat'room fee. . . . I'll reset the Cyclone an' automatically decapitate a buncha dollars from each check so y'don't gotta drop Susan B. Anthonies in the slot every five seconds—"

"*Thanks.*"

"I mean, y'might need change at some real incornvenient times."

"*Right.*"

"An' there's wit'holdin' taxes. You'll be glad you're gettin' paid less. The more y'make, the less ya end up wit'. . .now, lessee. . .there's unemployment tax—pays *me* if I fire ya."

"*What?!*"

"An' there's our bare bones accidental insurance, so in case y'get hurt—or worse, heh, heh—*we* don't suffer."

Chills ran down my spine.

"Almos' forgot the mandatory county tax. Now, lessee, how much'll your first paycheck be? Hmmmm. . . ."

My breathing had become rapid and shallow.

Gneeecey looked up, grinning from ear to ear. "Works out per-fec'—won't even hafta cut'cha a check!"

"Huh?"

"Keep in mind, y'get paid every other WetNooodlesday—the pay period always ends the FriedEgg before. This week's check'll be for what'cha earn today."

"Okay. From my, uh, job description, I'll be working pretty hard today. So, uh, what's my total net then?"

His wagging tail thumped loudly. "That's FIFTEEN CENTS this week!"

CHAPTER 14

THREE EGGS, TOO BAD

SHELL SHOCKED, I STAGGERED into my "room" and collapsed. Didn't even take off my jacket. Just sat on the hard floor, slumped against the wall, staring into darkness. I'd barely survived my first workday at WGAS—a *13-hour* workday.

My heart sank through the soles of my feet when I heard Gneeecey, across the way, in the kitchen, blabbering on the phone that he'd discovered three freshly-laid, spike-covered chrome eggs in the goths' playroom.

Yammicles, he squealed, was thrilled. Soon he'd have brothers and sisters to play with.

Right. Soon feathery clouds of the teddy's innards would float out of his new siblings' steel snouts as they ripped his plush butt to shreds.

"Foun' the little eggs nex' to that chair they been eatin'," gushed Gneeecey. "MaybeVizzy been eatin' furniture 'cause she needed the extra nutritootion to lay eggs."

Down the hall, the goths snarled with joy. Maybe they were picking out baby names.

"Yeah. . .uh-huh," continued Gneeecey, "like I said, I'm workin' on it. Yeah. . . . I'll fix Imbroglio, too. Don't worry. Yuz won't be jus' a buncha planetless, floatin' eyeballs forever. I promise."

I sat up straight.

"An' sorry I was late. Got to the office late—the Ig hadda play foot-ball wit' the birds. She lost my sock ticket, too. Is she gonna pay!"

Groaning, I squeezed my eyelids shut.

CHAPTER 15

A SOCK IN THE HAND'S WORTH TWO IN THE PIANO

THE STINK SEEMED TO come from everywhere. Maybe some un-fortunate rodent lay decomposing under one of the vividly col-ored pieces of furniture that vied for attention in The Grate Room. I glanced at my watch. It was eight a.m., and the good director had yet to show his face downstairs. He'd been out late again—another midnight meeting with Mark. Third one that week.

Of course, our tardiness would end up being my fault.

I peered underneath Gneeecey's electric chartreuse, motorized gear-shifting easy chair and nearly jumped out of my skin when an unearthly, hyena-like voice screeched, "Igzed felopsaded!"

Adrenaline surging, I spun around.

"Bad mornin', Iggarooney," chirped Gneeecey. "Igzed felop-saded. . .igzed felop—"

"What language are *you* speaking?"

"I'm studyin' for my eye exam—memorizatin' the stinkin' chart so I do good."

"Speaking of your favorite word, *stinking*," I began, "do you smell something funny?"

"Nah, Ig, I don't smell nuthin' that makes me wanna laugh," he an-swered, admiring the unkempt character that grinned back at him from one of the room's fifteen mirrors. "But we're gonna be late, an' it's your fault. As usual."

"You're the one who got up late—"

"Why ain' cha lookin' for my spare socks? Gotta take 'em to Gus!"

"But, we're——-"

"An' y'better find that ticket! Gotta have them lucky socks back in time for the Grand Ooogitty-Boogitty's concert. His tail'll be in our neck of the woods any day now."

Even though Gus knew damned well which reeking pair of socks were Gneeecey's, he wouldn't release 'em. Rules were rules, he insisted.

"LOOK FOR 'EM, IG!"

"But we're late!"

He jammed his face in mine, assaulting me with morning breath. "FIND 'EM!"

"Well, don't blame *me* if——"

"If y'don't, you'll never see that poopfolio case of yours that I ain't got——"

Muttering, I dropped to my knees and began to search.

I was all too used to looking for stuff. Nights Gneeecey stayed out late, I hunted for my portfolio, determined to work my way up from the mansion's nightmare of a basement to its fourth floor.

The sound of Gneeecey's pogo stick, or his wet, rubbery nose honks, would send me hobbling back to my room highspeed.

I glanced over at him as he lounged in his chair, perusing the *Tims*. "Aren't you gonna look, too?"

"Nope. I'm readin' this article 'bout 'choo Earthlin's. Says the more garbage yuz manufacturate, the heavier your world gets."

"Puhleeease," I began, scrambling to my feet.

"One day, your whole lousy planet's gonna flop to the bottom of the universe. I always thought yuz should ship your trash to your moon— pockmarked ol' rock ain't good for nuthin' else."

I glared at him.

"Your planet's increased gravoovitational pull made y'bump our innocent planet."

"We're late. You just gonna sit there reading?"

"Hmmm. . .stoopid crosswords always get harder by the enda the week. Three down. 'Normal,' minus the L—a girl's name. . .hey, Ig, what's a——"

"Stop calling me 'Ig.'" As I moved closer to the piano, the unidentified odor became overpowering. I lifted the lid, and there were his spare socks.

"Yeah, okay, Ig. Now, what's a word for 'normal' wit'out the L—a girl's name?" A pencil dangled from his lips.

"Can't believe you're sitting there doing a puzzle," I hissed, tossing his socks into his briefcase.

"I SAID, the clue here says it's a five-lettered girl's NAME!"

"Norma!" I shouted, grabbing my jacket. "It's Norma! Now c'mon—"

"Nah, can't be. . .hmmmm. . .yeah. . .NORMA. . .that's IT—wait . . .it's not NORMAL!"

"It's not normal—it's Norma."

"It's not *normal*," he whined.

"It's *Norma*." I snatched the pencil out of his mouth, jammed a fresh health cigar in, and threw his briefcase into his lap.

"But it's only normal to add letters, not take 'em away," he protested, leaping out of his chair. "An' besides, then eight across, a person who sells propooperty, wit' a extra syloolable, won't fit!"

"What?!" I asked, as I dragged him into the hallway, by the neck of his T-shirt, wishing I had a choke collar and leash.

"REALILTOR—then REALILTOR won't fit!"

"For crying out loud—"

"Wait, Ig—seven down—a five-lettered girl's name wit'out a extra L added to its end, to make it the same as three down. . .I've GOT it. . .NORMA!"

"Burt, Mary—I'm so sorry," I whispered, as I gaped at their trashed bakery, still not believing what I saw. "Let me know if there's anything I can do—I'm here for you."

"Thanks, Nicki." Burt had aged a couple decades overnight.

"The Ig ain't got time to be here for yooou—she gotta be there for meee!"

"As a matter of fact," I added, ignoring Gneeecey, "we'll be passing by after work, as usual, to pick up Flea. I'll give you a hand then."

Gneeecey's eyeballs inflated like balloons. "Fleaglossitty's here every day?"

"We appreciate that, Nicki," replied Mary, as she swept up what had been Shisskey's front window. "Last time we were hit, it was messy— y'know, whipped cream all over—but they didn't destroy the place."

"Yeah," growled Burt, stepping over squashed strudels and crumbled cookies. "It'll take us weeks to come back from this. We're practically outta business."

"Hey, Mark, y'think it's the same perpoopetrator?" asked Gneeecey, as he slobbered up one of the few items that hadn't been stolen or smashed—his usual cherry-topped whipped cream concoction. "Din'cha say y'found some short black hairs in here—like las' time?"

The policeman adjusted his hat. "Yeah. Could be the same black-haired perpetrator."

"Maybe it's Flea," suggested Gneeecey, gawking at the Shisskeys like he was watching a movie. "He has black hair, he loves whoop cream, an' he's always here."

Mark rubbed his peeling chin. "Mrs. Shisskey, last time, the burglar left money on the counter, right?"

"Yes—we've told you over and over again, last time the burglar left two tens."

Gneeecey almost choked. "Twenny bucks—whadda chump!"

"But whoever did this left a coupla dimes," continued Mary, her red-rimmed eyelids narrowing. "Like we've been telling you for the past hour, whoever broke in before didn't vandalize us—or take more than what he paid for."

"Don't catch an attitude wit' me," drawled Mark, leering at Mary's shapely behind as she bent over to whisk up a mashed corn muffin. "I didn't rob yuz. Maybe this was an inside job—maybe business ain't been so good lately—black hairs were planted to make it look like a burglary. . .an' the dimes came from *your* register. I'm gonna take 'em in, along wit' some of these here crumbs, an' dust 'em for prints."

Burt marched over to Mark and poked him in the chest with a sturdy index finger. "Why don'cha go reread your notes? Then maybe you can stop asking us the same stupid questions and go catch whoever's been doing this—like a *real* cop."

Sneering, Mark backed away. "Easy, Shisskey."

Burt pointed to what was left of his door. "Time for you to leave!"

The yellow-eyed, amber-skinned officer chuckled as he hopped over a pile of debris and out onto the sidewalk. "Oh, an' Shisskey, your door's broke. Have a nice day!"

Burt stood in the entranceway, veins popping out all over his neck.

"THANKS FOR GIVIN' ME a copy of the police report," said Gneeecey, lean-ing out of the limo. "I'm savin' this Shisskey story for six o'clock—my evenin' ratin's been saggin'. A real robbery—how cool!"

"Yeah," replied Mark. "Cool."

Gneeecey flopped back into his seat and turned to me. "Y'makin' us late again."

"*Me*?! We had to find your socks—"

"Why din'cha look in the piano right away?"

"Oh, c'mon. And we had to stand around while you stuffed your face and eavesdropped on the Shisskeys and your strange cop friend—"

"Don't say 'strange cop'!" he shouted, as he gulped down the gooey waxed paper that had covered his treat. "That was my bes' friend Mark. Or Mark."

"Burt and Mary are supposed to be your friends, but to you, it's more important to use that police report that you're—you're *eating*—"

"WHAAAAAT?" he asked, swallowing it.

"The police report!"

"Whaddaboudit? BRAAAAAAAAP!"

"You just *ate* it!"

"LOOK WHAT'CHA STINKIN' MADE ME DO, IG—Y'MADE ME EAT THE POLICE REPORT!" He plunged his fist into his mouth.

"*I* made you do it?"

"YOOOU DISTRACTIPATED ME WHILE I WAS EATIN' MY WAX PAPER!"

"And what normal person eats wax paper?"

"Oh, NO—the police report!" Gneeecey exclaimed, gagging. "It's awready gone too far DOWN! Arm's not long enough!" He pulled his hairy elbow out of his esophagus.

I had to look away.

"NOW WE'RE GONNA BE REAL late—havin' to come all the way back 'cross town to headquarters for another copy of the report that—"

"That you ingested," I snapped, moving away from the splintery counter. "We've been waiting forty-five minutes. These cops are too busy eating to do any work."

"Don't pick on 'em—they're Mark's brothers. Can'cha see the re-semboooblance?"

"Yeah. I sure can." I watched a dozen or so waxy-faced, uniformed officers ignore ringing phones as they crammed cupcakes, turnovers, donuts and fancy whipped-cream concoctions like Gneeecey's into their big traps. The single bulb that illuminated the dark-paneled office cast eerie shadows and made their supernatural complexions glow.

Gneeecey held out his grubby palms. "Guys, got any extra?"

No one answered.

"Ig, maybe if yooou ask 'em——"

"Haven't you eaten *enough* today?"

"Shisskey report," boomed a black-haired officer, running his hand over his crew cut as he tossed a paper our way.

"Thaaanks," bleated Gneeecey, practically shoving me through the closed plate glass door.

"DUCK!" GNEEECEY SHOUTED INTO the intercom, "TURN OFFA THIS LOUSY BOULEVARD—RIGHT HERE—TAKE THE BACK WAY! WE'RE LATE!"

Culvert complied, instantly.

"AN' IG, STOP SAYIN' THE COPS BROKE INTO SHISSKEY'S!"

"Stop saying it's Flea!"

Gneeecey poked his head outside as we crept down the exit ramp, underneath a green-and-white sign that read, "The Back Way."

Backed up for miles, the alternate route was a multi-colored mosaic of bumper-to-bumper metal. Drivers stood outside their vehicles, conversing.

"DUCK—WHY'JA PULL ONTO THIS GIRDLE-LOCKED ROAD?"

"Jus' followin' orders," quacked Culvert, parking. Gneeecey flung his door open and flew out sideways, like a batty wet hen.

As I stepped out, my jaw dropped. The good diroctor had mounted the limo's front end. Gyrating and gesticulating hysterically, he resembled a hood ornament having a seizure.

Onlookers applauded.

CHAPTER 16

SHOPPING AT HOME WITH GAS

NEEECEY PULLED ME, BY my scarlet sweater's unraveling hem, into AM. Its walls were painted *pastel black*, as he described it. Swearing, he scurried over to the audio board and opened the microphone. "The deceased program's prerecorded," he shrieked, slamming his fist against a rickety reel-to-reel recorder, causing its PLAY button to pop off and spring across the room. "Got fifteen minutes—C'MON!"

As I followed him into the newsroom, I read the instructions he had scribbled on my clipboard. "Durin my newzcast," he wrote, "I'll signal ya to simulkast a sicks sekkond delay on FM wit a ate sekkond delay on AM."

"Diroctor, how can anyone simulcast a 6-second delay with an 8-second delay?"

"Do the math."

"But—"

"Thought'cha knew how to do radio." He raced over to the news wire and began to rip copy from the '80s relic, using the counter's sharp edge to tear and separate stories. "Yoooou shoulda done this. Stu did all your other mornin' junk."

"But—"

"C'MON!"

Something sharp slid under my heels, tilting my whole body backward. Next thing I knew, I was flying down the corridor on wheels, at breakneck speed. "Whaaa—"

"Y'been eatin' too much, Ig—I can hardly push this here handcart!"

"ROOT, ROOT, ROOT FOR your planet! Cheer, cheer, cheer for your schoooool!" sang the cheerleaders, blasting their way out of WGAS-FM's ON AIR speakers. "PUNI! PUNI! RAH! RAH!"

"To register for the coming post-Blirg semester at Perswayssick University of New Ideas," whinnied a dorky voice, "or to take advantage of our continuing Eccchs-centric Adult Education Program, call 999-333-3334. That's 438-555-9876."

I must've looked confused.

"Those are sub-numbers, Ig," said Gneeecey. "You'll learn all 'bout 'em when y'spend lunch telemarketin'."

"Telemarketing? On my *lunch?*"

"I'm sicka you an' Cleve takin' breaks together!" Fussing with frayed wires and a patchboard, he flung a program log in my face. "Okay, got AM an' FM runnin' together simultaneousfully. Engineer my newscast!"

Reluctantly, I sat down at the controls. Everything around me, from the disintegrating '70s-style console to the walls and carpeting, was colored electric diarrhea-brown.

Gneeecey sprinted into FM's shoebox of a news booth, glared at me through its smudged window and stuck his tongue out.

I popped a StomQuell antacid tablet and opened his mike.

"Bad mornin', everyone," he began, shrill enough to shatter bulletproof glass. "You're in Gas Radio Newsmaker Territory!"

A bulky, old-fashioned tape cartridge sailed over my head, crash-landing on my held-together-with-duct tape audio board. Wincing, I shoved the projectile into a battered "cart" machine.

The START switch fell off as I pressed it. "This mornin's news," screeched the prerecorded Gneeecey, "is brung to ya by Bogelthorpe's Bweeeek Emporium, purvooverator of fine, repossessed Earth automobiles, located on 345 Drip Drive, in Snurddles Township, near Snott's Landing."

Bweeeek? I glanced down at the log. It read *Buick*. I didn't even want to know how they'd obtained vehicles from my dimension.

I reopened Gneeecey's microphone and watched, puzzled, as he made a series of wild slashing gestures at his throat.

"BRAAAAAAAAAAAP!" Gneeecey's elongated belch lasted exactly six seconds—on AM *and* FM, for all the county to hear.

If looks could kill, I'd have been traveling horizontally in a black Caddy station wagon, clutching daisies and heading to St. Vlad's, to be dumped—quite unceremoniously, I'm sure—six feet underground.

"Any mistakes yuz folks hear are the fault of the Iggleheimer engineer who ain't followin' instructions," he growled, flashing me an "I fixed you" look.

"Today in sports," he continued, "yesterday, Planet Eccchs's Sportin' Commission ruled that if two teams play equally lousy, they tie for a loss. Tension at the meetin' was so thick, y'could cut it wit' a balloon. GET IT? HA, HA, CUT IT WIT' A BALLOON!"

I wondered what halfwit had written that copy.

"An' accordin' to uninformed sources, the commission plans to indict Gregg Gronkle into the Zorgle Hall of Fame. Now, there'll be weather today, an' plenny of it. The prevoovalent winds are blowin' in from the east-west, an' tonight'll be sunny, wit' heavy traffic. Tune in later at six, for igsclooosive details on the Whoop Cream Bandit's latest excitin' robbery!"

"I'M NOT COVERING A spitting contest—"

"Look, Clevooveland, I'm stinkin' boss—"

"Send Stu—his first initial and last name spell 'spit.'"

"Stop pickin' on Stuey. An' anyways, I need him to set up merchoochandise for home shoppin'."

Eyes fixed on the half-fallen drop ceiling, Cleve didn't notice the lopsided figure executing cartwheels as it sang, "I love my job!"

"I wish everyone here was like yooou, Stuey. Y'remindicate me of myself when I was young."

"Thanks, Boss," replied the panting intern. "And thanks for all the overtime!"

Stuart Pitt was about five foot five and a little out of shape. He sported a carrot-red crew cut and a ponytail that wagged at the nape of his meaty neck. His scarlet, mule-like ears matched his annoying knob of a nose.

His face was moon-shaped, except for one sharp chin that jutted out of six others. A dense mask of freckles surrounded his beady eyes.

"Don't know what I'll do with that extra nickel!" he exclaimed, patting his short-sleeved polyester shirt's pen-populated pocket.

Gneeecey smiled.

Stu pulled the mustard slacks, that matched his eyes, up to his chest, exposing doughy, hairless calves and white socks half-swallowed by scuffed brown oxfords.

Gneeecey handed him a roll of duct tape. "Fell outta your pocket when y'were demonstratin' your very depreciatin' corpooporate enthusiasm an' team spirit."

"Thanks, Boss—got that at Squiggleman's!" Stu possessed the voice of a young jackass vaulting its way into puberty on a pogo stick.

"Great place," said Gneeecey. "That's where I purchoochased my Electronic Water Cyclone 3000."

"Y'know, Boss, the safest place to be during a thunderstorm is on a toilet!"

"Yeah—I never once been hit by lightnin', sittin' there."

"And thanks for letting me do the voice-over on that PUNI commercial!"

"Stuey, good junk comes to desiccated employees. The more ya do for me, the more I'll do to you."

"And the hotline rang this morning and I didn't answer it!"

Gneeecey patted his intern's flabby back. "Atta boy!"

"Plus, I figured out a better way to set up cameras than how Cleve taught me!"

"Bet'cha stinkin' did!"

Cleve adjusted his tie and limped out of the studio, muttering something about going downstairs to blow up master control.

"An' Stuey, show the Ig here how to do a six-second delay."

"Hurry, Ig—go help Stu set up merchoochandise in Studio A. An' fill the carousels in FM, take a transmitter readin', an' stop in my office—check my e-mails."

"Okay."

"An' run back to AM—check the transmitter readin'—then go up to duplooplicatin'—xerox these logs. An' throw a few gloortworms to the goonafish. An' check the alkookalinity in their tank."

"Uh-huh."

"But before ya do anythin', get to TV right away, to help Stu. But do all that other stuff first. But don't stop to do a single thing before ya go help Stu."

He hurled a reel of audio tape at me. "An' make this here half hour radio program into a two-hour TV show. Have it on my desk after lunch."

"But—"

"Y'don't hafta be a rocket surgeon to know TV's jus' radio wit' pictures. Now do all that junk, but get to TV *right away*, to help Stu."

THERE WAS STU PITT, bustling all over the set with armfuls of shrink-wrapped digital drapes.

He'd assembled a strange, one-wheeled bike in front of Studio A's fake, drape-covered bay window. Five long, thick red rubber bands dangled from the machine's pulleys. There was no seat. Just a small, curved platform, labeled "detachable chin rest."

The intern waddled toward me. A small office shredder hung from his puce necktie. "Icky!"

"That's *Nicki*," I replied, gulping for air, having just dashed from FM to Gneeecey's office to AM to duplicating to the goonafish tank, and finally TV. "Uh, what happened to your tie?"

He giggled. "Oh, I was just multi-tasking again. Aren'cha gonna thank me for doing all your work this morning?"

I bit my lower lip. "Thanks, Stuart."

He yanked his tie out of the shredder. "Check this out, Icky! We've turned this place into a cool on-location studio—won't hafta bother goin' places anymore!"

"Really."

"We got backgrounds for indoors, outdoors, day, night, city and country—*and* this spiffy wind machine that blows the boss's ears around!"

"Really cool, Stuart."

"And look at these babies here," he cried, ponytail wagging as he pointed to a panel of multi-colored buttons and switches. "We can make it rain and snow inside!"

"You're a real, uh, technical wizard."

Blushing, he dumped a load of drapes onto a card table positioned near the peculiar exercise contraption.

"Stu, what still needs to be done?"

"Nuthin', Icky—I've already set everything up—"

"That's *Nicki*—"

"Oh, and I got a little tip for ya, Icky—boss doesn't like when y'get to work late. Working in the broadcast biz is a real responsibility. I'm just telling you 'cause you're new—I'm sure y'wanna stay on his good side—"

"Didn't know he had one."

Stu's head turned. "What?"

"Uh, nothing."

"Speaking of the boss," continued the intern, regarding me with raised brows, "he loved my joke about the tension being so thick, y'could cut it with a balloon! Get it? So thick, y'could cut it with a balloon!"

"Yeah, Stuart, I get it all right."

"Ig!" shouted Gneeecey, blustering into the room like an ill wind. "Why're y'jus' standin' there? Aaah, good boy, Stuey—everythin's set up."

"I did it all myself."

"Ig, y'can learn from Stu. He's only been internin' six months an' he awready knows little more than when he first came here. He's ready to be promotated!"

Stu grinned. Gneeecey scampered behind the sagging card table and set down his tumbler of Slog. "Let's get this road on the show, like people from *her* planet say."

"People from her planet actually talk like that?"

"Yupperooney, Stuey. They certaintaineously do."

As Gneeecey and Stu conversed, I lobbed the wad of gum I'd been chewing into Gneeecey's drink. The pink blob splashed in and sank to the bottom. I still had good aim.

"Nice tie, Stuey," commented Gneeecey, just noticing the mutilated mess hanging from his intern's neck. "Now, be sure an' come in tight on me wit' that camera at the very *enda* the show. Someone's waitin' for me to give him a special Morse code message usin' them drapes behind me—it's a matter of life an' *deaf!*"

"Okay, Boss!" Stu positioned himself behind the camera and lifted his pudgy hand, cuing Gneeecey with what resembled an obscene gesture on *my* planet.

"Bad mornin' everyone," began Gneeecey, peering into the lens. "Welcome to 'Shoppin' at Home wit' GAS.' As usual, this program's captioned for the sight-impaired. We got lotsa specials today, an' we'll be takin' testimonials.

"Did'ja know it's Plaaastic Appreciation Month? Buy any two plaaastic products an' you'll receiverate a free gift—a portable, genuine plaaaastic Freak O'Nature umbrella, complete wit' that famous three-headed hawk logo!"

Stu trembled and twitched as he visualized shielding himself from his on-location studio's electronically-generated elements, with his very own Freak O'Nature bumbershoot.

The more vividly he daydreamed, the more he squirmed—and the more tangled his right foot became in the rubber bands attached to a second, partially-assembled exercise machine.

"Okay, folks," said Gneeecey, sipping his Slog and screwing up his snoot, "we got this authentic plaaastic replooplica of Earth's Stonehenge that I happen to be wearin' on my wrist. It's a space-age watch, wit' a light-sensitive sundial. Even works in the dark! An' it's only 99.95!"

Stu studied his wrist, unaware that the rubber bands had wrapped themselves halfway around his calf.

"Call quick, folks—we got a limited supply!" warned Gneeecey. "Dial 'G - I - M - M - E - E D - A -T.' Our opooperators standin' by in Hemlock Heights'll take your order. An' stay tuned—we'll be right back wit' our new non-acoustic laundry detergent—for that clean quiet y'jus' love to hear—plus a bran' new produc' specially formulizated to soothe your nauseous feet!"

GNEEECEY HELD A PAIR of three-legged, kelly green pantyhose up to the camera. "Lemme cut through the sizin' confusionism for yuz. The small-large is small, the medium runs large, but the large-medium's smaller than the large, even though the large is small."

Whenever I attempted to signal Stu that a half-dozen rubber bands had wrapped themselves around his leg, he and Gneeecey shushed me.

I decided to mind my own business.

"An' now," announced Gneeecey, "here's a testimonial! Hi, Aboobigail, where y'callin' from?"

"I'm calling from New Buttzville, and I'm thrilled to be talking to yoooou," gushed a contralto female. "This pantyhose is great! I use the third leg as a tailwarmer!"

"What a faboobulous idea! Thanks, Aboobigail! Now, on to our nex' produc'!"

When my empty stomach roared, Gneeecey and wiggling Stu shot me dirty looks. Well, Stu wasn't wiggling all that much. Gneeecey was hawking something that didn't really interest him—the strange machine just like the half-put-together one, whose rubber bands were climbing his right leg.

"It's the amazin' BlabbaFlabb Exercise System! Blab your flab away! First, this master plaaastic elaaastic band attaches to your jaw—one size fits all! Nex', ya attach these other four miercolated bands to your hands an' feet. Y'can use this here chin rest, or y'can go freestyle, like me," suggested Gneeecey, tossing the piece over his shoulder.

"Then," he added, "y'go 'bout'cha business—y'won't even know y'have it on. I'm gonna wear it for the resta this show!"

Gneeecey's arms and legs whipped around in fifty directions as each syllable spewed out of his blabbering snout. He resembled a malfunctioning windmill. "Order now an' we'll send ya some fries to chew on— *free!* Whole thing's just 299.99!"

Stu, perking up at the notion of food, resumed wriggling, and the rubber bands climbed above his knee.

"Time for our las' item," declared Gneeecey, the BlabbaFlabb's pulleys spinning so fast they were barely visible. "This is the produc' that enaboobled me to start this network—our Digital Drapes! We got an overstock, so today, we'll be offerin' 'em at jus' 19.95!"

As Stu danced, a rubber band crossed over from his right ankle, to his left. He didn't notice.

"What a great produc'!" exclaimed Gneeecey. "How many times have ya asked yourself, 'What time is it? My clock has stopped an' my watch is broke! If only I had curtains that tol' time!'"

Enraptured by his boss's passionate presentation, Stu wept softly.

"An'," added Gneeecey, "how many times have y'said, 'My calendar's busted! What day is it? What's the tempooperature outside? If only my drapes *knew!*'"

Stu nodded his prickly head in agreement.

"Not only will our Digital Drapes give ya a read-out of the time, date, an' tempooperature—they'll even play Planet Eccchs's anthem— at the top of every hour!"

Stu sighed.

"You'll feel more secure too—they automatically open an' close every ten seconds, whenever you're not home! Plus they'll open your bottles an' cans, do your taxes, fry your goonafish, an' dice your veggies!"

Stu continued to sob.

"But wait—there's more! Their sturdy plaaastic rod makes 'em ideal for hangin' everythin' from wet underwear to decorative poultry, like dead rubber chickens! Plus y'can use 'em to dry your hands, wipe your nose, polish nearby furniture, an' clean up spills!"

The intern began hyperventilating.

"Not available in any store, Digital Drapes come in the followin' colors: yellowed green—which y'see hangin' behind me—an' burgundy blue! An' y'know what? I'm gonna lower the price today, jus' 'cause I like yuz!"

Stu gasped.

"How much," asked Gneeecey, "d'ya think you'd hafta pay for a pro-duc' packed wit' so many spectakookular features?" For emphasis—and with great effort, as his rubber bands had other plans for him—Gneeecey pounded a fist on the mound of drapes heaped in front of him.

What happened next was sheer poetry in motion.

As the overloaded table collapsed, his flailing limbs became entan-gled in the display curtains that had begun opening and closing behind him. He and the entire rapidly fluttering set, rods and all, tumbled to the floor.

Arms and legs revolving, Gneeecey poked his head out of the mess. "HELLLLP!"

Coming to his boss's aid, a bug-eyed Stu Pitt lunged forward, only to be snapped backward with equal force by the thick red rubber bands that had become his newest, most affectionate friends.

On the rebound, he flew back in his howling boss's direction, then shot sideways, with sudden violence. Braying like a terrorized mule riding a roller coaster, the hapless intern managed to grab hold of a nearby lever.

A split second later, a trapdoor in the ceiling opened and dumped a half-ton of snow—*real* snow—on Gneeecey's noggin.

Only the camera remained upright, running.

CHAPTER 17

ASK NOT FOR WHOM THE ELECTRONIC WATER CYCLONE FLUSHES

*I*T WAS THE WORST of times; it was the worst of times. Punching my pillow, I continued my predawn review of my miserable existence at 3 Bimbus Crack Drive. The only place I ever found peace was the bathroom—unless Gneeecey already sat enthroned upon his high-tech john, geared up for another marathon session.

He never closed the door. When I'd pass by, his bloodshot eyes would peer down at me from over the top of some tabloid whose headline proclaimed that an albino alien had given birth to a dump truck driven by a one-legged, opera-singing werewolf in drag.

The insomnia-stricken Poe crow's recent relocation to the window ledge outside—shrieking "Nevermore!" at all hours—did little to alleviate the good diroctor's chronic constipation. Or bad moods.

Lately, Gneeecey's moods were blacker than ever, especially after those midnight meetings with Mark. Or Mark. Or Mark.

The arrogant creeps never spoke to me. Whenever one showed up at the house—and they did frequently, usually unannounced—I'd head for my room, muttering, "Thanks for asking. And how are you?"

Then, with an uncharacteristic tremble in his voice, Gneeecey would stammer, "Where she comes from, they ain' got no stinkin' manners."

I slugged my pillow again, harder. My waking hours—when I wasn't preoccupied with work—were spent worrying. About my mom, Alex, and Dave. And my jobs and apartment. And my creditors. I'd been gone for over a month. Everyone must've given up on me. Except my creditors.

I'd fantasize about bursting in on my own memorial service and transforming it into a joyous homecoming—a bash filled with hugs and tears. Maybe Carlos's band would be wailing away in my honor.

A relieved Rico would shake my hand and say, "Place is still yours—always knew you'd be back!"

Fernández would rehire me on the spot. Never one to offer an outright compliment, he'd simply grumble, "That temp just couldn't cut it."

Scratching a plane bite on my arm, I chuckled.

"And," the not-quite-smiling Fernández would add as he handed me a thick envelope, "we took up a collection. Put it toward your bills."

One thing was for sure—I'd have no shortage of strange stories to tell.

Second thought, I'd be wiser to concoct some believable explanation for my absence. The truth would, most likely, get me put away. "*Me pondrían en el manicomio*," as my mom would whisper, whenever she stashed away a particularly way-out abstract painting she'd done—*they'd put me in the nuthouse.*

I sighed. My legs were as gimpy as when I'd arrived. Even if I found my portfolio, traveling home anytime soon was out of the question. As much as I loved my dad, I wasn't ready to meet him yet. Or Julio.

Every day, I did die a thousand deaths, visualizing the awful moment that Gneeecey might slip his slimy paws into my case's secret sleeve and discover my 10G. He'd prance back and forth, flashing my cash, screaming, "FINDERS KEEPERS, LOSERS WEEPERS!" Then, with my luck, he'd dematerialize into some other dimension. Maybe the one where his missing sock ticket was hiding.

And work. Work sucked more than ever. Gneeecey had just purchased some advanced news-guessing software. You'd enter his pre-approved list of names and places into the computer, then click on the "FINANCIAL," "SHOW BIZ," "SCIENTIFIC," "SPORTS," or interchangeable "POLITICAL" and "SCANDAL" icons, and bingo, the program created an infinite variety of so-called news stories. An infinite variety that, according to the program's manufacturers, had a fifty-fifty chance of being true on any given day.

Invariably, the logged-on user's name—usually Cleve's or mine—popped up in the fabricated copy, instead of Justin Imbroglio's or Frank Salvador's, or whomever else Gneeecey intended to slander.

The good diroctor would snatch the faulty copy from our hands as he sprinted into the news booth, bellowing that there wasn't enough time to make corrections. It was probably a blessing in disguise that I was known 'round those parts as "the Ig"—I'd long given up on being called by my actual name.

Of course, only Stu operated the software properly.

And even more despicable than WUGG's monotonous musical rotation was the nausea-inducing string of "Top 10 Hits" that spewed out of WGAS-AM and FM, day and night. To my horror, I found myself humming along with King Cholesterol's "Our Love Unraveled Like A Cheap Sweater," The Invasive Procedures' "Before You Scream Again," and Noble Gases' "Dancin' on the Third Rail."

My clock's thumping tail interrupted my cheery thoughts.

Ugh. . .six a.m. I smashed the piece of junk against my cardboard-thin door.

Next thing I knew, Gneeecey was spraying me with spittle. "Ingratitooodinous Iggleheimer—how *dare* ya abuserate that poor, innocent clock!"

MY EMPLOYER'S HIDEOUS CACKLING cascaded down the corridor. I reached under FM's dusty console for the bottle of antacid Cleve and I had stashed away, and took a long swig.

Just as I was about to air The Metabolites' "Klogged Lint Filter" for the four-millionth time that day, something rammed my chair.

I flew sideways, slammed into the wall, and landed flat on my back, dazed. Then, a dirty sneaker stepped down on my neck.

The red high-top's owner, oblivious to my plight—and FM's resulting dead air—chattered away on his orange phone. "Yeah, Mark, like I tol' yuz guys las' night—over an' over again—I'm sorry! I meant to signal yuz that I don't got it quite yet. . .I know I made yuz jump the gun wit' your boss, an' now we gotta go faster! I know it's gonna cost me."

I managed to grunt. To no avail.

"Y'saw what happened wit' them lousy curtains," continued Gneeecey. "It was beyond my control. . .uh-huh. . .there won't *be* a nex' time. . ."

"Take your foot," I croaked, "off my *throat!*"

"Yeah, Mark. . .uh-huh. . .changin' the subjec', the nerdologist did one of them brain scans on me, an' he didn't find nuthin'. Yeah. . . yeah, I'm severely happy 'bout it."

The sneaker pressed harder. I could barely breathe. "Ow—would you please—"

"Oh, him. . .he's a Slogaholic. . but his toilet's so clean, y'can drink from it. Yeah. . .uh-huh, like I promised, it'll be soon, I swear! An' I want the resta what yuz ain't finished givin' me."

"Ow—Diroctor—"

Gneeecey looked down. "Her? She's the one who turned our shoppin' show into a real disaster—it's her fault everythin' got messed up! An' now she's layin' down on the job. Eavesdroppin' on our conservation. I'll dock her." He kicked me. "GEDDUP, Y'LOUSY IG! WE GOT DEAD AIR ON FM!"

GNEEECEY SKIPPED DOWNSTAIRS, TWIRLING Yammicles above his head. The two sported identical orange-and-green plaid footie pajamas, complete with buttoning rear trap doors. "Hey, Ig, ya like our nightie suits? UniGeeks hadda order 'em special."

"Really?" I muttered, rubbing the sneaker sole imprint on my throat.

"For five extra bucks, they threw in a coupla DreamPaks—matchin', battery-powered dreams that plug into my headboard!"

"Uh-huh." I lowered my weary bones into the only chair in The Grate Room he permitted me to sit in—a mud-colored, inflatable piece of plastic that had sprung a leak.

"Y'certaincerely ain't got no depreciation for fine taste, do ya?" Scowling, Gneeecey climbed the ladder of his vibrating, two-tier, drink-mixing, envelope-licking, hair-combing, back-scratching electronic char-treuse recliner-on-wheels.

Seventeen yardstick-sized gear shifters grew, like weeds, out of each overstuffed arm.

With great care, he propped Yammicles up in a corner. The usually limp bear was bursting at the seams.

"Diroctor, Yammicles looks like he's put on some weight."

Gneeecey bared his teeth. "How dare ya incinerate that Yammicles is fat? He got big bones."

"Maybe it's just his, uh, outfit."

Glowering, Gneeecey shifted the chair's gears. Pretending to drive the tiny white Porsche he kept in his limo's trunk, for emergencies, he sped in circles, leaving tire tracks all over his lime green "Oriental" rug.

"I've certaincerely earned all this luxuriatin' after such a rough day bossin' everyone 'round. VROOM! VROOM!"

He jammed on the brakes and began fumbling with several remote controls. "Chair's software's incompatipoopable wit' the TV an' curtains," he complained, squinting down at me from his padded perch. "Jus' to watch a little telooolevision, I gotta push all these difooferent buttons!"

With a couple clicks, the living room drapes—the digital, yellow-green ones that told time, opened cans and wiped your nose—retracted, transforming the north wall into an expansive azure sky dotted with scores of parachuting humans and canine-humanoids. All played violins and chewed gum.

"Welcome to Channel 3½'s live telecast of the Fourteenth Annual Freak O'Nature Fiddabumbling Championships," rumbled a deep voice, competing with a zillion badly-tuned, plummeting fiddles that screeched a zillion poorly played, plummeting tunes.

Gneeecey sipped a blue fizzy drink his chair had handed him, and smiled. "This is las' year's championships."

"I'm your host, Wursty 'Gum Bottom' McGurkey, here with you for the next eighteen hours, bringing you this exciting sport that originated in Planet Eccchs's famous mountain range, the Yelps. Today, we'll experience the sheer beauty and dazzling grace of one-hundred-and-thirteen of Perswayssick County's most outstanding fiddabumblers, all competing for that coveted two-hundred-pound Freak O'Nature bubble gum trophy.

"There's no snow or skiing involved here, but what skill it takes—in addition to jumping out of a plane, competitors must finish fiddling their association-approved selections *before* executing mandatory vertical landings, or face automatic disqualification. What a disappointment that is, for so many."

"A big disapperntment," mumbled Gneeecey.

"And," continued Gum Bottom, "size matters. The judges award those crucial extra points according to the size of bubbles blown *before* competitors hit the ground."

Sure enough, gigantic pink bubbles, some as large as basketballs, protruded from parachuters' pursed lips.

"Of course," added the gravel-voiced commentator, "that's unenhanced *regulation* Freak O'Nature bubble gum. Ah, the weather's just spectacular here this afternoon at scenic, mile-high Point Goozey—"

"Been there, done that, got the T-shirt," growled Gneeecey, aiming the remote like a pistol and silencing Gum Bottom.

I glanced up at him.

"It's harder than it looks," he said, addressing Yammicles. "A real mess when ya land on your face."

Biting my lip, I rose.

"By the way, Ig, me an' Culvert are sicka drivin' y'round. Got a stinkin' surprise for ya."

"One day," I hissed through clenched teeth, "I'm gonna surprise you, you mangy fleabag."

"What? Y'surprised me an' made me some tea wit' a bag? Nah, I don't want none—awready got this drink my chair made me."

I stood, shaking my head.

"Go to your room, like a good Ig. Flea's comin'—we gotta rehearse for the big concert. Meet me out on the driveway tomorrow mornin'."

CHAPTER 18

WAMPUM PHYSICS

LIFE WASN'T WRETCHED ENOUGH, working thirteen-hour days, eight days a week, then trying to catch a few sorry winks of shut-eye on a lumpy, spring-popping mutant of a mattress two-thirds the size of my worn-out body.

Now I had to suffer through Gneeecey's late night rehearsals for the upcoming concert honoring the Grand Oogitty-Boogitty. The sacred spud—(I'd seen his official photo)—was due to arrive any day, as Gneeecey declared daily, with a mixture of reverence, dread, and certainty.

I stuck my fingers into my ears and squeezed my lids shut, managing to drift off as Gneeecey's tooth-shattering electric violin howled across the hallway in The Grate Room. Howled as it was murdered by the out-of-tune, two-ton combination laundry hamper-upright piano that tone-deaf Flea played.

"EEEEEEEEEEEEEEEEEKS!" shrieked Gneeecey, jolting me out of my cacophony-induced coma.

"WHAAAAAAAAAAAAAAAAA—" counter-shrieked Flea, in a high, nerdish voice that bore an eerie resemblance to Gneeecey's.

"That stinkin' TREE! I swear, Fleaglossitty, he's STALKIN' me!"

"Jus' keep playin' your violin. Let's take it from where the kazoos come in wit' the resta the orchestra. Right after the note you let Flub-bubb play—"

"I CAAAAAN'T keep playin' my voaline! That tree's watchin' my every move—like a police! He's walkin' 'round the yard—starin' at me through that window!"

Flea leapt off the piano bench. "I don't see anyone."

At that moment, Gneeecey's combination-locked refrigerator's overly sensitive, motion-detecting alarm screeched. The one that always detected rogue shadows the moment I fell asleep.

Gneeecey jumped six feet into the air. "Mr. Tree's in the backyard again!"

Flea flinched. "Probably jus' your Redecoritis flarin' up. Y'take your meds?"

Gneeecey pointed to my cracked door. "The Ig forgot to remindicate me. But them pills don't help anyways—how can they take away a whole tree? Listen—he's laughin' at me again! Laughin' so hard he's coughin'!"

"A *coughin'* tree?"

"Don'cha hear peals of coughter comin' from the backyard?"

"How d'ya know it's the tree? In fac', how d'ya know the tree's a tree?"

Gneeecey scratched his noggin. "Once my friend Mark, y'know, the cop wit' the blond hair an' big nose whose fraternically identical twin brothers got smaller noses an' brown hair—"

"'Zig, I wouldn't trust those guys—I don't think they're your friends. I've tol' you before, they're after somethin'—"

"THEY LIKE ME FOR WHO I REALLY AAAAAAM!"

Flea flopped into an orange beanbag chair.

"Now, I'm trynna tell ya—once Mark was a tree that wasn't a tree!"

"Huh?" Flea's glazed eyeballs spun in opposite directions.

"He went, y'know, incognizant—as a tree—to one of them costume parties. So, *he* was a tree that wasn't a tree."

"'Zig, my question was rheumatical. How d'ya know the tree's really a tree?"

Gneeecey smacked Flea's head with his frayed moose hair bow.

"OW! An' if it coughs, an' no one's around to hear it, is it really coughin'?"

Gneeecey looked at Flea, puzzled.

"I mean," continued the superhero, "what if it's like they say, y'know, that matter can be either energy waves or particles, dependin' on whether or not it's bein' observed?"

Gneeecey grinned. "Wampum physics?"

"Now y'got it."

"Well, if particles can wave, so can trees!"

"No, 'Zig—I meant, maybe it ain't really a tree when nobody's lookin' at it. So don't look at it. Then it can't hurt'cha."

"What I wanna know is, if the tree ain't lookin' at me 'cause I ain't lookin' at him, does that mean *I* don't exist?"

"Well, 'Zig, when I'm not lookin' at someone or thinkin' of 'em, they don't exist for me at that moment."

"Fleaglossitty, this here has real implooplications. What I asked before, 'bout *me* not existin' if the tree ain't lookin', was jus' hypoopotheatrical. He's always lookin' at me, so I don't gotta worry for myself—"

"Huh?"

"But if yoooou say the lousy tree don't exist, that means he can't see you neitherwise, so yoooou don't exist. I jus' proved *yoooou* don't exist!"

Down the hall, a couple of Gneeecey's latest acquisitions—Rodin's Balzac, complete with an analog clock implanted in his belly, and a life-sized chrome Harley that sported a similar timepiece in its stomach—rumbled and vroomed, respectively.

Flea glanced at his watch. "Four-thirty a.m.—gotta go."

Gneeecey smashed the piano lid down. Startled, his exotic orange-and-green-checkered Monotony birds squawked, "Bore, bore, bore, bore, MONOTONY! MONOTONY!"

The good diroctor ripped off a high-top and hurled it at their gilt cage, stunning them silent.

Head shaking, Flea whisked his music back into his briefcase.

Gneeecey crouched down and yanked a filthy piece of loose rubber off his other sneaker. "Y'know Fleaglossitty, if y'go home, y'won't be here to play that lousy piano. If y'don't play, I don't gotta look at'cha. Then I won't thinka ya neitherwise."

"So?"

"I'll prove ya don't exist, for a second time."

Flea shuffled out of the room. "Bad night, 'Zig."

"Bad night, Fleaglossitty. Y'know, I usually only thinka myself. Now I'll thinka myself even more. I'll exist *forever*."

The door slammed shut.

"Fixed that Sooperflea," laughed Gneeecey, snatching Yammicles off the couch. "I'm a PUNI graduate—y'can't argue wit' *me*. Let's go to bed, Yammy."

"EEEEEEEEEEEEEEEEKS!"

Gneeecey froze. "What the stinkin'—"

"Tree IS movin'," shouted Flea, outside, pounding his fists on the side door. "DANCIN'—WIT' A BUNCHA FLOATIN' EYEBALLS!"

Gneeecey's teddy slipped through his hands.

"LEMME IN, 'ZIG! LEMME BACK IN!"

"NOT ON YOUR STINKIN' LIFE!" screamed Gneeecey, as he tore into the kitchen and dove under the table.

I bolted out of bed, to save Flea.

CHAPTER 19

MY STINKIN' SURPRISE

MY JAW DROPPED SO far down, it darn near fractured my collarbone, when I beheld the gargantuan orange-and-purple hunk of dented-up metal cringing on Gneeecey's driveway. I hadn't seen fins like those since the day my grandfather dumped his old '57 Plymouth.

Now, years later, this psychedelic dinosaur sat in front of me, sagging mournfully on four bald, colorfully patched tires of various heights and widths. The jalopy's cross-eyed headlights gazed heavenward and its toothless grille grimaced as if gasping for oxygen.

"Y'like it, Ig?"

"Isn't that Altitude's old delivery car?" I asked. "You know, the one he uses for Gneeezle's?" I'd never seen it close up.

"Not no more. It's yours, now," replied Gneeecey, with that usual ain't-I-wonderful look smeared all over his unwashed kisser. "Y'can start drivin' it today. Take Fleaglossitty home—if he ever wakes up."

"I—I don't understand," I mumbled, still freaked out, remembering how a catatonic Flea had fallen through the door, into my arms, hours earlier.

"Look, Ig, Altitude ain't gonna be usin' this here very nice automobile no more. He'll be ridin' his bike for the forstinkable future. Traffic court judge jus' regurgitated his license."

I couldn't take my eyes off the old wreck.

"So, I thought, why should this ol' bomb—I mean, this lovely 1975 Splodge—jus' be sittin' here, uglifyin' my beaudiful new driveway—"

"What?"

"I mean, jus' be sittin' here feelin' unwanted when I could be makin' a prof—I mean, jus' be sittin' here when a transpooportationally challenged Ig like yoooou could use it? Y'can't afford nuthin' else anyways."

Three words somersaulted from my nearly paralyzed vocal chords. "Does it run?"

"HAAAAH? WHAAAA'? Speak up, Iggleheimer, speak up! I know you're overchrome wit' emotion."

Chrome is certainly more than the ol' Splodge had. Clearing my throat, I tried again. The words tripped hoarsely from my lips. "Does it *run?*"

"Only when y'drive it."

"Oh for God's sake, I meant—"

"It don't jus' take off wit'out'cha. Usually it waits for ya to start it up. Wit' jumper cables. Or that concraption I invented, in the garage."

I wondered if I'd ever see my Mustang again.

"Look, wit' any car, there's never no quarantine that nuthin'll never go wrong, no matter how ol' or new it is, y'know, Ig, y'know?"

I knew. I knew.

Gneeecey strutted over to the rusty rattletrap. "Don't brush a gift horse's teeth—I'm givin' it to ya."

"*Giving* it to me?"

"For a price, of course—everythin' comes at a price."

"Well then you're not *giving* it to me, are you?"

"I am, Ig—I'll jus' take a little more outta your pay each week." He grinned.

"I only get paid—if you can call it that—every two weeks."

"Well, if I take somethin' out every week, you'll pay it off twice as fast."

"Oh, geez—"

"It's this, or walk, Ig."

So, it was this, or walk. Mass transit in Perswayssick City was so unreliable—if you missed a bus or train, you might have to wait a couple hours for another. And out in suburban areas like St. Bogelthorpe Parke, public transportation was practically nonexistent. I just stared. My tear ducts had long gone dry.

"Nope," Gneeecey mused, bending over to look the Splodge in its desperately flared nostrils, "Altitude won't be drivin' this thing for six whole months. This ol' heap—I mean, very nice automobile—will pro-boobably be in pieces by then."

He kicked one of its tires, and a loose piece of fender crashed to the pavement, as if to punctuate his sentence.

<h1 style="text-align:center">CHAPTER 20</h1>

<h1 style="text-align:center">PURPLE DAZE</h1>

MY DAYS WERE LONG, my pay was short. And Blirg had begun, midday on Octvember 40th. Time itself flowed in reverse, turning my already wacko life totally upside down. I didn't think I'd ever get used to having dinner before lunch, or coming home from work and eating breakfast before bedtime.

The season's high-pitched primordial hum, caused by the dimension's axial reversal, made me want to crawl out of my skin.

It never truly got dark. Day and night, a fluorescent purple glow permeated solid structures, even my windowless utility closet of a room.

Holiday season was in full swing. In Perswayssick County's violet-tinseled, dead rubber chicken-decorated stores, the same three Grimace carols blasted from speakers, as frenzied shoppers agonized over which purple rubber wallet to purchase for whom.

Try as I did—and I *did* try—I couldn't understand what was so thrilling about giving or getting such a gift. Whenever I dared question the custom, Gneeecey would state, "Whoever has the most at the end wins."

Flea, who seemed to have blocked out all memories of his terrifying encounter with the dancing tree and floating eyeballs, mentioned that canine-humanoid and human youngsters—and their pet dogs—went nuts for peanut butter-flavored, squeaker-imbedded models. The superhero himself favored flat billfolds.

Not that there were that many styles of wallets—or anything else—to choose from in the places *I* frequented.

I usually ended up sifting through heaps of pawed-through seconds at Seemingwhale's, or picking through mounds of irregular merchandise at OddLottz, the outlet famous for one-armed garments, magazines with missing pages, and tape that never stuck.

The pennies I pinched three different ways were sucked up by constant repairs on the Splodge, and by the only-game-in-town Purple Pelican car insurance that the ever-helpful Gneeecey "paid" for by taking massive deductions from my pay.

My clock's tail hadn't yet thumped, but as I was awake—"blirged out," as Cleve called it—I thought I might as well just get up and eat an early supper.

"Hey, Ig! Got good news!" screeched Gneeecey, flinging my door open. "It's your lucky day!"

"*What?*" I asked, alarmed. Gneeecey's definition of "good" usually didn't match mine, and any luck to be had was usually his—at my expense. "And shouldn't you knock?"

"IT'S WETNOOODLESDAY!"

"Guess I should be thankful you don't try to force me to work upside-down anymore—not that my whole life's not upside-down and screwed up—"

"IT'S PAYDAY!"

"Why should *that* excite me? I kill myself working, then every other Wednesday—"

"WETNOOODLESDAY—"

"Every other *WetNooodlesday*, you reach into your shirt pocket and throw me a coupla bills and coins. Then, for two more weeks, I work like a dog—"

His snout crinkled.

"I mean, I kill myself for two more weeks, then we do it all over again. Why should I be excited?"

"Don't be so oogdimonious. This is the first actual check we're cuttin' ya. Ya owed so much when y'started, that after all my decapitations, I ended up givin' ya—"

"You didn't *give* me anything—I *earned* it—"

"Whatever. Ya earned so little, I paid ya from outta my pocket. But this pay period, ya get a little more—it's more cornveeenient for me to issuate ya a actual check."

I almost smiled. A few extra bucks couldn't hurt.

"Don't get too excititrated, Ig—it ain't gonna be that much more. In fac', y'wanna know why you're gonna hafta take your check to the bank?"

"To cash it, I'd assume."

"No—'cause it's too little to go by itself!"

"Yuz two fraternalizatin' again?"

"No," snapped Cleve. "We're sharing antacid—*again*."

"And this super-sized bottle's almost empty. Third one since MondiStink," I added, slumped over Fraxinella's desk. "And I couldn't imagine why."

"Yuz don't live right," replied Gneeecey, washing down another health cigar with a can of Diet Slog. "An' Cleeevooveland—"

"Uh, that's *Cleveland*—"

"That's what I stinkin' said," muttered Gneeecey. "Here's your check, Cleeevoooveland."

Cleve wrinkled his nose as he peeked into his envelope.

"Whatsamatter? Y'look like y'smell Cross-Eyed cheese."

"I do."

"I'll ignauseate that remark, Cleeevoooveland."

"That's *Cleveland*."

"That's what I SAID! Why they named ya Cleeevoooveland when y'was born in Cincinnati, I'll never understanderate. Cinncinati Wheeler —has a nice ring to it."

"Uh-huh."

"Oh—Cleeevoooveland, I'm meetin' Mark. He invited me to one of them fancy luncheon meats in New Nork. They'll be servin' horse divorces, like baloney-filled dumpooplin's."

"Really."

"So y'gotta work through lunch," continued Gneeecey, smiling from ear to ear. "Stay here an' run things."

Cleve groaned. "Oh, man—I had plans—"

"Don't worry—I'll be back a coupla hours ago, before breakfas'. Then y'can go out on your *own* time. An' Ig, here's your first regoogoolar check." He tossed an envelope my way.

"Thanks. . .I *think*. . . ."

"An' Ig, since yours was issued by our Knapsackville home office, y'can only cash it at Stummix Bank's main branch on North East Stummix Avenue."

"Where?"

"It's down by the northwestern-southern service spur of the East Stummix junction."

"*Where?*"

"If y'don't cash it today, our home office'll nulloolify and invaloolidate it."

"*What?*"

"Go on your lunch. Before breakfas' you'll be doin' more volunteer work at the Shoppin' Cart Orphanage—I signed ya up to help 'em dekookerate for the upchuckin' holidays."

"You *what?*"

"Don't worry. If y'miss breakfas', y'can make up for it yesterday by havin' brinner."

I gulped down some more antacid.

"An' when y'finish there, pick Flea up at Shisskey's. We gotta rehearse again."

"How," I growled through gritted teeth, "do I get to this, uh, Stomachs Bank?"

Gneeecey reached into his pocket and threw me a crumpled ball. "Jus' happened to have this map on my grand personage."

He didn't notice the daggers shooting through my narrowed lids. As a matter of fact, his face lit up. "Here, use summa *my* deposit slips. But get'cher *own* wit'drawals. Why're y'lookin' at me all oogdimonious?"

He waddled out into the corridor, trailed by several feet of toilet paper, stuck to his left heel.

Cleve and I snickered.

"Cleeevooooveland," I shrilled.

"His speech impediment's getting worse."

"Seriously."

"And now lunch is wrecked. I was hoping we could eat in Plutonium Park again."

I nodded. "We can always count on Gneeecey to screw things up."

"Thanks to that little creep, I've gotta stay here while you try to cash that hopefully not-bogus check. Wish I could go with you."

Gazing outside, I folded a voided outvoice into a paper plane. "Who'd even expect it to be sixty-eight degrees this late in Octvember? I mean, it's already the forty-eighth."

"Blirgian summer's not gonna last. Tomorrow's supposed to be cold. Might even snow."

"Flea'll be happy—he can't wait till that whipped cream finally falls from the sky."

"Yeah—I think he's depressed 'cause it hasn't yet."

"Look at us, talking like it's normal to expect the season's first snow to come down as whipped cream."

Cleve loosened his tie. "I'm so freakin' sick of that mangy furball always trying to break our spirits."

"Look on the bright side—he'll be gone for a coupla hours." Staring as a high-flying, soon-to-die purple-and-orange plaid butterfly fluttered past our window, I flew my outvoice into Fraxinella's wastepaper basket. "We can vent!"

Cleve grinned. "I never finished telling you 'bout the run-in our dear boss had with that airplane."

"He ran into the cafeteria and interrupted us—as usual. I'm dying to hear the whole story!"

"Well," began Cleve, unbuttoning his collar and rolling up his sleeves, "like I was telling you, one morning, he was doing a couple errands—y'know, in the days before you did everything for him."

"I would've liked to have seen him back then."

Cleve chuckled. "I was in Shisskey's, shooting the breeze with Burt and Mary, munching on a donut, and I look outside and see this small commuter jet—mind you, not one of those mutant flies, but an actual airplane—flying straight for—oh, geez—" Cleve dropped to his knees.

"*And?*" I coaxed him, shoulders trembling.

"And," Cleve continued, with great difficulty, "it was flying low, only a coupla feet above the sidewalk, straight toward Gneeecey—and as usual, his big, fat kisser was wide open, and—and—the plane zoomed right in!"

"It didn't!" I cried, nearly falling off my chair.

"And it got stuck! It's rush hour on Murgatroyd Avenue, and he's jumping up and down, trying to pull this plane out of his mouth."

Tears streamed down our faces.

"Burt and I go running outside to help, and he starts kicking us."

"Shut up—he didn't!"

"You could actually see his skin through his fur—it was blazing scarlet."

I couldn't breathe.

"Burt and I tried to pry the plane out, but it wouldn't budge. You shoulda seen, traffic was at a complete standstill."

"Little jerk," I spluttered, clapping gleefully.

"We grabbed him and ran toward Florence Ferguson—their ER entrance is right on Fredwill Avenue. Meanwhile, Mary had called the cops and paramedics, and the fire department too."

"I love it!"

Cleve took a deep breath. "We beat all of 'em to the hospital. They threw the little jackass onto a Gurney and took turns yanking. Took about twelve doctors, nurses *and* orderlies just to hold him down, and another dozen to remove the plane, with these giant forceps."

I thought I'd pass out.

"Almost felt sorry for the dope." Roaring, Cleve threw himself across Fraxinella's desktop.

"Then what?"

"They gave him a walker, to help his big, fat mouth get around—"

"They didn't!"

"Nicki, I kid you not!"

"He must've looked like a real fool!"

"You know it. And as he slowly recovered—and it wasn't slow enough for *me*—he threw away his walker and went yakking around on crutches. Chin got sore, and that only made him more evil—y'know, the padding on those armrests is only *so* thick—"

"You're making this part up!"

"Nope—I've got actual video of him doing a newscast, with his jaw supported by these two little crutches. I swear!"

"Cleve," I gasped, "I'm dying!"

"And toward the end of his recovery, he blabbered around the office on a cane."

"What about the plane?" I asked, cheeks cramping.

"An article in the *Tims* said it was piloted by a deranged squirrel."

"No!"

"He couldn't look me in the eye for six months."

"Our boss is a real piece of work."

"And poor you—you *live* with him."

"Y'know, Cleve, hanging out with you is about the only thing that keeps me sane."

"There's so much more I wanna tell you. Maybe tomorrow, even if it's snowing whipped cream, we can still have lunch—"

"YUZ LOUSY IGGLEHEIMERS! I DIDN'T LEAVE YET—I WAS OUT IN THE HALL, LISTENIN'!"

Cleve and I stood paralyzed.

"Heard every stinkin' WORD—yuz even made funna my speech impedipoodiment! I'll fix it so yuz don't stinkin' SEE each other no more! An' Ig, wait till y'get HOME—ain't finished WIT'CHOOO! AIN'T EVEN STARTED!"

THE SPLODGE SNORTED AND backfired, threatening to stall as I backed out of the tight, impossibly angled parking space Gneeecey had assigned me. Ugh. Manual steering—straight out of the first half of the last century . . .just my luck to be driving history on wheels. Prehistoric history.

As I hadn't quite gotten used to the ol' heap's reversed pedals, I had a tendency to gun the gas when I thought I was flooring the brakes—and vice versa. Poor, hunched-over old Lenny the security guard ran for his life whenever he saw my bomb rolling his way.

Maybe Flea wasn't such a bad driver after all.

The Splodge finally picked up some speed as I left the lot.

Flying down the uncharacteristically unconstipated Vompt Boulevard, I peeked at my cheap, purple Blirg watch. I'd punched out at noon and had a good chance of making it back by my lunch's end at eleven-thirty, if traffic remained light and lines at the bank weren't long.

It was a gorgeous day. Even The Irons glistened as they reached for the lavender heavens, and a gentle breeze tousled my needing-to-be-dyed-again hair.

All was good—or as good as it could've been, under the circumstances—until I made the mistake of visualizing the vengeful Gneeecey I'd have to deal with when I returned home.

I scooped up the remaining half of my King Oggle's eggplant parmesan-like oogdenplantzil hero, left over from the previous afternoon's Plutonium Park picnic, and took a greedy bite. Even cold, it was scrumptious.

Eleven-fifty—I'd only been on the road ten minutes and had reached the very last exit—the Stummix District exit. I was practically there.

Swallowing the last mouth-watering morsel of my sandwich, I turned onto the northwestern–southern service spur and peered down at Gneeecey's map. It indicated that I should turn left onto North Stummix Avenue.

But I couldn't make a left—North Stummix was a one-way. Reluctantly, I turned right, onto West Stummix Place—another one-way leading onto a never-ending elevated ramp that dumped me back onto the other side of Vompt Boulevard—heading north, back to the office.

I socked the steering wheel, and my horn squealed like a hyena being crammed into stilettos three sizes too small.

There didn't seem to be a U-turn for miles. It was eleven-forty—I'd never make it back ten minutes ago.

By the time an exit materialized, traffic had begun building. My stomach churned as I hit the brakes, then the gas, then—oops—the gas again, almost rear-ending a bus.

As I cursed the reversed pedals, lilac-tinted midday sunlight poured through my crazed windshield, making me queasy.

Crawling down the ramp, traveling south again, I exited the boulevard and turned onto the northwestern-southern service spur, for the second time. And pulled onto the shoulder and buried my face in the map.

Horns blasted me, one after another, and a cocker spaniel-like canine-humanoid zoomed past, shouting, "NO STANDING!"

"I'M NOT STANDING," I screamed, "I'M SITTING!"

I still couldn't turn onto North Stummix Avenue, but I did manage to make a left onto a street I hadn't seen before, the half-hidden Northeast Stummix Circle, a one-way triangle that gave me an opportunity to turn onto North Stummix Avenue, where I should've been in the first place.

My next task was to locate North East Stummix Avenue. The crappy map insisted that it was accessible from the northwestern-southern service spur of the East Stummix junction.

The entire district seemed to be a maze of clogged arteries, bearing names like East Stummix Street, West North Stummix Avenue, Stummix Boulevard South, North West-eastern Stummix Lane, and every other Stummix permutation possible—along with a couple odd non-Stummix streets—all twisting and tangling like strands of spaghetti in a bowl. One-way strands, garnished with grime.

There was a West Northeast Stummix Avenue, but there didn't seem to be a North East Stummix Avenue—except on the map. The paper-clip-shaped North Stummix Avenue led into Southwest Stummix Place, and after three or four long lights, turned into West Stummix End, a *dead* end.

My only alternative was to turn around and travel the wrong way on a one-way street for a block or so, then veer right, onto Tinkey Street, and ride north on Old Southeast Stummix Road. Drive the wrong way I did. Lucky for me, the street was empty.

The Splodge's oil light had begun flashing, and its temperature gauge was rising. So was mine. I popped a couple StomQuells and glanced at my watch. Eleven twenty-five. Game over. My lunch had ended five minutes ago.

I pulled over and popped the car's hood so its overworked, under-sized engine could cool down.

Absentmindedly, I turned Gneeecey's piece-of-garbage map over, and saw, scribbled in his childlike handwriting, a *different* set of directions—"korrekt direckshuns two bank."

Flames shot through my gut as I turned my warping key in the ignition and pumped the accelerator until the Splodge retched back to life.

To access the East Stummix junction and North East Stummix Avenue, I had to take the next-to-last exit on the boulevard, the Horoscope Avenue exit.

According to Gneeecey's diagram, it ran parallel to the northwestern-southern service spur and merged right into the northwestern spoke of the distorted wagon wheel of a junction.

I'd have to retrace my steps back to Vompt Boulevard, drive north, search for a second U-turn—north of Horoscope Avenue—then cross over, travel south on Vompt, exiting finally on Horoscope Avenue.

There was only one slight problem. I couldn't retrace my steps. All of the streets I'd just driven on were one-way streets. Busy ones.

I wondered if I'd ever see my lumpy little mattress again. Tears clouding my vision, I drove down South Stummix Avenue to West Stummix Boulevard, which morphed into New Southeast Stummix Drive.

A few blocks later, I came to a fork in the road. An actual fork, of stainless steel, held up by a life-sized granite kangaroo that rose from the pavement, dividing the otherwise nondescript road.

I took the fork. Turning left onto First Street, I held my breath. Maybe there would be more numbered streets.

No such luck. After First Street came Northwestern Southeast Stummix Lane Loop.

I parked, grabbed my purse and lunged out of the car. "Could you tell me," I begged, staggering across the street to a PassGass service station, "how I can get to the main branch of Stummix Bank—the one on North East Stummix Avenue?"

The blond, amber-skinned attendant pointed up the road. "Take Eastwestern Stummix Street two blocks up north-south—make a right onto West Stummix. Since it's one-way, you'll make another right, then a left—after two or three lights—onto South Stummixville Terrace. But since that road runs the opposite way, you'll make another left, after a coupla more lights, onto the southeast corner of Northwest—"

My eyes had glazed over. "I think I'll just walk."

"Then y'cut straight through there," he drawled, motioning toward a cluster of electric-blue weeping willows. "Cut straight through Stummix Park—you'll find yourself a coupla blocks from the southwest corner of North East Stummix Avenue. Make two rights."

"One other thing—"

"Bank's closin' any minute," he advised.

"Can I leave my car here?"

"Guess so—*I* don't own this road." He kicked an empty Slog can in my direction.

"These streets are really set up kinda crazy, aren't they?"

"Not really," he replied, strolling back to his gas pumps. "Whole district's only a square mile. Only an Iggleheimer could get lost."

CLUTCHING A LIME-GREEN envelope containing a tiny wad of bills—and a few clinking coins—I stumbled back through the park, toward my Splodge. It had begun to rain. Legs threatening to give way, I collapsed onto a bench.

On my way in, I'd spotted a sullen Altitude, straddling his wreck of a bike, wedged between two cars, waiting his turn at the drive-thru. I'd waved and he'd looked away.

As drizzle dampened my head, I studied a larger-than-life statue of an elegant gentleman perched atop a rearing stallion, proudly hoisting his briefcase skyward.

A plaque below indicated that Perswayssick City's business district had been named for revered latrine magnate, Drummond A. Stummix.

The bronze monument had turned green and listed to the south. It appeared to be well-worshiped by pigeons.

It began to pour. I glanced down at my hard-won Stummix envelope. Sometimes less was more, more or less, and other times, more was less—much less than you'd hoped for. Drenched to the bone, I rose.

Slogging through soggy tartan plaid grass, I checked my watch. Ten-thirty. I'd be docked double time, as was Gneeecey's policy during Blirg.

Cleve was probably swigging antacid and wondering where I was. Even if he'd been tempted to punch my time card for me, he couldn't. Gneeecey had installed seventeen surveillance cameras, aimed with precision at the flashing, beeping clock. Stu, no doubt, was covering my duties plus his own.

One thing was for sure. Next payday I wouldn't have to worry about finding my way back to any bank—I'd probably have to give Gneeecey money from *my* pocket.

Crossing Northwestern Southeast Stummix Lane Loop, my heart sank when I spied a helmeted cop planting a ticket under the Splodge's rusty wiper.

I broke into a lopsided trot. "Officer! Officer! I didn't see any signs saying I couldn't park here—the guy over there at the gas station said—"

"Oh, *you*." First time a Mark—and I recognized this one as a frequent visitor to the mansion—had lowered himself to speak to me. Ocher eyeballs looking me up and down, his thin lips curled contemptuously.

"Please, Officer, show me where there's a sign that says I can't park—"

"*You* should know *better*." His waxy complexion glowed in the rising lavender fog.

I snatched the summons from my windshield. "*Two-hundred dollars? Court appearance required?*"

"Have a great day." The policeman turned on the heels of his gleaming boots and swaggered over to his chrome chopper.

CHAPTER 21

THE TWO Ks

MOUSE, DON'T SCRATCH YA bimbus when y'work wit' food," admonished Gneeecey, scratching his bimbus as he disappeared into the kitchen. Still scratching, Altitude climbed onto a stool and leaned against the greasy wall.

Just as he began to snooze, Gneeecey thundered back through Gneeezle's new stainless steel doors, reached into his apron pocket and slammed a dozen greenish-brown patties onto the sizzling grill. "Watch these here jackass burgers while I clean the terlit."

"Okay," drawled the mouse.

SMOKE FILLED THE DINING ROOM.

"SPLOGGLE-BRAIN!" yelled Gneeecey, fanning the fumes with a shovel-sized spatula. "I TOL' YA TO WATCH THEM LOUSY BURGERS!"

"I did," spluttered Altitude. "I watched 'em burn."

I ran outdoors, coughing.

"Back in here, Ig!" ordered Gneeecey, as he dashed after me.

"Maybe," I suggested, gulping in fresh air, "I can take an early lunch—"

"Y'got too much to do. You'll be havin' breakfas' soon, anyways."

"But—"

He yanked me back inside. "Smoke's clearin'!"

Wheezing, I lumbered back to the booth where I'd been updating menus—hiking prices and pasting in various warnings. "Director, I'm supposed to add seven bucks to your fried scloggs? *What* are scloggs?"

"Any dope knows they're three-legged, sneaker-wearin' mollusks."

I hated my unpaid, part-time gig at Gneeezle's even worse than weekdays and weekends at WGAS. And this hideous Toostank, as punishment for mocking Gneeecey, I had to work at the restaurant all day, while Stu assumed my regular duties—and received my pay.

But my heart suddenly flip-flopped with joy when I remembered that the following Someday and Snatturday, Gneeecey would be away. He was the scheduled keynote speaker at some business conference in Booolabeeezia, out in the county's far reaches.

Miraculously, my dear boss had neglected to pre-structure my time during his absence. When Cleve asked me what I planned to do with those two blank days on my work "schedoodle," I'd mentioned something about rearranging my sock drawer.

"Stop dreamin', Ig! An' when y'set up the tables, remember our new polooolicy."

"What new polooolicy—I mean, *policy?*"

"From now on, we only use plaaastic cutootlery—too many customers are eatin' the silverware. I'm sicka doin' the hemlock maneuver every five minutes."

So, it wasn't just the food that made people choke.

"It's okay if they eat these plaaastic utensicles," he growled, irritated by my Mona Lisa smile. "They dissolve."

"What?"

"Mark says," he whispered, "if anyone chokes, this special mierkolated plaaastic's impossibooble for medical examiners to trace, in them forensical autopoopsies they do when someone croaks for no reason."

My jaw dropped.

"An' here—paste these in every single menu."

I glanced down at the printed, adhesive-backed labels he'd just dumped in my lap. "This food is full of undeclared nuts." "Gneeezle's recycles all unconsumerated garnishings onto future consumerators' plates." "You may be ingesting small pieces of black plastic."

Shaking my head, I began to separate the tiny tags by color.

"See, Ig—we really *do* care 'bout our lousy customers."

"Oh, uh, Diroctor, I meant to ask you, what's wrong with all our lava lamps?"

"Whaddaya mean?"

"All the blobs inside 'em seem hyperactive. That red one over there's grinning—it's creepy!"

Blirg's unnatural glow, along with the black light-lit clumps of purple tinsel and sparkly rubber chickens Altitude had hung helter-skelter, reflected off scores of wildly percolating lava lamps, transforming Gneeezle's into what looked like the set of a one-and-a-half-star psychedelic horror movie. I shuddered.

"Ain't nuthin', Ig. Jus' the electronical gravoovitational disruptications caused by Blirg's magnetical polaric reversal."

"But—"

"Makes the lamps think they're hungry."

"What if—"

"Don't look at 'em. Then, like Flea says, they won't exist."

I took a sip of coffee from my "official team merchandise" Gornks thermos. (Some bootlegger had misspelled the team's name. Made Altitude nuts every time he saw it.)

"But," continued Gneeecey, "if any of them meat-eatin' lava lamps do start chasin' ya, RUN FOR YOUR STINKIN' LIFE!"

I scalded my tongue.

"I'm takin' the afternoon off—gotta prepooperate for our Quality of Life meetin'. You're takin' minutes. I'll be back to pick ya up. An' get ready—we're gonna be up close to the enda night."

I groaned. "I hate Blirg."

"You'll jus' hafta get used to sleepin' backwards."

"But—"

"Time used'ta go backwards on your planet. One of your ancient Greek guys lived from 620 to 560. *He* managed okay."

"Yeah. Right."

"Mouse!" barked Gneeecey.

Altitude flew three feet into the air. "Whazzup, Boss?"

"Cook everythin' in one pot, so y'have less to clean."

"'Kay," replied the groggy mouse.

Gneeecey smacked his head. "I'm trynna teach ya 'bout the two K's—cookin' an' cleanin'."

"Uh-huh."

"An' stop wearin' that hideossical ol' shirt."

"But, Boss," whined the mouse, "it's my lucky shirt—it got Gronkle's number on it!"

"Can'cha find no better rolled models? Why can'cha dress normal, like Burt an' Mary?"

The rodent leapt down off his stool. "I ain't gonna wear no dress like MARY!"

I spit coffee through my nose.

Perswayssick City Councilperson Verna Vlott strolled over to the counter.

Pretty, a bit on the plump side, the sixty-ish human's reddish-blond curls complemented her fair and remarkably unlined complexion. She wore a dove-gray, horizontally pin-striped power suit, and her immaculate ivory athletic shoes matched the strand of pearls adorning her rose-colored silk blouse.

Her saucer-like emerald eyes widened with concern. "Oh my—was there a *fire* in here?"

Altitude yawned. "Uh, no Ms. Vern, uh—"

She chuckled. "You've got us mixed up, too. I'm Councilperson Verna Vlott—people always mistake me for my twin sister, Vlotta Vern, the freeholder."

"Uh-huh."

"Even though she's a couple years older, we're an awfully lot alike, right down to our dreams for this great county's future. We also exhibit a rare poetic synergy."

Not giving a deck of vlecks, Altitude stared into space.

"Well, young man, *was* there a fire? I do hope our recently revamped fire department responded quickly! Was anyone hurt?"

"Nah, Ms. Verna, uh, Vlott," answered the mouse, still wearing the bent spatula his boss had wrapped 'round his singed noggin. "We was cookin' Cajun style."

"Are you sure everything's okay? *I* can help, you know."

"Yeah. Can I take your order now?" mumbled Altitude, in what sounded more like a statement than a question.

"Yes, I'd like some lunch."

"Whatever. Wanna use the bat'room? We cleaned it."

"No thank you, dear." Smiling my way, the councilperson perused the graffiti-like fluorescent-chalked specials scrawled all over the violet wall. "I'll never forget the first time I saw this young man. I jumped up onto one of these tables, screaming, 'EEEEKS, A MOUSE!' Then your Diroctor Gneeecey so kindly helped me down. 'No,' he assured me, 'this is Altitude. He works here. He'll be your waitress tonight!'"

"Whaddaya WANT awready?" demanded Altitude, yanking the spatula off his head and hurling it, just missing his distinguished customer's delicate, upturned nose.

Ignoring the mouse's rudeness, Ms. Vlott set down her delicate, simulated-goonafish-skin attaché case, only to snatch it back immediately, disgusted by the fine layer of slime coating the counter.

"Young man," she began, inspecting her thankfully unscathed brief-case, "I'll have one jackass patty—but not *too* well done—with blue cheese dressing—but not *too* awfully blue—and a plain, quarter-pound jackass burger, with a squirt of zurt on the *side*, not *on* the burger—"

"Zurt'll cost ya a extra buck," warned Altitude.

"Okay. And a goonafish melt for my sister—"

"She ain't here."

"Excuse me—"

"I SAID, ain't nobody else here WIT' CHA, lady!"

"I'm bringing it to her. I'll also have one Gnautical Seafood Wharf-Barf Salad Combo—but go easy on those sand dollars. And give me a chicken-flavored O'Gurt—those probiotics are *so* important for good health. And to drink, maybe some clean water."

"Clean water'll cost ya—"

"I assure you, I can afford it," snapped the usually good-tempered councilperson. "And please throw in a generous slice of sloggenberry pie—make that two. One for my sister, too."

"Awright, lady, but like I tol' ya, ya sister the county freeloader ain't here—an' two of somethin'll cost y'twice as much as one of somethin', an' a whole lot more than some of nuthin'."

"And, oh my, that bag of Rindom Doodles is nearly as big as you! My sister the *freeholder* and I could snack on it at this morning's meeting. How much is it?"

"If y'hafta ask, y'can't afford it."

Her twinkling eyes darkened. "I told you, I can most definitely afford anything in here. As a matter of fact, I'll take *two*. That completes my order."

"Is that," inquired Altitude, "to stay, or is it for here?"

"It's to go."

"Didn't ASK y'that!" Altitude tapped his foot impatiently. "Is it to STAY, or is it for HERE?"

"It's to *go*."

The mouse ripped some loose threads off his jersey. "Y'don't UN-DERSTAND me, DO ya?! I ASKED ya, is that to STAY, or is it for HERE?"

"I *said*, it's to *go*."

Before Altitude could ask again, his boss planted his size thirteen sneaker square in the middle of the rodent's ratty backside.

"OW! Y'came in through the back, Boss?"

"Y'gingivitis-head! Y'HEARD her—it's not for HERE an' it's NOT to STAY! If it was for stinkin' HERE, it would be to STAY an' not GO! If it wasn't to STAY an' not GO, it wouldn't be for HERE an' not to NOT stay, stinkin' WOULD it?! Conversically, if it was to STAY an' not GO—"

"Bad morning, Director," chirped Councilperson Vlott.

"Bad mornin', Vlotta—"

"That's Verna."

"Oh, heh, heh. Sorry 'bout this little Iggleheimer here."

"Don't worry, I'm sure Mr. uh—what is Altitude's last name?"

"He don't have a last name—can't afford one."

An expression of intense pity washed over Verna Vlott's kind face.

"Anyways, Verna, you're lookin' lovlier'n ever!"

Gazing down at her silver-trimmed Cross Trainers, the councilperson blushed.

"I take it, this beaudiful mornin', yuz'll help me kill Question 345, right? We even got a chance to removerate it from the ballot!"

"Diroctor, my sister and I actually support 345. So do all the freeholders, the city council, and most of the Merchants' Association."

"But—but—I *promised* I had it all sewn up—I mean, yuz *gotta*—"

"No, Director, I certainly don't think you'll have the constitutionally mandated three-quarters majority required to amend the ballot this morning—or any other."

Gneeecey's egg-shaped eyeballs sprang from his sockets.

"See you earlier, Diroctor," warbled Mrs. Vlott, as she scooped up her five bursting-at-the-seams smiley-face take-out bags, and dropped a thick wad of greenbacks into Altitude's grungy palm. "Keep the change, young man. Everyone should have a last name!"

Altitude's beady red eyeballs sprang from *his* sockets.

CHAPTER 22

DEMOCKOOKRACY IN ACTION

MERCHANTS, BANKERS, POLITICIANS, AND concerned citizens jammed the stuffy old Knapsackville courthouse, packing it to its rotting rafters. Gneeecey poked his fists into my kidneys and shoved me through the crowd. "Bad mornin', Burt an' Mary. . . Squiggleman, how's the terlit business? Y'sittin' priddy? Hey, Verna an' Vlotta—or is that Vlotta an' Verna? Whichever one o'yuz is whichever one o'yuz, yuz better do right this mornin'."

"We'll do right," sang the look-alike sisters, pushing past him, "even if we hafta fight!"

Hands visibly shaking, Gneeecey grunted.

"Hiya, 'Zig!"

"Whazzup, Fleaglossitty? Hey, Flubbarooney. Cleeevoooveland, didn't know you were civoovically minded. Stuey, set up the mikes, like a good boy."

"Anything y'say, Boss. Hi, Icky."

"Stuart," I asked, high-fiving Cleve, "who's back at Vompt, running things?"

"We're on autopilot," answered the intern. "Boss invented this endless bloopy-loop—automatically runs AM, FM and TV. He never screws up."

"*He?*"

"Mr. Bloopy-loop."

"So much for job security," I muttered, following my elbow-high boss, as he worked his way to the front of the room.

"Bad mornin', Gus!" Gneeecey's tail, limp and droopy these days, began wagging. "How're my lucky socks?"

"Hangin' by their necks till dead," quipped the deadpan tailor.

"WHAAAAAAAAT?!"

"But they'll live, most likely," added Gus, seeing the panic written all over his most steady customer's face.

"Don't scare me like that! Now when can I have 'em back?"

"When y'bring me a ticket."

"But'chooo *know* the stinkin' socks are mine!"

"They're impounded till y'bring me a ticket."

"The *Ig* lost it—y'shouldn't punish *me*."

Gus's frigid blue eyes settled on me. I wanted to sink through the creaky floorboards and disappear.

"Pleeeeze," begged Gneeecey. "I gotta have 'em back for the Grand Oogitty-Boogitty's concert!"

"Sorry," replied the old man. "Rules are rules."

Gneeecey punched my kneecap. "Ya Ig! Oh, hi, Seemin'whale— good talkin' last night. Like y'said, I'll fix 'em *all* this mornin'! An' looky here—Justin Imbroglio! Who let'chooo in? You're a reporter!"

"Yup," answered the olive-skinned thirty-something human, tapping the press pass clipped to his lapel. "Y'know what we in this business say—'the people have a right to know.'"

Gneeecey swallowed his cigar. "Know stinkin' whaaat?"

"About whatever affects their well-being." The six-footer's almond-shaped hazel eyes bored into Gneeecey's.

The good diroctor broke eye contact first. "Get a stinkin' haircut, why don'cha?!"

Imbroglio smiled at me. Wavy jet black locks framed his angelic face and tumbled down onto his square shoulders. "Hi there."

"Hi," I replied, mesmerized.

Gneeecey jammed his clipboard into the small of my back. "Y'ain't permutated to talk to reporters. 'Specially not *this* one. I'll have him thrown outta here!"

Imbroglio grinned.

"I'll swipe that smile offa your face—when I *buy* that muckracketin' yellow rag y'write for."

"Really."

"Then you'll be workin' for meee—that is, unless someone torches yuz first."

"I'd rather someone torched us." Laughing, Imbroglio turned to me. He was fine, and knew it. "Whadda you think?"

Before I could answer, Gneeecey kicked me. Hard. "C'mon, y'lousy Ig!"

"IG," Gneeecey screamed into my ear, "I GOT A REAL DILEM-NOONICAL PROBLEM!"

"What? I can hardly hear you!" I looked down, from the judge's bench where we sat, at the sea of noisy humanity—and canine-humanoidity—still pouring into the courthouse's main room.

Gneeecey gulped down another unlit health cigar. "I SAID, I HAVE—"

"Diroctor, should you be eating all these cigars? I don't even think they're helping your, uh, y'know, *problem*—"

"DON'T TALK 'BOUT MY STINKIN' BAT'ROOM PROBLEM—"

Stu had just pumped up the volume on Gneeecey's mike.

All chatter ceased instantly. Except for a few stray snickers, it was so quiet, you could hear a Rindom Doodle drop.

"GIMMEE A MINUTE HERE, PEOPOOPLES!"

Once folks had resumed coughing and yakking, Gneeecey elbowed me. "I *said*," he repeated, covering the microphone, "I got a stinkin' *problem.*"

Sick of dealing with nothing but problems, I groaned. "Now what?"

"I caaan't start the mos' important parta this meetin'—the 345 part—till Mark an' them get back from the Mierkolatory."

"Why not?"

"None of your bees' droppin's."

"Well then, how do you expect me to help you?"

"Who stinkin' *asked* y'to?"

"And what are they all doing at the Mierkolatory?"

"WHAAAT? Did I say THAT? Pretenderate y'never HEARD that, or I'll dock your crummy little checks more'n I do awready!"

I gazed up at the water-damaged ceiling and counted to ten, slowly.

"Ig, how can I waste time?"

"I dunno."

"*I* know—I'll bring up a buncha other junk." Gneeecey scooped several fistfuls of shredded paper out of his T-shirt pocket and dumped them next to his laptop—the one with the slashed screen.

Forcing a toothy smile, he smashed his gavel three times. "ORDER IN THE COURTHOUSE, FLUBBUBB WANTS TO SPEAK! SPEAK, FLUBBUBB, SPEAK!"

Squinting, the obedient head of Perswayssick County's useless Near-sighted Committee shuffled up to the mike.

"Take down *everythin'*," Gneeecey ordered me, "unless I tell ya not to."

"My indistinguishable fellow citizens," began a squirming, throat-clearing Flubbubb, "it is my indubitable honor to commence this suspicious occasion by introducing our great and tragic county's equally tragic Quality of Life Commissioner an' newly-elected Grate Gizzygalumpaggis, under whose expedient stupervision we've suffered the extreme enjoyment of untold an' awful—"

"SIDDOWN! An' that's Grate GIZZY—stop wastin' all them 'spensive letters! You'd APPRECIATE all your consonants an' vowels if ya hadda EARN 'em, like *I* did."

Flubbubb trudged back to his chair, dragging his magnificent tail behind him.

Gneeecey smashed his gavel with such vigor that wood chips flew in his face. "Bad mornin', ladies an' gentootlemens," he shrilled, spitting and blinking. "Welcome to our county seat, located on the shores of scenic Buzzard's Breath Bay."

Polite applause echoed through the gray-and-institutional-green sardine can of a room.

"We'll start wit' a few items that need to be started wit', before we can start wit' other items that can't be started wit' till they can be started wit'."

Picking through his tattered notes, Gneeecey scoured the room for any signs of Mark, Mark or Mark. Or even Mark or Mark.

There were none present.

"Before I start wit' what needs to be started wit'," he continued, flashing a dirty look at Cleve, who sat conversing with Justin Imbroglio, "I wanna rekookognize the folks from MierkoZurk Minin's subsidoodooary, PassGass Petroleum. An' I wanna welcome my friends from Stenchover an' Associates, the Potts' Chamber of Commerce, an' also our Windsock Preservation League, of which I'm a proud, foundin' member.

"An' last, but certaincerely not least, the members of a coupla civoovic orgooganizations I chair—S.C.R.A.M., our Shoppin' Cart Rescue an' Aid Mission, an' the Society to Prevent Cruelty to Antennas."

All present clapped courteously.

Gneeecey plunged his fist back into his scrap pile. "I must also acknowledge this commission's vice commissioner—over there, somewhere—he's also the president of the prestigoogious Alphabet Exchange, on Zugzwang Street, where I trade daily. An' a worn welcome to the Mal de Mer Yachtin' Club, of which I'm a rail-huggin' member—"

"STOP WASTIN' TIME!" shouted a hulking canine-humanoid.

Gneeecey pounded his gavel so hard, it shattered. "Now, I propose a propooposition proposin' we regoogoolate county birds." He glanced around the room again. Still no Marks. "I say we charge all birds—exceptin' exotic pets, of course—a seven percent tweetin' tax, to increase county revoovenues."

"Instead," interrupted the usually bashful Flubbubb, making his way up front, "why don't we do somethin' 'bout all the nasty little planes that fly 'round biting us? *Kill* 'em!"

Choruses of "KILL 'EM! KILL 'EM!" followed Flubbubb's impromptu recommendation.

"We've had this conservation before," said Gneeecey, whipping a spare gavel out of his shirt pocket. "Perswayssick County's a wildlife refuse. Ya kill all the planes, ya wreck the food chain. Birds'll starve—they'll croak an' put the frogs outta work. Then it's a real uphill swim for the resta us."

Flubbubb shuffled back to his seat, head bowed.

"Any better suggestications to improooverate our crummy quality of life? You, human, wearin' the green-an'-a-half necktie—step up to the mike. Identificate yourself."

"Manny Meantwell here. We at Good Intentions Paving wanna underwrite free hearing testing for all residents—"

"Nah," snapped Gneeecey, "we don't usually like what we hear, so why would we wanna hear it more? An' our friends at the Center for Selective Hearin' Loss wouldn't be too happy neitherwise."

The only person scribbling faster than me was Justin Imbroglio, still grinning.

"Okay," declared Gneeecey, "since this here's demockookracy in action, I'll throw up some topics. We'll disgust whichever ones get 'ayes.' First one: if new cars' headlights always stay on, how'll we know when there's a funeral procession? Shouldn't local government step in?"

A couple disinterested 'nays,' and several loud yawns, erupted.

"Uh, lessee. . . ." Eyes darting about, Gneeecey reached for another crumpled piece of paper. "How 'bout I elect Fleaglossitty to be in charge of our Oversight *an'* Hindsight committees?"

"I'm honored," responded Flea, as he stumbled over a chair. "But 'oversight' means I'll forget stuff."

"But then, Fleaglossitty, when you're leadin' the Hindsight Committee, you'll look back at what'cha gonna forget."

"If y'say so," replied Flea, rubbing his sore eyeballs. He'd spent the day cramming for his chiropractor's exam and helping the Shisskeys install an alarm system in their newly repaired shop.

"Okay, I unanimooosly elect Fleagossitty Floppinsplodge to both posts. Now that we got that deciderated. . .hmmm. . .okay, let's talk 'bout pet dogs. Mine lives in his own condo. But what 'bout all them strays who built their own homes? Whenever one of 'em's adopted, he abandons his house. Shouldn't we TAX 'em? Abandoned dog hice bring down ALL our propooperty values!"

A ripe tomato sailed over Gneeecey's head and splattered against the wall.

"ORDER! ORDER! How many of yuz keep unicorns as pets?"

Verna Vlott strode up to the microphone. "Why are we discussing mythical creatures and other nonsensical matters, when we have 345 to consider? It's nearly dawn!"

She received an ovation.

"ORDER!" cried Gneeecey, pulverizing another gavel. "Nobody's proven unicorns don't exist—there's a fifty-fifty proboobability they do. We even got laws protectipatin' 'em. But do they care 'bout *us?* At least the goonafish let us *eat* 'em."

"Bizzig," called out Mary Shisskey, "let's get down to the nitty-gritty—most of us have been working since before dusk."

"Okay, I'll speed things up. Now, it was brought to my detention that Candlestein Park needs more illuminization at night. Wouldn't it be more cost-deficient if we jus' learned to walk through there makin' believe our eyes were shut?"

Attendees jeered.

"Nex' item. I'm studyin' reincarceration—y'know, the fac' yuz may have lived before. We could invent a new agency to investigate who everyone was in their prevoovious lives—thinka how we could utilize that info to make increasements in county revoovenues!"

Gneeecey's idea was met with boos and hisses.

"But if we could find out who owes back taxes an' deboobits from past lives an' make 'em pay up *now*, I bet'cha banks an' credit card companies would pay finder fees!"

A pie whizzed, like a cream-covered frisbee, over Gneeecey's ducking noggin.

"ORDER! Guess I'm presidin' over a buncha deadbeats. Okay. How 'bout we build a cobooblestone goth path in Plutonium Park? Ya know, wit' encloserated areas where they could relieve themselves in pieces? Meantwell, I'll award yuz the contract—"

"NAY!"

"How about," suggested Burt Shisskey, "we catch the Bakery Bandit?" Everyone cheered.

"Our cops are workin' on it," replied Gneeecey.

Burt's nose wrinkled and Mary shook her head.

"Now, peepooples, this nex' item's excitin'! I foun' the cure for chicken pox in my own stinkin' 'frigerator!"

Everyone gasped. I began to gag.

"Geee whizzicles, I said, chicken pox mus' be related to chicken salad! Anyways, I'm offerin' innoculizations, cheap—"

"As long as we're wastin' time," hollered Flubbubb, "let's limit the number of ecnalubmas allowed to park in fronta Gneeezle's. There's never any room for us payin' customers."

"WHAT'S A ECNALUBMA?"

"One of them white trucks wit' sirens that takes people away from the restaurant after they—"

"SIDDOWN!" howled Gneeecey, straining to be heard over all the hoots and hollers.

A hush came over the crowd when a couple dozen waxy-faced men burst in through the side door, wearing three-piece steel gray suits, white shirts, and winking, luminescent spider's web-patterned ties.

Gneeecey wiped the perspiration from his brow. "Welcome Mark, Mark an' Mark! An' Mark, Mark an'—"

"Let's get on with this!" demanded Steve Squiggleman, the tall, gaunt human proprietor of Squiggleman's Plumbing.

"Jus' a minute!" Five Markmen—as Cleve and I had begun calling them—approached Gneeecey, bearing armloads of pamphlets.

Three others surrounded Justin Imbroglio. A tall, brown-haired Markman bent down and whispered something that drained the blood—and wiped the grin—from the reporter's face.

As Imbroglio leapt to his feet, a blond, big-nosed Markman jabbed something concealed under his jacket into the newspaperman's ribs, and escorted him out of the courtroom.

Gneeecey watched, smacking his palms together with glee.

From across the room, Cleve's eyes met mine. He glanced over at Imbroglio's empty seat and shrugged. No one else seemed to notice the journalist's forced departure.

"Since it's so early," announced Gneeecey, stuffing papers back into his shirt, "we'll hafta tempooporarily table my propooposition to rename the Leopold Underpant Causeway after me, in order to make it a hysterical landmark."

Squiggleman stood. "Let's get to 345!"

"345!" chanted attendees, clapping in rhythm. "345! 345!"

"ORDER! We'll disgust our final item, this whole no-brained issue of the upchucking election refooferendum, Question 345—"

"345! 345!"

"ORDER! Accordin' to this latest informative information I've jus' receiverated, from very reliarable sources," said Gneeecey, waving one of the Markmen's brochures, "zodd's hazardous—to us, an' our county's aminals an' plaaants."

"Can you document that?" inquired Verna Vlott and Vlotta Vern, as they rushed up front.

"And," asked Verna, "are aminals a new type of organism indigenous to our county?"

"Yeah an' yeah. Zodd stinks, an' aminals are real new an' indigoogenous." Gneeecey tossed a couple booklets at the identically dressed women.

Vlotta examined her leaflet, then frowned. "You're just pulling these statistics out of a hat!"

"Yes," agreed Verna, scanning her tract. "Why, zodd couldn't hurt a cat!"

"No, dear sister, not like the bite of a ravenous rat!"

"Nor the nip of a slovenly, Slog-swigging gnat!"

"Or the surreptitious nibble of a bureaucrat!"

"Not even one wearing a blue bowler hat!"

"By our uncle's carbunkles, we'll both swear to that!"

"Yes, to change our minds, you'll need a report very fat—against *this* bunk, we'll *both* go to bat!"

"HEY!" protested Gneeecey. "YUZ TWO CAN'T—"

"You'll have to take us down to the mat—we assure you of that!"

"AY!" boomed five-hundred other voices.

Heads held high, the councilperson and county freeholder marched back to their seats.

Gneeecey hammered his gavel. "I'll sanitize yuz both for contemptible replooplication of vowels an' consonants!"

All twenty-four Markmen stared the sisters down as they chomped on Rindom Doodles.

Gneeecey spat his cigar to the floor and began chewing up and down his right forearm.

I STIFLED A YAWN. My writing hand had gone numb.

Massaging his shaved, cucumber-shaped head, Steve Squiggleman tapped his gold watch. "Look what *time* it is."

"I've gone without breakfast," complained Manny Meantwell's brother Harry, patting his protruding belly, "and won't get any sleep before dinner."

"We've been fighting for hours," said Burt Shisskey. "Let's just leave this for Election Day—let the *people* decide."

"With all due respect," added Mary Shisskey, "these pamphlets are just glossier editions of the old ones—they're not saying anything new."

"Or," called out Verna, as she marched back up front, "anything that makes sense!"

"Right," concurred Vlotta, pointing to Gneeecey. "Some folks are so dense!"

Applause thundered through the courtroom.

Gneeecey, who'd run out of gavels, removed his left sneaker and pounded it until reeking clouds of dust obscured his face. "Vlotta an' Verna—or whoever yuz stinkin' are—I'm sicka your snarkasm. I'm citin' yuz for contemplation!"

"Yeah?" shrilled Verna, competing with Stu's screechy feedback.

Jaw clenched, Vlotta sprinted back up to the microphone. "Y'think we're that mealy?"

"You," the twins crooned, "wanna find out what we're made of, really?"

"Yuz two threatootenatin' meee?" asked Gneeecey.

"Enough!" proclaimed Jacob J. Qwertyuiop, portly basset hound-like canine-humanoid president of the Alphabet Exchange, and the commission's usually affable, if not invisible, vice commissioner. "Like Mr. Shisskey says, leave 345 on the ballot—let the people decide. Seems we've got a vocal minority here that just won't quit. We'll never reach consensus this morning."

"Morning's over," grumbled Squiggleman. "It's past dawn."

"I do want to go on record," added the bespectacled Qwertyuiop, "and state that I agree with what most of our citizens say in the latest poll—"

"Whaaat poll?" demanded Gneeecey.

"The *Pooper-Scooper* poll that came out today—says we're not happy eating, drinking, breathing, or wearing mierk. My son Jacob, Jr. is only six, and his fur's coming out in patches. His teacher says he's having trouble concentrating. Mierk's poisoning our—"

"Look, Qwertyuiop," interrupted Fred Seemingwhale, the Humpty Dumpty-like CEO of MierkoZurk Mining. "Y'say we should stop arguing, then y'start all over again—"

"A man's allowed to express his opinion," countered Qwertyuiop, "and his concern for his family and community."

"Mierk's safe—our Grate Gizzy, a scientist himself, says *zodd* poses the real threat—"

"Seemingwhale, you mine miercoles, and you process it in that polluting eyesore of a Mierkolatory, then you pump the by-product, the mierk, into *everything*—"

"You lie!"

"You slop up the riverbanks and cause inversions," continued Qwertyuiop, remaining cool. "In fact, the other day, on the thruway, the mogg was so thick, I couldn't see the nose on my face, much less the car in fronta me—"

"We wish we couldn't see the nose on your face—"

"You and your companies are posting record profits," charged Qwertyuiop. "Why in Bogelthorpe's name would *you* want to change anything?"

"And you just happen," added Squiggleman, "to be a voting member of this commission. Smells like a conflict of interest."

"Our employees have been coming down sick," said Manny Meantwell. "Might be from working with mierk. Let's get to the bottom of this! I make a motion calling for full public disclosure of MierkoZurk *and* its subsidiaries' financial records, plus the names of all board members, officers and major stockholders."

"And silent partners," chimed in Harry Meantwell. "I've always said we need a regulatory oversight agency, y'know, like that SEC they have on Earth!"

Gneeecey began gnawing on his wrists.

Qwertyuiop nodded. "I second the motion."

Squiggleman sprang out of his seat. "Passed! And I move that Mr. Seemingwhale recuse himself from today's vote!"

Seemingwhale leapt up. "Hey!"

"I second that motion!" exclaimed Manny Meantwell. Seemingwhale's beady eyes inflated to the size of grapefruits.

"Passed!" snapped Qwertyuiop. "We need to change how we do business around here!"

Gneeecey's mouth finally opened. "Change is DANGEROUS," he wailed, wringing his hands. "Change is BAAAAAD!"

"CHANGE! CHANGE!" roared the crowd. "NO MORE MIERK! NO MORE MIERK!"

"ORDER IN THIS CRUMMY COURT!" screeched Gneeecey. "Let's read our pampooplets again—everybody, turn to page two."

"How mehny tiams can vee keep rrreadin' deeese tings? Vhut eeet saids herrre is naughtin' nyeeeuw," objected Ingabore Scriblig, proprietor of Ingabore's Meatball Express. The stocky, gray-haired human, born in the Bozovian region of Yuckenstadt—proud home of legendary composer Zirbert Shriekensobb, and Flea, Flubbubb, and Gneeecey—hadn't lost her heavy Eccchsian accent.

Squiggleman threw his hands up. "We agreed to call it quits!"

"Look, Steeevoooven," said Gneeecey, "we'll vote to removerate 345 from the ballot. Then all the trouble'll be over—we can go home!"

"Surely," Vlotta Vern shrieked, "he doesn't think he'll have the three-quarters majority needed!"

"Evidently," added Verna Vlott, "my lunchtime remarks went unheeded!"

"Okay," began Gneeecey, "all in favoovor of remooveratin' 345, shout 'ay'! If we all say it fast—wit'out even thinkin'—we can leave!"

The good diroctor's nerdish, soprano "ay" contrasted with the Markmen's deep, unearthly rumblings, and Seemingwhale's defiant, elongated tenor utterance.

Everyone else remained silent.

"Don't hear no 'nays'!" whooped Gneeecey. "'Ayes' GOT it!"

Mary Shisskey jumped up. "Just a minute! You never gave anyone a chance to say 'nay'! And those guys in the gray suits aren't members—they're not authorized to participate."

Burt Shisskey popped out of his chair. "And as Grate Gizzy—and head of the commission—you're not supposed to vote either."

"And neither is Mr. Seemingwhale," added Mary.

Grinning, his eyes narrowed, blond, big-nosed Mark aimed a plump index finger at the Shisskeys and pulled an imaginary trigger.

Squiggleman rose. "Diroctor, you sure tried to pull a fast one!"

Gneeecey's kisser opened wide, but his vocal chords didn't vibrate.

"Keeping 345 on the ballot," explained an impassioned Verna Vlott, "lets the *people* decide whether or not to enforce a moratorium on mierk, and clean up our shameful waste sites!"

"Yes," agreed an equally fervent Vlotta Vern. "Mierk bites! Let the people decide whether or not to redevelop our riverbanks and make them beautiful once more!"

"Yes," said Verna. "Let the people say what they're for! Removing 345—no way!"

"I hereby move," proposed Vlotta, "to have all members *not* in favor of removing 345 from the ballot, shout 'nay'!"

Verna smiled. "I second that motion—then we've all got a say!"

Jacob Qwertyuiop rose. "I third it!"

"ORDER!" squeaked Gneeecey. "Yuz can't dooo this—yuz ain't followin' corrugated parloolimentary proceeedure!"

"We *are*," replied Verna. "All members in favor of *not* removing Question 345 from the ballot, say 'nay'!"

The naysayers nearly blew the roof off the old courthouse.

Victory flashing in their pie-sized eyes, Verna and Vlotta joined hands and pranced in circles, singing, "A coupla strong daughters, way more'n three-quarters! We won, we won, we hit a home run!"

Gneeecey's yapper opened so wide, a 747 could've zoomed in.

Qwertyuiop adjusted his steel aviator frames. "Election's on Octvember 68th. I move that we meet Octvember 64th, to begin official proceedings, demanding full disclosure, as Mr. Meantwell moved, from MierkoZurk, PassGass, and everyone else involved here. I also move that we adjourn and go home!"

Burt Shisskey raised his hand. "I second both motions!"

Fred Seemingwhale shot Gneeecey an icy glare, then marched toward the side exit.

"Qwertyuiop," yelled a middle-aged man, "for Grate Gizzy!"

"An' whaddabout gettin' us home, back to our planet?" shouted a Rottweiler-like canine-humanoid.

"We want Verna an' Vlotta!" cried several beagle types, raising their fists.

"*They'll* get us back!" squeaked a Chihuahua-like woman.

"WOOF!" exclaimed Gneeecey.

"C'MON, YA IGGAROONEY," SNARLED Gneeecey, sneaking out through the courthouse's back door.

He stopped short when he saw the mob of Markmen puffing away on cigarettes in the dark, dumpster-scented alley.

Red-haired, broken-nosed Mark—a frequent visitor to the mansion—loosened his flashing necktie. "Y'tol' us y'had all the votes lined up."

Gneeecey wedged his left sneaker underneath one of his wet armpits. "Thought I did."

"You'll hafta do better'n *this*," warned a tow-headed Markman, whose Blirg-lit buzz cut glowed lavender.

"Yeah," agreed a curly-haired, graying Markman, looking Gneeecey up and down. "Y'got beat up by a coupla girls."

I bit my tongue.

The redhead blew smoke in Gneeecey's face.

"Careful wit' them cigoogarets," advised the good diroctor, coughing as he pulled his left sneaker back on. "Yuz guys catch fire easy. I *eat* my cigars."

"Don't worry 'bout *us*," replied blond, big-nosed Mark, unbuttoning his tight vest.

"An' we're thinkin' 'bout chargin' ya for them pamphlets," said the brown-haired creep who had cooed sweet nothings in Imbroglio's ear.

"An' your driveway," added the blond. "Even your good buddy Seemingwhale jus' tol' us ya better get'cha act together, or else."

One by one, each scowling Markman stepped up to the curb, stamped out his cigarette, and stole away into the Blirgian night.

As Gneeecey fumbled with his laces, a blue-helmeted sparrow—

chased by two green-clad adversaries—slammed into his snout. Their microscopic football bounced into his wet eyes.

"Lousy birds!" he yowled, walloping his schnozzle until the feathered footballers rocketed up into the violet, cloud-streaked skies.

"C'mon, Dirrector," I whispered. "Let's go home."

A tear trickled down his dirty cheek.

CHAPTER 23

NUTHIN' BUTT THE TRUTH

I LOVED HAVING THE mansion all to myself. Not that I'd planned to throw any wild parties. A Gneeecey-less weekend simply meant I'd enjoy a respite from brain melting stress. And Markmen. The miscreants had been populating my nightmares ever since that last Quality of Life meeting, chasing me down mogg-covered riverbanks, guns drawn. I'd run for my life, but they'd close in, shedding their skins.

Paralyzed—unable to scream—I could only watch as their disembodied eyeballs floated toward me.

I'd bolt out of bed and tear down the hall, waking fully once I spied Gneeecey, in the gloomy shadows, enthroned upon his Water Cyclone, glaring my way with wide-open, bloodshot eyes.

Drenched with perspiration, I'd slink back to my room, shivering.

Surprisingly, he never mocked me.

This Someday afternoon, I tried to push it all out of my mind—even the shocking news that the *Pooper-Scooper's* offices had burned to the ground the morning of the meeting. Frank Salvador's 98.6 *Normal Radio*—where Cleve and I recently filed applications—had been housed on the third floor.

I have to admit, I'd become good—way too good—at compartmentalizing my life. Heading toward the kitchen, I felt almost giddy. Not actually happy, mind you, but as close to not unhappy as I'd been since my second arrival in Perswayssick County.

Refreshed, I relished the thought of sleeping in again, on Snatturday. I was even getting used to time traveling backwards.

Klunkzill watched warily through a jagged slit in the shower curtain, as I padded past the bathroom. He wasn't any trouble—a greased bike chain and bowl of motor oil kept him happy for hours on end.

As usual, the goths snarled and butted their heads against walls, furniture and each other. But I wasn't worried. The charred oil furnace Gneeecey had flung into their playroom would keep 'em busy for days.

Much to my delight—and Gneeecey's utter dismay—their eggs had not hatched. Dr. Quackagoo—a goth fertility specialist located two hundred miles away, in Spittle's Spray, on ritzy Telephone Book Hill—dared to suggest that an infuriated Gneeecey use the lifeless orbs as paperweights.

Chuckling, I entered the kitchen, where instantly, my appetite evaporated. I did a three-sixty and shuffled back to my room, wondering if I'd make it back home in time for my twenty-fifth birthday—November 29th—or Octvember 60th, according to Gneeecey's Blirg calculator. It was a little more than a week away.

My legs were stronger, and this weekend I could search for my portfolio in peace.

I'd worked my way up from the creepy, cavernous basement to the fourth floor, picking through piles of petrified T-shirts and ankle-deep layers of newsprint, and strange-titled tomes like *Your Local Arthropod: Golf Buddy or Meal?* and the gored-up *Good Goths' Collection of Bedtime Prayers*.

Along the way, I'd encountered a six-foot-long periscope, welded to a sofa on skis, and a commode that had been converted into a planter on wheels. Spoked alloy wheels. A dead cactus resided in the red-striped racing bowl.

Up in the third floor library, I'd unearthed a cache of rusted surgical instruments, several colossal orthopedic devices, scores of test tubes, and miles of tubing clogged with substances of all hues imaginable—and some not so imaginable.

Gneeecey had told the truth about one thing—the only functional toilet in the house was the first floor's Electronic Water Cyclone 3000. (The basement's recently-used "facility"—a round hole cut into the cement floor, complete with carved indentations to accommodate long feet and tails—didn't count.)

The good diroctor's parting words still echoed in my mind. "No compoopany!" he'd warned, as he schlepped his Monotony birds' ornate cage and two bulging, electric-brown suitcases out of the living room window and down the front steps. "Don't want nobody comin' in my house while I'm gone!"

The second he left, I latched all the windows and locked all the doors. And leapt into the air, giving myself a high-five.

It was quiet.

So, adrenaline burned new pathways through me when I heard rhythmic rapping, coming from The Grate Room.

I grabbed the bent-into-a-U-shape putter Gneeecey had hurled, in a fit of after-game fury, into a psychedelic, quasi-Hellenic urn. Wielding the club like a bat, I limped into the room on rubbery limbs.

My jaw dropped, and my weapon fell to the floor.

There, on the other side of the picture window, stood Cleve, grinning. On the top step, by his sneakered feet, sat two King Oggle's take-out bags.

"Bad evening, Madam," he greeted me, still tapping his keys on the glass.

Straining, I slid the sash open. "What a surprise!"

"I brought dinner—or is that breakfast?" Roaring, the six-footer stepped inside and bear-hugged me.

"What's that?" I asked, as he dragged in a rectangular mahogany box and set it down on a chair.

"Thought we could rearrange our sock drawers together," answered Cleve, mischief sparkling in his ebony eyes. "You think Gneeecey'd mind?"

"Proboooobably," I shrieked, in a nerdish voice.

"If he finds out," he squealed back, "he'll schedooodle us for hangin', by the guillotine!"

"Hangman's sharpenin' his ax!" I shrilled.

We hung onto each other, doubled over.

Once we'd caught our breath, Cleve tossed his fleece-lined denim jacket onto Gneeecey's recently purchased ten-piece lime green sectional. "C'mon, Nicki, let's eat before it gets cold."

"We'd better hurry—he can probably smell this all the way from Booolabeeezia!"

Sitting cross-legged on Gneeecey's new circus-yellow shag carpet, we scattered two foil-wrapped heroes, a couple cups of freshly brewed coffee, a pair of pie-shaped dessert containers, and dozens of utensils, all over Gneeecey's mustard, faux-marble—actually heavy-duty, mierko-lated-plastic—coffee table.

My mouth watered as I unwrapped my oogdenplantzil hero, smoth-ered with melted Parmesan-like cheese.

Cleve hoisted his Styrofoam cup. "To our beloved boss in Booolabeeezia, benefactor of this humble feast!" he proclaimed, faking a pretty good English accent.

I lifted my steaming vessel. "And to 98.6 *Normal Radio* and the *Pooper-Scooper*. May they find new headquarters—fast!"

Cleve frowned. "I'll drink to that, even though it's not gonna hap-pen."

"Why not?"

"Something real strange is going on."

"Something real strange is *always* going on, isn't it?"

"Well, playing back some of my conversations with Justin Imbroglio, I'm beginning to put a few of the pieces together."

I leaned forward. "Pieces of *what?* Have you seen Imbroglio since the meeting?"

"Nope. I did run into his brother, Ethan. He's a cop—looks just like him. Says Justin's left town."

"Left town?"

"Yup. And Ethan's thinking of quitting the force—said something 'bout being outnumbered by creeps."

"Can't say that surprises me—when we stopped by the Squirrel Squash Road precinct, I got a pretty good look at some of our county's cops. Markmen are taking over."

"For real. I still can't get that picture out of my mind—them sur-rounding us, at the courthouse. Imbroglio and I were just minding our business."

"Our wonderful boss didn't like *that* too much—did you see the look he gave you?"

"Uh-huh," answered Cleve, sipping his coffee. "I saw from clear 'cross the room. And speaking of looks, I didn't like the looks those Markmen gave me, either. That stocky blond with the big nose strikes me as being particularly vicious."

"They all strike me as being particularly vicious." I laughed nerv-ously. "Maybe they burned down the *Pooper-Scooper* building."

Cleve's mouth opened.

"I mean," I continued, "you can't always believe what you read—"

"The *Tims* said it was faulty wiring—that is a buncha bull. That rag, and all its puppet editors, have been in Seemingwhale's pocket forever— he's been a major stockholder since the beginning of time. Imbroglio was on to something."

I picked up the other half of my sandwich. "Sounds like you know something I don't—"

"Imbroglio and I'd been running into each other, every day, at Shisskey's. He's okay, once you get past that egotistical exterior—once he lets his defenses down."

I listened, rapt.

"We'd usually sit by the front window. He'd joke about how he was getting on certain people's nerves, giving voice to the environmentalists' side of the 345 controversy."

"Just Imbroglio's being at the courthouse made Gneeecey mad."

Cleve took another bite of his hero.

"He threatened," I remembered, "to buy the *Pooper-Scooper*, saying then Imbroglio would have to work for *him*—unless someone *torched* them first."

Cleve stopped chewing.

"Cleve, you don't think—nah, he was probably just joking—"

My friend gave me one of his famous, piercing "ya never know" looks. "Imbroglio said he was on the verge of breaking a real scandal. Involving some big names."

"Did he mention any?"

"Seemingwhale, his guys at MierkoZurk and PassGass, and the folks who run the Mierkolatory and Freak O'Nature."

"Interesting."

"And—get this—our own dear boss!"

I dropped my sandwich. "Whoa—when were you ever gonna tell me all this?"

"I was—I swear—"

"With the *Pooper-Scooper* gone, where'll Imbroglio break all this—if he ever surfaces?"

"Dunno," replied Cleve. "Now, the *Tims* is the only game in town."

"And WGAS owns the airwaves. But when Salvador finds a place and hires us—picture Gneeecey's face when we both give notice—then Imbroglio can come on board too and—"

"Ain't gonna happen."

I crumpled my foil. "Why not?"

"Even if Salvador finds new digs, Gneeecey'll tie him up with so much red tape, he'll look like a freakin' Christmas present. With our boss sitting up in Knapsackville, it'll be impossible for *Normal Radio* or the *Pooper-Scooper*—to start up again."

Groaning, I popped a StomQuell. Gneeecey could ruin anything, even a good meal, from miles away.

Cleve looked down at his empty paper plate. "Last Someday, I decided to go check out the Mierkolatory. After operating hours. Imbroglio was right—something's going on there."

"Cleve, be careful—I've got a feeling something really bad's gonna go down—"

"Tell me. There were lights on in the basement—just like Imbroglio said. I saw a buncha guys rolling barrels outta the rear entrance, and loading 'em onto trucks. Freak O'Nature trucks."

"You recognize anyone?"

"Nah—it was so dark, and. . . ." He stared across the room, at the digital drapes. The stupid things were on the fritz again, flashing times like *86:73*.

"And?"

"Someone took a potshot at me. Actually, several. As you can see, they were *bad* shots."

My coffee went down the wrong way, and I spilled the precious brew all over Gneeecey's table.

Cleve slapped my back. "You okay?"

"Yeah," I spluttered. "Aside from almost drowning in my coffee, and you being shot at. And I might as well have drowned—when *he* sees this table—"

"Don't worry—that's why they're called coffee tables."

Trying a little too hard to be funny, Cleve poured the rest of his java on top of mine.

"Who'd shoot at you? And why?"

"I didn't stick 'round to find out. Truth is, I ran like my butt was on fire!"

"Don't go back—don't go getting yourself killed—"

"I'll try not to," he whispered, stroking my hand and giving me that "let's not talk about it anymore" look that I knew so well.

Just as the curtains began blinking *00:00* and *RESET*, something slammed against the side of the house.

Cleve jumped up. "What the *hell* was that?"

As the blood rushed from my head, I realized it was just the goths, going at each other. "Thank goodness, he triple-locked that playroom before he left."

"Man!" exclaimed Cleve, wiping his brow. "How d'ya live here at Three Bimbus Crack Drive, without going nuts?"

"I dunno. And I hate this idiotic address—you should see the looks I get when I fill out forms."

"I can only imagine. And now, you're living with the enemy—not that you *weren't*—"

"Cleve, promise me you won't go back."

"Back where?"

I crossed my arms.

"Hey, Nicki, whaddaya say we try some of this sloggenberry pie?"

"Okay. That shouldn't kill either one of us."

Ignoring my remark, Cleve hopped up onto the table. "Let's not stand on ceremony—let's stand on this instead!"

I couldn't help but crack up as Cleve smooshed a glob of cheese into Gneeecey's fake marble, with his heel. "Improves it, don'cha think?"

"Absolutely."

He bent down, stabbed a white plastic fork into a slice of pie, and handed it to me.

"Y'know," I began, savoring my first mouthful of the strawberry cheesecake-like dessert, "I wonder whatever made Gneeecey so rotten in the first place?"

Cleve jumped to the floor. "We both know, as a kid, he was a super geek. And it didn't help that his fiancée jilted him—"

"*Fiancée?* I can't even picture him having a girlfriend!"

"He did—back on Planet Eccchs."

"Get out!" I scraped up some sloggenberry sauce with my flimsy utensil.

"Her name was Goonafina Blopperdang. She was a golden retriever-type. A doctor. When she found out he was stranded here, she jilted him—by e-mail."

"Cleve, how long have you been stuck here?"

He put his fork down. "Five years."

I was speechless.

"Five long-ass years. And my limp hasn't gotten any better. It's worse."

"I never think of you as having a limp—I mean, only when you mention it do I ever become aware. And even then—"

"That's sweet of you—"

"I mean it—I never see you as moving with a limp."

"But I do. And I've seen what happens when you try to leave here before your legs heal. . .like my buddy Julio. . . ."

"Is that the Julio that Flea and Gneeecey always talk about?"

"Uh-huh," Cleve replied, eyes watering up. "Julio Rivera was my best friend. We were both ten when Grandma, my sis and I moved to Hackensack, from the Bronx."

"Where in the Bronx?"

"Good ol' banana-shaped Kelly Street."

I sat up straight. "That's where my mom and dad grew up—I lived there till I was two! Y'know, so many great musicians came from there—Manny Oquendo, Orlando Marín—"

"Y'know, I think I own every recording those guys ever made."

Goose bumps spread down my arms. Cleve's heroes were mine. Cool guy.

"Getting back to Julio and me," continued Cleve, "we loved messing with chemistry and electronics—almost blew up our building."

"You *what?*"

"We were trying to invent an electronically powered, organic hybrid vomit monster."

"Maybe you invented Gneeecey," I suggested, throwing a handful of napkins over the spilt coffee.

"Maybe! Anyway, lucky for us, our little explosion—food coloring and all—fizzled out pretty quickly. But we gave everyone a major scare, with all the smoke."

"I'll bet."

"Green smoke that smelled like exhaust, with a dash of rotten eggs. After the firemen left, Grandma Eleanor grounded me for a year. And Julio's mom grounded him. But we managed to get 'round the rules."

"I'm sure you did."

"In high school, we started our own band—the Latin Hackensoul Brothers. A real garage band—we practiced inside Santos' Auto Repairs, at night. Julio played percussion, and I played guitar."

"Wow!"

"There's this green beauty I've been paying down on, practically ever since I came here—over at Murgatroyd Music. Looks just like the Gretsch Country Club waiting for me back home."

"You must miss it."

"I think I'm finally gonna go pick that baby up. You wanna take a ride downtown, one day next week?"

"I'd love to."

"Great!" Cleve paused for a moment. "Julio and I did college radio, like you. And we both ended up working in Manhattan, at WZXL-TV. And then. . .we both ended up *here*."

Sighing, I picked crumbs off Gneeecey's carpet.

"Julio always had a shorter fuse than me. And Gneeecey was even worse back then."

"Worse?"

"Trust me—he's mellowed."

I shuddered.

"Anyway, Gneeecey had just told Julio his paycheck had been held up—again. Then he threw one of those old-fashioned reels of audio tape at him and ordered him to make it into a TV show. Before lunch. And in the same breath, he told him he'd be working weekends—indefinitely."

"Little jerk—"

"Julio threw that big ol' reel of tape back in Gneeecey's face and told him to stuff it—in English and Spanish. Then he tore outta the building."

My stomach was killing me. I knew this story didn't have a good ending.

"I ran outside and pleaded with him to come back," continued Cleve. "We'd only been here a coupla months—we were both kinda weak, with shaky legs. The dimension burn had hit him extra hard."

Chills ran through me.

"But Julio shouted out those words and. . . ." He studied Gneeecey's newly-painted cadmium yellow ceiling. "My best friend vaporized— right in front of me." After a moment of silence, he smacked his thighs. "Dunno if I'll ever leave here. But I don't want *you* to try before you're ready, y'hear? I don't wanna lose another best friend." He wiped his wet face on his sleeve.

I couldn't speak.

Cleve pulled a blue plastic tube out of his sock drawer. "I know you—nobody's gonna talk you outta leaving when you think you're ready. This is a special salve—rub it into your legs before you go to sleep. It's meant for sore muscles. Counteracts some of the numbness."

"Thanks." I unscrewed the top and sniffed. "Smells like lavender."

"It'll help you more."

"Why's that?"

"You're younger."

"C'mon, by two years. I mean, big deal—so, you were falling off your tricycle when I was born."

"Or turning it into some kinda monster."

I smiled.

"One more thing, Nicki. Remember I told you 'bout my kid sister?"

"Uh-huh. Lauren. You said she's seventeen now."

He nodded. "I call her whenever I can—I'm always trying to explain why I can't just pick up and come home. And it kills me when she says I need to try harder."

"This whole dimension thing's hard enough for *us* to wrap our minds around."

"You got that right. And Grandma, she's pretty progressive, if not a bit unconventional—I think I told you, she's a retired office manager, and now she's into astrology. Has clients."

"Yeah, I remember you mentioning that."

"But she'd never believe any of *this*. She'd slap me through the phone! She thinks I'm away on some secret assignment, working for the government." He reached for his wallet. "This is the last photo I have of Lauren. She was twelve when I disappeared."

I looked down at the face of a bright-eyed preteen, wearing a white blouse and gray plaid school uniform, and an expression of innocence. Impish innocence, framed by shoulder-length braids. "She's beautiful. You have the same eyes."

He beamed. "She's always been wise beyond her years. Says she wants to be an astrophysicist, so she can bring me home. Loves chemistry, too."

"Just so she doesn't almost blow up any buildings, like, uh, someone I know."

"Grandma and Lauren still live in that same apartment." He shook his head. "Lauren was a newborn when Mom and Dad were killed. Now, here *I* am—gone out of her life, too."

"You said you still talk to her."

"Except now, when we can't call outta here."

First thing I planned to do—if I was still stuck in Gneeeceyland when Blirg ended—was phone my poor mom.

Cleve walked over to the window. "See that star?"

"That big bluish one?" I asked, joining him.

"Yeah. If I look at it long enough, I swear I can see Earth circling 'round it."

"I think I can almost see it," I agreed, squinting.

Brushing his lips against my cheek, he squeezed an arm around me. I slipped mine around his waist. "Every time I talk to Lauren—usually when it's nighttime, back home—I tell her to look outside and pick the most brilliant star she can find. Then I tell her we're both looking at the same one."

We gazed through Gneeecey's smudged window, out into space. Whenever I was with Cleve, I forgot about Carlos.

"I was wondering, Nicki, if you get back home—"

I raised an eyebrow.

"I mean, *when* you get back home, could you do something for me?"

"Sure—anything!"

He removed a small box from his sock drawer and lifted the lid. "Could you make sure Lauren gets this?"

"Of course."

"Eighteen carat," he said, as he clicked open a heart-shaped locket, attached to a shimmering box-link chain.

"I've always said, you've got great taste."

"Better not be spelled 'g-r-a-t-e'."

"No, it's not. And look whose picture's inside."

"Don't want her to forget me. And here's our phone number. I know you'll find a creative way to make contact."

My stomach fluttered as I stuffed Cleve's tiny scrap of paper into my pocket.

"You're gonna leave on a whim, one day after you've found your stuff, and Gneeecey pisses you off—"

"Cleve, I don't wanna leave *you*—you'll come home soon—"

"I dunno," he replied, fastening the delicate chain around my neck.

"But when you leave all of a sudden—like I know you're gonna—you'll have this, and I'll be with you."

I tucked the pendant inside my maroon blouse.

"But don'cha *dare* leave before your birthday—we're going out to celebrate!"

A blaring nose-honk rattled the windows. We froze.

"He's not supposed to be back till tomorrow—I mean, yesterday," I whispered.

"Someone's with him! I can't tell if the voices are coming from up the hallway, or right outside the window here."

"Quick, Cleve—hide!"

He grabbed his sock drawer and sprinted behind Flea's white piano. "Phew, I'm gonna die—somethin' back here stinks!"

"Sssssh—they're coming!"

Gneeecey's blabbering grew louder. "Y'know what else, Mark? They suggesticated I change Channel 3½'s slogan to 'Gneee-TV'. But I tol' 'em, nah, that wouldn't really be me."

"Speakin' of changin' stuff," growled the Markman, "y'got lotsa minds to change before the nex' meetin'."

"Don't worry. I'm plannin' to distractipate folks—I'm gonna propose we change our county bird's name. A woodpecker should really be called a couldpecker 'cause it can!"

Gneeecey's suggestion was met with stony silence.

"I mean, I aaam workin' on it," insisted the good dirroctor.

"We both know y'ain't tellin' the truth."

"I aaam tellin' the trooooth—nuthin' *but* the trooooth! Look—I jus' dumped twenny shares on a coupla sucker salesmen from New Kerhonkson."

"Gotta do better'n that," snapped the Markman.

"Well," replied Gneeecey, in a martyred tone, "I lef' Booolabeeezia a whole stinkin' day early, to get ridda more."

"Who else y'gonna dump'em on?"

"Thought I'd drive down to Upper Revolta—I know more'n a few idiots in that village."

"Yeah?"

"An then, I'll relax by Lake Gizzagoola. Do a little goonafishin'."

"Y'better watch out," rumbled the Markman, "or they'll hafta go fishin' to find *you*."

"Why'd they hafta do *that*? *I* don't live in water."

"Y'don't do right by us, you're obsolete."

"Leggo of my shirt—you'll bust it!"

"We ain't jokin'—y'know?"

"Y-yeah," stammered Gneeecey, chewing on his left wrist as he and blond, big-nosed Mark entered The Grate Room.

"A deal's a deal, Doc."

"Jus' gimme a little more time!"

I held my breath. Neither Mark nor Gneeecey seemed to notice my presence—or Cleve's muffled cough.

"Bore, bore, bore, bore, MONOTONY!" squawked Gneeecey's birds, spooked when he dropped their cage to the floor.

Mark scowled. "Can'cha shut dem stupid things up?"

"Don't wanna insultipate 'em—they got delicate constitutions."

"So do *you*."

"IG!" Gneeecey jumped so high that the slowly-revolving, rhinestone-studded ceiling fan nearly whacked his head off.

"Director. . .you're back early—or is that *late*?"

The Markman's steely eyes bored through me. His skin was peeling.

"What'chooo doin' in here, Ig? Ain'cha s'posed to be somewheres else, doin' somethin' meanin'less?"

"Uh, no, Director, not according to this week's schedule—"

"Well, get'cha dumb Ig garbage outta here." He glanced down at his disfigured putter. "Y'been playin' golf?"

"No—I heard a noise and—"

"Who said y'could eat in here? Get all this junk offa my table! An' look at all them wet napoopkins! What in Bogelthorpe's name did'ja spill?"

"Uh, sorry—I cleaned it up. Your table's okay—"

"Stinkin' better be—or you'll be payin' that off, too. She looks real funny, don't she, Mark?"

"Yeah," he replied, shifty eyeballs scouring the room. "An' looky here—why's there *two* of everythin'? *Two* cups, *two* dishes, *two* forks. . . someone else here?"

"The Ig always eats like that—she's a real hogwash!"

I spotted Cleve's jacket, crumpled on the couch. My hands trembled as I whisked the remnants of our feast into the two take-out bags.

Mark strode over to the sofa, grabbed Cleve's garment and held it up to the light.

I tried not to look in the direction of the piano.

"Kinda big for *you*, ain't it?" he asked.

Before my shorted-out brain could come up with an explanation, Cleve coughed again. Klunkzill clunked over to the upright and began sniffing vigorously.

I thought I'd lose my meal. "Dir: your uh, goths, you'd better check on 'em—they've been, uh, hacking their heads off. Maybe it's that old oil furnace—all the carbon build-up."

Gneeecey's peepers bulged with concern. Klunkzill, who'd wandered behind the piano, scampered out, hackles raised.

The Markman unbuttoned his trench coat, exposing a compact Saturday night special. "Whatsamatter wit' Klunky?"

Gneeecey stuck an index finger up his nostril. "Dunno."

Mark whipped out his weapon and took aim at Flea's keyboard. "I shoot first—an' ask later."

I flinched.

Detecting my discomfort, Mark's smirk grew into a grin. "Got one of dem Kalashnikovs in my car. I'll go get it."

"Y-y'mean," stammered Gneeecey, still picking his nose, "one of them okay-47's?"

"Yeah. One of *dem*."

"Y'know," I began, unable to control my quivering voice, "I'll bet Klunkzill smells the director's socks—that pair we couldn't find the other day."

Mark's cheek muscles twitched. "Y'don't expect me to fall for *that*."

I hobbled over to the piano and began fumbling with its hinged wooden top. It crashed down on my fingers. The ensuing, dissonant chord sent Klunkzill scurrying out of the room.

"Nice Z-minor chord," squealed Gneeecey. "Didn't know y'could play!"

The pain radiated all the way up my arms. Ticker hammering out sixty-fourth notes, I lifted the lid again. The gods were with me. Gingerly, I plucked a ripe pair of purple-and-green-striped socks off the not-so-twinkling ivories.

Forcing a face-cracking smile, I handed Gneeecey his polyester skunks. Mark recoiled as the rank foot-coverings passed beneath his overgrown schnozz.

"Now we won't have to waste time looking for 'em," I told Gneeecey. "Maybe we'll get to the office on time, for once."

"Those ain't my lucky socks, Ig—y'better find that ticket before the concert. Now, GIT!"

"Okay," I answered, moving slowly, hoping they'd leave the room first. "I'm gitting—I mean, going. Just have to pick up all my stuff."

"Mark," squeaked Gneeecey, "could'ja get them new pampooplets outta your car?"

The Markman stuffed his firearm back under his too-tight belt. "Whatever."

"I'll meet'cha back here in a coupla minutes. Jus' gotta run up to the fourth floor an' check on Yammicles. He's on my bed, restin' in his new sleepin' bag."

Mark watched Gneeecey disappear up the spiral staircase, then walked briskly toward the side door.

"Cleve," I whispered, pushing the front window open with all my might, "they're gone!"

He leapt out from behind the piano, sock drawer in hand. His red sweatshirt was soaked.

"Hurry! The Markman's headed for the driveway—don't let him see you! Where's your car?"

"On Drivel Drive." He snatched his jacket and flew down the mansion's misplaced front steps.

CHAPTER 24

A LITTLE CELESTIAL CROSS-TRAININ'

MANGY MEGALOMANIAC MUTT," I hissed, pulling my itchy, yolk-colored blanket up over my head. Out of habit, I clicked Cleve's palm-sized radio on. One of the few things I looked forward to was listening to "Normal Commentaries" under the covers.

Now 98.6 broadcasted static.

Sighing, I yanked the plug out of my ear and stashed the receiver behind the cardboard box next to my mattress. Still couldn't afford to buy a night stand—or a radio.

I sandwiched an ice pack, wrapped in paper towels, between my two sets of throbbing fingers and tried to push the vision of blond, big-nosed Mark and his pistol out of my mind.

Gneeecey was across the hall, raiding the refrigerator, noisily stuffing his food-sucking face with three-week-old goonafish salad, moldy molderberry pie, and rusty nails. Rasputin had nothing on him.

As usual, he jabbered away on the telephone, spitting food bullets all over the mouthpiece. "Well," he shouted, probably at another reporter who had obtained his unlisted number, "redivloppment's divloppin' an area that's awready been divlopped!"

I could hear his high-top tapping.

"An'," he added, "that ain't smart, redoin' somethin' that's awready stinkin' been done. So go redivlop ya MOTHER!"

He slammed the phone down.

It rang again, two seconds later. "WHAAAAAT?! Oh, Stuey— everythin' okay? WHAAAT?! They promised me a five-foot banana that would squeak on-air! Squeeze it again. . .still won't? Shove it in the engineerin' closet—the Ig'll write up an outvoice."

My lids closed.

"WHAT'RE YOU DOING?"

"Whatever I want—as usual." Eyeing me defiantly, Gneeecey hoisted his golf bag up over his shoulder.

"But," I protested, hugging a nearby maple, to keep from flying off the spinning golf course as it hurtled through blackness, "you can't *do* that—"

"I'LL DO WHAT I WANT!" He caught Earth's cratered moon as it flew by his nose, and plunked it into a plastic hole. It clunked loudly.

"HOLE-IN-ONE!" he declared. "Pockmarked thing deserves to stay in that matter-eatin' black hole—ain't even green. An' it ain't made of cheeeeese—almost busted a tooth!"

"Diroctor—"

"There weren't no man in it neitherwise. It's jus' a crummy rock."

The tree I clung to disintegrated, and I tumbled to the ground.

"Look," squealed Gneeecey, sprinting down the disc-shaped field. "Snatturn—the planet named after Snatturday!"

I stumbled to my feet and lumbered after him.

He snatched the volleyball-sized sixth planet's famed ring and slapped it over his head. "A halo!"

Still rotating, the grooved band slipped down around his stubby neck.

"Now," I observed, watching Saturn roll away, "it looks like a noose."

"Not no more!" he yelled, yanking it up over his noggin and tossing it with all his might.

I shivered as the glittering, multi-banded swirl of rocks and ice sliced through space, like a glow-in-the-dark frisbee.

"Pluto's a *real* nuthin'!" he whooped, racing over to the edge of the lush, diaphanous green. "No wonder yuz demoted it."

He leaned forward, plucked the frozen pebble out of its elliptical orbit, and took a bite.

"Stop!"

"It's actually a chockookolate-covered raspoopleberry truffle. Sloppy, but tasty."

"You don't eat *planets*—"

Gneeecey sucked what was left of the picked-on, former planet into his big yapper. "BRAAAAAP! 'Scuzipate me."

"Don't think I will," I replied, shaking my head.

He pulled a nine iron out of his bag. "Time for a little celestial cross-trainin'. Lessee. . .Jupoopiter's nex'—red spot on its belly always did get on my nerves. I'm also gonna off that other gasbag, Neptune."

"Diroctor—"

"Neptune an' nuthin' both got N's an' U's, but borin' Big Blue here don't deserve 'em."

"I'm freezing and dizzy—"

"Watch, Ig. I'm puttin' them two losers in the side pocket—utilizatin' that rusty planet over there as the cue ball. The one yuz Earthlin's named after a candy bar."

Gneeecey snapped his fingers, and a spray can materialized.

"Gas hardener—makes planets bust up better," he explained, squeezing the nozzle and coating Jupiter and Neptune with a lacquer that smelled like apple pie.

He aimed his iron like a cue stick and smashed Mars into Jupiter, shattering the red planet into a zillion jagged shards. Meanwhile, the spot-bellied sphere whirled, at supersonic speed, toward ol' nuthin' Neptune, pulverizing it.

The explosion sent me flying sideways. Multi-colored, sun-lit remnants of the destroyed bodies scattered slowly.

"Put lotsa English on that one!" he screeched.

"You didn't put 'em in the side pocket."

"This was even better—my own Big Bang!" he shrieked, skipping down the fairway. "Too bad we'll be runnin' outta planets soon."

"C'mon—stop—"

"Nex', I'll whack Uranus right offa the face of the universe. It don't deserve its N's an' U's neitherwise—although I do appreciate its heavenly methane aroma."

He plunged his honker into the green clouds that covered the gaseous basketball, and snorted vigorously. "Mmmmm! What a simpooply divine fragrance—might decide not to off this baby after all. Second thought, UniGeek's stocks methane-scented aftershave—they sell it wholesale."

Gneeecey grabbed his fixative and sprayed Uranus.

I moaned. "You're sick—"

Swinging his club like a bat, he smacked the tilted planet out into the stars. "HAT TRICK!"

"You're destroying my solar system!" As I fell flat on my face, I discovered that each blade of grass was translucent. "What's this, ghost grass? I can *see* through it."

"Astroturf, ya Iggarooney," he replied, zigzagging over to Venus. "Hot potato! Hot potato! CATCH!"

"Are you *nuts?*" I shouted, leaping to my feet and running for my life.

"Stinkin' thing's hotter'n it looks! Ain't really a star neitherwise—your dopey sister planet's a imposter. I'll confisticate her N an' U."

"You are nuts."

"Take THIS, y'backward-spinnin' greenhouse," he roared, slamming the brilliant body into a hole. "BIRDIE! GO FISH! OL' MAID!"

Jubilant, he swung at golf ball-sized Mercury three times and missed.

"You've struck out!"

"Stinkin' asteroid threw me off." He blew a cluster of stray stars over his shoulder. "It's a do-over."

"C'mon—"

"Merkookury, y'piece of charcoal," he muttered, slapping at a tiny comet as it whizzed by his ear. "Take THIS, y'hotheaded dwarf!" He gritted his teeth and smashed the sun's nearest planet out of sight, hollering, "HOMERUN!"

"Ground rule double," I said, just to annoy him.

"Nah, that was a grand slam touchdown! Din'cha see my imaginary runners on base?"

"I don't see any runners or bases."

"*I* make the rules," he replied as a rocket ship sped by.

"Diroctor, Earth there's the size of a softball, and that sun's only as big as a beach ball. I read that the sun could hold 1.3 million Earths—plus it's about 93 million miles away. This solar system isn't real—it's not to scale."

He turned toward the only body still orbiting. "Oh, it's real."

"NO!" I cried, instantly regretting having mentioned my planet.

"Now looky here at this dopey blue ball—it's all wet!" He whipped an aluminum tennis racket out of his suddenly red T-shirt pocket. "Briney lumpa mud's infected wit' Igs like yooou."

"Please—*don't!*"

"Hafta! I get a dime for each planet I whack."

"Earth's populated," I protested. "Teeming with life—just like Planet Eccchs! You can't *do* this!"

"Nebberd-kinnezzard tell me I can't do somethin'." He splashed his pinky into the sparkling Atlantic. "Better be carefoofal—don't wanna lose a finger in that lousy Bermuda Triangoogle."

He withdrew his soaked digit and licked it. "A bit on the salty side. An' this little boat here tastes like a cruise ship."

"STOP IT—NOW!"

"Want me to make Earth safe for demockookracy?"

"JUST LEAVE IT ALONE!"

"It is alone, Ig—*all* alone. Finally get to use this here aluminizated, official replooplica of a Wimboobledon tournament racket."

Whistling, he lobbed Earth out of the solar system.

As the shimmering planet sailed over my head, an arcing trail of chilly ocean water sprayed my cheek. Reflected brilliantly in each drop were all the colors of the rainbow.

I picked a transparent, ant-sized porpoise out of my eye and placed it in my left palm.

And watched helplessly as the feathery layer of clouds that encircled my runaway world streamed away, flinging a microscopic flock of birds into oxygen-less oblivion.

"Well Ig, like they say, y'can never go home. An' now, y'never *will*."

I gazed out into the frigid heavens, then down at my hand. My squealing porpoise had morphed into a lifeless, cellophane facsimile of itself—a smiling, cartoon-like creature.

"Got a evergreen stuck in my teeth," complained Gneeecey, picking his fangs with the edge of a bent scorecard. "Prickly—tastes like brockookoli."

"Diroctor," I stammered through chattering teeth, "I can't breathe!"

"That's 'cause there ain't no air here."

"But you're breathing—"

"How many times do I gotta tell ya? *I* make the rules."

He bopped up to the sun. Blazing brightly, it hovered about a foot above the center of the golf course.

"Glad it's night!" He flashed a devilish grin. "Couldn't do this durin' daytime."

"NO!" I screamed, shielding my eyes.

"Y'big spotted furnace—y'ain't as hot as y'think. I'm not even breakin' a sweat. Okay, here goes—"

"NO! Diroctor, I *beg* you—"

"No more solar acne flare-ups for yooou—it's curtains, big guy."

I stood paralyzed.

Gneeecey winked as he extracted a gigantic pair of mirrored sunglasses from his pocket and clamped them over his snout. The sun's blinding image reflected off each lens.

He rubbed his palms together. "Awready made eighty-five cents—they'll only gimme a nickel for Pluto an' the moon—but I'll get a whole buckerooney for puttin' out this bad boy!"

"NOOOOOOOOO!"

"Adds up to a buck-eighty-five. Plus, today I discovered that secret compartment an' found all *your* mon-ney."

"WHAAAAAAA—"

"Once I put the kibosh on your lousy sun, I've actually earned ten-thousand-one bucks an' eighty-five cents. Not bad for a day's work, huh, Ig?" A gold hoop earring suddenly sprouted out of his left ear.

I crumpled to my knees.

He puckered up, and with ease, blew out Earth's mighty five-billion-year-old star, extinguishing it forever.

Sobbing, I rolled off my mattress, onto the floor.

CHAPTER 25

LET'S DO LUNCH

"HOLY CRAP!" I HOLLERED, knee-deep in rubbish. "I DON'T FREAKIN' BELIEVE IT!" My rapture was tempered only by the slight dread that I might be hallucinating. Maybe the oxygen was thinner up on the fourth floor.

Swaying, as Gneeecey's pigsty of a bedroom spun 'round me, I flopped onto his bare, striped king-size mattress.

I had to get my act together. He'd be home any minute—he was taking me out to lunch for my birthday, at the exclusive Tricycle Club. Don't ask me why.

Forcing myself up, I crept forward, past half a tire, an empty pizza box, and a heap of soiled, smelly aqua T-shirts. When I reached Gneeecey's spit-stained pillow, I froze.

I wasn't dreaming. There, right out in the open, in front of my very eyes, sat my maroon leather portfolio, Yammicles stuffed inside.

A hand-scrawled sticker taped to the case read, "Camp Bingaboonga sleeping bag." I yanked at the teddy, finally dislodging him after a half-dozen attempts. He'd really plumped out since I'd last seen him. According to Gneeecey, he had big bones. And an eating disorder.

I licked my quivering lips. Oh, God. Please let it be there. Let it *all* be there.

Eyesight pulsating in tandem with my pounding heart, I reached inside the main compartment. Pulled out my passport and shorthand outline of my novel. Both had been marked up in red pencil. The little hairball had even defaced my photo—he'd scribbled a handlebar mustache under my nose.

I held my breath and slipped my fingers into the secret compartment, hidden behind an open seam at the bottom of the case's silky—and thankfully waterproof—lining.

And gasped.

Nothing?! Nothing there?! Dirty thief!

Wait. . .wait a minute. . .I'd made the same mistake before. There were *two* hiding places—one on each side.

I plunged my fist back in and groped around, this time surfacing with four bulky wads of cash. Exhaling, I rifled through each bundle. Twice.

It was all there. *Thank you, God*, I whispered, tears burning down my cheeks. *I am so outta here!*

I began to howl. Until I became aware of a white-coated golden retriever canine-humanoid, glaring down at me from Gneeecey's prescription bottle-infested night table.

A stethoscope hung from her neck. Stitched red letters on her pocket indicated that I was staring up the snooty black nostrils of Dr. Goonafina Blopperdang.

Ah, Goonafina.

A pair of Bend-A-Britch-stained briefs, polka-dotted with dimes, hung from one corner of the tarnished frame. Splashed across the seat was the slogan: "Stummix Bank: We Cover Your Bimbus!"

As I stuck my tongue out at Goonafina's glossy image, a faint boinging underneath the window—possibly that of an unlicensed fugitive kangaroo, or more likely, Gneeecey's pogo stick—grew louder by the second.

I crammed my cash and passport into four inner pockets of my zillion-zippered jacket, and jammed my other papers into a couple roomier outer pouches. I would look hippy but didn't give a deck of vlecks.

After scooping supermarket tabloids off the floor and stuffing them into the empty portfolio, I ran out into the hallway as fast as my nearly normal legs could carry me.

Just as I reached the staircase, a blaring nose honk informed me that indeed, Gneeecey had returned.

The moment my foot hit the first step, I realized I hadn't replaced Yammicles in his "sleeping bag." Cursing colorfully, I sprinted back into the bedroom.

"GET IN AWREADY!"

I pointed to the microscopic white Porsche idling on the driveway. A tail-on-a-spring wagged on its trunk. Vigorously.

"Director, I told you, I won't fit."

"TRY, DAAAAAAMMIT!"

I moaned. "Can't we use the limo?"

"She's dislocated—waitin' for parts they hadda special order all the way from Slipshodville."

"Dislocated?"

"Yeah. Her automatic GPS dragged Culvert through the swamps an' halfway up the river—"

"He couldn't override the system?"

"Nope—I designed it foolproof, to cut wear an' tear."

"Is Culvert okay?"

"Proboobably."

"*Probably*?!"

"He'll be outta the hospoopital in a coupla weeks. Which is per-fec'—limo won't be ready till then."

My eyes widened.

"Aaaah—ducks always land on their bimbus." He glanced over at his Porsche. "Lucky I remembered to roll this baby outta the trunk be-fore Zeke put the limo in traction."

He stomped over to the vehicle and pointed to some dark, baseball-sized globs. "Poe crow's been defooficatin' on my car!"

"Gee—"

"Now, get IN!"

"How come," I asked, stalling for time, "there's a tail on the trunk?"

"Anti-gravoovitational antenna. Now if y'don't stinkin' get in awready, we'll be early. Durin' Blirg, The Tricycle Club charges for bein' early. It's a very igscloosive joint—hadda make resuscitations three weeks ago."

"I can't roll myself up small enough to—"

"That kangoogaroo I brung home fit—I cleaned up his little accident offa your seat—"

"You brought home a *kangaroo*?"

"Thought if I brung one of our county mascots to our nex' meetin', it'd take people's minds offa other junk—"

"He's in the *house*?"

"The marsoopoopial's locked up in the third floor lyberry. There's plenty of stuff to color up there."

"But—"

"NOW, WILL Y' GET IN THE CAR AWREADY!"

Couldn't go in my Splodge—it was in the shop again. It had a seizure. On Murgatroyd Avenue, during rush hour. For twenty minutes, I'd cringed while the backfiring jalopy—jackass horn honking nonstop—

heaved and shuddered, hurling rusty fender bits sky high. Screaming pedestrians had run for cover as pieces rained down on their heads.

Had to talk my way out of a ticket—for pollution. And Zeke himself had to come cut the ignition wires before he could cart the piece of junk away.

He still couldn't figure out what was wrong.

Crouching low, I backed into the Porsche's Gneeecey-sized bucket seat and, with difficulty, swivelled around to face the bird-bombed windshield.

The stale-smelling vehicle's ceiling scrunched my head so far down, my chin touched my collarbone. To see straight ahead, I had to roll my eyeballs upward.

My knees, pinned by the blood-red dashboard, jutted up around my ears. I was a living pretzel.

"Y'look like a pretzel," observed Gneeecey, plopping down onto the county phone book duct-taped to his seat. "A fat one."

I grunted.

"Even hidin' in that dumb coat," he added, turning on the wipers and creating a gaggy mess, "everyone can tell you're gainin' weight. Y'ain't foolin' nobody."

Little did *he* know whose turn it was to be fooled. I smiled.

"Another thing—why d'ya keep smilin'?"

"Uh, I dunno." I bit my lip. Hard.

"Somethin's gonna wipe that grin right offa your Ig face. Now, lemme concentrate—gotta back all the way down this here driveway. Forgot how stinkin' big this car is!" He could barely see over the dash.

"Isn't it dangerous to *back* all the way down such a long, curvy—"

"Drivin' backwards, y'don't burn as much gas," he mumbled, slugging me as he slammed the gearshift into reverse.

"THAT TREE!" I SCREAMED. "You're gonna HIT it!"

"Don't worry, Ig—it's a one-way tree."

The Porsche grazed the fracas's lumpy bronze trunk, then bounced back into the street.

"By the time I was old enough to drive," said Gneeecey, flying down Femur Avenue, "I was rich enough to hire folks to do it for me. But don't worry—I've watched Flea."

"*Oh.*"

"Y'know," he continued, screeching onto Triple Bypass Lane, "I read that if y'were born durin' Blirg, you're actually two months younger."

"Younger than what?"

"Normal people."

"Oh."

"An' y'know what else?"

"No."

"Well, Ig, when we get back home before lunch—"

"Yeah—"

"As I was sayin', before y'rudely interrupticated—"

"*I what?*"

"There y'go, doin' it again."

"Doing *what?*"

"Don't make me change my mind, Ig. As I was trynna say, I'm givin' ya a surprise birthday party—earlier, when we get home." He almost wiped out, turning onto tree-lined Diaper Pin Drive.

"It's not a surprise anymore, is it?"

"*I'm* surprised." Gneeecey floored the gas, forcing a group of elderly pedestrians, hobbling on walkers and canes, to clatter to safety. "I'm surprised I'm givin' ya one."

"Second thought, I am surprised," I said, straining to look his way. "You're actually cracking your wallet open for me, aren't you?"

"Don't worry—the bathroom guest fees alone'll cover my expenses—I'll turn a nice profit."

Surprise, surprise. . .Gneeecey had an agenda. Well, boy, will *he* be surprised when I'm history. Could be any day now. . .maybe even yesterday. I peeked down at my bulgy pockets.

Gneeecey cleared his throat. "You're smilin' again."

"Uh, must be 'cause you're giving me that party, and it's not even gonna, y'know, dent your wallet."

"Speakin' of wallets, I 'spect folks'll bring me over lotsa purple rubber billfolds—"

"Huh?"

"Y'know, as host gifts, this bein' so close to Grimace."

"YAAAAAA—you hit that blinking purple reindeer—on that lawn, by the house you just sideswiped—"

We'd entered Curdlecrumm Township, decked out to the max with lit, inflatable purple wallets, and miles of matching lights and glitter-sprayed dead rubber chickens.

"Y'see that reindeer there?" asked Gneeecey, as he knocked over a mailbox.

"The one you hit?"

"Yeah. See its horns?"

"You mean, its *antlers?*"

"Yeah. Reindeers were made that way on purpoopose, wit' antelopes, so y'could hang tinsel on 'em."

That moment, a cluster of disembodied eyeballs drifted by.

"LOOK!"

"What now, ya Ig?"

"By that telephone pole you just scraped—more floating eyeballs!"

"I don't see nuthin'," replied Gneeecey, as he flung a bottle of Repulsid at me. "Here, take one—it'll make all your little eyeballs go away—"

"YIKES!"

"NOW WHAAAT?!"

"THAT MAN—YOU JUST RAN OVER HIS FOOT!"

"That guy in my rearview mirror?"

"Aren'cha gonna stop and see if he's alright?"

"He's okay—he's usin' the foot," snapped Gneeecey.

"Huh?"

"He's hoppin' toward us on his left foot—the one I thought I ran over."

"In your mirror, left and right would be *reversed.*"

"Aaaaaah—he's proboobably some actress my insurance company hired, to trick me." Snarling, he clicked a switch, and a TV screen embedded in the center of his steering wheel came to life.

"My favorite epoopisode of 'Angry Little Airplanes'—y'know, where Daddy Airplane's ridin' his half-donkey-half-cow through a blizzard in the tropics, to buy his son the last two tickets in town to see Spit Wit'out Color's farewell concert. But, the boy awready bought 'em, to surprise the half-donkey-half-cow."

"Huh?"

"But he was half-goat too—ate the tickets when the mailman's uncle-in-law stopped by to borrow some recycled toilet paper—"

"You're watching TV while you drive?!"

Head rotating with each turn of the wheel, Gneeecey didn't answer. "YOU TRYING TO KILL US?!"

"I'm starvin'!" He extracted a box from his T-shirt pocket, ripped it open, and submerged his snout. "Mmmmm—I love aminal crackers! But I'm not gettin' at 'em fast enough!"

He turned the cardboard container upside-down, over his head. Its flaps covered his sloping shoulders.

"Are you nuts—driving with a box over your head?!"

"Don't worry," he reassured me, as horns blasted us. "I can still see— a little."

"Take that off your head or we'll end up—"

"End up what?"

"DEAD! You're weaving all over the place—we're gonna be ROAD-KILL!"

"Stuff like that only happens on the news. Besides, I always snack on the road."

"Yeah, while *Culvert's* driving!"

"He's in the hospoopital."

"That's where *we're* gonna be—"

"Yeah—if I drive wit' low blood sugar—"

My heart flew into my throat. "OOOOOH MY GOD," I croaked, "WE'RE HEADED STRAIGHT FOR THAT BIG—"

"—MILK TANKER," SHOUTED THE officer, as he bent down to get a better look at Gneeecey. "I SAID, YOU HIT THAT BIG MILK TANKER!"

"So that's what that nerve-racketin' noise was." Prying the box off his noggin, the good diroctor leapt through his open window and shoved past the policeman.

"Excuse me, sir—where exactly d'ya think you're going?" The deep-voiced six-foot human bore an uncanny resemblance to Justin Imbroglio.

Gneeecey skipped over to the silver rig, as it lay on its side in an ocean of white, smack in the middle of Plunger Road. "Lemme get to that moo juice, 'fore it freezes!"

He began to dunk his crackers and shove them, two-fisted, into his salivating trap.

The officer turned to me and shook his head. "What's with your, uh, friend?"

"Oh, he's not my friend—he's my boss."

"I'm sorry."

"Me too."

"I've gotta check on the other driver. His tanker's cracked in half."

"Is he okay?"

"Yeah, but pretty traumatized. Are *you* alright?" The policeman leaned so close, I could smell his musky aftershave. Had to be Justin's brother, Ethan. Shorter hair, but same face. And same rippling physique —hugged by a close-fitting, jet-black uniform.

He kept staring. "Anything you need?"

"No, no thanks," I lied, forcing a weak laugh.

The officer smacked the Porsche. "Not a scratch—must be made of rubber."

"Must be," I agreed, shivering uncontrollably.

His hazel eyes brimmed with concern. "It's warm today, but you're freezing. And you look so uncomfortable. Do you need medical attention?"

Only if you're the doctor, I thought.

"Would you like me to go back to my cruiser and get a blanket?"

"Thanks, but—"

"I'm back," whooped Gneeecey, massaging his distended belly. "Ran outta crackers 'fore I ran outta milk. So I asked the driver if he had any."

I winced. "You didn't."

"If he's transpooportatin' milk, he mus' carry cookies. Anyways, he said somethin' 'bout stuffin' 'em. Guess that was his way of sayin' he awready ate 'em all. But I comforted him anyway, even though he couldn't be of no use. See him there?"

"Yes."

"Tol' him not to cry over spilt milk."

"Is that why he's slapping himself in the face?"

"No—I tol' him to cry for Argentina instead."

My jaw dropped.

"Musta really touched his nerves." Grinning—a brilliant milk mustache contrasting with his grimy, off-white fur—Gneeecey chucked his empty container onto the pavement.

"If you don't go pick that up right now," warned the policeman, flexing his biceps, "I'll cite you with a 3379.26, section BS-45, article 3.9— littering a public thoroughfare."

"Someone else'll pick it up," said Gneeecey as he climbed through his window, back into the Porsche. "Someone else always does. Now, I'm real busy an' important! GOTTA GO!"

"Wait a darn minute, sir—I don't care *who* you are. You can't just leave the scene of an accident. I'm already citing you for reckless driving, operating a motor vehicle while wearing a box on your head—that's a 759.06, section 4A, article 13, and—"

"An' stinkin' whaaat? *I'll* tell y'what! Y'look jus' like someone I hate!"

The cop clenched his fists. "And who might that be?"

"Can't remember the chump's name—but'chooo look jus' like him. Lookin' at'cha dumb badge, I think yuz even spell your crummy names alike."

"Imbroglio would be the name," the cop replied, his exquisitely sculpted cheek muscles twitching.

Gneeecey turned his key in the ignition. "Y'ain't one of my regoo-goolar cops, are ya? *They* always do what I say."

"I need to see your license, registration and insurance," demanded Officer Imbroglio, articulating each word clearly. "Take 'em out slowly."

"Ain't showin' y'nuthin', 'specially not slowly. Y'know who I *am*? I'M GRATE GIZZYGALUMPAGGIS OF THIS HERE COUNTY! I SIGN YOUR STINKIN' PAYCHECKS!"

"I know who you are," replied the officer. "You leave the scene of this accident and I'll charge you with a 1096.27, section 78, article 3, and put out a countywide APB on you—"

"KISS MY LEFT FOOT!" Gneeecey stuck his sneaker out of the window, up toward Officer Imbroglio's nose, then gunned the gas. The Porsche farted down the road on its two rear tires.

"SEE, IG, I TOL' Y'SOMETHIN' was gonna wipe that grin offa your face."

"I don't freakin' believe this," I wailed. "My legs were almost normal—now I can hardly walk!"

"Guess yoooou ain't goin' nowheres for a while. Not that'cha thought'cha were."

A couple of Tricycle Club busboys snickered as I clutched their arms and negotiated my way around the piles of shattered glass that had enclosed the establishment's distinctive art deco-style lobby.

"Sorry," bleated Gneeecey. "Didn't mean to actually drive *into* the place. The Ig here was distractipatin' me."

Yeah, right. Adding insult to injury, I'd been thrown from the vehicle. Just missed the fountain.

"You certainly know how to make an entrance, Diroctor," said a waxy-faced, silk-suited gentleman, poking his silver head through a doorway. His tone was icy.

"Sorry, Bob. Put it on my account."

"Will do. And I'll have the valet guys come get your, uh, *car* down off the top of our vending machine. One of my, uh, smaller guys'll put it in the lot."

"Thanks."

Bob's electric blue eyes narrowed with contempt. "Lady Luck isn't exactly on your side these days, is she?"

Gneeecey stuffed a health cigar in his mouth and peered up at his Porsche as it rocked on its roof, tires still spinning.

"WHY WON'CHA LET 'EM hang your coat, Ig? Nobody'll steal that stooopid thing."

"I'm cold."

"Mus' be sevooventy degrees—real warm for Octvember."

"But it's chilly in here," I insisted, hobbling into the dimly lit dining room.

Glistening bicycle frames—aluminum and titanium—and reflectors, sequined saddlebags, silvery rims with ornate spokes, and every other accessory imaginable, adorned the walls, from top to bottom. Hundreds of handlebars, sprouting lit streamers, sparkled as they hung from the black ceiling.

"Interesticatin' place, huh, Ig?"

"I've never seen anything like it," I answered, craning my achy neck. "WHOA—WHAT THE—"

"Y'gotta watch the ground. Bob almost ran y'down."

Sure enough, patrons and staff zoomed around on bikes. There wasn't a table or chair in sight.

"Sorry, miss," apologized Bob, grinning down at me from atop a unicycle. "I'll show you to your bicycle. We've reserved a red three-speeder for you—over there, in that cozy corner. And Diroctor, your usual two-wheeler's waiting for you. Follow me."

"*Bikes?!*"

"Forgot to tell ya, Ig—everyone eats ridin'."

"How," I asked, dodging a fast-moving cyclist, "can anyone *eat*, riding a bicycle?"

"Everyone is—even the little kids. Handlebars got these little grooves in 'em to hold your tray in place."

"I can't eat riding a bicycle," I protested, as a unicycling waiter sped through someone's spilt beverage and splashed me like a city cab on a rainy day.

"You'll jus' hafta try, Ig."

"Can't we sit at the bar?" I pointed to a row of stools, topped by shiny, red bike seats.

"Can't eat there—that's only for drinkin'. Bob, can we get the Ig here some trainin' wheels?"

"Sorry, Diroctor," he replied, regarding me with amusement. "We don't have any—we just assume that our customers, uh, *ride*."

"Maybe she could use the kickstand," suggested Gneeecey, swerving so as not to collide with another diner who refused to make way. Everyone was too busy playing chicken to eat chicken.

"She can use her kickstand," agreed Bob, "if she stays in that corner and doesn't ruin other customers' meals."

"Well, hapoopy hatchday, Ig! Order anythin' y'want."

"Anything?" I asked, slumped against the wall, astride my two-wheeler.

"Yeah—I'll decapitate it from your nex' paycheck."

"In that case," I replied, "I'm not hungry."

"C'mon, Ig—don't be a soiled sport."

"You said you were treating."

"I said I was takin' y'to lunch, not payin'. There's a difooference."

My stomach rumbled so loud, folks turned to look. "How much," I wondered aloud, pointing to what looked like the only edible item on the menu, "is the Vegetarian Platter Number Five?"

Gneeecey chuckled. "If y'hafta ask, y'can't afford it."

An athletic, white-shirted young human glided over on his unicycle. "Bad afternoon. My name's Wade. I'll be your server."

"How much is the Vegoogitarian Platter Number Five?"

"14.95, sir," replied Wade, as he pedaled in place like a swimmer treading water. "Excellent choice."

"Wouldn't Numbers Four, Three, Two, or One be cheaper?"

"Sir, we only have a Number Five. If you'd like, I'll guide you to something more affordable—"

"Don't bother—the Ig here's payin'."

"My name's *Nicki*, and yes, I'll have the Vegetarian Platter Number Five."

"She's one of them vegoogitarians," explained Gneeecey. "Blindfolds her plants when she eats broccoli."

"One Vegetarian Platter Number Five. Excellent choice, Iggy. And you, sir?"

"Well," answered Gneeecey, as he rode his mountain bike in circles, "I'll have one of them Frummidge Melts—nah, wait—doctor says I awready got too much cheese in my blood. I'll jus' have one of them bread sandwiches."

"Excellent choice, sir."

"An' gimme a bowl of fully simmered ice block soup. An' some bloonked parrumph, wit' extra blurdle sauce. On the side. An' bring me a chain an' some grease."

"Trouble with your bicycle, sir?"

"Nah—jus' want an apoopetizer."

"Very good, sir," replied Wade, studying Gneeecey with jade eyes. The auburn-haired, thirty-ish waiter's demeanor was that of an actor-in-training, tolerating his lowly job until he landed his first big break.

"Wow!" I gaped, transfixed, as a waitress unicycled by, juggling flaming desserts.

"They charge more," warned Gneeecey, "for juggled food."

"IG," BEGAN GNEEECEY, SLURPING his soup, "Redo that Bweeek commercial. Bogelthorpe himself called to say the music bed ya used made his voice sound fat."

"Uh-huh." I pushed some wilted parsley around on my spoked chrome plate.

"I can't afford to lose that account."

"Uh-huh." I couldn't take my mind off my legs—my numb, newly injured legs.

"I'll have good ol' Stuey redo it."

"Uh-huh. Okay."

"Cleeevoooveland's too busy workin' unpaid overtime."

Mr. Bloopy-loop had self-destructed. Looked like Cleve and I would never get out to celebrate my birthday. Or drive downtown to pick up his guitar. I threw my fork down.

"Stop playin' wit' your food!" admonished Gneeecey. "You'll knock your tray offa your handlebars."

"Uh-huh. Yeah. Y'know, Diroctor, I was wondering, how's Spot?"

"Who?"

"Oxymoron, up in Seemingwhale Towers," I replied, stunned.

"Oh, him. Dunno—he ain't called lately."

"Why don't you keep him at home? I mean, why bother to keep a dog?" I'd been unable to convince Gneeecey to let the poor pup come live in the mansion. Cleve had even offered to look after him, in his tiny studio apartment.

"Why keep a dog," answered Gneeecey, "when y'can bark yourself?"

"What?"

"That's one of our Grand Oogitty-Boogitty's wise sayin's—I wouldn't 'spect yooou to understand." He dipped his chain into his cup of grease, threw the clanking thing up into the air, and caught it his yapper. And swallowed it whole.

"Why," I asked, taking a sip of bad-tasting, lukewarm water, "do they call this The Tricycle Club? I haven't seen a tricycle yet."

"Well, ma'am," answered Wade, rolling up with Gneeecey's bread sandwich and bloonked parrumph, "our chefs ride 'em. That's why our food's so known for its excellence—they don't have to expend energy balancing while they cook."

"Oh."

"Only busboys walk," added Gneeecey. "They gotta *earn* their wheels."

Wade nodded.

"Weird," began Gneeecey, "y'forgot—"

"That's Wade. *Wade.*"

"Way Weird?"

"No. Wade."

"No way?"

"Name's *Wade,*" growled the waiter, doing a slow burn.

"It is weird. Now, y'forgot my side of blurdle sauce. An' gimme another crappucino. Gotta stay awake this mornin'. 'Kay, Weird?"

"I'll get that right away, sir," answered the scarlet-faced waiter.

I TAPPED MY WATCH. "You were in the men's room for twenty minutes."

Gneeecey glared at me. "Timin' me while I pee?"

"I thought you decided to stick me with the check—maybe you climbed out a window."

"Tol' y'before—I'm takin' this outta your pay."

"Diroctor," I began, anger crackling in my voice, "you're not getting by with this—"

"Yummy!" He stabbed his fork into his chin-high mound of parrumph. It smelled like cauliflower gone bad, seasoned with sulphur and a dash of skunk.

Smiling, he dipped a huge glob of the mashed potato-like mush into his headlight-shaped cup of pungent purple sauce, then shoved it into his kisser.

Half a foot of the tie-dyed mess hung from each corner of his mouth, moving upward as he chewed. Some remained glued to his fur. I had to look away.

"Here's your extra parrumph," announced Wade, banging another dish onto Gneeecey's gumped-up steel tray.

"I'll try an' finish it," squealed the good diroctor, as he steered in lopsided circles. "But I'll wanna take home any manevelins."

"Manevelins?"

"Leftovers."

Wade frowned. "I'll get a doggy bag."

"Nah, guy-wit'-the-weird-name, I ain't sharin' this wit' Spot. Hardly ever see him."

"Whatever, sir. I'll just bring you a waterproof receptacle so you can bring your *manevelins* home."

"Good—the stuff's comin' outta my ears."

The parrumph was actually pouring out of his ears, onto his shoulders.

"Whattsamatter, Ig? Ain'cha never seen someone eat till it came outta their ears?"

"Can't—can't say I have."

"Hey, Doc, whaddaya say?" shouted redheaded, broken-nosed Mark, flashing by on a gunmetal ten-speeder.

Gneeecey almost fell off his bike. "Uh, *Mark*, whazzup?"

"I expect you'll tell *us*."

"Y-yeah," stammered Gneeecey, as he knocked his meal to the floor and rode through it, leaving tire tracks.

CHAPTER 26

HAPOOPY HATCHDAY

O NE BY ONE, THEY filed in through the first-story window, bearing gifts. "Into the dinin' room," ordered Gneeecey. "Ain't got all mornin'—let's move!" And so they did, obediently—Flea, resplendent in his satin-caped dress uniform, followed by Flubbubb, glowing in his new Save-the-Goonafish T-shirt, and Stu, decked out in his usual mustard, geek-chic sartorial splendor.

Always trying to score points, the intern strained visibly when he saw Gneeecey watching him push Freak O'Nature Foods Chairman of the Board, B.M. Bonbeeederhead, down the hallway.

Bonbeeederhead was an actual chair, mind you—a living, kvetching hunk of oak. His soulless cue-ball eyes protruded from a saggy-jowled backrest, presiding over a stump of a nose and a down-turned mouth. And splintery seat. One nobody'd dare sit in—or want to.

A chrome-yellow numeral, known simply as Nine, marched in behind him, on nearly invisible legs. The dapper digit sported sheer tails, and a gleaming smile. He tipped his transparent top hat and presented me with a crystalline rose.

Bringing up the rear, wearing his dilapidated Gnorks jersey, was the only guest who'd arrived empty-handed—a sulky Altitude.

"Uh, where's Cleve?" I inquired, trying to sound casual.

Gneeecey grinned. "Ain't comin'."

My heart sank.

"Cleeevooooveland's workin' through breakfoofas', past bedtime, an' into the enda dinner."

"Doesn't Cleve deserve a little—"

"If Cleeevooooveland came, Stu couldn'a. *Someone* gotta reap the grim harvest while mice make hay. Y'know, a stitch in time saves—"

Nine flinched.

"What I'm trynna say," explained Gneeecey, "is that unpaid overtime is a most noble pursuit. In our Grand Oogitty-Boogitty's *Grand Bookitty of Sayin's*, he says other people workin' hard is character formulizatin'."

Bonbeeederhead nodded. "For *them*."

"An' his tail'll be in our neck of the woods any day now."

"That's as sure," stated Flubbubb, "as the fact that pie are square."

"Pies can't never be square," argued Gneeecey. "They're fulla round three's."

Flubbubb scratched his head. "But, in math class—"

"Forget school—I seen a piece of molderberry pie under one of them new subanatomical moleculizatin' telescopes, an' it was made entirely of stringy green round threes."

A green string theory might certainly explain things. I bit my lip.

"What'chooo laughin' at, Ig?"

"Uh—"

"Speakin' of threes an' their multipooples, I invited Nine here to entertain us."

"Merriment's not cost-efficient," grumbled Bonbeeederhead, knotty legs screeching as Stu shoved him down the corridor.

"I'd never pay anyone to amuserate us," replied Gneeecey. "'Specially not at a Ig's party. Nine owed me."

"Yep," agreed the six-foot-high number, twirling his chrome-yellow cane.

"Y'see," continued Gneeecey, eating a paperclip, "when I updated my menus—y'know, hiked prices for no reason—I didn't round nuthin' off to zero. Didn't eliminizate any nines. Real incornvenient—means I gotta use my dopey head. Plus, I gotta keep purchoochasin' batooteries for my calcoocoolator. But I done it all for Nine, outta sincere friend-shipperism."

"Business and friendship," scowled Bonbeeederhead, "don't mix."

"LET'S GET THIS OVER wit'," said Gneeecey, as the eight of us gathered in front of the dining room's stone fireplace. "Hapoopy hatchday, Ig. An' here's to Esophagus, the Greek god of swallowin'."

Raising delicate Booolabeeezian crystal champagne glasses above their heads, all chanted, "There, there! Where, where? Here, here!" and guzzled their sky blue fizzy drinks noisily.

The cautious sip I took set my sinuses ablaze.

"I love carbonated rindom!" exclaimed Stu, his seven chins shaking. "Happy birthday, Icky!"

"That's *Nicki*."

"Oh, and Icky, I redid that music bed on your Buick commercial. Y'know—the one everyone hated."

"Okay folks," shouted Gneeecey, knocking back the rest of his bubbly. "An' a one an' a two an' a three—"

On the count of three, following their gracious host's lead, Flea, Flubbubb, Altitude, Stu, Nine and Bonbeeederhead smashed their fluted vessels against the fireplace.

It collapsed.

As elephantine gray boulders tumbled, and charcoal clouds of ash swirled toward the ceiling, the goblets rolled about, not so much as a stem broken.

"Your—your—fireplace," I stuttered.

Gneeecey laughed. "Trick glasses, Ig."

The others had begun seating themselves at the mile-long table. Covered by yellow rain slicker-like fabric, it stood in the midst of the otherwise stark, fluorescent-lit room, on a gray-tiled floor. With a shower drain.

"Ooooh!" exclaimed Flubbubb. "I sit nexta 'Zig!"

Gneeecey scrambled over to his rococo mini-throne. "Someone musta moved your lousy place card. *Stuey's* sittin' on my right, an' Bonbeeederhead's on my left."

Gloating, Stu fastened his napkin around his neck, like a bib.

"So," growled Gneeecey, "go siddown by Altitude an' the Ig."

Flubbubb trudged down to the far end and lowered himself into a lawn chair.

"This ain't breakfoofast," warned Gneeecey. "We're only havin' horse divorces an' cake. But we *do* got sevooveral complooplimetary cases of Dalmation Beer."

Stu's face lit up.

"They always donate produc' after it's jus' past its date."

"A real tax write-off," boomed Bonbeeederhead, clapping his crudely-carved hands.

"We do it all the time at Gneeezle's—y'know, donate ol' stuff to customers. But *we* make 'em *pay*."

Bonbeeederhead nearly cracked a wooden smile. "You've learned well."

"An' folks," continued Gneeecey, "we got a bowla Slog punch, too—unfermented, non-alkookaholic. Drink up—bat'room's down the hall. If y'run outta Susan B. Anthonies, I'll make change."

"Heard ya thinking," whispered Flea, leaning close to me. "Don't be so hard on yourself—when y'climbed into 'Zig's Porsche, y'had no idea you'd mess your legs up."

"And now," I answered, glancing about furtively, "even though I finally found my stuff—"

"YOU FOUND YOUR STUFF?!"

"Sssssh—thought you knew *everything*."

"Nah—my ESP's spottier than a leopard wit' measles. But I *do* know you're thinkin' of leavin' before you're ready—"

I shook my head.

"Uh-huh," he said under his breath, shaking his head up and down.

"Mmmm-mmmm," I murmured.

"Will yuz two stop whispooperin'? Ain't polite," admonished our host, wiping his runny honker on the water-repellent tablecloth.

"What should we do first?" asked Stu. "Presents or food?"

"PRESENTS!" everyone yelled, drowning out the grumpy Bonbeeederhead.

Altitude addressed me directly, for the first time. "Nobody tol' me I hadda bring nuthin'."

"Almost didn't," creaked Bonbeeederhead, heaving three packages my way. "But when I spotted these in our stockroom, I realized I could write 'em off."

Forcing a smile, I unwrapped the silver-papered projectiles. Three identical, three-headed Freak O'Nature hawks grinned up at me from three identical, battered boxes. All the Rindom Doodles, Slug Nuts, and Rotzels I could possibly eat. Ever. Times three. "Uh, thanks."

"What a waste," complained Gneeecey, "givin' stuff like that to *her*. She only eats stuff that comes from them vegoogitarian tofoofuaries."

I ripped the containers open. "Please everyone, help yourselves."

Flubbubb popped a doodle into his mouth. "They are stale, Mr. B. But'cha still coulda sold 'em."

Gneeecey shot Flubbubb a withering glance.

"At my job," continued Flubbubb, perking up, "we always sell stale loaves. We have different colored twist ties. Yellow for old, blue for older, green for moldy, an' red for——"

Gneeecey hurled a rock-like Slugnut at Flubbubb, just missing him. "We're so sicka how yuz twist them ties. Bread's moldy by the time y'get to it!"

"That's on accounta most of us being left-handed. Speaking of that, Murgatroyd Music promised to deliver my left-handed triangle in time for our big concert——"

"Y'ain't playin' wit' me an' my voaline——"

"*Violin*," interrupted Flea.

"That's what I said! An' furthoothermore, Flubbubb, y'still think you're better'n us, 'cause *your* family had the only plaid lawn in town!"

Flubbub's disc-like eyes welled up.

Flea leapt up. "Leave him alone!"

Foam spraying from his mouth, Gneeecey flew across the table and grabbed the startled superhero by his throat.

Flea freed himself quickly. As the good diroctor thrashed around, trying to land a punch, he caught his shoelace on the ornate brass candelabra. Down it came, flames and all, setting the purple holiday centerpiece—spray-painted dead rubber chickens—and Gneeecey's behind, on fire.

The rest of us—except for combustible Bonbeeederhead—took turns whacking Gneeecey, in an effort to extinguish the blaze.

After about thirty seconds, the good diroctor plunged his smoldering hindquarters into the overfilled punch bowl, splashing scarlet liquid all over the place. He swore softly as his crossed eyeballs rolled up inside his head.

The stink of burnt fur hung in the air.

FLEA POINTED TO THE dingy hairs floating in the crimson fluid. "We'll hafta dump the punch."

"Why?"

"For Bogelthorpe's sake, 'Zig, you were, uh, *sittin'* in it."

"Awright—break open the Dalmation Beer."

I marveled as Flea poured the milky suds into his mug. Its dime-sized, inky spheres remained evenly suspended.

The superhero took a swig, and in an instant, morphed into a spotted negative of himself.

Gneeecey gulped his down, in two seconds flat.

"Look, 'Zig,'" observed Flea, "your nose is chalk-colored, an' covered wit' dark spots!"

"So's yours! BRAAAAAAAP!"

Gneeecey's white hair had turned black, except for the snowy discs dotting it. His honker matched his ears—as did the formerly-jet fur that capped each side of his head.

"Not bad," he squealed, studying his image in a hand mirror he'd yanked from his shirt pocket. "Good if I hadda, y'know, leave town all of a sudden—unreckookognized."

"You 'spectin' to hafta do that anytime soon?" asked Flea, as Altitude reached past him for a bottle of brew.

"None of your bees' droppin's, Fleaglossittty. An' here, ya underage rat—yooou get a Diet Slog."

Pouting, Altitude snatched the can.

"Now," began Gneeecey, "I hear it's bad luck not to give your host his gifts first."

Bad luck for whom?, I wondered.

"Don't worry, not *you*," replied Flea.

I gaped at the superhero, who watched as everyone but Altitude pelted Gneeecey with purple rubber wallets. The good diroctor scooped them up and hugged them to his chest. My eyes remained fixed on Flea.

He squirmed.

I decided then and there, I'd attempt to block his ESP.

Intertextuality, I thought to myself, concentrating hard. *Intertextuality*. *Intertextuality*.

"Interestin'," answered Flea, glancing my way as he tossed a poop-colored object in Gneeecey's expectant face. "Which novels were you considerin', in terms of literary juxtaposition? For me, *Moby Dick* an' Plato's *Republic* come to mind, although some may say it's a far stretch—"

"Stop," I pleaded. "Please!"

"I minored in lit."

I looked at Flea, amazed.

Gneeecey jumped up onto the tabletop. "SHAAADDUP! Now tell me, Fleaglossitty—"

Flea frowned. "How in Bogelthorpe's name d'ya 'spect me to tell ya anythin' if I hafta shaaaddup?"

"Jus' shaaaddup 'bout everythin' I don't wanna hear an' only answer me what I'm askin' ya to tell me."

Flea crossed his arms. "Well then, tell me what'cha wanna hear so I don't answer ya 'bout what'cha not askin' me to tell ya."

"Now, we're gettin' somewhere," proclaimed Gneeecey, scrutinizing his pal's gift under the fluorescent chandelier's harsh light. "Now, what *is* this bright brown rubber wallet y'threw in my face?"

"Y'jus' answered your own question."

"But it wasn't a answerin' question—it was a askin' question. Now, what is this bright brown rubber wallet y'threw in my face?"

"A bright brown rubber wallet."

"Why din'cha answer the first time?"

"I DID!"

"DID NOT!"

"DID TOO!"

"DID NOT—Y'MADE ME ASK!"

Flea marched over to Gneeecey. "Anybody can see, it's a bright brown rubber wallet."

"Why brown?"

"They say brown's the new purple."

"It is a priddy color, but I can't count it in my final Grimace tally. So, y'wasted your mon-ney."

Flea shuffled back to his seat, past Flubbubb, who grabbed his arm and whispered something about a plan to present a wagonload of purple rubber wallets to Gneeecey, on stage at the Grand Oogitty-Boogitty's concert.

"Maybe *then* he'll appreciate me," concluded the percussionist, loud enough for all to hear.

"Oooooh—can we go in the drawing room?" begged Stu. "Lemme at those crayons an' doodle pads!"

"Flubbubb could draw somethin'," suggested Flea, "an' we could all guess what it is—"

"No," interrupted Flubbubb. "I make a picture, then everyone hasta figure out what I drew—"

"Isn't that what I jus'—"

"Let's play 'Drip Dry' instead," proposed Stu. "We all throw water at the wall an' take bets on whether the drops'll dry before they drip!"

"No," insisted Gneeecey, "we'll watch my video from the Mierk Down Fest an'—WHAAAT THE—"

His half-chewed cigar fell to the floor as a storm of blue-black feathers swished past his snout, shrieking, "NEVERMORE! NEVERMORE!"

"WHICH ONE OF YUZ IGS OPENED THE BAT'ROOM WINDOW?"

Stu blushed.

"WELL, WHOOOOOOO?!"

Spooked by Gneeecey's grating voice, the turkey-sized raven swooped down and plunged its beak into Stu's beer. The intern dove under the table.

As the crow slopped up the drink, he turned snow-white, save for the ebony polka-dots decorating him.

Altitude sprang out of his seat. "Groovical!"

"BORE, BORE, BORE, BORE, MONOTONY! MONOTONY!" screeched Gneeecey's birds, caged in The Grate Room.

Grinning, the mouse grabbed Flea's stein and dashed toward the door.

"DON'CHOOO DARE," bellowed Gneeecey. "Mess wit' my birds an' I'll see to it that'cha end up back in that soup factory, splittin' peas!"

"Reminds of the time we dissected a pea," recalled Flubbubb, as Altitude stomped back to his chair. "In tenth grade. Took five buckets 'fore y'got it right—remember?"

Gneeecey raised his hand to smack Flubbubb, but flopped over Klunkzill, who vroomed past, lunging at the Poe crow as it fluttered around like a demented moth.

Before the good diroctor could uncork his foul mouth, a booming blast shattered our eardrums. "HOLY SAINT BOGELTHORPE!" screamed Gneeecey, flying under the table. "WHAAAT WAS THAT?"

Ozzy and Vizzy charged into the room, jagged hunks of their playroom door impaled on their spikes.

"We'll go after the goths first!" shouted Flea, racing toward them. "They're dangerous! C'mon, 'Zig!"

"How dare ya incinerate that Ozzy an' Vizzy are dangerousical?"

"They *are*!" yelled Nine, whacking Ozzy with his cane as the chrome beast ripped the cape off Flea's neck.

"NEBBERD-KINNEZZARD!" shrilled the corvine, soaring out into the hallway, trailed by Klunkzill, Vizzy, and Ozzy.

As they disappeared, a walleyed kangaroo wearing a skimpy orange-and-purple "KOUNTY BIRD" sweater hopped through the doorway.

THE GETAWAY THAT GOT AWAY —213—

Pouch stuffed with encyclopedias, he made a beeline for the Dalmation Beer.

"THAT SHOULD DO IT," declared Flea, shuffling back into the dining room, Ouch-O Strips plastered all over his face and fingers. "Crow's back out on his ledge, Klunkzill's in the kitchen, kangaroo's back upstairs, an' the goths—"

"I don't think lockin' 'em in the GAZE BOW is a good idea," warned Gneeecey. "What if evil Mr. Tree kidnaps 'em?"

My heart skipped a beat. "Isn't the gazebo too flimsy?"

Gneeecey's jaw tightened. "Y'lousy Ig—if y'weren't afraida them, they could have the runna the house."

"Boss, wait till y'see the giant hole in their door!" exclaimed Stu, breathlessly.

"Yeah," said Flubbubb. "You'll hafta replace it."

Gneeecey's eyes flashed with contempt. "Wouldn't that kinda be like shuttin' the horse's mouth after the barn door escapes?"

The corners of Flubbubb's mouth turned down.

Flea handed me a book. "Anyway, happy birthday, Nickels. This'll fit right into one of your coat pockets."

"Thanks," I replied, admiring my new, compact *Webster's Dictionary*.

"Webster started runnin' outta words by the time he got to the enda the alphoophabet," stated Gneeecey. "Y'ever notice how there's so few words in them las' X, Y an' Z sections?"

Stu's mouth opened in amazement. "Wow, Boss, you know *everything!*"

Altitude puffed out his belly and began mimicking Stu.

"An' Ig," began Gneeecey, ignoring the mouse, "these are for you." He shoved a mountain of packages under my nose.

"For me?"

"Yeah. I kinda gotten used'ta havin' ya 'round—in fac', I hope ya never leave."

I pinched myself. It hurt.

"You do all the work, I get mosta your paycheck. It's almos' like havin' my own indenturated servant."

"I'm touched," I replied, unwrapping what appeared to be a one-armed cardigan. "Oh—a sweater."

"Oooooh, Boss," gushed Stu. "It matches the new wallet Flea gave ya!"

"Yupperooney—it's a lovoovely color. They say it's the new purple. My Aunt ReeeUmpa once knitted my mom a couch in that same shade. Nice, Ig, ain't it?"

It ain't, I thought, biting my lip.

"I put it in a Nurdsen's box," continued Gneeecey, "but I actually got it at OddLottz, 'cause they sell cheap junk. An' they got a humane shoppin' cart policy."

"Really."

"Sweater was originally two bucks, but they marked it down to twenny-five cents. I lef' the tag on in case y'didn't believe me."

"Open the next one, Icky," suggested Stu.

"That's *Nicki*. Hmmmm. . .what an interesting, uh, gift. . . ."

Gneeecey smiled. "It's a comboobination birthday-Grimace present."

The coffee-stained Seemingwhale's box was filled with seven empty wooden spools, a peach pit, and a decomposing hot dog, stuck to a half-melted purple rubber wallet.

"Cleaned out my junk drawer."

"How very thoughtful."

"Open this one nex', Ig."

Three pea-green knit snakes peered up at me from inside a yellow UniGeek's bag. "My, what do we have here?"

"Tail warmers—got 'em on sale in Seemin'whale's, but I put 'em in the UniGeek's bag 'cause I awready used the box they came in for the stuff I gave ya from the junk drawer."

"Which Seemingwhale's?" inquired Flubbubb. "The one on From Road, near To Street?"

"Nah—the other one, up the street from To Road, on the way to From Avenue."

"Oh."

"Nex' year, we'll all chip in an' buy the Ig a tail!"

I groaned. If I was still stuck in Perswayssick County, I'd deserve one.

Flea shot me a sideways glance.

"This las' one's the coop de grass," announced Gneeecey, rubbing his palms together. "Thought you'd enjoy the disapperntment of receivin' it."

Curious, I tore the toilet paper off a Martian's box and lifted its warped lid. My mouth opened wide. "Diroctor, this stuff's already mine!"

"Foun' it in your room."

"*You* were in my *room?!*"

"Lookin' for my sock repair ticket—an' while I was in there not findin' it, I foun' some extra stuff to give ya. Knew you'd like it, bein' it's awready yours."

"How dare you—"

"Look," continued Gneeecey, holding each item up. "Your red sweater, your waste-of-mon-ney deodorant, a toothbrush y'ain't used yet but I tried, plus summa your underwear—"

Altitude snickered as I slammed my possessions back into the box.

"Well," said Gneeecey, "at least y'know it's really yours—y'got it twice."

"Yeah, right."

"Oh, I almos' forgot." He tossed a tangled mess into my lap. "Free gift."

"It's not a gift if isn't free, is it?"

"Could be, Ig."

I raised an eyebrow.

"Irregoogoolars," he whooped. "Three-legged pantyhose—thirteen pairs!" Kelly green, like the ones he hawked on TV.

I said nothing.

"OddLottz's said I could jus' take 'em—said I'd be doin' *them* a favor." He smiled. "See? It was a free gift."

NINE PLACED HIS TOP hat at his feet, upside-down.

"Y'ready to perform?"

"Yes, Diroctor," he answered, as he positioned his cane to his right, with a flourish. "Here goes, all you non-numerals!"

Gneeecey's mouth opened wide. "You're a nineteen!"

Nine laid down his stick and launched himself into an upward trajectory that culminated in a ceiling-grazing somersault. It deposited him headfirst into his hat. The clear headgear created the illusion that he floated a foot off the ground.

"A six!" roared Gneeecey, pounding the tiles with his fists. "I caaan't staaand it!"

Nine picked up his cane and held it to his left.

"A sixteen!" shrieked Stu.

Flubbubb gasped. "Now he's a sixty-one!"

Nine flipped again and landed upright. He looked queasy. "A bit rough on a full stomach," he said, patting his gold cummerbund. "But I'll carry on—"

"You *integer*," barked Gneeecey. "Y'stinkin' better not—"

Flea and Flubbubb gawked at their pal.

"I *am* a whole number, factored by myself, plus a distinguished prime, and One, who humors me by standing in as my patient sidekick, enabling me to parody double-digits," declared Nine, raising his walking stick. "And that he does faithfully, rather than exercising his more, I'm sure, preferable prerogative, that of recusing himself from these proceedings, hilariously colorful as they might be."

Gneeecey chucked a bucketful of Styrofoam peanuts at the numeral. "Go home and square yourself!"

Nine's face glowed a deep orange. "I shall not discuss exponents— or any of my rather fascinating multiples."

Twirling his cane, the digit leapt into the air and hovered, for a split second, before executing a quadruple-flip and touching down lightly, as a ninety-one.

Flea clung to me, doubled over.

Flubbubb fell to his knees. "Be sixteen again!"

"No!" yelled Gneeecey. "Not in *my* dinin' room!"

"That's it, folks," proclaimed Nine, dusting himself off.

Everyone clapped, except Bonbeeederhead, who snored in a corner, a frilly, rose-colored lampshade topping his knobby noggin.

Knowing I hated eating noises, Gneeecey shoved a handful of packing peanuts into his yapper and, smiling triumphantly, crunched them in my face.

"You don't eat that!" I exclaimed, aghast, as the others crammed fistfuls into their mouths.

Flea tugged gently on my sleeve. "My good friend," he said, chomping, "the questions *are* the answers."

Silly me.

"Uh, t-to whadda w-we owe the p-pleasure of your visoositation?" stuttered Gneeecey, as blond, big-nosed Mark and tall, brown-haired Mark swaggered into the disaster of a dining room.

"We let ourselves in," replied the dark-haired Markman. "Livin' room window was open. As usual."

"Well now, whadda we got here?" inquired the blond, surveying the scene.

His humorless buddy stomped his cigarette out on the floor. "Decadent debauchery, no doubt."

"Yup," agreed the other one, adjusting the strap on his canvas backpack. "You'd think Doc had more important stuff to worry 'bout, these days."

"We—we was jus' havin' a hatchday party for the Ig," stammered Gneeecey. "Guess it *is* a waste of time."

The gray-suited men glared at me, then turned to him. "We were in the area," said the yellow-haired one, "an' we needed the bat'room."

"Yuz certaintaineously know where it is. Here's a coupla Susan B. Anthonies."

"An' Doc, we fixed that ticket for ya—the one that punk Imbroglio issued ya."

"Y'mean when all the milk spilt?"

"Yeah, that would be it. An' we fixed Imbroglio, too. He handed in his badge."

"Yeah," said brown-haired Mark. "We kinda, heh, heh, ripped it offa his shirt."

"Glad yuz got ridda him, but I can, y'know, fix my own tickets— me bein' the all-powerful Grate Gizzy an' all," replied Gneeecey, a trace of humiliation evident in his tone. "Hadda good defense—low blood glucosamine."

"Whatever."

Gneeecey held out a tray of vintage, cream-topped Matchbox-like cars. "Want a horse divorce? I call these 'Trafooofic Jam in a Blizzard.' Used whoop cream from last year's first snowfall."

Gingerly, Flubbubb reached for a froth-slathered, red-and-white '57 Chevy.

Gneeecey slapped his hand, and the car crashed to the tiles. A tiny wheel flew off and rolled out of sight.

"Look what'cha done, y'dope!"

Flubbubb stooped to pick it up. "Sorry, 'Zig—I didn't mean to—"

"SIDDOWN! I was ofooferatin' these to Mark an' Mark—not yoooou!"

Flubbubb backed away slowly, looking daggers at the Markmen. Altitude sneered, overjoyed to see him spurned once more.

Jaw clenched, the golden-haired percussionist watched as blond Mark devoured a green '66 Chevy Nova and brown-haired Mark wolfed down a white '75 Caddy.

Licking their fingertips, the two headed for the Electronic Water Cyclone.

"Okay folks," announced Gneeecey, "time for cake!"

Everyone scrambled back to the table. I didn't know Stu could move so fast.

Gneeecey slid a lopsided tower of gray, half-baked batter under my chin. "Made it myself. Cheaper."

"Uh, thanks."

"The half wit' soap flakes an' salt that was in the colder parta the oven rose up an' sunk after the other half—wit' the lard an' rotzelberry rind—rose," he explained. "That's why it came out a little uneven. Stinkin' make your little Ig wish an' blow out the candles."

Squeezing my lids shut, I made my wish.

When I opened my eyes, I saw Flea pouting.

"BLOW OUT THE CAAAANDLES AWREADY, YA IG!"

There were only three. Three puny, purple candles.

I took a deep breath and blew. And blew. And blew and blew and blew.

Gneeecey could barely speak. "HEH HAAH, HEH HAAAH—TRICK CAAAANDLES!"

"WHAT'D THE CUSTOMER SAY," asked Gneeecey, "when the waiter spilled soup in his lap?"

Flea shrugged. "Dunno."

"There's soup on my fly! Get it?"

The superhero yawned. "Yeah. Uh-huh. Ha, ha."

"Did'ja know," interrupted Flubbubb, "chocolate's a vegetable?"

"An' so are yooou," growled Gneeecey.

I stared into space. This would be a rough day for my family. I rolled a red, cream-laden '65 Corvette down the table. "Still can't believe you guys eat these."

"Ig, y'ain't seen nuthin'. Once I devooverated a whole motorcycle."

I sat up straight.

"He had help, as I recall," piped in Flea. "'Zig, Flubbsickles an' me were sophomores at the University of Hardenoxx, back on our planet. Crammin' for finals—pretty stressed out."

Gneeecey swallowed the Corvette. "Sophoophomoronic stress."

"One night, we put down our books—for Flubbsickles and me, it was lit an' conversational Booolabeeezian, and for 'Zig it was marketin' an' proctology. We went down to Rasputin's Revenge to grab a bite."

Sighing wistfully, Gneeecey crammed bubble packing into his mouth. "That was Bozovia's most popoopular hangout for collogical kids. Best-tastin' hardware this side of the universe—we at Gneeezle's still ain't come close to dooplooplicatin' their secret recipoopeys."

"Anyway," continued Flea, "we ordered coffee, to stay awake."

"Then we got hungry," said Gneeecey.

Flea chuckled. "We ordered a custom Harley Sportster—cherry red, chrome-plated."

"An' you guys convinced me to put the whole tab on my folks' EccchsCorp credit card," added Flubbubb.

Gneeecey grunted. "We stinkin' paid for it in the end. That nex' summer, we hadda work it off at Camp Bingaboonga—"

"That's on our moon Cronon—"

"Stop interrupticatin', Fleaglossitty! As I was sayin', we spent the whole crummy summer cleanin' orgnocks."

I pushed away my uneaten slice of cake. "Orgnocks?"

Gneeecey glared at me as if the whole thing had been my fault. "Cronese latrines."

"That Harley had a 1200 cc engine," remembered Flea, reaching for a doodle. "The three of us picked all night—finished off the whole bike."

"Hadda floss with steel cable that night," recalled Flubbubb.

I laughed. "Like I said, I can't believe the stuff you eat. Look at the gray rocks you're munching on, Dir100r. Package says, 'Avoid contact with mouth.'"

"That's a disclaimer—y'can't take them serious. Even transmission fluid'll make y'sick if y'drink too much. Yuz Earthlin's are the weird ones."

"Don't Earth people name their kids after hurricanes?"

"Yupperooney, Flubberooney, they certaintaineously do."

"Really?" Stu's open, cake-filled mouth resembled an overstuffed, front-loading washer, as its contents revolved in full view.

"Her people even named one of their presidents after a vacuum cleaner. Or was it a resoosevoover? Musta been Hoovoover Resoosevoover, 'cause it rhymes."

"Leave her planet alone, 'Zig," ordered Flea, tilting backwards in his chair.

"Bust my chair an' I'll send ya up in one of them heloolicopters you're so afraida."

Stu flew out of his seat. "Can I fly it? Pleeeeeeeease?"

"An' furthoothermore, Ig," added Gneeecey, paying his intern no mind, "a chicken witnessed your whole sky fallin'."

"Any of you guys," interrupted Flubbubb, "hear 'bout that headless chicken named Sievehead, over in Cashville? The one wit' the plastic funnel stuck down his neck?"

"For Bogelthorpe's sake, I was makin' a point—"

"They say after living on diet lemonade while tap dancing to belly-dancing music for forty-five days, he laid a egg an' bit the crust!"

"Y'dope—"

"Bye, Doc," sang Mark and Mark, poking their faces through the doorway.

Gneeecey waved a trembling hand. "Want some cake 'fore y'go?"

"Nah," answered the blond, slinging his knapsack over his shoulder. "See ya at the meetin'."

Brown-haired Mark stuffed a bottle of Dalmation Beer in his pocket. "Let's hope y'got'cha act together by then."

"I will! I aaaam! I mean, I promised yuz!"

"We'll let ourselves out. As usual."

"Thanks again," stammered Gneeecey, as he bit up and down his arm, spitting out clumps of fur, "for thinkin' of me when yuz needed the bat'-room!"

"We always do."

"Don't know if I'll make this next meeting," said Bonbeeederhead, stretching his stiff oaken arms. "I'm being refinished."

"I hope y'can make it—they're persecutin' us. We're jus' trynna protect our way of life!"

"Don't worry, Diroctor—things usually stay the way they are."

Altitude tapped Gneeecey's shoulder. "Know what I heard, Boss?"

"What?"

"We're gonna have competition."

"Compoopetition? What'cha mean, Mouse?"

The rodent yanked a thread from his jersey. "I overhearded this guy who got outta this shiny black limo tellin' Mr. Qwertyuiop that a Rasputin's Revenge is openin' on Murgatroyd Avenue, 'cross the street from Gneeezle's—right after Grimace."

"WHAAAAAAAAAAAAAAAAAAAAAAAAAAAAAAAAAAAAAT?!"

CHAPTER 27

MY VERY EDUCATED MOTHER JUS' SERVED US NUTHIN'

YAWNING, I WATCHED OUR guests stagger into the hallway. It was almost time to get up for dinner. The table lay overturned, near what had been the fireplace. A chandelier no longer hung overhead—Gneeecey and Stu had ripped it out of the ceiling, reenacting Tarzan episodes. I sat atop a stool and gazed out the dining room's one slit of a window, at Cleve's blue star.

He had called to remind me that we'd have our own celebration. And he mentioned, rather casually, that someone had messed with his brake lines. But not to worry—he'd fixed them himself.

And Ethan, who he'd seen the day before, would be on the case.

"Hey, Ig!"

My tall seat nearly toppled.

"What'cha lookin' for out there? Your dumb planet?"

"Stop raggin' on Earth," admonished Flea.

Gneeecey kicked an empty Diet Slog can across the room.

"Flea," I half-whispered, "I see *three moons* out there—and I didn't drink anything but water."

"There are three," he replied. "One's yours, an' the other two are our twin moons, Cronon an' FishVendor 4."

Maybe Cleve's star *was* Earth. I was afraid to ask. Or even think it too loudly.

"FishVendor 4," added Flea, eyeing Gneeecey, "is home to several re-form facilities for selfish people."

Gneeecey hurled a bent fork Flea's way.

"An' the only day outta the whole year," continued a ducking Flea, "that y'can see all three moons happens to be your birthday."

Squinting, I studied the silvery spheres.

"They float through each other when their orbits converge—somethin' to do wit' negative Blirgular particulization."

"It's when the perceptabooble gravoovitational pull of our moons is intensified expooponentially by the interdimensional factorization of the transgressor planet," added Gneeecey, smiling smugly. "An' that transgressor planet is Earth!"

"'Zig—"

"Her people go 'round wreckin' worlds!"

"C'mon, Diroctor—"

"Yuz Earthlin's don't even realize how lucky yuz are. Our planet rotates a zillion times faster'n yours. We've hadda live wit' stuff fallin' offa shelves, for boingtangs."

I looked at him. "*Boingtangs?*"

"Sort of like your centuries," explained Flea. "But longer."

"Planet Eccchs was always fulla broken knickknacks," continued Gneeecey, "an' folks were always floppin' over slippery frippery. But our top engineers divlopped the advanced tekooknology to build tilted shelves. *Yuz* couldn't even deal wit' Y2K."

"Oh, we dealt with it—"

He spat on the floor. "An' now that yuz demoted that bag-of-ice Pluto, what'll Earth kids say? My very educated mother jus' served us *nuthin'*?!"

"'Zig—"

Gneeecey's eyes bulged out of their sockets. "Now her kids get nuthin' to eat insteada the nine stinkin' pizzas she used'ta serve 'em!"

I imagined that pretending to be nice to me for an entire day had gotten to the good diroctor.

"You're right, Nickels," whispered Flea. "He couldn't handle it."

"One day, Ig," screamed Gneeecey, through the same twitching lips that had once, presumably, smooched Goonafina Blopperdang's, "your crummy sun'll be free of all its orbitin' debris. It'll fizzle out an' leave yuz in the dark—"

"*Our* planet," interrupted Flea, "was actually the transgressor."

"You're WRONG, Fleaglossitty—they devooviated from THEIR course an' crashed into US! When it comes to scientical junk, y'got everythin' bimbus-backwards—as usual."

"No, 'Zig—it's true—"

"You're jus' lyin' 'cause it's her stoopid hatchday!"

Flea turned to me. "Your sparklin' blue planet looked so lush an' invitin', even from halfway across the universe."

Gneeecey clenched his fists. "IT DID NOT!"

The superhero tilted his head thoughtfully. "Us Eccchsers were more'n a little surprised when we finally saw Earth close-up."

"How's that?" I asked.

"From space, you'd never dream that such a jewel of a planet was fulla moldy shower curtains, expired dairy products, an' folks stealin' bicycles."

"Plus," yelled Gneeecey, arms revolving like a whirligig, "so many drinkin' glasses comin' outta dishwashers wit' SPOTS on 'em!"

Flea picked his shredded cape up off the floor. "Bad night, or whatever it is, 'Zig. I'm heading' home. An' happy birthday again, Nickels— hope your legs feel better."

I'd hoped he *knew* my legs would feel better.

Gneeecey trudged over to the one candelabra that had, miraculously, landed upright when he tackled Altitude. Its remaining lit candle cast long shadows. Winking, Gneeecey puckered up and, with ease, blew out the flame.

I broke out into a cold sweat.

CHAPTER 28

YES, THE GRASS *DOES* MIND

HE'S MISSIN'! MIIIIIIISSSSSSSIN'!" I raised my head. There, framed in FM's doorway, stood Gneeecey. "*Who*," I asked, not really wanting to know, "is missing?"

"YAAAMMICLES!"

Before I could dive under the console, he flew at me, fists revolving.

"Whaddaya think you're—"

"YAAAMMICLES IS MISSIN'!" Gneeecey pressed his face into mine. His breath was putrid enough to knock out a sumo wrestler with sinus problems. "KIDNAPPED!"

"Well, don't take it out on me—"

"I'm priddy sure yooou know somethin' 'bout this," he screeched, pulling my hair. "An' y'better tell me 'fore I—"

I grabbed him. "GET OFFA ME—"

"Boss," called Stu, waddling into the room, "sorry to interrupt your conversation with Icky. Police are on line three."

Gneeecey hopped down off my shoulders. "Bet they foun' him!"

"Oh, an' Boss, y'seen Cleve? He's not here yet—I was s'posed to go home ten minutes ago."

"I'll double-dock him!" Gneeecey snatched the phone up off the counter. "Mark? Tell me y'foun' him! Y'did? Where?"

Gneeecey's face went ashen—through his fur. "*WHAAAT?!*"

"Hey, Icky, shouldn't the boss look happier?"

I shrugged. "You'd think so—"

Gneeecey winced. "In the river? *Dead?*"

Stu began biting his stubby nails.

"Don't worry," I assured the intern, "after the, uh, boss pops him into the washing machine, he'll come out looking good as new—"

The receiver dropped to the floor and Gneeecey stumbled back-

ward, into the CD player airing The Asthmatics' "Holdin' My Breath."
The song began skipping.

I reached over to steady the machine. "They found him?"

Stu's voice rose several octaves. "In the *river*?"

Gneeecey's usually-jabbering yapper opened wide. But no words
spewed forth.

I crossed my arms. "Well? They found him?"

"They stinkin' foun' *Cleve*. Floatin' in the river. Dead."

THE ACRID SMELLING SALTS jolted me conscious. Sprawled flat on my
back in the FM studio, I peered up, through swollen slits, at Gneeecey
and a cop.

"C'mon, miss. Like I said, y'got questions to answer."

"Yeah, Ig—stop faintin'!"

"I—I wish to invoke my Miranda rights," I stammered.

"Fuggeddaboudit—ain't no lady runnin' 'round here wit' fruit on
her head," replied Gneeecey.

"Now," continued the young Markman, "what was your car doin' at
the scene of this, uh, mishap?"

"It couldn't have been mine," I insisted, still too numb to process
what I'd been told. Surely, Cleve was in the next studio, and in a few
minutes, we'd be laughing and swigging antacid.

"It *was* your vehicle."

"Yeah," agreed Gneeecey, moving closer to Mark.

"Miss, I'm losin' patience."

Gneeecey nodded. "That's why I switched from medicine to entre-
preneutership."

The Markman's yellow irises bored through me. "We found *your*
Splodge on the riverbank, yards from where Wheeler was floatin', face
down—"

"My car's been in the shop for days—Zeke himself can't even get it to
start—"

Gneeecey turned to Mark. "She knows 'bout Yammicles, too."

I groaned. "Can't you both just leave me alone?"

The cop snickered. "She's gonna pretend to pass out again."

Gneeecey kicked my arm. "This time, it better be for real."

Mark gritted his fake-looking teeth. "Look, miss, that '75 Splodge
is yours—vehicle identification number matches up."

"Diroctor—tell him—*you* know my car's been sitting at Zeke's for days! I've been with you all that time—never out of your sight!" I dabbed at my suddenly wet eyes with a disintegrating tissue.

Gneeecey remained silent.

"There were Rindom Doodles on your seat," said Mark. "Medical examiner says someone—probably you—was feedin' Wheeler doodles till he began chokin'. We found 'em stuck in his throat. Then he jumped into the Perswayssick an' proceeded to drown himself."

Energized by rage, I leapt to my feet and jammed my face in the Markman's. "That's the most ridiculous crap I've ever heard! I've just lost my best friend—someone better tell *me* what happened!"

"Funny," mumbled Gneeecey. "Cleeevoooveland always said he wouldn't be caught dead eatin' a Rindom Doodle. . .yet he *was*. . . ."

THE NEXT AFTERNOON, I limped through Thistlethwaite Memorial Home's lobby, watery eyes fixed on the sea-green Oriental rug.

"C'mon, Nickels," said Flea, chin trembling, "he's in there—Room Three—"

I froze. A sleek, steel-gray casket—a dark-suited figure reposed inside—glistened at the far end of the spacious room, bathed in the golden glow of an enormous brass chandelier.

A hint of embalming fluid hung in the chilly air, mingling with an almost oppressive floral fragrance. Eerie music piped softly through ceiling speakers.

As we entered, I tightened my arm around the superhero's shoulders, and we inched forward, past rows of cherry wood chairs, our feet cushioned by plush indigo carpet.

Then I raised my head. And gasped.

"Whattssamatter, Ig?" shrilled an all-too-familiar voice.

Jaw dropping, I pointed to the coffin. "My God—somebody *close* that!"

"That, uh, happens when you've, y'know, been in water too long," whispered Flea, squeezing my hand and looking away.

Laid out in front of us was a hideously bloated man, stuffed into a navy suit—recognizable only by his monogrammed maroon tie and distinctive wristwatch. The one with the white-gold band and rectangular, ultramarine face.

The one that Gneeecey tore off the deceased, with gusto. "No use buryin' this baby!" he shrieked, as he slammed the lid shut. The ensuing metallic thunderclap sliced through the stillness.

"Well, he don't need to know what time it is no more."

Flea snatched the timepiece from Gneeecey and handed it to me. "Cleve would've wanted *Nicki* to have this."

Stifling a sob, I slipped the watch onto my wrist.

A STRICKEN MARY SHISSKEY knelt in front of Cleve's coffin. "He was a lovely man."

Unable to speak, Burt just grunted.

Gneeecey chuckled. "I certaincerely hope nobody never says nuthin' like that 'bout meee."

"Don't worry, Boss. Nobody never will," replied Altitude, shredding a yellow pencil in his fangs, as the Shisskeys filed out, heads bowed.

Gneeecey's eyes shot down to the pile of shavings that had accumulated at Altitude's feet. "Mouse, I'd watch where I displayed that rodential heritage. If they charge *me* for cleanin' up that mess, I'll decapitate it from your pay."

Unmoved, Altitude continued grinding away.

Tears trailed down my cheeks as memories of my dad's untimely death rushed back. He had drowned, too. In the Atlantic, one perfect August afternoon. *Luis Rodriguez Loses Life Saving Son*, read our local paper's headline.

"I heard," began Altitude, glancing Cleve's way, "he shot himself in the head—fifteen times!"

"Didn't know he had a gun," replied Stu, as he squirmed in a tan polyester suit, several sizes too large.

"I heard it was a computer-assisted suicide," chimed in Flubbubb, knocking over a huge spray of white lilies.

"Stop passin' rumors like y'was passin' gas," admonished Gneeecey. "Cleeevooveland choked on Rindom Doodles an' he couldn't stand the pain so bad, he drownded himself to death in the Perswayssick."

"*Really?*" asked Flubbubb, as he bumped the casket. "Oooops— sorry, Cleve!"

"Ya dope—Cleeevoooveland hates when people bump him!"

Flubbubb backed away, upsetting another floral arrangement.

"An' there's more," announced Gneeecey.

Altitude, Flubbubb and Stu gawked at him, expectantly.

"Well," Gneeecey continued, flashing a conspiratorial grin, "Mark an' them foun' the Ig's Splodge by where Cleeevooveland drownded himself! An' they foun' Rindom Doodles all over her seats!"

The four looked my way, brows raised.

Head held high, I stared back.

Gneeecey spat his chewed-up cigar onto the carpet. "Mouse, gimme a burger."

Altitude lobbed a small, greasy package in his boss's direction.

"Lousy throw," complained Gneeecey, nose honking as he ran into the ivory grass cloth wall. "Got fries?"

My blood was boiling. So was Flea's. He rose slowly and strode over to the foursome, who stood gobbling up mini-jackass burgers, directly underneath an unobtrusive sign that read, "No Food or Drink Permitted."

Flea whisked Altitude's soda off the casket. "Don'choo people have any respect? Or manners?"

Gneeecey threw his half-eaten patty down at Flea's feet. "*You're* the one who ain't got no stinkin' manure, shoutin' in a house of dead people! You'll wake 'em!"

"'Zig—"

"Can'cha see? I'm worried 'bout Yammicles! BRAAAAAP!"

Flea jabbed an index finger in Gneeecey's chest. "Your breath stinks of fermented Slog!"

Before Gneeecey could answer, the black-suited, white-haired Thornton Thistlethwaite himself—a lanky skeleton of a man—appeared.

His dusky, sunken eyes settled on the good diroctor. "Excuse me," he began, in a voice barely audible. "Is there a problem?"

"Nah, Sistleswaiths, everythin's jus' groovical," replied Gneeecey, smacking the coffin. "I'm the self-appointed executioner of his estate. Give ol' Cleeevooveland here anythin' he asks for—'cept a Rindom Doodle, of course."

"Y'THINK," ASKED FLUBBUBB, CLIMBING up the tombstone-dotted hill, "the grass minds when we walk on it?"

"It might," replied Gneeecey, as he tossed a crystal salt shaker over his left shoulder. "It's proboobably the only thing alive here at St. Vlad's—'cept for *us*."

Flubbubb's spinning eyes widened. "I better walk softer."

"Whatever works for you." Gneeecey threw his half-eaten cigar to the ground, hopped three times on each foot, jumped twice, spun clockwise, then counterclockwise, and clapped his hands, chanting, "One potato, two potatoes, three potatoes, four, rub-a-dub-dub, five ghosts in a tub, Mother, Father, spirits won't bother—spilt salt in a cemetery's no one's fault!"

My calves began to cramp. As I slowed to a stop, my eyes wandered over to the graveyard's spiked gates, and the meandering Perswayssick. This day, the river resembled unflushed toilet water.

Shivering, I resumed my ascent, startled when the city's skyline popped up, larger than life, on my right. The skyscrapers always reminded me of hypodermics. Rows of them, standing on end.

The City of Screams. That's what Cleve and I called it.

"Y'didn't bury him without me, did'ja?" inquired a sweaty, red-faced Stu, as he tripped over his sleeves.

"Nah," answered Gneeecey, chewing gum noisily. "Like in life, he ain't goin' nowheres till *I* stinkin' say he is."

"'Zig,'" called out Flea, regarding him with pure disgust, "I jus' realized—back at Thistlethwaite's, on that easel, all the photos were of you. Not one of Cleve. Whazzup wit' that?"

Gneeecey sucked a collapsing super-bubble back into his snout. "He worked for meee all these years."

"A POLICE IS RIDIN'" a horsey up the hill," observed Gneeecey, as he stuck his wad of gum on a headstone. "Soon I'll be ridin' one, too—in that parade after the big concert!"

An orange-haired Markman—the same creep who had interrogated me—galloped over atop a piebald steed. "Miss, don't leave town."

"Don't worry," barked Gneeecey. "She ain't goin' nowheres till *I* stinkin' say she is."

Before I could protest, scores of Markmen motorcycled into our midst.

"M-Mark," stammered Gneeecey, gnawing on his wrist. "An' Mark, Mark an' Mark! Didn't know yuz cared."

"We do," answered blond, big-nosed Mark. "More'n ya know."

Gneeecey pointed to Cleve's casket. "Can yuz guys do me a favor?"

"Depends, Doc."

"Could yuz open up that caskooket an' make sure Yammicles ain't inside?"

Thornton Thistlethwaite stepped forward. "Excuse me, Dir.ector. As funeral director, and as the individual who prepared Mr. Wheeler, and checked the coffin forty-nine times, at your request, I personally guarantee that no one else—and *nothing* else—is inside there, except for Mr. Wheeler."

"Pleeeease, Sistleswaiths," cried Gneeecey, wringing his hands, "help me out here, an' I promise, I'll throw a little business your way—"

"Consider the coffin—and the matter—closed," snapped the mortician, as he tapped his watch. "It's already midday. The interment must be completed by eleven-thirty."

Four hard-hatted men stood nearby, leaning on shovels.

I clicked Cleve's locket open. A lump rose in my throat as I glanced down at his smiling face, then at the cold metal box that contained him.

His grandmother and sister had no idea that anything was amiss, and wouldn't, until he didn't call. Or until I did. And what would I say? Cleve's death was as senseless as his parents'—the cops never did find out who mowed them down, that sultry summer night, years ago, on the Grand Concourse. I squeezed my lids shut, as if doing so could make it all go away.

"Look at her neckooklace!" shouted Gneeecey. "I knew all along— the Ig an' Cleeevoooveland had somethin' goin'! Well, they won't be fraternalizatin' no more!"

"They might be," said blond, big-nosed Mark, "if she don't come clean."

Gneeecey smirked. "Cleeevoooveland couldn't swim, an' she can't neitherwise. Watch out, Ig—hangman's sharpenin' his ax! Whaaat, Fleaglossitty—why're y'lookin' at me like that?"

GNEEECEY YANKED A CRUMPLED sheet of paper out of his T-shirt pocket. "I am now gonna deliver the urology."

Flubbubb blew his honking nose and raised a fist into the air. "Cleve is dead—long live Cleve!"

"What's *that* stinkin' mean?"

"That's what Earth folks say when kings die—"

"This ain't Earth." Gneeecey squinted my way, hatefully. "Let's get this over wit' so we don't gotta pay them dirt shovelers overtime. Okay, we're gathered here to say a final g'bye to our good fiend, Cleeevoooveland."

Flubbubb sobbed softly into Flea's cape.

"So," continued Gneeecey, "y'might be wonderin' why we didn't give

Cleeevoooveland no ceremony at Saint Bogelthorpe's. Well, those of us who knew him good know he didn't like standin' on ceremonies."

That scene played back in my head, of Cleve mashing food into Gneeecey's tabletop with his sneaker. "Let's not stand on ceremony," he'd said. "Let's stand on this instead."

"Ig—y'think it's funny?"

My half-smile became a jaw-clenching scowl.

"Anyways," continued Gneeecey, as he cleared his throat, "I thought we'd skip all that mess so's we could put him to sleep quicker an' get back to the restaurant for the finger san'wiches Altitude has managed to prepooperate, wit' such short notice."

Slumped up against a gravestone, the bimbus-scratching mouse beamed. "Had less'n twenny-four hours to make 'em!"

"So, Cleeevooveland, rip—whatever *that* means—an' don't let the bedbugs bite." Gneeecey glanced down at his watch. "Okay, guys—y'can go ahead an' deep-six him, now."

"This is gettin' horribuller and horribuller," blubbered Flubbubb.

The four gravediggers trudged over to Cleve's casket and threw down their shovels. Positioning themselves with precision, they lowered him into the ground.

Flea caught me as my legs buckled.

CHAPTER 29

BAD DAY AT THE OFFICE

GRIEF PULSED, LIKE A caustic fluid, through the chambers of my raw heart. I tried to convince myself that Cleve and I were only working different shifts, and in a few minutes, we'd bump into each other, just long enough to share a joke or a hug. Or a grievance.

Whenever that fragile fantasy crumbled, or some trivial, everyday thing reminded me of him—a swig of antacid, a good cup of coffee, or a song we'd made fun of—I'd end up hightailing it to the restroom.

Cleve hadn't been buried for twenty-four hours.

Those who might have been able to help me get to the bottom of what really happened—like Frank Salvador or the Imbroglios—were missing in action. Or having their own problems, like Flea, whose ESP now malfunctioned ninety-nine per cent of the time.

As for my mysteriously mobile Splodge, Zeke said that someone had authorized its release a couple days before Cleve's death, but he couldn't— make that wouldn't—tell me more.

Meatball maven Ingabore Scriblig had just, this day, sold me her elderly Aunt Cookitha's only-driven-to-St. Bogelthorpe's-on-Somedays Splodge Nebulizer—a slightly newer, more compact model than my missing monstrosity. Grayish-pink, or "grink," as Mrs. Scriblig described it, it had smaller fins and less rust.

But like its predecessor, it was allergic to wet weather, frigid temperatures, stop-and-go traffic, and, as Mrs. Scriblig had also warned me, anything but the highest grade fuels. And it was prone to backfiring. I couldn't complain, though—I'd paid pennies for it. Didn't want to dig too deeply into my 10G for a ride I'd be ditching soon.

In less than a week, right after the Oogitty-Boogitty's concert— during the pre-parade confusion—I planned to steal away and attempt a return home. I'd be gone by Decvember 1st.

Stomach flip-flopping, I gazed at the outvoices heaped on Fraxinella's still unmanned desk. According to Gneeecey, they were my fault, too.

Speaking of Gneeecey, things weren't going all that well for him either.

Neither Yammicles nor his sock repair ticket were anywhere to be found. But he did discover his goths, the misty morning of Cleve's funeral, frozen in combat, their cast-iron inner fangs and twenty-three collective metallic limbs tangled and rusted, under the tree that stalked him night and day.

Their demise was my fault, too. If it wasn't for me, the flesh-eatin' little darlings could have had the run of the house after they demolished their new, priority-delivered and installed plate-armored playroom door.

But, as they say, when one door shatters, another opens. Recently, Twisty the Tornado, an associate of evil Mr. Tree, had entered our lives.

Only Gneeecey could actually see the grinning, spinning, chin-high funnel cloud. And he seemed to be its lone victim, mercilessly blown about Bimbus Crack Drive's rolling, plaid acres when no one else was around.

Chalking it up to anxiety, his neurologist, Dr. Idnas, had bumped his

Bumpex up 2,000 milligrams.

As for anxiety, there was no shortage. Pro-345 environmentalists, and just plain, disenchanted citizens, picketed outside the Vompt Pavillion daily, since the Quality of Life meeting.

Their bullhorns blasted loud and clear, all the way up to our building's 250th floor, right through WGAS's supposedly soundproof walls, and interfered with live programming.

Also heard 'round the county were more than a few whispers, calling for the resignation of Grate Gizzy You-Know-Who, and the appointment of Jacob J. Qwertyuiop, to finish out his blighted term.

Tragedy had even struck inside the mansion, when Flea hung Gneeecey's prized acoustic Stradivopoulos on what turned out to be a fly on the wall. Freaked out, the superhero had dashed through a closed window. Like a duck on fire.

Speaking of ducks, Culvert, released from the hospital earlier than expected, had just called to inform Gneeecey that he had found himself a less stressful job on some farm in New Peapack, closing turkeys' mouths when it rained.

I shook my head and plucked an outvoice from the top of the pile, and scanned the "fourth and final" notice stapled to it, threatening to refer the matter to a collection agency. Why would we contest a 5.95 invoice from Dinwiddie's Inflatable Squeak Toys & Broadcast Supplies? Oh, well, *whatever*. . .I reached for a pen.

"IG!" shrieked Gneeecey.

Exhaling slowly, I traipsed into his office, for the nineteenth time. Since lunch.

As soon as I opened my mouth to ask what he wanted, his phone rang.

"Bad mornin'," he hollered into the mouthpiece. "Yeah, Gregoogory . . .uh-huh. . .we're adjusticatin' to the bigger workload. Thank Bogelthorpe I got someone like Stu, now that Cleeevoooveland's desiccated." Gneeecey glared at me.

Through stinging tears, I glared back.

"Uh-huh. . .thanks for your 'spressions of grimpoopathy—an' thank everyone at the Board of Guesstimates for the fruit basket. G'bye."

I tilted my head. "Grimpoopathy?"

"Yeah, Ig—comboobination of grief an' sympoopathy."

"Now, uh, what did you want?"

"NUTHIN'! Why're y'standin' there? Git back to work—look at all them outvoices!"

His hotline began wailing. I looked at him like I'd never seen him before.

"GIT!" he ordered me.

I returned to Fraxinella's desk.

"IG! GET IN HERE!"

Teeth clenched, I marched back into his office. "*Yessssss?*"

"Remember my last visit to the opoophthalmologist?"

"*Yessssss.*"

"I memorized that eye chart for NUTHIN'!" he shouted, spraying me with spittle.

"What," I asked, recoiling, "is the problem?"

He leapt up onto his desk. "MY NEW GLAAAAASSES AIN'T NO GOOD!"

Just then, I noticed he'd put his socks on over his sneakers. And they didn't match.

"I CAAAN'T REEEEEEEAD!"

"Uh, Diroctor, I think you, uh, put on your, uh—"

"I KNOW my socks don't match—now read this e-mail for me!"

"This message saying your support group for ex-laxative abusers meets today?"

"NOT THAAAAAT ONE," he yowled, yanking on my sleeve. "THI-IIIIS ONE!"

My eyebrows shot up. "It says the MierkoZurk stocks you swore you never owned, but recently divested and put in Flubbubb's name—behind his back—are plummeting."

Knotty veins popped out, visible beneath his fur.

I backed away, slowly. "When you thought you'd be found out, you put 'em in Flubbubb's name, without even asking him?"

"Jus' till this 345 mess blows over. He's a natural for a straw man—he ain't got no brain!"

I crossed my arms. "Isn't that called cheating?"

"Only if y'look at it that way."

"I think *I'm* beginning to put some of the pieces together, now."

"GET OUTTA HERE! AN' WHO TOL' YOU TO READ MY LOUSY E-MAILS ANYWAYS?" He slammed his door so hard, the glass panel popped out and exploded before it hit the carpet.

GNEEECEY SAT PERUSING *SPLOGGLE Digest,* unaware that the publication was positioned upside-down, as were his new glasses.

Sighing, I reached for a stapler.

"IG! GET IN HERE—NOOOW!"

I groaned.

"Don'chooo understanderate the meanin' of NOW?!"

I stepped over what had been his office door.

He hurled his spectacles across the room. "Din'cha think I'd find out 'bout your little plan to rent that room over that Scriblig woman's meatball shop?"

I gaped at him.

He stuffed a cigar in his kisser. "Well, y'can forget it—her tenant ain't leavin' after all. Seems *someone* convinced the guy he should stay."

I stared down at the maroon pleather pumps I'd bought in OddLottz the other day.

Gneeecey's telephone rang again. "Grate One here. . .yeah, Flub-bubb, thanks for tellin' me I'm welcome for the thank you card y'sent. G'BYE!"

I cleared my throat. "Anything else, Diroctor?"

"Yeah—stop interruptin' me."

I PICKED UP THE Dinwiddie's outvoice. And glanced sideways at Gneeecey, yakking on his phone.

"Yup, Mark," he squeaked, as he chewed on his knuckles, "jus' three more installments an' I'll deliver it myself. But I gotta add a surcharge, 'cause I suffered a loss recently—y'know, Yammicles. An' yeah," he continued, looking my way, "sooner or later, we'll get her to talk. G'bye!"

Squirming, I checked off both of the outvoice's preprinted no-pay options, "product defective/service unsatisfactory" and "notice of counterclaim/possible lawsuit."

"IG!"

My eyes rolled up to the ceiling, then back down to my mountain of paperwork.

"IG! IG! IG!"

I limped into his office. "*What?! What?! What?!*"

"Order me a gallon of copy paper."

"How can I—"

"Don't question me—jus' do what I say! An' call Dr. Idnas. My pills ain't workin'—I think the pharmacy's substitutin' lower-costin' place bows."

"Yes, Diroctor." I didn't mind talking to Dr. Idnas. She *understood*.

And I needed to inform her of Gneeecey's latest plot to kill Mr. Tree. The good diroctor intended to inhale a bushel of rindom-laced pepper and sneeze the oak down.

"Stop lookin' at me like that, Ig!"

"I wasn't—"

"An' I need—wait, Ig—gotta take this call. Yeah, stinkin' hello! What? Another bakery break-in? CheeseQuake's, out in Stuperville? An' y'wanna know, as Grate Gizzy, what I'm gonna do 'bout it? Well, uh, the situational requirements that this situation requires are, uh, situational. I'll address situational requirements at our nex' meetin'. G'BYE!"

"Diroctor, you were saying you wanted me to—"

"Those drapes over there—see how they're starin' back, real funny-like?"

"Did you take your last batch of pills?"

"Pills ain't gonna stop them curtains from comin' to get me when I ain't lookin'."

I knew had to distract him, and fast. I pointed to an old newspaper floating on his desktop. "Look at that *Pooper-Scooper* headline—isn't that your photo underneath?"

It worked. He smiled.

I shoved the paper under his snout. "It says, 'Perswayssick County's Rich are Getting Richer.' But what about the poor?"

He scratched his head. "What 'bout 'em? Oh, Ig, you're poor, an' that reminds me—y'gotta go back downtown an' exchange the new equipment y'jus' picked up."

"*What?*"

"Stu did another sound check at the auditorium—says we need the more 'spensive Glavorzian 320x wires. The thicker ones wit' them mierk-tensilated input-output repellent gizmos on each end."

"Send him." I stamped my foot, and my shoe ripped.

"I need Stu here. *You're* goin'." He threw a cable-filled bag at me.

"I've been to Schweinzimmer Electronics six times in the past week! Buying stuff, returning stuff, buying more stuff, returning more stuff—they think I'm nuts!"

"Everythin' hasta be perfoofect for His Holiness. His tail will be in our neck of the woods, any day now."

I popped a StomQuell. "That trip downtown is murder—my car's gonna overheat in all that traffic—"

"Who tol' ya to buy that ol' vehickookle from that Scriblig woman? Y'know what the law says. Buyers beware—emperors got cadavers. Y'shoulda let meee find ya another good car."

I clasped my hands behind my back, so as not to strangle him. "I'll go. But you'll have to give me something from petty cash to cover the price difference."

"Yes, I won't."

I forced a smile. "Is that yes, you will, or no, you won't?"

"Yes, I said yes I won't. An' also, no you will."

"I will, but you won't? If you don't, I can't—and *won't!*"

"I awready said yes, I ain't, but then y'said I said yes I won't, so y'can't. An' won't. So, yes, I ain't."

"Isn't that what I asked you—if you said *yes*, you're *not?*"

"Yeah, y'did, an' yes, I did, an' yes I'm not—aren'chooo? If y'don't, then I won't not, not unless you do."

"You let me know when you figure it out," I replied, tossing the sack back at him.

"Anyone ever tell ya, Ig, you're dense!"

"IG! GET IN HERE—ON THE DOUBOOBLE!"

I threw the Dinwiddie's outvoice up in the air.

"NOOOW!"

I popped my head through his empty door frame. "*What?*"

"Nuthin'," he replied, looking at me like I was chained to a cup-clutching chimp as I stood on my head, playing an accordion.

"Why'd you call me in here then?"

"Can'cha see I'm busy? Go process your lousy outvoices!"

"I'm trying to."

"An' Ig, din'cha hear me callin' ya? Get in here—take a letter."

Muttering, I stepped back into his office and sat down. He threw a pad and pencil onto my lap. "It's to John Smiff, Equestrian."

I looked up. "What?"

"Our new attorney. Now take this down. Dear Mr. Smiff: Imagine my horrification when, today, I was accused of falsely untrue—"

The ol' horn rang again. He grabbed it. "Yeah? Bad mornin', Qw-ertyuiop. HAAAH? WHAAAT? WHAAAT POLLS SAY 345'S GONNA PASS BY A LANDSLIDE? HUH? YUZ MET BEHIND MY BACK AN' GOT A SUBPOENA, REQUESTIN' *MY* FINANCIAL RECORDS?!"

Gneeecey's peepers popped out of his head like a pair of fly balls. "AN' I GOTTA REACCUSE MYSELF AN' LET YOU RUN THAT SPE-CIAL MEETIN'? WHAAAT? Y'MEAN I CAN'T DEFEND MYSELF TILL AFTER ELECTION DAY? RE-READ OUR BYLAWS—THAT AIN'T LEGAL. . . . IT STINKIN' *IS?*"

He whisked the entire handset off his desk and pitched it over my ducking head.

CHAPTER 30

AIRPLANES IN HIS PANTS

AIRPLANES IN MY PANTS!" howled Gneeecey, as he tore into The Grate Room. I chased after him with a can of plane repellent. "Spray 'em!"

"IT'S NOT BUGS—IT'S REEEEAL PLANES!"

"You can't *possibly* have real airplanes in your pants—"

"I DOOOOO!" He ran around the coffee table, clutching his keister. "AN' THEIR PROPELLERS ARE SLASHIN' UP MY UNDER-PAAANTS!"

"Uh, sit—no, second thought, *stand* right where you are. I'll call Dr. Idnas."

His eyeballs spun in opposite directions as he performed a strange belly dance, incorporating elements of hip-hop. "PLANES ARE KILLIN' ME!"

"I'm sure they'll, uh, run out of gas."

"YES, DOCTOR, I'M LOOKING in the freezer." Phone wedged between my chin and shoulder, I balanced a dozen cartons of Mrs. Dammit's Sloggenberry Pie in my frostbitten left hand, and, with my right, held back an avalanche of freezer-burned jackass patties, several plastic containers bursting with frozen ice block soup, and a couple hairy, egg-shaped green things.

Gneeecey shuffled into the kitchen, wimpering. "Y'were right, Ig. They ran outta gas."

That moment, the ice pack I'd been searching for landed on my foot. "*Found* one," I informed Dr. Idnas, as I hopped up and down.

Gneeecey tugged on my sleeve. "Tell her I take Sleepoopex 'cause the Bumpex keeps me awake, an' I swallow it wit' this purple coughin' syrup, but then I get too sleepy an' get a headache—"

"SSSSSSH! Yes, Doctor, I'll make sure. Thanks so much."

Gneeecey kicked me in the shin. "Don't stinkin' shooosh me in my own house!"

"She has a heavy Eccchsian accent—I wanted to make sure I understood everything she said. Now, I'll cut an extra Bumpex in half for you, and here, she wants you to sit on this for fifteen minutes." I wrapped the ice pack in a dish towel and placed it on his chair. "Sit."

He lowered his embattled runway of a behind, then sprang up. "TOO STINKIN' COLD!"

"Dr. Idnas says icing it'll desensitize the, uh, area," I replied, guiding a razor blade down the center of a tiny, scored Bumpex tablet. "And she also told me something kinda scary."

He settled back into his seat. "What?"

"She says recent studies have linked mierk exposure to Redecoritis."

He jumped up. "You're lyin'!"

"No, I'm not. She says that in autopsies, they're finding high mierk levels in the tissues of people with Redecoritis and Redecoritis-infected speech—"

Gneeecey hurled the ice pack into the sink. "What does *she* know? She ain't never done no autopoopsies on *me*!"

"She says more and more patients are presenting with neurological symptoms. She's already treated a couple dozen Good Intentions Paving employees."

"They did my driveway."

I handed him a glass of water, along with his extra dose of Bumpex. "Yeah—those three miles of miercolated pavement that surround this house. Manny Meantwell said many of his workers have been coming down sick—remember?"

Gneeecey kicked his chair over. "I don't believe none of this—it's them 345 people, saboobotagin' the election."

"And," I continued, "she said that Evoovelyn Jefoofrey's husbooband, who works for Freak O'Nature proboobably—"

My mouth was still open and moving, but my vocal chords had quit. A burning, prickly sensation spread from my scalp down to the soles of my feet.

Gneeecey almost choked on his pill.

CHAPTER 31

FRENEMIES

"I US' VOTED!" PROCLAIMED GNEEECEY, swaggering out of the bathroom. Determined to stick to single-syllable responses, I just grunted.

"I SAID, I VOTED—'GAINST 345!"

"In *there?*"

"My Electronic Water Cyclone 3000 has a feature that allows me to cast a electronical ballot from the privoovacy of my own bat'room, an' it has a special flush function so's I can cast a backup paper ballot."

"Realooly—ugh!" I stomped my left shoe so hard, the heel broke off.

"Your shoe's broke."

"YEE HAW—THINGS ARE GOIN' MY WAY!" exclaimed Gneeecey, as he lounged in his motorized recliner. Its robotic arm held a blue fizzy drink up to his mouth, freeing his fists to pummel the armrests.

I cupped my hand to my ear. "Whaaa—TV's too loud!"

"I SAID," he shouted, pumping the volume even higher, "EVERYTHIN'S GOIN' MY WAY!"

"And," I muttered, "I suppose the corn's as high as an elephoophant's eye—ugh."

"WHAAAAAAT?!"

"Uh," I replied, biting my lip so hard I tasted blood, "nothoothing—ugh—"

"Y'better not be mockin' our election system." He crammed a fistful of Rindom Doodles in his kisser.

"Dirokooktor—ugh! That's *you*—on TV!"

Gneeecey didn't hear me—he was too busy admiring himself. "Our latest returns," shrilled the prerecorded him, "show 345 losin' by a mierkslide!"

"How," I demanded, "can you prerecord election results?"

"I look real sharp, don't I?"

"Wit' ninety-nine percent of precincts an' toilets reportin'," continued the Gneeecey-on-the-screen, "we got forty billion 'gainst 345, an' only twenny-three-an'-a-half for it!"

I tapped him on the shoulder. "There aren't forty *million* peopoople —ugh—in all of Perswaysoossick—ugh—County."

His eyes remained glued to the set. "Accordin' to our uninformed Channel 3½ exit polls," continued his wall-sized twin, "a hundred-forty-two percent of them unpatriotical twenny-three-an'-a-half yes-votin' dopes might be impropooperly registered. An' the other ninety percent might be disqualified 'causa votin' irregoogoolarities, right, Stuey?"

"Yup, Boss," whinnied Stu, offscreen. "Do the math—it's g'bye zodd!"

"How," I asked, choosing my words carefully, "can you air this? You don't know how this election's turned out—"

"How many stinkin' times do I gotta 'splain it? Either stuff hapoopens, or it don't."

"What if someone else airs or prints the truth?"

Gneeecey smiled. "Wit'out *Normal Radio* an' the *Pooper-Scooper*, WGAS an' the *Tims* are the only games in town."

I sighed. His words reminded me of a conversation I'd had, not so long ago, in that very room.

With the TV blasting, Gneeecey didn't hear the persistent banging on his always-open-until-lately front window. Outside stood a rain-slicker-clad Flubbubb, and a plastic-caped Flea, the latter holding a *Shopping at Home with GAS* umbrella over his head. It wasn't raining.

Gneeecey's snout wrinkled. "Whaddoo *they* want?"

"Re-hear-sal," I answered slowly and deliberately, letting them in.

"Yuz two hypotenuse-heads," snarled Gneeecey, turning the sound down, "I tol' yuz to use the side door."

"Someone stole the doorbell," replied Flea, stumbling into the room.

"Anyone wit' brains knows if y'pull the two wires outta that hole in the bricks an' touch 'em together on your tongue, it'll still ring."

"How can it ring if it's gone?" asked Flubbubb, scratching his head through his yellow hood.

"Same stinkin' way you're gonna ring when you're gone."

"Huh?"

"Now, shut that window so's Twisty an' Mr. Tree can't get in. They proboobably stole the bell to trick us into usin' the window an' forgettin' to close it."

Flea and Flubbubb exchanged worried glances.

"An' look at yuz—whoop cream all over your dopey faces."

"We, uh, stopped at Shisskey's," answered Flea, smiling sheepishly. Gneeecey and Burt were no longer speaking. They'd fallen out—over 345.

"Don't blow all your dough in that zodd-lover's dump. YOU OWE ME BIG TIME, REMEMBOOBER?"

Flea gazed down at his high-tops, splattered with white goo.

"Wit' what'chooo earn, it'll take ya forever-an'-a-half to replace my unreplaceable voaline."

"Y'know," interrupted Flubbubb, sliding his new left-handed triangle out of its red velvet case, "I feel sorry for anyone who hasn't dumped their MierkoZurk stocks—those babies have taken a real dive."

Flea smiled. "I'll bet 'Zig's glad he kept all his eggs in one basket— in consonants an' vowels."

"Alphabet Market's a lot less volatile," agreed Flubbubb. "Slow, steady nickels are better'n fast, fickle dollars."

Gneeecey peered at him. "Yooou follow the markets?"

"Everyone's heard 'bout MierkoZurk," replied Flubbubb, shining his gold-tone triangle with gold-tone, left-handed triangle-shining cream. "I'm sure glad I don't have any—not unless someone secretly put some in my name."

"LISTEN UP," ORDERED GNEEECEY, spreading diagrams of the Perswayssick Civic Auditorium along the length of the dining room table. "Grand Oogitty-Boogitty'll sit up in the main balkookony, on a custom-made porcelain throne."

The three of us nodded, dutifully.

"Orkookestra's in the center, as usual," he continued. "We've put our kazoos on the left, 'cause we'll need lotsa space for the bazooka section—"

"Y'mean *bassoon* section?" asked Flubbubb, inspecting his triangle.

"That's what I said, ya Flubboobleheimer. Bazookas'll be shootin' nonstop durin' that twenny-two gun salute at the very enda Shriekensobb's 'Suite for Artillery'—"

I bolted upright. "*Shooting?*"

"Proboobably jus' blanks," replied Gneeecey.

Acid burning my esophagus, I popped a StomQuell.

Gneeecey flattened a complicated schematic that kept curling. "Okay. Stuey an' the Ig'll meet at the audooditorium before anyone else gets there yesterday mornin'—right, Ig?"

"Yes, Dirrector," I answered dreamily, visualizing my mother's honey eyes widen as I burst through her door.

"Pay detention! You an' Stuey'll make sure them cables are set up propooperly, before doin' preliminary, intermediate, *an'* final sound checks."

How many freakin' sound checks needed to be done?

"Stinkin' got somethin' to say, Ig?"

"Uh, no."

"One more thing, before we go back into The Grate Room for our last rehearsal—"

The telephone rang.

Gneeecey nearly ripped it out of the wall. "What?! Shisskey's? A *fire?* An' they foun' whoop cream sneaker prints leadin' away from the crime scene?" He looked at his two pals.

Flubbubb gawked back, but Flea avoided eye contact.

"Well," barked Gneeecey, "that's what they get, bein' 'gainst 345. 'Kay, Altitude, thanks for notificatin' me. An' carefoofal on that bike— y'don't wanna get bicycler's bimbus."

"Everything seemed normal when we left Shisskey's," said Flubbubb. Flea stared down at his lap.

I gasped. "Poor Burt and Mary! How horribooble—ugh—"

Flea and Flubbubb's mouths opened wide.

Gneeecey grinned. "Ig's come down wit' Redecorotis-infected speech!"

"Ooooh!" exclaimed Flubbubb, "Redecoritis an' ooglitis are devastating auto-immune disorders—"

"Y'smart-bimbus Iggleheimer, how come you're not as stoopid as usual?"

"Been going to school," replied Flubbubb.

Scowling, Gneeecey turned to me. "We'll visit a Redecoritis ward, after the holidays."

Fat chance, I thought. *After yesterday, I'll be history. Just hope I won't go home talking funny.*

Flea's ears perked up.

"Ain't priddy in them nervological hospoopitals," added Gneeecey. "Furniture's prohiboobited—everyone's rollin' on the floors screamin'—plus there's these big killer trees watchin' yuz through the windows—"

"Stop, 'Zig," admonished Flea. "Her ooglitis is proboobably jus' tempooporary—"

We gaped at the superhero.

"Boy," declared Flubbubb, shaking his head, "I'm sure glad I don't eat all the crap *you* guys do!"

The phone rang again, and Gneeecey skipped across the room, taunting me. "Hey, Ig, maybe that's Mark callin' again, to interrogate'cha 'bout Cleeevoooveland!"

Not a day went by without Markmen concocting outlandish theories and accusations, and demanding answers to idiotic questions. I searched my pockets for another StomQuell.

"Grate One speakin'," cackled Gneeecey. "Qwertyuiop—whadda yoooou want? How'd I think I'd get away wit' whaaat? Us here at WGAS are jus' doin' our lousy job as usual—keepin' our good snitizens informed—"

Qwertyuiop's staccato syllables fired out of the earpiece like bullets spraying out of an automatic weapon.

Gneeecey's teeth began to zigzag up and down his left arm, like a sewing machine gone haywire. "Whaddaya mean, what planet am I livin' on?!" he asked, spitting out fur. "You're a stinkin' LIAR—jus' like y'were back in third grade!"

The telephone slipped through the good diroctor's fingers and crashed to the tiles. He lunged forward, then staggered backward into the wall.

Our eyes were fixed on the black cloud that had formed above his noggin.

I'd never seen anything like it.

"345 was approved," whispered Flea, as he cringed under his bumbershoot.

Flubbubb adjusted his hood. "By a landslide. Din'cha know?"

Flea moved closer to me, positioning his umbrella over both our heads. "Everyone else sure seems to know."

Before Gneeecey could reply, a lightning bolt, about a foot long, shot out of his personal storm cloud. The searing arrow found its flea-bitten target in a flash, embedding itself square in the middle of his behind.

"EEEEEEEEEEEEEEEEEEEEEEEEEEE!" he screeched, as he ran in lopsided circles. A thunderclap exploded overhead, accompanied by a sudden downpour.

As it rained sideways, the upside-down-again table floated toward the rebuilt fireplace, surrounded by a soggy flotilla of drowning diagrams. Flea's umbrella blew inside out.

"FLEEEEEEA!" hollered Gneeecey, unable to touch the solid, blistering hot shaft. "HELLLLLLP!"

Slogging though the flotsam, the tight-jawed superhero rolled up his sleeves and pulled on the fiberglass gloves he kept clipped to his utility belt. "Bend over, 'Zig."

Gneeecey complied instantly. Flea grasped the spear and tugged this way and that. Finally dislodging it, he tossed it into the water, where it sizzled for a good sixty seconds, then fizzled out.

"Excalibur is freed at last," declared Flubbubb, as ankle-deep waters swirled down the room's shower drain. "An' Flea is king!"

ALTITUDE'S MOUTH HUNG OPEN. "Wha' 'appened?"

"Don't ask," answered Flea, drying his ears with Gneeecey's pistol-shaped blow dryer, in The Grate Room.

"Mouse, why're y'talkin' funny?" asked Gneeecey.

"Tongue's buzzin' from ringin' your stolen doorbell."

"Uh, Diroctor," I began, "you want me to drive you down to Florence Fergoogooson—ugh—*Ferguson*—to get that, uh, wound treated?"

"Nope," he replied, turning his nose up at me. "Lightnin' booboos cauterize themselves."

I continued brushing my hair dry. What did *I* know?

"An'," added Gneeecey, applying another Ouch-O Strip to his injury and eyeing Flubbubb hatefully, "the real Excaliboobur popped outta some lousy medievooval dragon-infested lagoon, not outta some normal person's bimbus."

"I know, Bizzig," responded Flubbubb, fluffing out his tail. "I been taking classes at PUNI—"

"YOOOU CALLED ME BIZZIG!"

"Huh?"

"ONLY FLEA CAN CALL ME THAT!"

"Call y'what?"

"CALL ME BIZZIG!"

"Jus' did."

"Y'CAAAAN'T!"

Flubbubb threw his towel down. "Y'jus' tol' me to."

"I DID NOT—AN' WOULD NOT—'CAUSE YOU AIN'T FLEA! GET IT?"

"I know I'm not Flea. I'm Flubbubb."

Gneeecey jammed his face in Flubbubb's. "YOU AIN'T STINKIN' FLEA, ARE YA?"

Flubbubb backed away slowly. "You're kiddin', right? You *know* I'm not Flea—"

Flea clicked the dryer off. "'Zig, we know you're upset 'bout the election—"

"I'M STINKIN' GONNA GET IT OVERTURNED!"

"'Zig—"

"I got faith," said Gneeecey, speaking in a softer tone, "that my faith in the Grand Oogitty-Boogitty'll get me through this crisis. After the parade, I'll invite him to lunch here at the house an' convince him to—"

The telephone rang. Gneeecey knocked over two floor lamps on his way to the answering machine. Panting, he switched on the cheap, leopard-spotted device—a *Shopping at Home with GAS* overstock item—and cranked the volume up.

"Bad morning, Diroctor," droned a middle-aged female. "This is Francine F. Fruesenfrauffel, President of the Perswayssick Preservation Society. I'm afraid we've got some rather bad news."

Gneeecey began gnawing on his wrists.

"Our board members," she said, "have voted *not* to grant you a permit to chop down that magnificent oak in your backyard, and furthermore, we must inform you that you've exhausted all avenues—"

"Boss," whined Altitude, slinking back into the room, "we got a problem—"

Gneeecey spun around so fast that he knocked over another lamp and a paisley spittoon. "WHAAAAAAAAAAAAT?"

"I—I jus' flushed the sploggle," stammered the rodent. "By accident."

"MY PLATINUM SPLOGGLE?!"

"Sorry, Boss—when I was sittin' there, that crow out on the ledge was shoutin', 'Son of a bitch, son of a bitch,' an'—"

Gneeecey lifted the mouse up by the scruff of his neck.

"Boss—I said I'm sorry—"

Winding up like a pitcher with a three-and-two count in the last out of a tied World Series, Gneeecey raised Altitude high above his head.

"Stop," I pleaded.

"Put him down," ordered Flea.

"AN'," shrieked Gneeecey, preparing to hurl Altitude through a closed window, "HE PROBOOBABLY NULLIFIED MY VOTE, TOO!"

Flea threw his hands up. "Election's over, 'Zig. It's a done deal. Now, put Altitude down—"

The phone rang again. Gneeecey dropped the mouse on his head.

"Hey, Doc," boomed blond, big-nosed Mark's instantly recognizable voice. "Things didn't 'zactly turn out the way y'promised, did they? Ya know what *that* means. Heh, heh. . .catch y'later—an' we *will*."

Gneeecey fell to the floor and began chewing his sides, like a flea-ridden hound.

FLEA SAT DOWN AT the piano. "'Zig, the peopoople—ugh—*people*—have spoken. You'll hafta get used to zodd."

"NOOOOOOOOOOOOO! I'll petition His Holooliness to overturn this fraudulent election, for the good of demockookracy throughout the universe," proclaimed Gneeecey, removing his left sock.

"What'cha doin'?" asked Flea.

"Y'wanted a cuppa coffee."

"So, uh—help me out here—why're you takin' off your sock?"

"I'm fresh outta filters. This works jus' as good—"

Flea extracted a wad of sheet music from his briefcase. "Forget it. Let's jus' get on wit' this last rehearsoosal—ugh—rehearsal."

"Intermittent ooglitis, without prior symptomology," observed Flubbubb, blowing a speck of dust off his triangle. "Probably temporary."

"What makes you an expert on tempooporary sympooptomology —or anythin' else?" demanded Gneeecey.

"I think Flubbubb's right," I chimed in, unwrapping an oogdenplantzil hero I'd stashed in the refrigerator.

Gneeecey studied me through narrowed lids.

"Hopoopfully—ugh—we'll regain our normal speech patterns," I added, pounding my fist on my thigh and squashing my sandwich. "Like Flubooboob—ugh—said, we don't have any other sympooptoms— ugh—"

"Who *asked* ya? An' what's that you're holdin' in your hairless Ig hands? Takeout? I been meanin' to ask—where y'been gettin' all this extra mon-ney?"

"*Extra money?*"

"We both know I don't pay ya 'nuff to buy all this extra stuff, like that new Splodge—"

"I told you—it's not *new*. I paid pennies for it. I need it, to get to work—"

"Whaddabout'cha new shoes? An' new box of *brand name* tissues? Y'can't afford such luxuries."

I threw my hero down. "*Luxuries?!*"

"Where's all the extra mon-ney comin' from?"

My no-longer-purple face was burning. "I have no idea what you're talking about—"

"Y'know," added Gneeecey, head cocked with suspicion, "I even think y'know what hapoopened to Yammicles."

Man, I thought, *when I blow outta here yesterday, it won't be a second too soon!*

Flea looked my way. I flinched.

"Leave her alone, 'Zig. Let's get on wit' this so we can get some sleep before we gotta play for real."

Altitude clicked his violin case open, revealing a smooshed cheese sandwich, a two-stringed violin, half a hairless bow, and dozens of chewed-up pencils. He glanced over at his boss's electric Stradivopoulos, propped against the wall.

"Don't even think of it," warned Gneeecey. "That's my only workin' voaline!"

Flea yawned. "C'mon awready."

"Gotta tune up," replied Gneeecey, plucking a series of sour notes. "An' actually, I do got another voaline, but it's still broke."

"Can't it be fixed?" asked Flubbubb.

"Nope. No matter how many parts they replace, each time I get the lousy thing back—an' I musta got it back two hundred times awready—it still don't play J.S. Batch's music propooperly."

Flea glanced at his watch.

"My first teacher, Miss Connie, did say I might be able to play Batch's 'Doubooble Voaline Concerto' if I clone myself," added Gneeecey.

Shuddering, I zipped up my jacket.

"So," concluded the good diroctor, "until I get time to start on that little project, I'll concentrate on Shriekensobb. Y'don't gotta play *his* notes exact."

"'Zig!"

"Okay, Fleaglossitty, we're startin' yesterday's program wit' Shriekensobb's 'Three-legged Waltz.' An' a one an' a two an' a—"

Altitude raised his wreck of a fiddle to his chin and positioned his half-bow over his two flaccid goonafish-gut strings.

"*You* ain't playin'!" thundered Gneeecey. "Y'coulda, but'cha ain't never tried to learn nuthin' from me."

Altitude crouched down to tie one of his dirt-colored high-tops. "I've learnt lots—y'teached me if y'sell your house to yourself an' buy it back cheaper, y'can make a ton of money! Y'could probably get a ton for this place—"

"Get outta here—I don't wanna see your ignoramical face till yesterday!"

The rodent scooped up his musical debris and scampered away.

Flea frowned. "'Zig, y'coulda been a little less vicious."

Gneeecey stuffed a health cigar in his mouth.

"Hey," inquired Flubbubb, "are those smokes helping your, y'know, problem? I mean, they sure as hell smell like what they're supposed to make happen."

Gneeecey snatched Flubbubb by his plush throat.

"Sorry!" spluttered the percussionist, fighting to free himself. "Now, lemme go—"

Flea flew into the fray. "Leggo of him!"

"NO—YOU STINKIN' LEGGO OF MEEE!" hollered Gneeecey, losing his grip and landing on his honking bimbus.

"OKAY," BEGAN GNEEECEY, "A one an' a two an' a—FLEEEEA! YOUR MUSIC'S UPOOPSIDE-DOWN!"

"It is," replied Flea, doing a quick handstand to make sure. "But I don't really need it—I awready know it."

"Y'better follow it, or you'll stinkin' end up playin' aheada me again. Now, a one an' a two an' a three an' a three-an'-a-half—"

Gneeecey's bow hit his electrified strings. Everything went black.

"FLEAGLOSSITTY, YOOOOU UNPLUGGED MY VOALINE!"

"I didn't unplug nuthin'. Your cheap amp tripped the breakers."

"DOOOOOO SOMETHIN', FLEAGLOSSITTY—THE CONCERT'S YESTERDAY!"

"I'm trynna find my flashlight so I can go down to the basement wit'out breakin' my neck."

A couple clicks and clanks later, the superhero—and a compact yellow beam—moved across the room and out into the hallway.

"IT'S YOUR FAULT, IG!"

"Huh?"

"Y'BRUNG ME NUTHIN' BUT BAAAD LUCK SINCE YA INVADED MY LIFE!"

"You've gotta be kidding—"

Before I could finish, the lights flashed back on.

"'Zig," complained Flea, trudging back into the room, "I wish y'didn't have that prehistoric toilet carved into the floor down there."

"Well, I certaincerely hope y'wiped your feet."

"I did, after I fell over Klunkzill. An' you're welcome."

"I am?" asked Gneeecey, crawling around, plugging in another amplifier. "Jus' so I know, what did I *do*?"

"Forget it. Jus' don't blow that amp."

"Pay detention to your *own* playin'. An' a one an' a two an' a three an' a three-an'-a-half—"

The lights stayed on this time, as Gneeecey's instrument mimicked the cries of pigeons being electrocuted.

As best as I could tell, Zirbert Shriekensobb synthesized Earth's classical European styles of the 18th and 19th centuries with more than a touch of 20th Century dissonance. The music made my teeth hurt.

Suddenly, "The Three-legged Waltz" screeched to a halt, much like a subway train whose emergency brakes had been slammed on.

Flea was messing up again—his on-again-off-again ESP made him anticipate entire passages before their time.

"YOU'RE PLAYIN' AHEADA ME AGAIN!"

"Sorry, 'Zig—my ESP seems to work mostly when I'm playin'."

Gneeecey stomped over to the upright and slammed down its lid, nearly amputating the superhero's fingers. "IF THE GRAND OOGITTY-BOOGITTY AIN'T IMPRESSED, HE WON'T HELP ME!"

Flea shrugged.

Gneeecey pounded his knuckles on the piano. "TURN OFF YOUR CRUMMY ESP!"

Flea jumped up in Gneeecey's face. "I CAAAAN'T!"

"OH, YEAH?!"

"YEAH!"

"YEAH?!"

"YEEEEAAAAH!"

The two stood toe-to-toe, fists clenched, crazed expressions plastered across their mugs.

Flubbubb and I held our breath. "C'mon, guys," he pleaded, "we're all friends!"

After a minute that stretched into next year, Flea marched back to the piano.

Gneeecey picked up his violin. "An' a one an' a two an' a—"

The phone's shrill ring sent him flying into the air, where his bow remained—stuck to a gooey strip of airplane-dotted flypaper that hung from the ceiling.

He froze as a raspy voice growled through the answering machine's tinny speaker. It was blond, big-nosed Mark's worse-tempered associate—tall, brown-haired Mark. "Pick up, Doc. We see ya. An' we hear ya, too. That lousy music you're playin' sounds like how *you're* gonna sound when ya hit the third rail!"

Gneeecey dropped down on all fours and began chasing his tail.

"Stop, 'Zig," begged Flea, wincing.

Flubbubb recoiled, disgusted. "Our residual canine tendencies were supposed to have been trained out of us back in elementary school."

"'ZIG," BEGAN FLUBBUBB, "I hate to bring it up again, but 'Suite for Artillery' calls for use of prepared percussion—as its title *an'* Shrieknsobb's notations imply."

"Since when are *you* usin' big words?"

"I'm jus' saying—"

"You're lucky I'm lettin' y'play a sixteenth note on that fancy-schmancy triangle."

"But," insisted Flubbubb, opening a volume the size of two county phone books, "it says right here—"

"Shriekensobb never called for puttin' shoes in washin' machines to make percussionary rhythm. Not even in his sacred kazoo music."

Flubbubb shoved the encyclopedia under Gneeecey's muzzle. "We should play it the way he intended it to be played. It's all 'bout musical integrity—after I'm dead, I gotta live with myself."

"You'll be dead sooner than y'planned if y'don't do things *my* way—"

Flea inserted himself between the two. "That's enough, 'Zig!"

"NO IT AIN'T!"

"Y'should be kinder to Flubbubb," he whispered, leading Gneeecey away by an ear. "He really looks up to you—y'heard 'bout his plan to present'cha wit' a wagon load of purple rubber wallets durin' the concert."

Gneeecey's face lit up.

"Let him use his washer/dryer. Jus' for that one number."

"NOOOOOOO!"

"'Zig—"

"He'll still gimme them wallets—he kisses the ground I sit on."

"But—"

"Y'know, Fleaglossitty, I'm hungry. No offense to ol' Culvert, but I wish I had summa that Bombay duck. I don't usually like to eat nuthin' that quacks, but—"

"Most people know Bombay duck's really *fish*," interrupted Flubbubb. "So y'don't hafta feel bad, like you're eating Culvert or any of his family—"

Gneeecey smacked Flubbubb over the head with a music stand. "YOU ACTIN' SUPERIOR TO MEEEEE?"

"Ow—I was trynna make y'feel better 'bout—no—don't throw that book! I borrowed it from PUNI's library—"

Flea grabbed the tome. "Time to chill, 'Zig!"

"STINKIN' STAY OUTTA THIS!"

"No!"

Gneeecey spat in the superhero's face.

"Hey," spluttered Flea, "you're s'posed to be my friend!"

"I AAAM!"

"You're not treatin' me like one."

"I treat everyone alike—friends an' enemies," replied Gneeecey, air-boxing. "But I'm startin' to thinka yooou more like a frenemy."

"*What?*"

"A enemy who used to be a friend."

Flea grabbed his briefcase and busted umbrella and headed for the window.

"I hope," said Flubbubb, "*I'm* not a frenemy."

"Nah," replied the good diroctor.

"Whew!"

Gneeecey blew his snoot in the drapes. "Never thoughta ya as a friend in the first place."

"I'M GLAD THEM TWO dopes finally lef'. Gotta shine up my horsey saddle for yesterday's parade."

Gneeecey's dark, darting eyes spooked me.

"An' you watch," he whooped, rubbing his palms together gleefully. "That stinkin' Flubbubb won't get one lousy winka shut-eye, worryin' 'bout the concert!"

CHAPTER 32

PRE-SHOW JITTERS

MEANWHILE, IN A TINY furnished flat across town on South Alamoochy Avenue, a yawning, pajama-clad Flubbubb turned out the lights and tucked himself into bed.

"*Whatever. . .*" he mumbled, as he rolled onto his stomach, fell fast asleep, and snored loudly and continuously for eight hours.

CHAPTER 33

OCTVEMBER 69TH: D-DAY

A FTER TOSSING AND TURNING for hours, I shot out of bed. The mansion's thermostat had been set so low, I could see my breath. In semi-darkness, I pulled Cleve's icy watchband onto my wrist. The afternoon before, I had knelt at his grave and placed a red rose next to a temporary marker that read, *Wheeler, C.–Plot 7408s.*

I was glad I'd never see the headstone. I would be unable to bear the sight of it.

Heart aching, I fought the urge to open Cleve's locket. I had to stay focused. After the concert, as Gneeecey saddled up and St. Bogelthorpe's off-key bells tolled, signaling Blirg's end, I would disappear into the woods and say those four words.

I strapped on my cheap, plastic Blirg watch. Soon, I wouldn't need a second timepiece.

Dressing with more care than usual—choosing my maroon turtle-neck and least dilapidated pair of jeans—I wiggled into my navy jacket, triple-checking that my dough, passport, outline, and the Wheelers' phone number were zipped securely inside inner pouches. Couldn't even imagine what I'd tell Lauren and Grandmother Eleanor—*if* I got through this.

I felt as if I was wearing a fat suit—probably looked like I'd gained twenty or thirty pounds overnight. Inhaling one last whiff of the room's caustic chemical odor, to remember it—don't ask me why—I headed for the door.

As I crossed the threshold, I scrambled back to my cardboard dresser, yanked its drawers open, and rifled through some of the hard-won possessions that would be left behind.

I plucked out a silky, black V-neck—an all-too-rare, two-armed garment I'd managed to find in Oddlottz—and crammed it into one of my remaining empty pockets, along with a fleecy red pair of Flea's socks.

Suddenly, I sprinted behind my "night table" and scooped up Cleve's radio, amazed that I'd almost forgotten it.

A split-second later, it dematerialized in my hands. I stared until, mysteriously, it reappeared.

"Sleep deprivation," I muttered, jamming the receiver into an inner pocket.

Dismayed by the possibility that I might be losing my mind—and alarmed by a tingly sensation spreading from the soles of my feet, up to my thighs—I stumbled out into the hallway.

"DIDN'T SLEEP GOOD," SNARLED Gneeecey, as my swinging fist collided with his skull, in the lavender-lit corridor. "OW!"

"Sorry," I mumbled, caught up in my own thoughts.

He looked me up and down. "Y'musta gained twenny or thurdy pounds overnight!"

"Like Yammicles?" I whispered.

"WHAAAAAT?"

"Uh, nothing."

He scowled. "I'll hafta put one of them newer comboobination locks on the 'frigerator door."

"Uh-huh."

"Now remember Ig, soon as the concert's over, yooou come back here an' throw up all them Grimace dekookorations—they're in that crate there."

"Yeah," I replied, studying my new cobalt-trimmed gray Mierk-Tracker sneakers.

"Make sure there's tinsel on every chair in this house."

"Right."

"Things better look real Grimacey—His Holooliness gotta be impressed." Gneeecey stared me down. "It's my *laaast chaaance*—after lunch, he jumps back on his comet an' goes gallopin' 'round the universe for a whole 'nother year!"

"Uh-huh."

"EVERYTHIN' GOTTA GO PERFOOFECT!"

"Okay." I couldn't look him in the eye.

"By the way, Ig, the civoovic center jus' called. After all them sound checks yuz did, a buncha wild kangoogaroos broke in an' chewed up the wirin' an' bit gigantical chunks outta the stage—"

"*What?!*"

"Y'gotta stop at Schweinzimmer's—gotta replace them wrecked Glavorzian 320x cables."

"How," I asked, slumped against the wall, "can I go all the way downtown, then make it back to the audooditorium—ugh—"

"Jus' do your job," he snapped. "Leave the thinkin' to *me*."

"Can't Stu—"

"Nope. He's awready there, testin' out the seats. An' I tol' him to go get dinner. Wit' Blirg endin', poor kid'll miss breakfoofas'!"

Doing a slow burn, I held out my hand.

He looked at me like I had several heads. "Why're y'holdin' your hairless Ig hand out?"

"Last time I picked up caboobles—ugh—at Schweinzimmer's, you never reimbursed me."

"Never said I'd *reimburse* ya."

"You said you'd pay me back."

"Pay y'back *twice?*"

"Huh?"

He sighed. "I mighta said I'd *imburse* ya—that means payin' y'back *once*. Reimburse means—"

"You never paid me back *once*—you owe me fifty dollars, plus what I'll lay out now."

"I'll imburse ya after the parade—when me an' His Holooliness come back to the house for lunch."

My heart sank. By then, I'd be history. And out a hundred bucks.

He belched. "What'chooo lookin' at?"

"Uh, nothing." When I thought about it, a C-note was probably a pretty cheap ticket out of hell.

"Oh, an' Merry Grimace, Ig."

"Yeah. You too."

"NOW GIT!"

"Uh-huh." I'd be gittin'.

ARCTIC AIR SLAPPED MY face as I gazed into lilac heavens. The low sun's rays streamed through breaks between dramatically shadowed cumulus clouds.

Sympathy card skies.

Slowly, my eyes wandered down to the ground. A blanket of white covered everything in sight.

"FIRST SNOW OF THE SEASON!" shrieked Gneeecey, as he tore through the yard like a hyperactive third grader. "WHOOP CREAM!"

Snow would complicate everything. I hated the stuff.

He stuck a finger into the chilly mess. "MMMMMM—I WAS DREAMIN' OF A WHITE GRIMACE!"

"Uh-huh."

"AN' NOW I'LL BE ABLE TO SEE MR. TREE'S FOOTPRINTS— HE'S BEEN CHASIN' ME FASTER LATELY!"

I pulled out my car keys.

"YEE HAW!" he howled, submerging his snout in the glop.

"You'll get sick," I warned.

"Nah," he replied, surfacing between slurps. "Gotta eat up 'fore it spoils—this whole county's gonna smell priddy funky in a coupla days!"

I'd timed my departure perfectly.

"Now, git yourself down to Schweinzimmer's!"

My "as seen on TV" MuckGrabber soles were no match for the slick surface—my first mincing steps landed me on my knees, and I whizzed down the driveway, right past my creamed-over Splodge.

Struggling to my feet, I executed a backward triple axel, followed by what must have looked like a quadruple klutz.

"PERFEC' FORM!" whooped Gneeecey. "DO ANOTHER!"

CHAPTER 34

CUTTIN' EDGE MUSIC

DRIVING IN THE WHITE crap proved to be no less hazardous than walking in it. Just a gentle tap on the brakes would send my Splodge veering sideways into the exhaust-blackened curb, or into the path of another skidding vehicle—usually an oncoming tractor-trailer, or a county bus filled with bug-eyed passengers.

My journey to and from Schweinzimmer's—typically a ninety-minute round trip—had snowballed into a harrowing three-hour expedition.

When, at long last, I turned into the Perswayssick Civic Center's lot, there was nowhere, absolutely nowhere to park, except for an extra space reserved for Gneeecey. It appeared to have been shoveled out with a teaspoon.

Rather than waste time searching for a spot on gridlocked, one-way Oink Avenue, I pulled in beside Gneeecey's Porsche.

Schlepping two five-ton Schweinzimmer's bags, I skated right past the theater's rear entrance, distracted by the sight of an idling Freak O'-Nature tractor-trailer half the length of a football field.

"WHERE WERE YA, Y'LOUSY Ig?"

"Where do you think?"

"An' where's His Holooliness?" My bimbus-scratching boss looked up at the Grand Oogitty-Boogitty's vacant throne. "An' where's Flea-glossitty?"

"Dunno," I answered, dumping a sack of cables at Stu's feet. "C'mon, we'd better get started."

"Soon's I finish dinner, Icky. Carpenter's still fixing the stage." The intern plunged his dimpled mitts into a Krappy Korners Deli bag.

"Oh, no you don't," I protested, dragging him away by an ear.

We must've looked like quite the pair, on elbows and knees, running lines all over the place and shouting into mikes—me, garbed in cream-splattered sneakers and jeans, topped with that bulky jacket, and Stu, swimming in the ill-fitting suit he had worn to Cleve's funeral.

"HURRY, YUZ TWO," bellowed Gneeecey, chewing on the hand he'd just used for scratching, "OR I'LL FIRE YUZ!"

Stu's face went so scarlet, it blended in with his raccoon mask. I almost felt sorry for him.

Gneeecey looked just as petrified. I almost felt sorry for him, too. Almost.

He did crack a slight grin when Flubbubb rolled his red MierkFlyer, heaped with purple rubber wallets, over to Flea's piano.

The percussionist dashed backstage, then reappeared, pushing a compact white washer/dryer-on-wheels, topped with a clear, thirty-gallon trash bag, filled with shoes of all types.

"Y'CAN'T USE THAT!" yelled Gneeecey.

Whistling Shriekensobb's screechy "Plight of the Goonafish," Flubbubb parked his appliance next to Gneeecey's violin.

"NEBBERD-KINNEZZARD," shouted Gneeecey, "DID SHRIEKEN-SOBB CALL FOR PREPOOPERATED PERCUSSION!"

Folks in the audience giggled nervously.

Gneeecey stomped onstage, waving his fists in Flubbubb's face. "AN' I KNOW MUSIC INSIDE-OUT—IN MEDICAL SCHOOL, I SPENT SIX STINKIN' SEMESTERS PRACTICIN' COLONOSCOPIES ON FRENCH HORNS!"

As a shrugging, gum-chewing Flubbubb removed his triangle from its case, Gneeecey spotted Altitude below, decked out in a three-piece gray suit, accessorized by a flickering spider web-patterned necktie. "Hey, Boss," called out the mouse. "Whazzup?"

Blinking faster than the rodent's battery-powered tie, Gneeecey lost his footing and tumbled into the orchestra pit. His butt blared loudly. Amid the chuckles and chortles, Flea—whipped cream smeared all over his mug—scuttled out from behind the stage's glitzy violet curtain. As the superhero flopped over his piano bench and landed on his honking schnozz, Gneeecey crawled out of the orchestra pit, squinted up at the floodlit balcony, and gulped.

There sat His toga-clad, scepter-toting Holiness—garnished with a diamond-studded platinum crown, and a sprig of parsley the size of a small sapling.

Everyone oohed and aahed.

To me, the Grand Oogitty-Boogitty looked like nothing more than a freakishly overgrown Idaho tuber. With a little bling.

"Your Grand Celestial Hynesty," squeaked Gneeecey, knees quaking, "we greet'cha most revooverently."

The whipped cream-intoxicated audience clapped itself silly, but Planet Eccchs's lumpy, multi-eyed spiritual leader remained expressionless.

Gneeecey glared at Flubbubb, who'd just blown a baseball-sized bubble. "We'll begin this momentical event by preforatin' the works of Zirbert Shriekensobb."

The Grand Oogitty-Boogitty stared into space. Vacantly.

Blond, big-nosed Mark and a couple dozen of his cronies began pounding their fists on the stage. "Get to da lousy music awready!"

"Yeah," shouted Altitude. "Get to da lousy music awready!"

Gneeecey's notes spilled to the floor. "Your Royal Holooliness, we, your humbooble servoovants, will now entertainerate your High, Indisposable an' Excellent Hiney—uh, Highnesty—wit' Zirbert Shriekensobb's 'The Three-Legged Waltz.'"

His High, Indisposable and Excellent Highnesty still stared into space. More vacantly than ever.

The Markmen stared at Gneeecey. Intently.

Gaze fixed on the refrigerator-sized spud, Gneeecey slid in a puddle of his own sweat as he reached for his Stradivopoulos. "Your Primeval Imperiality, we will play this compooposition in Z-minor," he continued, on his knees, making no effort to get up. "Okay, orkookestra—FARTIS-SIMO!"

Someone in the wind section passed gas. Rather loudly.

Unhinged, Gneeecey snatched up a saw that had been left onstage and positioned it over his violin, like a bow.

Everyone gasped.

"It *is* cuttin' edge music," proclaimed the good diroctor. "An' a one an' a two an' a three an' a three-an'-a-half—"

The blade made contact and sawed back and forth, popping the fiddle's ill-tuned strings one by one, until there were none.

Oblivious, Flea banged his white baby grand's ivories faster and faster, playing miles ahead of the music, even improvising on future passages.

Poised to strike his sixteenth note, Flubbubb stood frozen, triangle suspended in midair.

Concert master Zlonkhammer Zlannker leapt up, and the entire Perswayssick Civic Orchestra fell silent. "Diroctor!" shouted the distinguished, white-haired human. "You're—you're—"

"SHAAADDUP, ZLANNKER," barked Gneeecey. "YOU'RE JUS' JEALOUS!"

Realizing something was amiss, the vamping superhero swivelled around. "'Zig!"

"NOT NOW, FLEAGLOSSITTY—CAN'CHA SEE I'M PLAYIN'?!"

"Diroctor," I pleaded from below, "*stop*—"

"SHAAAAAAAADDUP, IG!" Gneeecey ordered, as he sliced his Stradivopoulos in half.

It's severed lower belly—chin rest, bridge, and all—clunked to the floorboards, raising a storm of white dust. The fingerboard and upper portion slipped out of his left hand and smashed to the floor.

The two wooden chunks—weedy shoots of string still attached—bounced, step by step, into the orchestra pit, sounding forth more melodically—and more rhythmically—than ever before.

Everyone gaped, stupefied.

The Grand Oogitty-Boogitty appeared to be reading the Sunday comics.

"GIMME DAT!" Gneeecey yanked the violin out from under Zlannker's chin.

The concert master jumped to his polished black shoes. "You can't just—just—"

Gneeecey examined Zlannker's red-toned instrument in the footlights' warm glow. "Ain't electronically ampooplificated, but if I play hard 'nuff, I know I can make these goonafish gut strings *scream!*"

Face flushing, Zlannker marched out of the orchestra pit.

Gneeecey threw the violinist's music in the kazoo master's round face. "Here—yooou stinkin' take over!"

"Excuse me," protested the young human, "but I have no idea what—"

"JUS' DO IT—IF Y'WANNA KEEP YOUR JOB!"

"OKAY, YOUR PROVERBIAL PRIMATE," squawked Gneeecey, clutching what was left of Zlannker's fiddle. "We hope ya enjoyed Shriekensobb's 'Bozovian Rhapoopsody' in E flat-sharp. He wrote it for harpoopsichord, tympoopani, an' cello, but we took the libooberty of substitutin' a piano, jackhammer, an' voaline. Ol' Zirbert won't mind—he's dead!"

After three hours, the Grand-Ooggitty Booggitty still sat, devoid of expression. His sprig of parsley had wilted.

"Okay, your High Muck-a-muck," continued Gneeecey, "we'll now present Your Gracelessness wit' our final number. We're endin' wit' a real *bang*—Shriekensobb's 'Suite for Artillery!'"

He positioned Zlannker's violin underneath his chin.

On the count of three-and-a-half, a lopsided military march—written for Bozovia's legendary three-legged infantry—limped off the stage, staccato sharps blasting into the air like torpedoes, shooting down short-lived, off-beat flats.

The more dissonant the piece became, the more it wowed the crowd. After a sweat-dripping Gneeecey produced a particularly grating screech, the audience delivered a standing ovation.

Spurred on, he played Zlannker's bundle of splinters—held together by a single string—louder and harder. After he completed his caterwauling cadenza, he cued the bazookas. And watched, helplessness etched on his face, as Flubbubb rolled his washer/dryer center stage.

Cracking his gum, the percussionist set his appliance's wash cycle on "Gentle," opened the lid and dropped in a pair of oxfords. Boonk, boonk, boonk—boonk, boonk, shook the shoes, in an Afro-Cuban 3-2 clave-like rhythmic pattern, creating a driving, multi-layered syncopation, when coupled with the rapidly firing weapons.

Flea's runaway piano sounded jazzy—only thing missing was a Puerto Rican horn section's wailing trumpets and trombones.

I really missed my Salsa. Grabbing Stu's pudgy hand, I began to dance a mambo out in the aisle. What the heck—everyone else was jumping up and down. "Cool—*chevere!*" I exclaimed, moving to the conga drum-like beat.

"Icky!" shouted the intern, breaking loose. "What the hell d'ya think you're doing?"

"Nothing." Deflated, I flopped into a velveteen seat.

Onstage, Flubbubb peeked at his music, picked three pairs of stilettos out of his bag, and threw them in the washer. Boonkitty-boonk, boonkitty-boonk, boonkitty-boonk—boonkitty-boonk, boonkitty-boonk banged the footwear, in double-time.

Gneeecey's face matched the curtains behind him.

Flubbubb switched his dial from "Wash" to "Dry," selected a heavy-duty cotton cycle, and plopped in two pairs of loafers.

Boonka, boonka, boonkitty-boonk—BOONK—boonka, boonka, boonkitty-boonk—BOONK—knocked the shoes, in tandem with the bazookas' fiery pow, pow, pow.

An ear-splitting end-of-cycle signal buzzed, just as the rockets blew a hole through the theater's sparkling indigo dome, exposing almost-blue skies above.

It was all over. Except for the wild cheering.

"Flubbubb! Flubbubb!" chanted the crowd.

The percussionist raced over to his wagon and began to toss wallets out into the audience—concentrating his efforts on an attractive group of female golden retriever types.

St. Bogelthorpe's bells tolled in the distance. Time to cut out. Heart fluttering, I rose.

As I made my way toward the backstage entrance, Gneeecey scooted his bimbus across the length of the stage, like a mutt with an itchy butt.

CHAPTER 35

MARKED AND BOBBED

Y'RUINT THE WHOLE CONCERT!" yelled Gneeecey, pummeling my kneecaps backstage. "What's your problem?" I asked, backing away.

"Y'BRUNG ME BAAAD LUCK!"

"Yeah," piped in Altitude, as he leapt into the air and ripped his trousers, trying to to kick me. "An' look—she jus' busted my pants!"

"Oh, and uh, Stu's gathering all the cables," I volunteered, pushing past the two of them. "He'll bring 'em back to Vompt." All seven of the intern's chins had bounced to his chest when I stuffed that crisp twenty in his palm.

"Okay," snapped Gneeecey, on my heels. "Now git back home, like I tol' ya, an' get everythin' ready!"

"YEAH!" screeched Altitude.

"Whatever," I mumbled, striding past a strange, four-wheeled receptacle that towered over me.

The moment I stepped into the corridor, someone grabbed me from behind and dumped me, head first, into the crate. As I flailed around, something large and furry crash-landed on me, screaming, "WE'RE ALL GONNA DIE!" A split second later, something small and furry struck me, crying, "YEAH!"

A lid thundered down from above, and we rumbled away, in blackness. Then, a constant gnawing below caught my attention. Could only be a rat, I thought, heart thumping through my chest.

"C'mon," shouted someone outside, "help me get this big sucker out the door!"

We tumbled into the midst of what sounded like a dozen marching bands tuning up, accompanied by the plaintive, high-pitched neighs of a horse.

Gneeecey kicked my chin. "MY HORSEY! HELP! GEMMEE OUTTA HERE—I GOTTA GO LEAD THE PARADE!"

"Bye guys!" squeaked Altitude, as he squeezed through the tiny hole he'd just chewed. "I'm outta here!"

Gneeecey slapped me. "Dirty rat—desertin' a stinkin' ship!"

I slapped him back. "You're just jealous *you* don't fit!"

He jammed his face in mine. "I GOTTA GET TO HIS HOLOOLI-NESS 'FORE HE LEAVES!"

"Lets wheel this baby up the ramp," ordered a gruff voice outside. "Bob don't like to be kept waitin'."

Gneeecey stuck to my ribs like porridge on a winter morning as our dungeon-on-wheels trundled up a steep, notched slope. Moments later, doors boomed shut and a powerful engine fired up, vibrating beneath us.

After a lurch, our unsecured container slammed back and forth, nearly capsizing several times.

"Ig," whimpered Gneeecey, as his rancid breath wafted into my nostrils, "I don't feel good—think I'm gonna—"

"Don't you dare."

"AWRIGHT, YUZ THREE—OUT!"

The crate tilted forward, depositing us on a trash-littered warehouse floor. The dark place reeked of burnt mierk.

"Hey," snarled blond, big-nosed Mark, "I only see *two* of dem."

Gneeecey pointed to Altitude's hole. "Little rat escaped!"

The Markman whipped out his revolver. "He won't get far—an' neither'll yuz—so don't try nuthin' stupid."

"Y'know," began the double-jointed Gneeecey, chewing on his elbow, "if y'wanted to meet here in the Mierkolatory basement, all yuz hadda do was ask—y'didn't hafta go to all this trouble."

"On your feet—botha yuz," ordered tall, brown-haired Mark.

Gneeecey jumped up and began waving his hands. "BOB! BOB!"

The gray-suited figure ignored him.

"He's their *leader*," Gneeecey informed me, reverence in his tone. "His *socks* light up! An' backwards, his name's still *Bob*!"

The silver-haired gentleman strolled toward us, argyles flickering.

"Hey, Bob," began the good diroctor, "hope there ain't no hard feelin's, y'know, 'bout me bustin' up your lobby—"

"We've debited your account and rebuilt our entrance."

Gneeecey began sucking his thumb.

Bob's electric-blue eyes flashed my way. "And don't worry, miss, you won't have to ride any two-wheelers here."

I couldn't steady my knocking knees.

Bob crossed his arms. "Take 'em away—throw 'em in Interrogation One."

Blond Mark grinned. "Wit' pleasure."

Gneeecey fell to his knees. "Can't stay—gotta catch up wit' his Eviscerated Holooliness, 'fore he blasts back into space for a whole 'nother year!"

Bob yawned.

"*PLEEEEEEZE*, BOB—IT'S A MATTER OF LIFE AN' DEAF!"

Bob snapped his fingers.

The Markman jabbed his pistol into my back. "Yeah, Boss?"

"Don't waste my time till one of 'em talks."

CHAPTER 36

JUS' ZOGULATIN'

STOP POKIN' ME WIT' that gun," whined Gneeecey. "You're hurtin' meeee!" "Shaaaddup or I *will* hurt'cha," warned red-headed, broken-nosed Mark, as he shoved him through the basement, past rows of beige cubicles.

Each station contained an illuminated desk—a crystalline octahedron whose edges reflected all the hues of the rainbow, and then some.

Sleek silver keyboards, connected to gigantic, paper-thin, wall-mounted monitors, sparkled above the pulsating desktops.

"I see yuz upgraded your headquarters," bleated Gneeecey.

The Markman smashed the side of his revolver against the good director's head.

"OOOOOOOOW!"

"I said shaaaddup!"

Sick to my stomach, I shuffled along behind them, blond, big-nosed

Mark's firearm digging into my right kidney.

Studying the mierk-dripping barrels that lined the walls, I stumbled. Piled twenty-high, they reached all the way up to the painted-over, umber windows.

Blond Mark spun me around. "Ergzap, I tol' ya, don't try nuthin'!"

"Ergzap? What's—"

"*Inferior alien*," he explained, regarding me with contempt.

I gazed down at my left sneaker, stuck in a mound of mierk. "My shoe came off!"

"Y'won't need it," growled the Markman, pushing me up some stairs and past an open entryway, wide enough to accommodate a commercial jetliner. Frigid air rushed in through the sun-filled gap. Squinting, I slowed down.

"Don't even think about it," advised yellow-haired Mark, reading my mind. "Joint's crawlin' wit' guards—they been trained to shoot first an' ask later."

My shoeless heel hit something sharp. "Ow!"

Laughing, the Markman dragged me down some steps and hurled me through the steel-framed doorway of a room labeled "Interrogation One."

A split second later, Gneeecey whizzed past my cheek like a white-and-black, fur-covered spitball.

"Siddown—botha yuz!" ordered red-haired Mark, waving his weapon in the direction of two incandescent, scooped-out spheres.

Reluctantly, I sat.

Gneeecey lowered himself slowly, then flew up into the air. "Chair's burnin' up my bimbus!"

"SIDDOWN!" bellowed the redhead, flashing his gun.

Spooked by squishy footsteps coming up from behind, I sprang out of my butt-broiling seat.

"Easy," cautioned blond Mark, slamming me back down.

As I turned my head, a pair of sickly-yellow, disembodied eyeballs floated toward me. Lumpy, raised red vessels circled their shiny whites.

My mouth opened wide.

The ovals glowed and glimmered and dipped down low, intrigued as a glob of brown, rubbery mierk took on a life of its own, rising up from the filthy concrete and stretching itself into a taut membrane.

Gradually, the force made itself visible as a pair of amber-tinged hands, slathering and caressing more muck, building the eyes a head to live in. And a face. A waxy face, wearing an expression made malicious by its slanted, sardonic smile.

The hands grew arms. Muscular, chiseled arms. And legs. And a naked body that, pleased with having created itself, strode into the middle of the room, calling out, "Hey, Mark, whazzup?"

"Not much, Mark," replied the blond. "Whazzup wit'choo?"

"Nuthin'—jus' gotta go get my hair an' stuff outta my locker." He grinned at the redhead. "An' Mark, how you doin'?"

"Good. An' I'll be even better when these Ergzaps talk."

The undressed Markman resumed covering himself with goop.

"He's jus' zogulatin'," Gneeecey informed me.

"Gotta go zogulate, myself," said blond Mark, examining his flaky fingers. "I'm peelin'."

"Me too," snarled the redhead, his sewage-colored irises fixed on Gneeecey. "I tried that crummy zodd—it don't even seal our internal organs."

Gneeecey gulped.

Blond Mark glanced at his watch. "If I don't go zogulate soon, my lunch'll end up in my shoes again."

"Don't make me puke," responded the nude Markman, admiring his flexed biceps.

"WHAT'S THE CODE?" DEMANDED young, raven-haired Mark, as he booted up Interrogation One's computer. "Y'know, for the coordinates?"

The wall-sized screen fired up, illuminating the room.

"I told you," I insisted, "I have aboobsolutely—ugh—no idea what you're talking about."

"That's not what'cha friend here says," he said, sizing me up with merciless ocher eyes.

Gneeecey shrugged sheepishly as he shifted like mad in his hundred-watt seat.

"And what," I began, unable to control the tremble in my voice, "did my friend tell you?"

"That *you* got the code for the coordinates."

"Coordinates?"

"Don't play stupid wit' me—the coordinates on your planet."

I stared up at the sooty ceiling.

"He says only *you* can decipher the code." The Markman loosened his tie.

He wore civvies, but his thin-lipped smirk gave him away—he was the motorcycle cop who planted that ticket on my windshield, on Northwestern Southeast Stummix Lane Loop, the day I cashed my first paycheck.

The Markman pounded his fist on the desktop. "I ASKED YOU A QUESTION!"

I just looked at him.

He tapped his black oxford impatiently. "Well, you decide."

"Decide what?"

"Whether y'gonna walk outta here, or be taken out—y'know, horizontal."

"I—I don't—"

My muscle-bound inquisitor leapt up, sucked in his abs, and raised his right hand in a stiff salute.

"Ogblorg!" snapped a faceless, gray-suited being, blue eyes blazing in nothingness above his white collar.

"Ogblorg, sir," barked our Markman, standing straight as an arrow.

"They softenin' up?" inquired the headless entity, as he rolled a brown lump between two handless cuffs.

The young Markman cleared his throat. "Uh, not yet, sir."

"Pleeeeze, Bob," begged Gneeecey, "lemmee *go!*"

Bob's pitiless pupils remained fixed on his subordinate. "Y'like bein' off the streets, workin' on the inside, don'cha?"

"Yes, sir," answered our Markman, scrutinizing us through narrowed lids. "Guess I'll hafta start playin' rough."

"Do what'cha hafta. Blork!"

"Blork, sir!"

"I THINK I CAN handle this," protested our Markman.

"That's not what the boss thinks," replied tall, brown-haired Mark, as he motioned the rookie to make way.

"But he jus' said—"

"Bob wants results now, not some other day."

Grinding his perfect pearly whites, the young Markman rose.

Brown-haired Mark plunked himself down behind the keyboard and rolled up his sleeves. "Okay, Doc, y'lost the election after y'guaranteed it'd go our way—"

"Nuthin's really lost," squeaked Gneeecey. "Yuz'll find everythin' y'need on *her* planet! I'll stake her life on it!"

I bolted upright. "Now, you just wait a minute—"

Teeth bared, the younger Markman walloped my face with his meaty palm.

"Y'been hustlin' us," continued the senior Markman, ignoring me as I sat stunned. "Playin' us for fools."

"No!" insisted Gneeecey. "Nuthin' in life's for sure—everythin's fifty-fifty! We'd either win the election, or we wouldn't—"

"That ain't wha'cha was tellin' *us* the whole time—"

"I mean," spluttered Gneeecey, biting his knuckles, "y'know—"

"Don't eat your hand, Doc. Y'gonna need it to reach in your pocket an' return our deposit—all fifty-quadrillion bucks."

"*An'* thirty-seven cents!" shouted the younger man, wielding a translucent, flame-filled pole.

Gneeecey shrank back. "Not the one wit' the *red handle!*"

"Won't hurt me." The Markman's dead eyes came alive as he poked Gneeecey's left ear with the rod.

"OOOOOOOW!"

"Whattsamatter, Doc? Ain't real fire—not for *us*, anyway. It's jus' an eglonkerated field of emaxicated energy. We're talkin' elementary thirteenth-dimension physics. Here—let's try your other ear."

Gneeecey slid to the floor, howling.

"Stop!" I yelled.

"Lessee how *you* like it, Ergzap!" The rookie touched his stick to my down-filled sleeve.

The Markmen slapped high-fives as I beat out flames.

"Okay, Doc, give us back our moolah," ordered the senior Markman. "Every cent!"

"Caaaan't," Gneeecey wailed. "It's all tied up—y'know, investipated. An', uh. . .some's, uh, *missin'*. . . ."

The rookie aimed his fiery weapon at Gneeecey's nose.

"NOOOOO!" screamed the good diroctor. "*She* knows where the mon-ney is! An' all them codes are in her papers!"

"We're still waitin' for them papers."

"I'll give 'em to yuz, like I promised. But'cha gotta lemme outta here so's I can go get 'em."

"Nice try, Doc. But we got our own ways of gettin' what we want." The Markman's laser-like pupils burned through him.

"I swear," said Gneeecey, "sometimes it hurts when yuz guys jus' *look* at me!"

"An' what'choo lookin' at?" the older Markman asked me.

"I've nevoover—ugh—seen a computer mouse like that."

He rolled his luminous, crap-colored eyes. "Y'ain't never seen an optically-saturnated muridian zlooper?"

"No."

Gyrating geometric images raced up and down the screen as the Markman manipulated the neon-green outer ring of a gaseous orange sphere. He ran a hand through his greasy hair. "Doc, y'wanna see somethin' cool?"

Gneeecey leaned forward. "I love cool junk!"

Mark clicked the ring down and pumped up the volume on two silver cylindric speakers. "Check this out."

Gneeecey's mouth opened wide.

"There's your parade, Doc—goin' on wit'out ya."

A guttural sound escaped from Gneeecey's throat.

The Markman depressed his ring twice. "Let's zoom in an' see who's ridin' that pretty white horse."

Gneeecey's stallion pranced across the wall—ridden by a triumphant Jacob J. Qwertyuiop, an orange-and-purple satin sash draped across his barrel chest. Jacob, Jr. sat in the saddle with him, his young face lit up with joy.

"ONLY THE GRATE GIZZY'S S'POSED TO RIDE THAT HORSEY AN' WEAR THAT SASH!" shrieked the good diroctor, as he sprinted toward the door. "LEMME OUTTA HERE! NOW!"

The rookie scooped Gneeecey up like a ground ball and chucked him back into his chair. "You ain't goin' nowheres."

"We'll take care of them two witches," vowed the senior Markman, pointing to Verna Vlott and Vlotta Vern as they high-stepped their way down spectator-lined Veggie Burger Avenue, to a jovial, jazzed-up rendition of Planet Eccchs's anthem.

"Qwertyuiop, too," added the younger Markman, aiming his deadly pole at the screen, "*an'* his kid."

"Where's His Holooliness?" asked Gneeecey. "The Grand Oogitty-Boogitty always rides right behin' the Grate Gizzy, ontoppa that Squiggleman's barbecue float—"

"Your oogey-boogey man took off awready," replied brown-haired Mark. "Y'won't see him for a whole 'nother year—that is, if *you're* still around."

"But he always waits till after lunch to launch himself!"

"Let's rewind." Mark turned his ring counterclockwise.

There, up on the wall, the expressionless holy spud crackled and hissed, atop a state-of-the-art stainless steel grill, clutching his scepter and a Gnorks lunchbox, as the crowd chanted, "Ten, nine, eight, seven, six, five, four, three, two, one, BLAST OFF!"

Gneeecey's eyes glazed over as he watched his spiritual leader, and his hopes, disappear into the heavens.

"Let's fast-forward to the present," suggested Mark. "Hey, ain't that your buddy? The one all the chicks went nuts for?"

Gneeecey winced as Flubbubb marched past, striking his triangle with abandon. "Yuz guys ain't really my friends, *are* yuz? When I get outta here, I'm stinkin' gonna *get* yuz!"

Brown-haired Mark cleared his throat. "You threatenin' us?" He clicked on a lightbulb icon, and Gneeecey's hot seat vanished into thin air.

"Wha—wha' hapoopened?" inquired the good director as he tumbled to the cement.

Mark chuckled. "We don't play." Whistling, he brought my image—my live, three-dimensional image—up onto the screen. "Well, well, whadda we got here?"

The virtual me squirmed in her scorching seat, attempting to keep most of her weight on her insulated coat's thick bottom hem. Just like the real me.

Mark rotated the ring. "Looky."

I—and the shrinking series of virtual myselves up on the wall—gawked as the cursor dragged a shrinking series of dark objects out of a shrinking series of our virtual pockets.

Mark snapped his fingers.

My black V-neck blouse—the one I had stuffed into my pocket only hours earlier—unfurled and floated past my face, right into the Markman's slimy clutches.

Winking, he threw my garment into a pile of mierk.

"Whattsamatter, Ergzap Earthlin'? That was a pretty cool trick!"

"It was!" agreed an opportunistic Gneeecey. "Do it again!"

"We will—don'choo worry."

I began to black out.

"Okay, we'll try somethin' different." Rotating the ring clockwise, counterclockwise, then clockwise, the Markman double-clicked on my virtual jacket and snapped his fingers.

Breath nearly sucked out of me—the real me—I swooshed up toward the ceiling.

"Ig," whooped Gneeecey, clapping, "you're flyin'!"

An instant later, I landed hard, on my hands and knees. As I raised my head, I saw my jacket—my actual jacket—hanging from Mark's index finger.

"C-cool trick," I stammered, "but could I please have it back? I'm freezing!"

"Yeah, sure." He tossed my coat to the younger Markman. "After we search the pockets."

THE ROOKIE TAPPED GNEEECEY'S shuddering shoulder. "Not so freakin' hilarious when it's your turn, is it?"

"Get outta my house!"

The senior Markman moved his cursor up three staircases and maximized the view. "Ain't this fun, takin' a tour of your mansion, wit'out gettin' our dirty footprints all over your dirty floors? Let's check out your bedroom."

"NOOOOOO!"

"My, what a squalid mess," declared Mark, feigning astonishment. "It's a wonder y'can even find your shorts—y'know, them stupid-lookin' ones wit' dimes all over 'em?"

Gneeecey's snout wrinkled. "Leave my stinkin' shorts alone!"

"Whadda we got here?" The alien rolled his cursor over to Gneeecey's untidy pharmacy of a night table. "Ain't them your shorts right there— hangin' over that dame's picture?"

Scarlet face visible through his fur, Gneeecey grunted.

Mark clicked on the tarnished frame, enlarging our view of the photo inside. "Classy lookin' broad."

Gneeecey bunched up his fists. "Yuz stinkin' leave my Goonafina *outta* this!"

Mark snickered. "She's a real dog."

Gneeecey flew up into his amused amber face, kicking and punching. And missing.

The Markman hoisted him up by the scruff of his neck, then dropped him to the floor. "An' whadda shame y'killed them goths we gave ya, as a symbol of our fond an' everlastin' friendship."

"It's *her* fault," bawled Gneeecey, rubbing his behind. "The Ig here croaked 'em—*an'* their poor, unbornded babies!"

"Whatever," replied the Markman, highlighting Gneeecey's bed. "An' whadda we got here, parked up by your pillow? A red briefcase?"

I shot Gneeecey a withering glance. He turned away.

Noting my interest, Mark right-clicked on my portfolio, chose "cut," and left-clicked. And snapped his fingers.

It—my actual case—popped out of the screen, into his foul hands. "Another cool trick, huh?"

Pulse pounding in my eardrums, I stared across the room, at my jacket.

"Hey," suggested the younger creep, pointing his flaming pole at Gneeecey's virtual disaster of a master suite. "Let's do his place like we did Shisskey's—an' the *Pooper-Scooper!*"

Gneeecey cowered against the wall, his ratty knees knocking so loudly you could hear them.

"*Please?*" begged the Markman, aiming at Gneeecey's mattress.

"Maybe later," answered the senior Markman, absentmindedly, as he clicked on a green, leaf-shaped icon. In a flash, Gneeecey's cream-shrouded backyard covered the wall.

"Get offa my propooperty!"

Mark's cursor skidded to the foot of Gneeecey's icicle-dripping oak.

"MR. TREE!" screeched Gneeecey.

"Looky, Doc—I can make Mr. Tree dance twice as fast as usual."

Gneeecey's head whipped around. "See, Ig? Mr. Tree *has* been movin' faster!"

I scowled. "You guys have been making Mr. Tree—uh—this tree— chase him?"

"Nah. Not really. That lousy tree really does chase him—in his wacko mind. We jus' make it move a little faster—for fun."

I jumped up. "You call messing with someone's mind *fun?*"

"Yeah," he replied, as he clicked on a gold star at the bottom of the screen. "Here, Earthlin'—we got a little somethin' up our sleeve for you, too. We are gonna get that code outta you."

I stood face-to-face with my own virtual solar system.

"We're gonna have fun wit' this," continued Mark, pointing his cursor at Earth. "Even more fun than we had wit' Mr. Tree. Or them hungry virtual kangaroos we dragged to the auditorium right before your big concert—y'know, for kicks. Or even the time we tested an earlier version of this program, knockin' your car offa the bridge."

"No," I pleaded, acid pouring into my belly, "*not* my—"

Before the Markman could maximize my planet, Gneeecey stomped on his fringed designer loafers, with all his might. "Y'BEEN HELPIN' EVIL MR. TREE!"

Mark grabbed Gneeecey and smashed him against the wall. The good director fell to the floor, legs wrapped around his noggin.

"Time to make a new file," proclaimed the Markman. Teeth clenched, he minimized my solar system, opened another application, and dragged a folder into the screen's upper right corner.

Gneeecey watched through his knees, fascinated as Mark's fingers flew across the keyboard like amber lightning. "How 'bout we name this new file 'Doomed'? That'll be perfect."

"Yeah," agreed the rookie. "Perfect!"

"Now," continued the senior Markman, rotating his ring, "we would-n't want this new folder to feel empty an' unwanted, would we?"

I gaped spellbound as my portfolio swam above his head and merged with its gradually materializing onscreen image. As the Markman stashed my case away in his folder, my jacket drifted past me. The instant I reached for it, the coat coalesced seamlessly with its virtual likeness. He whisked it into "Doomed."

The blood rushed from my head.

"Doc," began the Markman, as he displayed a page filled with num-bered cubes, "pick any number, from two to ten."

Gneeecey's head tilted. "Threeeee."

"Three it is," Mark agreed affably. Clicking twice, he snapped his fingers and zapped Gneeecey off his feet, past my face, and into the screen. Another manipulation of the mouse shrank the good director down to the size of a large housefly.

"Shut'cha mouth, Ergzap—y'want planes to fly in?" Chortling, the Markman dragged the microscopic Gneeecey, kicking and screaming, into "Doomed," then deposited the dossier and its condemned contents inside Cube Three.

CHAPTER 37

TEA AND STRUMPETS

BROWN-HAIRED MARK HELD HIS pistol to my temple. "Let's go." "Where?" I asked, limping out into the dark hallway. He rammed his weapon into my ribs. "*I* do the askin'. Walk!"

"Why'd you bother kidnapping us if you could zap us here with your computers?"

"They were down. Y'always gotta have a backup plan."

I sighed. I didn't.

"Now stop askin' dumb questions. Move!"

The moment I stepped forward, a thunderous boom rattled beneath us, slamming me into the wall. I tumbled to the floor as a second explosion rumbled through the building. A series of short, rhythmic blasts followed, accompanied by metallic squeaks.

I sat shivering and perspiring at the same time. "What the—"

"Jus' the mierkolatin' pistons pumpin'," said Mark, checking his watch. "First production shift jus' came on."

"Oh."

"Y'know, I could blow you away right now—wit' all this racket, nobody'd notice." His eyes lit up.

Mine widened.

"Now geddup awready an' walk."

"I'm freezing," I whispered, staggering to my feet. "Wish I had my jacket."

"You'll wish y'had more'n that if y'don't come clean."

"I still don't understand—"

"Stop playin' stupid, Ergzap. Wit' everythin' we got on you, we can put'cha away for years—or worse."

"But—"

"Over here." He shoved me up against Interrogation Three's closed door. "You're next."

"OOOOOOOOW!" howled Gneeecey, on the other side. "STOP!"

Mark jammed his face into mine. He stank like a mixture of moldy mierk and gasoline. "They're whippin' him for *your* lies. You're gettin' a real beatin'—by proxy!"

"What's in the coat?" demanded a harsh voice inside the room. "This navy job here, wit' all them zippers?"

I clutched my sides.

"Go through her pockets," suggested Gneeecey. "*She's* the one y'want—*she* double-crossed us!"

"Oh, man!" exclaimed a muffled voice.

"Tie that tighter! Now, where are the codes?"

"How's 'bout we crash this little tea party?" asked brown-haired Mark, banging his gun on the door.

It creaked open slowly.

"Whadda nice surprise," gushed a falsetto-voiced, blond, big-nosed Mark, arranging an imaginary bouffant hairdo with one hand and clutching a .44 Magnum in his other. "If I knew yuz was comin', I woulda baked some strumpets."

"Well," replied the dark-haired Markman, "if I knew I was comin', I woulda brung somethin'. Oh—I did! I brung *her*." He jammed the barrel of his revolver into my spine.

I peered over the blond's beefy shoulder, as a whip sliced through the air. It hit its target, with an ugly, cracking sound.

"OOOOOOOW!" shrilled Gneeecey. I winced.

Murky eyes dancing with delight, blond Mark, gracious host that he was, moved aside. "C'mon in."

I wobbled into the room and stopped short.

There, tied up in a chair, sat Yammicles, hemorrhaging thousand dollar bills.

"IG!" yowled Gneeecey. "THEY'RE WHIPPIN' HIM!"

"That's *our* dough!" growled blond Mark.

Teeth gritted, redheaded, broken-nosed Mark turned his lash on the sea of magazines spilling out of my portfolio. "Doc, y'knew all along the codes weren't in here!"

"They stinkin' *were*—I swear! Someone musta stoled 'em!"

The Markman's swamp-green eyes flashed with desperation. "I'll ask ya one more time, where are they?"

"Why don'cha put the Ig into your computer there an' drag 'em outta her?" proposed Gneeecey.

"We'll deal wit' *her* later—as a matter-of-fac', we're plannin' to delete her."

I nearly dissolved into the floor.

Hate oozing from his mierk-dripping sockets, the redhead resumed whipping Yammicles.

The teddy's crossed peepers remained fixed on the room's half-fallen drop ceiling, as clouds of cash exploded from his bursting seams.

Gneeecey dropped to his knees. "STOP! YOU'LL KILL HIM!"

"We'll kill you, too!"

"Yeah," agreed the blond, arranging greenbacks in neat piles. "Let's waste them Ergzaps, right now."

"Wanna make sure my weapon's fully loaded," said brown-haired Mark, spinning his revolver's chamber.

The redhead threw his whip down and wedged my jacket under his arm. "Yup. These bullets got perspiration dates stamped on 'em—might as well use 'em all up 'fore they go bad."

"We'll go through their crap *after* we blow their brains out," declared blond Mark, as he opened a tall locker.

Gneeecey and I exchanged glassy-eyed glances.

Brown-haired Mark grinned. "I'm sure Bob'll figure it ain't *our* fault if a few zillion bucks turn up missin'—if y'get my drift."

"Any, uh, *excess*, could be split three ways," suggested the redhead, eyeing the banknotes on the floor. "Let's march these two out back an' get it over wit'."

The blond tossed AK 47's into his colleagues' quick-catching mitts. "Let's do this in style."

Numb, curiously detached, I stepped aside quickly as a steady, noisy stream of yellow splashed Gneeecey's high-tops.

So this was how it was going to end. My mother would really be upset. Come to think of it, she already was.

"Okay, yuz two," ordered brown-haired Mark. He kicked Yammicles' empty plaid nightie across the concrete. "Start walkin'."

A tower of cartons, stacked at the far end of the room, caught my attention. Marked *Do Not Store On Floor!*, they were exact replicas of the makeshift night table I had left behind.

I stared at the containers, concentrating on them until nothing else existed. With little effort, I convinced myself that they'd begun expanding and contracting. Breathing in, breathing out, ready to topple.

Suddenly, the boxes exploded outward in seventy-five directions.

Heart beating erratically, I ducked for cover. When I finally raised my head, I found myself gaping at Cleveland Wheeler, all six denim-clad feet of him.

Unshaven, mouth gagged, and ankles bound, he gaped right back. Behind him lay an upside-down chair, ropes still attached.

I collapsed into his outstretched arms.

Gneeecey pointed to my dangling left wrist. "Hey, Ig, now you'll hafta give his watch back!"

CHAPTER 38

DYIN' FOR A SMOKE

"IT'S TIME," ANNOUNCED BROWN-HAIRED Mark, loading his assault rifle. "Line up by the door—an' don't try no heroics." As Cleve hopped ahead of me, he snapped his left foot up over his right and freed it, in a single motion. They didn't notice.

He loosened his gag and let it drop.

Blond Mark whirled around and took aim. "Watch it, Wheeler—I'll plug ya right b'tween your eyes an' blow off *her* head—wit' one shot."

Cleve's jaw tightened.

The dark-haired Markman strolled over to Gneeecey and stepped down on his flaccid tail, hard.

"OOOOOOOOW!"

"I *said*, line up by the door."

Urine-logged sneakers squooshing, Gneeecey tiptoed past Cleve and me and fell into line.

My precious jacket still clenched under his arm, the redhead pulled a dilapidated pack of cigarettes out of his pocket. "Let's take these Ergzaps outside. I'm dyin' for a smoke."

The blond nodded. "Me too. Boss is too freakin' paranoid 'bout smokin' inside."

"Bob does take it a little too far," agreed the senior Markman. "Yeah, this is a miercoles refinery an' all, but our fire ain't like Ergzap fire—it can't hurt nuthin'."

Laughing, red-haired Mark stuffed a half-smoked butt in his fat kisser. "If it did, every time we lit up, this whole crummy place would—"

A brick-shattering blast cut him off mid-sentence, rocking the place to its foundations. The three Markmen's eyeballs bulged out of their wig-topped noggins.

"FIRE!" warned a sandy-haired young gray-suit, sprinting past our door.

"FIRE!" shouted Sooperflea, as he galloped down the hall, his scarlet cape ablaze.

A braying Stu Pitt flew after him. Flames consumed the seat of his too-short khakis.

Cleve and I dashed past our captors. As we raced for the door, he snatched my coat up off the floor and tossed it into my hands, like a quarterback throwing a lateral pass.

Frayed cord still attached to his right ankle, he caught up with Flea, dropped him to the ground, and extinguished the polyester-fed blaze.

The superhero just gawked.

I stood nearby, whacking Stu's charred posterior.

"Thanks, Icky!"

"It's okay, Stuart. You'd do the same for me—uh, I mean—"

"Guess what, Icky?"

"What?"

"I jus' flew Chopper Three-an'-a-half! Boss wasn't around to say no, an' being it was an emergency—"

"Follow me!" shouted Cleve, as the hallway filled with black smoke and expletive-spouting Markmen.

I pulled my jacket on and took off. "C'mon, Stuart!"

"Ergzaps crashed a copter into the joint!" yelled a Markman.

"There's one!" hollered another. "Get her!"

Running hard, I glanced over my shoulder and caught sight of Flea. They were on his tail, literally.

"Hey, Mister Know-it-all," taunted blond Mark, "your crystal ball tell y'what we're gonna do wit'cha when we catch ya?"

Before the superhero could come back with a witty retort, he stumbled sideways into a wall lined with missile-shaped canisters labeled,

"Warning: Unstable Accelerant."

The silver cylinders fell like dominoes, cracking open and releasing vapors that reeked like rotten eggs laced with ammonia.

Meanwhile, the Markmen began to scatter as thready trails of mierk ignited and set off random explosions.

Flea was still down. I tore toward him. "When these fumes reach those flames, we're goners!"

I snatched him up off the floor, pulled my turtleneck over my nose and peered through the haze. Didn't see any signs of Cleve or Stu. But I did spy a fresh group of Markmen, in the distance, barking orders at each other.

Flea in my arms, I lunged forward, then stopped dead in my tracks when, from out of nowhere, a tow-headed Markman, his jacket burning, ran straight at me.

As he clutched at my throat, he popped like a balloon. His smoldering clothes and hairpiece landed in a heap at my feet, and his lime green eyeballs and haunting howl floated up toward the ceiling.

"Y'know," began Flea, face hidden in my jacket, "I think my psychic powers are returnin'."

"Oh?"

"I'm pretty sure I was contacted by a dead person."

"Huh?"

"Cleve. He helped me when I was on fire. I heard spirits can do stuff like that."

"Cleve's alive," I replied, laughing and sobbing. "These creeps had him the whole time."

"Holy Saint Bogelthorpe!" exclaimed the superhero, climbing down.

The two of us scuttled up the fire-lit corridor, littered with empty gray suits and shined oxfords.

CLEVE STUCK HIS HEAD out through a slot in the blackened bricks. "In here—quick!"

I pushed Flea through the pinched aperture, slid in, then stopped short.

"C'mon," whispered Cleve.

Slinking back with dread, I studied the stone staircase ahead. It led into a *tunnel*.

"It's our only chance," said Flea. A herd of Markmen stampeded past us, on the other side of the wall. I couldn't tell whether they were shooting or popping.

I gritted my teeth and took Cleve's hand. Flea unclipped his flashlight from his belt and the three of us flew down the steps.

Once through the gloomy passageway, we found ourselves inside a cave-like room. A single shaft of sunlight streamed in through a fissure, illuminating a banjo-eyed Stu.

"Stu, you alright?" asked Cleve.

"EEEEEEEEKS!" screamed the intern.

Cleve sighed. "For the last time, Stu, I'm not *dead*."

"But I'm so *used* to you being dead!"

"Well, sorry to disappoint you."

"Cleve's alive," I proclaimed, riffling through my jacket's pockets and pouches.

Cleve nodded. "Undead."

Stu turned whiter than a sheet. One with freckles. "You're a *zombie*?"

"He's un-unalive," explained Flea, as he positioned his flashlight up on a slanted ledge, to provide more light. "As opposed to bein' undead."

"Oh," replied Stu, wiping beads of perspiration from his furrowed brow. "Why din'cha say so?"

"And I'm still waiting for Seemingwhale's to deliver my new living room set," said Cleve, "so please, everyone, just cop a squat. We'll order out."

Smiling for the first time in a couple of weeks, I lowered myself down onto the damp dirt floor and drew in a deep breath of musty air.

Cleve's twinkling eyes met mine. "There's a sneaker imprint on your chin. A long, skinny one."

I rubbed my jaw with the back of my hand.

He squeezed his arm around my shoulders. "Your coat's stuffed."

"Yeah."

"Everything still there?"

"I think so."

"You were leaving, weren't you?"

"Uh-huh. I *was*." I leaned my head against his chest.

"Ahem!" whinnied Stu, shifting from foot to foot.

Cleve and I looked up.

"Uh, guys, where's the boss?"

Cleve groaned. "*Gneeecey*. We gotta go back for *Gneeecey*."

"C'MON, DAMMIT!" PLEADED CLEVE, dodging flames.

"I'm untyin' Yammicles!"

Cleve scowled. "We don't have time!"

"Ain't leavin' wit' out him!"

"C'mon, Diroctor—let's get outta here," I begged, breathing through my turtleneck, "before your friends come back!"

Cleve ripped Yammicles up out of the chair like a weed. "In case you hadn't noticed, this room's on fire!"

Eyes narrowed, Gneeecey seized his teddy and began stuffing it with singed bills.

Cleve bent down low. "What don'cha understand 'bout 'let's go *now?*' You need us to call in a translator?"

"Ain't leavin' wit' out my mon-ney!"

"It's not yours, is it?"

"They gave it to us—right, Yammypoo?"

Cleve threw his hands in the air. "C'mon Nicki—let's leave his sorry butt here to burn."

"Yeah—let's go!"

"STINKIN' WAIT—WE'RE COMIN'!" Scooping thousands off the floor and shoveling them back into Yammicles' torn trap, Gneeecey scurried along behind us.

"OUCH!" I CRIED, AS Cleve and I scrambled through the basement. "Foot's killing me, but I can't feel my legs!"

"You're not ready to leave yet, Nicki, are you?"

I kept running.

"And what happened to your other sneaker?"

I chuckled halfheartedly. "Don't ask."

"Lemme see something," he mumbled, slowing down to pick up a long black lump. "Looks like your size."

It was an abandoned left shoe. A loafer. Gulping for oxygen, I slipped it on.

Cleve laughed. "You're really making a fashion statement there."

"Hope I don't catch their cooties and turn into one of 'em."

"Don'choo dare! And speaking of *them*—where *are* they?"

"Proboobably—ugh—regroupooping—ugh." I felt my face flush.

"Nicki—my God—"

"Dr. Idnas say it's hopoopfully—ugh—just tempooporary—ugh. I've been trying to use short words."

"Ig's got Redecoritis-infected speech," announced Gneeeecey, skipping up behind us. "An' it might not be jus' tempooporary!"

It was all I could do not to rip the smile off his face.

Cleve tapped my arm. "Let's get back to Flea and Stu—we've still gotta figure out how we're gonna break outta here."

We jogged up the hallway, elbow to elbow. Gneeecey trailed behind, huffing and puffing like the little train that couldn't.

"Smoke's not too bad here," observed Cleve.

"No," I replied. "They've been putting out fires like mad—look at all this water and foam—"

"Can't keep up wit' yuz!" shrieked Gneeecey. "Wait up!"

"Cleve—you hear a familiar voice?"

He grinned. "Must be the pistons squeaking."

"I'LL FIRE YUZ TWO LOUSY IGGLEHEIMERS!"

"C'mon, Cleve—we've got a real good reason to run!" We picked up speed.

"There they are!"

Cleve and I whipped our heads around. That wasn't Gneeecey talking.

"Get 'em!" ordered brown-haired Mark. "I'll call for backup!"

"Okay!" Redheaded Mark flew after us, an unlit cigarette jutting out of his mouth.

Cleve doubled back and grabbed Gneeecey.

"WAIT—I DROPPED YAAAMMICLES!"

Cleve whisked the bear off the floor. "Here, dammit!"

"WE'RE ALL GONNA DIE—YOU'RE GONNA DIE AGAIN, CLEEEVOOVELAND!"

"I swear," began Cleve, shooting past barrels of mierk, "when this is all over, I'm gonna—"

"Y'gonna *what*, big guy?" inquired the red-haired Markman as he hooked his arm around Cleve's neck, from behind.

Cleve grunted and smashed his head straight back into Mark's face. Bone cracked audibly.

The redhead crumpled to his knees, grasping his nose. "It's broke—*again*!"

Cleve set Gneeecey down. "Diroctor, gimme your phone!"

"WHAAAAAAAT?"

"Gimme your phone!"

"Why?"

"Just give it here—now!"

The Markman staggered upright. A Park Avenue plastic surgeon couldn't have done a better job straightening out his schnozz.

"Gimme your phone!" repeated Cleve. "Like *now!*"

Gneeecey stared at him. "My cell phone?"

"Yesss!"

"Y'mean, my orange one?"

Cleve held his hand out.

"My orange Binky the Clown cell phone?"

"Give it here!" As Cleve's foot tapped impatiently, the Markman trudged toward us, his cigarette still wedged between his greasy lips. The butt was broken, like his nose.

Gneeecey began digging in his shirt pocket. "The phone I light my cigars wit'?"

"Will you give it here?"

"Wait—here it is—no, that's my pocket plunger—remember that telescopin', all-purpoopose plunger I picked up durin' Squiggleman's pre-Grimace sale? Nah, y'wouldn't—y'were dead—"

"C'mon—"

"Wait, here it is—nah, that's part of a trombone I always carry in case I ever come 'cross one missin' that very same piece. . . ."

The Markman reached into his jacket.

"Gimme your freakin' phone already!"

"Here, Cleeevoooveland. An' careful—it's one of them limited edition jobs—BlunderBuxxComm busted the mold of Binky's face las' week!"

Cleve snatched the gadget.

The Markman took another step forward. Vile green slime oozed from his unhappy nostrils.

"Easy, dude," warned Cleve. "I actually did you a favor—fixed your nose."

The Markman drew his weapon.

"I should charge ya," continued Cleve, flipping Gneeecey's cell open.

The Markman wiped his snoot on his silk sleeve and raised his pistol.

As he did, "Pop Goes the Weasel" tinkled out of Gneeecey's phone.

"Don't answer!" begged the good diroctor. "It's proboobably some-one wantin' the mon-ney back!"

Cleve pressed Binky's red nose and a yellow flame shot out of the nozzle below. He held it up to the Markman's ciggie. "Hey, bro, you still dyin' for a smoke?"

Abject terror leapt from the redhead's mustard-flecked green eyes.

"Don't worry," Cleve reassured him. "I love performin' random acts of kindness."

As the Markman took aim, Cleve touched Binky's fiery tongue to his chin, and FOOM!—another one of Bob's boys blew up in our faces.

CHAPTER 39

KILL! KILL! KILL!

WE ZIPPED DOWN THE corridor, chased by a brigade of broken-nosed Mark's grieving buddies, armed with scarlet-handled poles. "Faster!" ordered Gneeecey, as he rode piggyback on Cleve's shoulders. "Their fire don't burn *them*, but it could hurt me an' Yammicles!"

Cleve and I exchanged sidelong glances. "As usual," he muttered, "we're chopped liver."

"An' all this stinkin' smoke's makin' me an' Yammicles sick," continued Gneeecey. "I think we're gonna barf!"

"Here's your phone," growled Cleve, reaching up, nearly jamming it in the good director's flapping yapper. "Make yourself useful. Any Markmen come near, pop 'em."

"Okay, Cleeeevoooveland! Me an' Yammy got your back!"

"How comforting."

That moment, raven-haired, pyromaniac Mark jumped out in front of us, aiming his flame-filled stick at Yammicles.

"Y'like playin' wit' fire?" Teeth clenched, Gneeecey flipped his phone open, clicked the red button, and torched the Markman.

The detective wailed as his eyeballs floated up over our heads, and his burning, bodiless suit dropped to the floor.

The other Markmen fell back.

"KILL! KILL! KILL!" screeched Gneeecey. "THIS IS FUN—I SURE HOPE MORE OF 'EM TRY AN' GET US!"

"Don't worry," I replied. "They will."

"There's a shortcut," said Cleve, zooming around the corner.

"Y'sure know your way 'round here, Cleeevoooveland—they must be right—you're a spy!"

"I know mosta this building. First day I was here, they musta marched me through every square inch."

As voices behind us became louder by the second, we ducked into a closet. "Gotta crawl through that trapdoor," whispered Cleve. "Leads to a passageway that'll get us back quicker. Kinda like a wormhole."

"Me an' Yammicles ain't travoovelin' like no slimy worm," protested Gneeecey.

"Suit yourself." Cleve dropped to his hands and knees, forgetting that his boss sat perched on his shoulders. When he inched forward, Gneeecey's honking beak slammed into the bricks above, and he spilled to the floor.

"OOOOOW!" squealed the good diroctor, as he crawled in after Cleve. "Y'ALMOS' DECAPOOPITATED MY DOPEY NOODLE!"

Chortling, I wriggled through the hole—no small task, wrapped in my bulky jacket. As I hoisted myself to my feet, my mouth opened wide.

There, up on blocks, nestled between two mierk-filled vats, sat my missing monster-finned jalopy. Same exact dents and bent Jersey plates, designating me "SKEEVEY 1."

"Nicki," began Cleve, "isn't that—"

"My Splodge. . .those dirty creeps. . . ."

CHAPTER 40

CONFESSING IN THE CAVE

W INDED, WE SPRINTED INTO our cave. "You're doing tunnels better," remarked Cleve. "And you," I replied, "you ran like a marathoner—a champoopion—ugh—"

Gneeecey pushed past us. "ME FIRST—I'M GRATE GIZZY!"

Cleve took my hand. "I wan'cha to keep my watch."

"Awww. . . ."

Gneeecey hurled a fistful of dirt at us. "YUZ ARE MAKIN' ME AN' YAMMICLES ALL PUKEY!"

"Sssssh!" warned Flea.

Gneeecey threw a rock at him and missed. "An' I'm gonna fire Altitude—that dirty ship-jumpin' rat! So ingratitoodinous—after all I done to him."

"'Zig," replied Flea, "Altitude's the one who came lookin' for us—said y'were in troubooble—ugh—"

"Altitude, schmaltitude! Y'got'cha ESP—y'don't need some little rat to tell y'when—"

"You know my ESP's failin'—"

"One thing's for sure," said Gneeecey. "Your piano playin' still stinks—an' I *know* bad music!"

"Maybe it sounds so bad 'cause Shriekensobb wrote my parts for harpoopsichord—ugh—not piano."

Gneeecey stuffed a health cigar between his lips. "Whadda yooou know, stoopid?"

Stu flinched.

"A harpoopsichord," declared the good dirroctor, "is jus' a stinkin' piano playin' a lousy guitar."

Flea lowered his head. "Changin' the subject, I dunno if we're gonna make it outta here. . . ."

Cleve's brow wrinkled. "I don't like hearing *you* say that."

"Whatever hapoopens—ugh, I wanna. . .have a clear conscience—"

"What, Fleaglossitty, y'ain't Mister Perfoofect?"

"By the way 'Zig, your shoelaces are yellow."

Gneeecey's eyes flashed down to his soggy high-tops.

"I gotta get this offa my chest," said Flea. "I never *stole* nuthin'. Always lef' money to cover whatever I ate. Right on the counter. Even lef' tips."

"Y'nevoover leave no tips in Gneeezle's! An' what'cha stinkin' talkin' 'bout, anyways?"

"I *love* Burt an' Mary," continued Flea. "I'd never hurt 'em. Nebberd-kinnezzard."

I gasped. "You're not saying that *you're*—"

"The 'Whipped Cream Bandit'?" spluttered Cleve.

Flea looked down at his knees.

Cleve rubbed his stubbly jaw. "But, the vandalism—"

"Whipped cream addiction—it's not a pretty thing. But I didn't do *that*." A glittering, pear-shaped droplet slid down the superhero's cheek.

"What *I* wanna know," asked Gneeecey, "is how come Cleeevooveland's alive? He's s'posed to be dead—that's what I paid for!"

Cleve jumped up so fast, he whacked his head on the low, stone ceiling. "OW—*you what?!*"

"Your funeral."

"I don't follow you."

"Y'didn't. We followed yoooou, in that black Caddy station wagon—"

"*What?!*"

"Lemme igsplain—"

Cleve's face hardened. "You'd better."

"I paid for your funeral—after y'choked to death on a Rindom Doodle—"

"You know I wouldn't be caught *dead* eating a—"

"Well, y'were—an' after y'choked to death, y'jumped into the Perswayssick an' drownded yourself—"

"That's the stupidest, most idiotic crap I ever—"

"An' when they foun' ya—"

Cleve folded his arms. "*They?*"

"Mark an' them."

Cleve scowled. "Figures. . . ."

"When they foun' ya, I hadda pay your final expenses. I mean, ya didn't have no necks of skin 'round here. All your people are back in Sackenhacky—"

"*Hackensack.*"

"Whatever. So I handled your derangements—buried ya in your favoovorite tie—"

Cleve groaned. "Tell me it wasn't the monogrammed silk tie—"

"Went real nice wit'cha new navy suit—Thornton Thistlethwaite himself hadda stuff ya into it wit' a shoehorn, becausin' you'd put on a little water weight."

Cleve smacked his forehead.

"After party was at Gneeezle's," added Stu.

"Too bad I missed it," said Cleve.

"Yeah," agreed Gneeecey. "Evoovidently, I paid for some Joe Schmo to be deep-sixed."

Flea leapt to his feet. "Shouldn'choo be hapoopy—ugh—that Cleve's alive?"

Gneeecey's snout wrinkled. "I'll make 'em disinterpret that other body an' gimme a full refund."

Even Stu's seven chins dropped.

"They can always dump him into one of them pottery fields," continued Gneeecey. "I hear that after you're disembodied, y'don't know the difference anyways. There, the guy'll have lotsa compoopany, for the resta his life."

"'Zig—"

"An' Cleeevoooveland, if y'weren't dead, why din'cha call in sick?"

"*They* wouldn't let me."

Gneeecey turned on Flea again. "An' what's this I hear 'bout 'cha crashin' Chopper Three-an'-a-half?!"

"*I* didn't. Stu did."

Gneeecey smiled. "Oh—*that's* difooferent."

Flea bit his tongue.

"Y'know, Flea," said Stu, "y'were brave to fly with me. 'Cept for paper planes, I never flown nuthin' in my dang life. But once I watched 'em fly this 747. On TV. Plane crashed and the survivors ran outta food and hadda—"

"Stuart," I interrupted, "that's enough."

CLEVE GENTLY BRUSHED A few stray strands of hair out of my eyes. "Assuming we get outta this, you still leaving?"

"I—"

"They're down this end of the buildin'!" hollered Flea, as he scuttled back into our cave.

Cleve jumped up, hitting his head again. "OW! Okay, back into the tunnel, and that other hallway—we'll have to climb up onto the Splodge and get out through one of those high windows!"

"Me an' Yammicles ain't goin' *near* that Splodge," protested Gneeecey. "I always said that piece of junk was a deathtrap."

CHAPTER 41

WE'RE ALL GONNA DIE, AIN'T WE?

CLEVE POINTED TO THE umber panes above. "I'll climb up and smash one out. Then I'll boost Nicki up and—" "I GO FIRST!" hollered Gneeecey, high atop Cleve's shoulders, brandishing his lit phone.

Then it happened.

Binky the Clown slipped through Gneeecey's hands, straight down into the mierk-filled vat that stood to the left of the Splodge.

Cleve jumped back as flames blazed to the ceiling.

Markmen's voices sounding in the distance, he peeled Gneeecey off his neck. "You're last."

"BUT I'M THE MOST IMPORTOOTANT PERSON HERE!" proclaimed the good diroctor, hugging Cleve's knees.

Cleve broke loose and scrambled up to the Splodge's battered roof. "Gonna break this sucker out with my arm," he said, studying a window.

"Wait!" I snatched a half-rotten two-by-four off the floor and tossed it up to him.

He swung the hunk of wood like a bat and shattered the glass, then leapt out of the way as the conflagration curved toward him, feasting on the fresh air that rushed in.

"Cleve," I yelled, "your sleeve's on fire!"

He beat out the flames, then sprang further to his right and smashed out another panel. "Okay, Nicki—"

Stu, plastered against the opposite wall, whimpered.

"Take Stu first," I said, drawing back.

"Pitt, get'cha butt up here—NOW!" ordered Cleve.

"C'mon Stuart," I pleaded, coughing. "Hurry!"

"No, Icky—the boss goes next!"

"Yeah!" agreed Gneeecey, as he clutched Yammicles by the throat. "The *boss* goes nex'!"

"DAMMIT, I SAID, C'MON, PITT!"

"But, my mom taught me never to eat strange berries or jump outta windows!"

"It's a *basement* window!" exclaimed Cleve, dodging sparks. "A six-inch drop!"

"You'll be fallin' *up* insteada down," explained Flea, choking into his cape.

Stu shrank back. "Gotta be mighty hot up there!"

"Ya got that right, Sherlock," replied Cleve, wiping sweat from his brow. "Now, in a coupla minutes, they're gonna be all over us—if we don't burn to death, first!"

Flea and I shoved the intern up onto the hood and looked on helplessly as Cleve pulled him up the caving windshield, and onto the roof.

Wheezing, he held his interlocked fingers in front of Stu's shins. "I'll boost ya up!"

"But—but—"

"STUEY, WILL Y'JUS' STINKIN' JUMP OUTTA THAT LOUSY WINDOW, FOR BOGELTHORPE'S SAKE!" bellowed Gneeecey.

Without further delay, Stu hopped up into Cleve's hands and bounced, head first, through the window frame. And got stuck halfway.

We gaped at his flailing legs.

Flea shook his head. "*Now* what?"

"Dunno," answered Cleve. "That was our only way out. Can't reach the next window from here."

Gneeecey threw Yammicles to the floor. "WE'RE ALL GONNA DIE, AIN'T WE?"

Flea squinted up at Stu. "Not today. Gonna try my hand at flyin'."

Gneeecey whisked his teddy off the cement. "Maybe that's your problem right there—y'gotta use more'n jus' your hand!"

"I feel a whole lot lighter than I did before," declared the superhero, as he lowered himself into a sprinter's starting position. "Guys, if we get separated, we'll meet behind Freak O'Nature's garage!"

"We'd be trespoopassin'," warned Gneeecey.

"Behind the garage it is," replied Cleve, as he pulled his blackened T-shirt up over his nose.

Flea zoomed up into the smoke and circled above our heads, a bit unsteadily until he picked up speed. Palms extended, he soared toward Stu's wriggling posterior.

Next thing we knew, they were both through. We heard Stu outside, bawling like a baby. One only a mother could love.

"I'M NEX'!" screamed Gneeecey. "I'M BURNIN' UP—CAN'T BREATHE!"

Cleve stared down at him. "Nicki's next."

"I'll fix yuz when we get outta here!"

"Cleve," I asked, "who's gonna boost you up?"

"I'll manage—Julio and I were always pretty good at getting outta jams and—"

"ME NEX'!" cried Gneeecey. "THERE'S A BUNCH MORE FLAMES COMIN' TOWARD US, FROM DOWN THE HALL THERE—LOOK!"

Sure enough, a roaring wall was fast approaching.

As the good director rocked back and forth, hugging his teddy, he resembled a frightened toddler. I scooped him up and deposited him, with a thud, onto the Splodge's hood.

Cleve shot me a puzzled glance, then grabbed hold of the fast-moving Gneeecey and hurled him through the window frame.

"C'mon, Nicki," he said.

Lungs on fire, I scaled the vehicle. "Cleve, hurry and get out—this ol' bomb's gonna go up!" The gas tank was practically empty. As usual.

Cleve pecked me on the lips, then crouched and offered me his cupped hands.

A door slammed down below as I flew up and out. I crawled back over to the window, through several inches of whipped cream-covered mierk, and listened.

"WHEELER!"
"OH, MAN!"
A crisp gun shot rang out. My heart stopped.

CHAPTER 42

LUXURIATIN'

MISSED!" SHOUTED CLEVE, SAILING past my face, as a thunderous blast threw me backward. I managed to hook my arms around a dead sapling, and ducked just in time, as a jagged hunk of orange-and-purple fender flew up through the basement window and whizzed over my head.

In its death throes, poignantly hideous, the old brown-bricked dinosaur heaved and shuddered, as it expelled Markmen, disembodied eyeballs, and billowing, black smoke.

"WHOLE PLACE IS GONNA BLOW!" shouted tall, brown-haired Mark, taking cover. Sirens screamed, and firemen slipped and slid, as they rushed up the cream-covered hill, lugging axes and hoses.

"ERGZAPS!" exclaimed blond, big-nosed Mark, waving his pistol. "OVER THERE!"

Bob, last to emerge, caught sight of us, too. "GET THE GIRL, AN' THAT LITTLE WHITE-AN'-BLACK GUY WIT' THE TAIL—HE'S THE ONE WHO RIPPED ME OFF!"

I THOUGHT I WAS smashing into trees all by myself, until I heard a high, nerdish voice. And it was talkin' to me.

"Hey, Ig," it advised, "jus' pretend you're skatin'."

"Okay." I'd never skated, but I'd become pretty good at pretending.

"Light, glidin' steps'll get'cha 'cross the surfooface of this slipoopery-but-savoovory whoop cream—keep ya from gettin' stuck in all the lousy mier—"

KABOOOOOOOOOOOM! exploded the Mierkolatory, flinging us to the ground and pelting us with debris.

Faces buried in our arms, we waited. After about fifteen minutes of skull-shattering pyrotechnics, there was silence. Eerie silence.

"Y'awright, Yammy?" bleated Gneeecey, as a fine, brown powder rained down upon us. "Good. Me too."

"Lousy mierk," I hissed, wiping a glob off my nose.

He raised his rubble-topped noggin. "Don't call it lousy."

"But you just called it—"

"DON'T CALL THE LOUSY MIERK LOUSY! AN' GEDDUP—STOP LUXURIATIN'!"

I leapt up. "Luxuriating?! Are you outta your—"

"Let's go! My life's in shamboobles!"

"*Yours?*" I asked, brushing ash out of my eyes.

"Gotta get back to Vompt to declare a state of disastrophy an' call a 'mergency meetin' at the courthouse—I wanna see Qwertyuiop's face when I come through that door an' table a motion to the floor to call it a wall an'—"

"Uh, Diroctor, aren't they still after you? Y'know, Bob and all his Marks?"

He removed a cracked-up computer keyboard from around his neck. "Don't worry. Ain't seen 'em in a while—EEEEEEEEKS!"

"Famous last words," I muttered, flying behind a fracas tree.

"Boy," whispered Gneeecey, as he took cover between my quaking knees, "I thought they were my friends."

"You thought wrong—fifty-quadrillion dollars wrong."

"An'," he added, hugging Yammicles, "thirty-sevooven cents."

"How long do you think we'll have to stay here before they stop looking for us?"

"Dunno, Ig—but I jus' rememboobered, I'm 'llergic to fracas—AH–HAAH–HAAAH-HAAAATCHOOO—HONK!"

The tree blew over, roots and all. We dove behind its trunk.

"Hey, Doc," yelled blond Mark, "we see yuz hidin' behin' that busted tree."

"Yeah," snarled brown-haired Mark, wielding a flame-filled pole. "An' we see your Ergzap friend too."

The blond reached into his jacket. "We're comin' to get'cha!"

Gneeecey and I took off, hand in hand.

"Faster," I pleaded, pulling him.

"Caaan't! Yammicles' stuffin's fallin' out—it's flammable!"

"So are we, dammit!"

Gneeecey broke free and tore off in the opposite direction. I flew after him and nearly collided with an oak. "C'mon—they're gonna get us!"

"But—my mon-ney—"

"It's not yours!"

"IT IS!"

"C'mon—"

"Look," he cried, scooping up bills, "here's s'more!"

"Pleeease—"

"An' s'more over there!"

"I swear—"

"An' here!"

The dark-haired Markman was fast on our heels. I swooped Gneeecey and his cash-vomiting teddy up in my arms and ran.

Just as I slithered down to the curb, the blond appeared, gun drawn. "Gimme dat bear—now!"

"Can't we, y'know, disgust this?" begged Gneeecey.

Mark took aim between my eyes and squeezed the trigger. The revolver just clicked. I began to shiver, uncontrollably.

"Whadda crummy time to run outta bullets!" The Markman hurled his weapon to the ground. The whipped cream swallowed it whole.

I watched saucer-eyed as he extracted a switchblade from his waistband. "Ergzap, put Doc down—real slow-like."

"No," I replied, cradling Gneeecey.

Mark's shiny, six-inch blade sprang up. "Put him down."

Out of the corner of my eye, I spotted three figures running toward us. Looked like Cleve, Ethan Imbroglio—in uniform, shield gleaming—and Flea.

"I said, put Doc down."

"No."

Mark lunged forward. "Okay, ya witch wit' a B—see how y'like this—"

"The Ig can't afford no extra consonants," interrupted Gneeecey. "Not even a stinkin' B."

Startled, the Markman sliced my left leg, below the knee, as he slipped and fell.

"Not on what I pay her," added Gneeecey, clutching me for dear life.

Stunned, I gazed down at the scarlet puddle pooling on the white cream.

"How 'bout we see if Doc likes *this*," suggested brown-haired Mark. Laughing so hard that he began to cough, he pointed his fiery rod at Yammicles.

"THREEEE FORDY-TWOOOO BLUUUUUE!" shrieked Gneeecey.

CHAPTER 43

'EFT, REALLY 'EFT

WHERE IN BOGELTHORPE'S NAME *are* we?" inquired Gneeecey, floating alongside me. "D-dunno," I answered. My teeth chattered as I studied the gray, ice-crystal-dotted haze that surrounded us. There was no up or down, or end in sight.

I pulled my sleeve up to check the time and did a double take—the hands on both timepieces whirled high-speed, helter-skelter, in clockwise and counterclockwise directions, making me dizzier.

"Ig, y'think we're suspenderated in some gigantical storm cloud?"

"It's like we're stuck *between* places," I replied. "In some nowhere land—maybe another dimension."

Gneeecey's eyes widened.

I chuckled. "I'm no stranger to that kinda thing."

He frowned. "What's so funny? Nuthin's funny *now*."

I looked at him. "Was it before?"

"Y'don't s'pose they zapped us here wit' them computers?"

"Nah." I zipped my jacket up. "You saw—the whole place, including their computers, blew to smithereens."

"Ain't that somewheres in Texas?"

"No—it actually means—"

"Mayboobee," he interrupted, "it's my Redecoritis playin' tricks."

"No—I don't think—"

"Soon's we get back, have my nervologist describe me Extra Strength Bumpex—mayboobe she has free sampooples—"

"It's not your meds. You really wanna know what I think?"

"Yeah, Ig. For once, I do."

"When Flea and I first discussed the finer points of dimension jump-ing—"

"Get to the stinkin' point—"

"Well," I continued, ignoring his rudeness, "he warned me to make aboobsolutely—ugh—sure I was alone whenever I said those four words."

"So?"

"When you said those words—screamed 'em—you were holding onto *me*—"

"Somethin' I'm really 'shamed of—an' always will be—"

"And," I concluded, searching my pockets for a StomQuell, "because you did that when we were, uh, physically connected, we most likely ended up stranded in some intermediate zone."

"Well, now we're 'eft—*really* 'eft!"

"*What?*"

"Don'cha understanderate English?"

"Yeah. It's actually my first language—been speaking it since birth. What did you just say?"

"Do I always gotta 'splain stuff? "Eft' is a whaddayacallit—contrap-tion of 'bereft.' More economical—two less consonants an' one less vowel."

"Oh."

"Reminds me. On my planet—an' all over Perswayssick County—we got these amphiboobious blue lizards. Unhapoopy little creatures, called efts, 'causa their misooserabooble igspressions."

"Really."

"Perhaphoops y'mighta seen some, back at Vompt. They've made nests inside sevooveral of our copy machines."

I shuddered.

"They crawl in through the paper trays."

"Charming."

"Y'know," he continued, "I had a pet eft named Screwball. One day when I was at school, my dog Wrecks ate him. Y'shoulda seen—all that was lef' of him was his lef'—"

"I, uh, get the picture."

"Y'think we're *dead*—like Screwball?"

"You mean," I asked, "is this the hereafter? I certainly hope not—"

"The *whereafter?*"

"The hereafter—"

"Oh then," he declared with authority, "that proboobably wouldn't be here now."

"What wouldn't be?"

"The hereafter. Cause we're here now, not after or before."

I felt a migraine coming on. "Well, it's all neither here nor there."

"But," snapped Gneeecey, "we know it's not the thereafter, on accounta we're here an' not there."

"Where?"

He groaned. "The thereafter! The here is *now* an' the after would be *then*."

"But even then," I countered, "you don't know that here couldn't be there."

"If it's anywhere," he replied, punching his fists in the fog, "it's here now! Y'don't see it *there* now, do ya?!"

"I hate to agree with you, but no, I don't see here there now—"

"But," he claimed, as he thrust a finger in my face, "it could be *after*! An' it coulda been *before*, jus' as well! Prove that it wasn't or won't be."

"I can't."

"See? Y'can't prove here wasn't there before—but it certaintaneously was unless it wasn't! An' y'can't prove here might not be there after—it's all fifty-fifty!"

I glanced down at my mismatched shoes.

"Y'really can't argue wit' mathematratical formulas," he screamed, "so, conversically, y'can't prove anythin' there was here—then, after, or now. Thereforthically, y'can't prove we're not dead."

I took a deep breath of icy air. And got brain freeze.

"So don't waste your Ig breath arguin' wit' meee—I'm a PUNI graduate. I can argue both sides!"

I popped a fuzz-covered StomQuell.

Gneeecey turned to Yammicles. "Ain't no gravoovity here. You okay?"

"Just my luck," I mumbled. "He's going even more loopy."

He shook the teddy. "He's traumatized, 'causa these cirkookumstantial cirkookumstances. Yammy, *speak* to me!"

"Surely, you don't expect an answer."

"Says he's okay."

Best to change the subject. "Director, do you think Cleve and Flea got away? Didn't you see them running toward us? You think Stu—"

"Who cares, nah, an' who cares?—in that order."

My jaw dropped.

He smiled. "In times of crisis, my spiritual beliefs direct me."

"Didn't know you had any."

He plunged a fist into his shirt pocket and surfaced with a worn hard-cover book and a crumpled yellow card. "Looky—here's that sock repair ticket y'misplaced."

Lost for words, I just growled.

He opened his copy of *Revered Utterances of the Grand Oogitty-Boogitty: A Celestial Bullfighter's Road Map for Hiking Through the Six-Lane, Poop-Splat-tered Asphalt Ocean of Life.* "You'll depreciate his universically-revered Hynesty's wise advice."

"Uh-huh."

"He writes, 'For it is what it is, an' not what it was, an' certainly not what it might be, if ever it wasn't.'"

I looked at him. He shrugged and tossed the purple tome over his shoulder. "What's a roasted potato know, anyhows?"

"There's one thing *I* know," I declared, blowing warm air into my numb, cupped hands.

"What?"

"You've got a whole lot of explaining to do."

"Can't—tongue's froze to the roofa my mouth."

"I've never known anyone like you."

"Thanks, Ig."

"That wasn't a compoopliment—ugh. And stop calling me Ig."

He plucked a stretched-out, oval scrap of mierk off his shirt, com-plete with eye and mouth holes. "Musta been one of their faces."

"Lovely." As I attempted to move closer, to examine it, I drifted fur-ther away. "Must be, for every action, there's an equal and opooposite—ugh—reaction."

"Or not," he shrilled. "Rememboober, everythin's fifty-fifty!"

"That may be," I answered, swimming away from him in order to re-turn to his side, "but what I really wanna know is, what'cha gotta say for your sorry self?"

"My feet are froze." Yellow icicles hung from his shoelaces.

I exhaled into my jacket in a feeble attempt to ward off hypothermia. I had always suspected that hell would be air-conditioned—you'd have to wear a sweater, and your nose would constantly run. "Diroctor, I asked you a question."

He remained silent.

I stared him up and down, suppressing a strong urge to kick him inside-out. "You've really got issues."

His fists balled up. "Who are you—Sigmoid Freund?"

"No, I'm Nicki Rodriguez, and I want answers. You damn near got us killed. Why?"

A look of shame washed over him. I almost didn't recognize the good diroctor.

"Well?"

"I dunno why I do summa the junk I do. I'm jus' me—can't really stop bein' me."

"Y'know, Diroctor—"

"Call me Bizzig."

My heart nearly ceased beating.

"Or 'Zig-Squared—that's like callin' me 'Zig-'Zig, but'cha keep one 'Zig as a spare."

"Well, 'Zig-Squared—"

He flinched.

"I've always believed," I continued, "that people can change."

"Not me."

"Why not?"

"Well, Ig—"

"Please stop calling me Ig."

"Yeah, Ig, awright. Y'know, I always been priddy modest, even though I am a genius—"

"What's your point? Do you even have one?"

"I'm igsplainin' things slow 'cause I know ya understanderate stuff slow."

"Okay, 'Zig-Squared—"

"An' don't call me 'Zig-Squared, 'Zig-'Zig or Bizzig!"

"But five seconds ago—"

"That was then an' this is now."

"Fine. And stop calling me Ig."

"Now, Ig, 'bout your poopfolio—"

I folded my arms. "Yeah?"

"First of all, y'nevoover thanked me for fishin' it outta the Perswayssick—"

"I'm still paying you! All you ever thought about was lining your pockets—with my money."

"True. But I also did it for the environment."

"Puhleeease. Don't tell me you ever gave a damn about the environment—no, I take that back—you gave a damn when you thought you could make a bundle by selling it out."

"Thought I could work things a few ways, plus make a profit. An' make you an' everyone else hapoopy."

"Oh, how's that?"

"I'm soooo brilliant, I can't staaaand myself—"

"That makes at least two of us—"

He scrunched up his snout. "My plan had a little somethin' for everyone. First, it helped the most important one, meeee—an' it made Mark, Mark, an' Mark, an' Mark, an'—"

"C'mon—"

"An' Bob, too—made 'em all hapoopy. Gave 'em false hope, after they destroyed their own planet—Planet of the Marked Men. I tol' 'em yoooou had secret codes, inside your poopfolio, to coordinates on Earth, where they'd find all the mierk they'd ever need."

Boiling, I unzipped my jacket.

"So," Gneeecey continued, his words forming clouds, "I arranged to sell 'em your papers—"

"Papers that weren't yours in the first place—"

"Yeah—them. Dopes paid me big bucks—up front, before I even delivered. Along wit' what they gave me to kill that lousy, no-good 345. An' that jus' kilt me—hapoopily, of course—them payin' me to do somethin' I hadda do anyways, for my *own* sake."

"We all know how well *that* went."

Gneeecey's eyes darkened. "Ain't my fault if our snitizens are selfish, paranoid, backward-lookin', unscientifical—"

"You've just described yourself."

"Lemme stinkin' finish. I also tol' 'em that only *you* could decipher the codes. That way, I'd get the mon-ney, but you'd be in danger."

"Heartwarming."

"An' here's a part that's good for yoooou—I kissed up to 'em, not 'cause I was afraid of 'em or nuthin'—"

"Of *course* not—"

"I wanted to keep 'em hapoopy, to help you an' your planet."

"My planet and I thank you—we'll award you a Nobel Prize."

"See," he squealed, "I *said* you'd thank me!"

"If you don't mind my asking, how exactly would all this help me and my planet?"

"I'll make up—I mean, get to that."

I zipped up my jacket.

"An' nex' time Zynnfandel calls—"

"Zynnfandel?"

"Our Planet Eccchs leader. I can finally answer that lousy, stinkin' hotline an' report that I'm makin' progress! Your papers do contain secret codes—for a formula that'll return us Eccchsers to our planet!"

"Oh, this just keeps getting better and better."

"I'm glad ya rekookognize that. I got a patriotical duty to help my people, too."

I scoured my pockets for another StomQuell. "What made you possibly think that *I* know how to get to Planet Eccchs?"

"I figured, since ya invaded our dimension in the first place, y'musta knew lots. Then I read your papers—"

"After you *stole* 'em—"

"Yeah. An' bein' the genius I am, I discovered them codes, hidden in your dopey shorthand. There's more'n a few *X's* encrypted in them notes. Got everythin' wrote down here." He patted his lumpy pocket. "What's so stinkin' funny?"

I didn't have the heart to tell him that Xavier Colón was one of the main characters in my novel. "If you'd come to me first, I could've saved you a whole bunch of time—and trouble."

"Great—I knew you'd decipher them codes for me!"

Bobbing around in nothingness had made me nauseous. "And what was all that bull about Cleve choking to death on a Rindom Doodle?"

"He was nosin' aroun' in other peopoople's business too much—guess he hadda be, y'know, neutralizated."

My jaw tightened. "And we both know, the Splodge wasn't even running—it was up on Zeke's lift. Who authorized its release?"

"Mark an' them needed it, bad. I felt sorry for 'em. Stop lookin' at me like that."

"You're amazing."

"I know. An' now, I'll make ya privoovy to the resta my plan."

"What's that—to stop dreaming up insane stuff?"

He laughed. "No, Ig—my geniosity an' generosity'll confounderate an' astounderate ya."

"Confounderated and astounderated I already am."

"See? Now, I've awready helped the environment, my people, Mark an' them, an' you an' your planet—"

"You never answered me—how did you help me and my planet?"

"Uh. . .hmmm. . .lessee. . .here it is—Mark an' them'll travoovel to Earth, spend mon-ney, an' enrich your economy."

"Talk about rationalizing."

"Yes, Ig—it *is* rational. You're finally gettin' it!"

"Right."

"Anyways, since I've helped everyone else, now it's my turn."

I was dying for a drink. Of anything.

"After you decipher them codes, outta sheer gratitoodinosity for all I done to ya, you'll lemme take full credit."

I rolled my eyes in the direction I thought was up. "*Of course.*"

"Why y'sayin' it like that?"

"As if I have such a formula—"

"Y'do. An' when us stranded Eccchsers finally return, I'll be hailed as a hero! I'll write a book—well, you'll ghos' write it for me—then I'll take credit an'—"

I longed to sit somewhere. Anywhere.

"Don't look so oogdimonious—it's all quite igcitin'!"

"Uh-huh."

"I'll do radio an' TV, an' tons of speakin' engorgements."

"Yeah."

"Wit' what I make from all that, plus what I made in Perswayssick County, plus what I got from Mark an' them, plus all the dough I got socked away back on Planet Eccchs—accumulatin' compounderated in-teres' for thirteen months all these years—"

"Boy—you really—"

"Bada-bing!" He jammed his wet honker in mine. "I retire! Rich an' infamous—bet'cha I even win back Goonafina!"

"Oh?"

"She's a goonicologist. Her name led her to her profession."

"What's a goonicologist?"

"A doctor of goonicology."

"Of course."

He grinned. "One of the things I love bes' 'bout my Goonafina is that she retrieves the gold! Speakin' of stuff like that, I done some research on yooou."

"Did you?"

"Your family's from Porty Rico."

"*Puerto* Rico."

"In Spinach, that means 'rich port'! You certaintaneously been that for *me*!"

I wanted to wring his filthy neck. "You are a real piece of work."

"Why, grassy ass!"

My fists wouldn't unclench.

"Don't look so oogdimonious—I've really helped ya."

"How's that again?"

He sucked in his teeth. "Do I really gotta igsplain it more? Ummmm. . . . I got it—I made y'feel *good* 'bout yourself."

"Really."

"I've allowed ya to help me help myself, an' evooveryone else. I mean, don't it feel real good to be used like that? Don't the beauty of it all make y'wanna cry?"

"Yes. It does."

"Your leg's bleedin' again."

I looked down. My wound was gushing like a fountain.

"Don't worry Ig, back in medoodical school—in heemahoology class—they taught us how to tie tournaments."

"Huh?"

"An' they reviewed it in Brain Surgery 101—y'know, in case we ever cut ourself wit' one of them sharp scalpoopels. Jus' hold on. . ." Gneeecey began to transfer fistfuls of cash from Yammicles' carcass into his shirt pocket.

Then, kneeling in nothing but icy vapors, he tied his limp teddy tightly around my leg. It stopped the bloody flow.

"Thank you, Director," I whispered, eyes tearing up.

"When we get home, we'll drop by Florence Ferguson an' have 'em take a look at that. An' I'll give Yammicles a long bath in some heavy-duty, acid-based detergent, mixed wit' boilin' water an' grain alkookohol."

"Diroctor, one more thing—"

"Shoot, Ig."

"You were dumping those MierkoZurk stocks like hot cakes—selling 'em off cheap, to anyone who'd buy. Plus, there's the bunch you put in Flubbubb's name—"

His cheek muscles began to twitch. "So?"

"You must've taken a real bath—"

"Ain't taken no bath in two years."

I shuddered.

"Yeah," he said, "I sold them suckers when they were goin' bust, but I used what little I made—plus summa what Mark an' them gave me—to purchoochase stock in ZIT."

"Zit?"

"Zodd Intertechnological Technologies. Froop an' Fritzl didn't raise no dummy—you're lookin' at ZIT's new majority stockholder. I own fifty-one percent."

"You mean—"

"Wait till we get home an' ya taste one of Gneeezle's new ZigZodd Burgers!"

"Speaking of going home, we'll have to make some sort of decision—"

"What'cha mean, Ig?"

"We can't just hover here in empty, frigid space—"

"This ain't space, Ig—if it was, we wouldn't be, y'know, respoopiratin'."

"What I'm trying to say is, we'll have to—"

"—say them four words again?"

I nodded. "And we won't know whether we'll end up back in Perswayssick County, or in my dimension—or, well, y'know, like—"

"Julio?"

"Uh, yeah."

His pupils dilated.

"And," I added, "we should proboobably—ugh—move away from each other before we—"

"Nah, Ig—let's stay together."

"You don't think, when you yelled those words, that your Mark buddies heard, and they'll—"

"Ig, you doin' that?"

"Doing what?"

"Y'know, movin' 'way from me?"

"No—well, yeah—"

"Try movin' in the opooposite direction—like before."

"I am—it's not working."

"OH, NOOOOOOOOOOOOOOO," he howled, "I'M MOVIN' TOOOOOOOOOO!"

"We're being tugged apart—by some invisible force!"

"IG," he pleaded, "COME BAAAAACK!"

"CAAAAAN'T!" I shouted, rocketing backward.

"YOU'RE THE SIZE OF A DIME!"

"YOOOU TOOOO!"

"I STILL NEEEEED YA—TO DECIPHER THEM CODES!"

He disappeared.

CHAPTER 44

HOME FOR GRIMACE

I HIT THE GRAVEL hard. It was pitch-dark. A flesh-stinging chill sliced through the air. I couldn't see past the idling freight train. As I staggered to my feet, it hit me—I was just blocks from home. But on the wrong side of the tracks. I'd have to go through that vermin-infested tunnel.

Muscles tensed, I descended into blackness.

"Hey," rumbled a deep voice.

I stumbled through the passageway, at breakneck speed, and scuttled up the steps. Lungs bursting, I threw my arms around a splintery utility pole. Couldn't feel my legs.

After a moment, I let go and started up Walnut Terrace. And came to a dead halt. Cardboard goblins taped to doors? Jack-o'-lanterns burning on stoops? In December?

"What," I mumbled, watching my breath cloud up, "do *I* know?" I did know I must've looked like a cream-splattered, muck-slathered vision from hell. Thankfully, I didn't run into anyone—TV screens flickered through almost every window on the narrow, maple-lined street.

Smoothing down my hair, as if I'd scare fewer people, I resumed walking. And upon reaching Rico's house, stopped short again.

There, on the driveway, sat my Mustang. I smacked its dented trunk, and hiked up the steep incline.

I realized my keys weren't on me.

Out of habit, I turned the knob. The door opened. Heart pounding, I limped downstairs, through the kitchen and into the living room. And stared.

Everything was just as I'd left it—my bookcase lay sprawled across the floor, its contents strewn about. Aristotle's pen-and-ink image—maybe I just imagined the amused expression plastered across his face—peered up at me from *Metaphysics'* disheveled pages.

As I entered the bathroom, I caught sight of myself. Gasping, I ran a damp washcloth over my smudged purple face, and yanked a brush through my cyclone-styled hair. The brilliant overhead lighting exaggerated its two months' worth of dark roots.

I lumbered back into the parlor and collapsed into my big chair. My bills lay stacked on my desk, unpaid—just as I'd left 'em.

Damned phone was wet—liquid trickled into my sleeve when I picked it up. Perplexed, I reached for a tissue.

Decided to check my voice mail. I clicked the charging base's PLAY button, and bit down on my lip as I listened.

"You have no new messages, and five saved messages," droned my personal female automaton.

Missing for all that time, and nothing? Not a word from my mom? Or siblings? Or bosses or clients? Or creditors?

Maybe I was dead and didn't know. If anyone else did, they didn't give a deck of vlecks.

I stared into space. When the telephone rang, adrenaline surged through me like lightning.

"Hello?" I answered, warily.

"Hola!"

"Who's this?"

"Me."

"Who?"

"Carlos."

"Carlos?"

"I'm not a guy with a monster ego, but please don't tell me you forgot me since this morning—"

I leapt up and knocked over my lamp. "*This morning?*"

"Just wanted to let'cha know, we won't be back till Sunday. Got another gig in Paris! So don't hold that spot for me on your show."

"What?"

"Go back to sleep, Nicki. I'm sorry—I forgot. It's nighttime back home."

"Did you just say—"

"Sweet dreams—*ciao!*"

As my head spun, my landlord appeared, concern etched on his finely-lined, tan face. "Door was open—thought I'd check on you—"

"Check on me?"

"Saw you runnin' down the block—a coupla hours ago—"

"A couple *hours* ago?"

"Yeah. Chasin' after some strange-lookin'—"

My mouth opened wide. "A couple *hours* ago?"

"Heard you come back in, an' I thought I'd see if. . . ." Noticing my toppled bookcase, his voice trailed off.

"Maybe—maybe tomorrow, Rico, you can help me with that?"

"Sure. Jus' gimme a holler—"

"And thanks for not putting my stuff out in the street—"

"Wha'choo talkin' 'bout, *mi'ja?*"*

"I know I owe back rent—"

Rico's coffee-colored eyes grew huge. "You jus' *gave* me the rent—ten days ago."

"Huh?"

He stood there in his paint-stained overalls, gawking. "You look kinda, well, purple. You sure you're okay?"

Reeling, I unzipped my jacket. "Just tired. Really tired."

"Nice coat."

"Uh, thanks."

"My granddaughter jus' bought one 'zactly like it."

I tossed the many-zippered garment at my chair and hobbled across the room.

"You selling watches?" he inquired.

---

* contraction of *mi hija* ("my daughter"), affectionate slang for "my girl," "home girl."

"Uh, no."

Rico pointed to my feet. "You're makin' a real fashion statement there."

My eyes traveled from my left wrist down to my messy Mierk-Tracker and crudded-up black loafer—and the lifeless teddy tied 'round my blood-spattered denim leg. A singed greenback jutted out of its mouth. A vague sense of anxiety gripped me.

Rico raised an eyebrow.

"Probably just—just need some sleep," I stammered, as I walked back to my desk, scooped up my bills, and hugged them tightly.

My landlord shrugged and headed for the door.

I smiled. "Rico!"

He glanced over his shoulder. "Yeah?"

"I just said *probably*!"

THE BIMBUS

CPSIA information can be obtained at www.ICGtesting.com
Printed in the USA
BVOW011642200911

271700BV00002B/12/P

9 780983 371144